A
LIFE
FOR
A
LIFE

ALSO BY CAROL WYER

Detective Kate Young series:

An Eye for an Eye
A Cut for a Cut

Detective Natalie Ward series:

The Birthday
Last Lullaby
The Dare
The Sleepover
The Blossom Twins
The Secret Admirer
Somebody's Daughter

Detective Robyn Carter series:

Little Girl Lost
Secrets of the Dead
The Missing Girls
The Silent Children
The Chosen Ones

Comedies:

Life Swap
Take a Chance on Me
What Happens in France
Suddenly Single

A LIFE FOR A LIFE

Detective Kate Young series

CAROL WYER

THOMAS & MERCER

Text copyright © 2022 by Carol Wyer
All rights reserved.

Published by Thomas & Mercer, Seattle

www.apub.com

Amazon, the Amazon logo, and Thomas & Mercer are trademarks of Amazon.com, Inc., or its affiliates.

ISBN-13: 9781542021074
ISBN-10: 1542021073

Cover design by Dominic Forbes

Printed in the United States of America

A
LIFE
FOR
A
LIFE

PROLOGUE

Ben lifted his face to the rear-view mirror and shouted, 'Oy! If you two don't pack it in immediately, I'll pull over and shove you both in the roof carrier box for the rest of the trip!' The squabbling siblings stopped arguing immediately, unable to see the twinkle in his eye.

Lisa, in the passenger seat, threw him a wink. He returned her a quick smile.

'Getting into practice for when ours plays up?' she asked, placing a hand on her belly, which strained against the seatbelt.

'No need. Ours is going to be perfectly behaved. Not like Rowena's brood.'

The woman behind him barked a laugh. 'Good luck with that. You wait. One sprog might be okay, but it'll be a different story once you've got four of them. They'll be exactly like this bunch – noisy, demanding and never listen to a word you say.'

'Mu-um!' Kathleen, sandwiched between her mother and younger brother, Archie, had inherited the same cheerful round face as her mother and uncle. 'That's not fair. I listen to you.'

'Okay. You and Grace *sometimes* listen to me, but your brothers definitely don't.'

'That's cos they're boys,' she replied with an indifferent shrug. 'Uncle Ben, is your baby going to be a boy or a girl?'

Ben didn't answer. Although he and Lisa knew they were expecting a boy, they didn't want to spoil the surprise for any of the family.

'We don't know,' said Lisa evenly.

'I hope it's a girl,' replied Kathleen, her attention swiftly turning to her mobile.

Traffic was heavy and Ben was mindful of the fact that they'd left home later than intended to reach the airport in time. He also hadn't factored in the impromptu stop to refuel the MPV, and half of the kids taking off to the shop to stock up on sweets for their long journey. He hadn't seen his sister, nephews and nieces in almost two years, and they'd made the most of the last ten days, visiting as much of the area as possible. Once the baby was born, he and Lisa would make the trip to Canada to visit them. They'd even talked about emigrating there themselves. It would be great to live close to his sister. He and Rowena had always got along well, and it would be nice for their baby to grow up with his extended family nearby.

'Ooh, look! McDonald's. Uncle Ben, can we stop?' The small voice at the back of the car came from five-year-old Grace, who was cuddling a soft toy unicorn with a pink mane.

'Honey, we can't stop again. We don't want to miss the plane, do we?' Her mother's voice was gentle. The little girl gave a dramatic sigh.

Ben smiled again. Grace was the baby of the family and with her large blue eyes and sweet nature had won a firm place in both his and Lisa's hearts. He wouldn't mind having another child after this one, especially if it was a little girl like her.

Lisa twisted around in her seat. 'You'll be able to get a McDonald's at the airport, Grace. There are lots of places to eat there.'

'Great! That means we'll defo miss the plane. She's a shopa-holic,' mumbled twelve-year-old Dillon.

Grace looked at her brother, who sat beside her in the rear seats. 'What's a shoppoholy?'

'Shopaholic, not shoppoholy. It means you always want to buy things.'

'Don't.'

'You do. The first day when we went to London, you spent all your pocket money on that stupid unicorn and then it was, "Mummy, can I have that teddy? I really want that doll. Can I have some money for that dog? Please, Mummy!"' he squeaked in a girly voice.

'Did not.' Grace puffed out her cheeks. 'You got things too. You got a new Switch and loads of games for it.'

'And you got a whole suitcase of silly stuffed toys.'

'I haven't!'

'You have.'

'Dillon! Stop winding up your sister,' warned Rowena.

Dillon reached for the toy unicorn, grabbed it from Grace's hands and held it away from her. She let out a pitiful wail. 'Give it back!'

Ben looked up at the rear-view mirror again. 'Dillon, give it to her.'

He turned his attention back to the motorway. The sudden flashing of red lights ahead confused him momentarily and his brain was a fraction too slow to register that traffic was coming to a rapid halt.

He jammed down the brake pedal with all the force he could muster. It was true what they said about time slowing. The brake lights ahead glowed like hot coals. Lisa gasped. A high-pitched squeak of terror came from Kathleen. They slid closer and closer to the rear of a pipe-carrying HGV. The honeycomb of metal poles that stuck out beyond the lorry bed filled the windscreen. The steering wheel was slippery with sweat, his foot feeble and inadequate as he drove it into the pedal. The car moved with a momentum of its own. His mind screamed for the vehicle to stop. The sound of his thudding heart now drowned out all other noises: the screeching of brakes, the children's horrified squeals. Finally, his prayers were answered and the people carrier drew to a halt, mere centimetres from the rear of the vehicle.

'Oh, thank good—'

His words were swallowed by the ringing of metal on metal. Time was suspended and in a blink of an eye he understood what was happening. A car had rear-ended his own and was propelling it forwards. Instinct turned him towards Lisa. The pain that ripped through his body was nothing compared to the utter terror as the windscreen imploded and a metal pole materialised, on a trajectory with his wife's face.

CHAPTER ONE

DAY ONE – TUESDAY

The pale-faced man with soaking-wet straw-coloured hair begged to be released. Prison guard Tom Champion twisted under his binds until a person wearing military fatigues appeared on the screen, the upper body out of camera shot, and poured water over his face. Champion spluttered and coughed, mouth opening and closing like a fish's, as he struggled for breath. He gulped lungfuls of air.

'Tell us,' said a disguised, robotic voice.

'No . . . I can't . . . No.'

The figure moved again, more quickly this time. Water streamed over the man's eyes, then his nose and finally his mouth. He retched and hacked.

'We can keep this up for hours. You can't,' said the robotic voice.

'Okay. Okay. I admit it. I killed Cooper Monroe and made it look like suicide.'

'Tell us exactly what happened.'

'He was in the shower. He didn't hear me. I crept up behind him, surprised him and slit his throat with a razor blade before he could react.'

'And then?'

'I got cleaned up, put on a spare uniform I'd already left in the changing area, and called for assistance.'

'Why did you kill him?'

He shook his head. 'Please don't make me tell you. I'll lose my job, everything.'

'You don't tell us, and you'll die. Which is it?'

The man didn't answer, and was waterboarded yet again. He struggled for air, lung-sucking wheezes followed by short, panicked inhalations. More water dripped on to his face, filling his nostrils. His eyes flew open in wild panic, gargles bubbling from his throat, as if it had been sliced open.

He panted dramatically until there was sufficient air to talk. Each word puffed from his lips. 'I was . . . paid . . . to make it . . . look like . . . suicide. I needed . . . the money. My dad's got . . . advanced . . . dementia. He needs medical care—'

'How much were you paid?'

'Thirty grand.'

'A poxy thirty grand for a man's life?'

'He was . . . a criminal!'

The man's legs and lower body bucked under the leather restraints as more water was poured into his mouth. He blew and gasped and blew again. The water stopped.

'Who paid you?'

'An officer.'

'A police officer or a prison officer?'

'Police.'

'Who was this police officer?'

'No. I can't tell you.' He was tortured again. This time he pleaded for his life.

'Give us the name of the officer who paid you.'

The man gave it up at last. 'Superintendent John Dickson.'

6

Kate rewound the video she'd watched numerous times, flinching as she did so. Tom Champion had been on the verge of death, eyes rolling back in his head. She shouldn't have agreed to such a barbaric method of extracting information from him, yet it had given her what she'd needed – the name of the man she'd suspected all along, John Dickson.

She wanted Dickson unmasked so badly it hurt. Not only was the superintendent corrupt, but she was also convinced he had been behind the murder of her husband, Chris. He might not have hired the hitman who had killed Chris, but he had undoubtedly convinced the person who did to do so. Unsure how dishonest Dickson was, she was gathering evidence, by whatever methods needed, to prove she was right.

Her attention turned from her phone as she watched the man who had tortured Tom Champion stride from his Range Rover. He had the air of somebody who'd seen it all and feared nothing. Bradley Chapman had spent fourteen years in the SAS. Even though he'd been a civilian for over twenty-five years, the driving-school instructor practised Krav Maga, a mixture of martial arts, combat techniques and self-defence, originally taught to the Israeli army. Kate was sure this was one of the reasons he walked with the confidence of a much younger man.

The door opened. Bradley climbed into her car, filling it with a light cologne. He looked ahead rather than directly at her, eyes on vehicles crossing the causeway, his face set.

'Well?' When he didn't reply she said, 'You rang me. Are you going to explain why, or shall we play twenty questions?'

His voice was granite-hard, his words more powerful than the violent punches he could throw. 'Champion's disappeared.'

'He's been *disappeared* for the last four months.'

'I mean properly disappeared.'

Even though the video confession, given under duress, would be inadmissible in court, Tom Champion was pivotal to bringing down Superintendent John Dickson. With her genuine concerns about Dickson and how far his corruption had spread within the force, Kate had been unable to entrust Champion to fellow officers, or have him placed in a safe house. The risk to his safety was too great.

As a consequence, for the last few weeks, Bradley and his ex-SAS cronies had kept Tom out of harm's way in exchange for his cooperation. He'd been on the verge of agreeing to stand up in court and speak out against Dickson, in exchange for continued protection and a safe passage from the UK for him and his family, immediately after any trial.

Kate had her own theory as to why Dickson had wanted Cooper Monroe dead. In prison for his part in covering up a sex-worker's death at a gentlemen's club, Cooper probably had information to incriminate Dickson in the crime or, more likely, information about what had happened afterwards. Her husband had got wind of underage sex-workers being brought into the club. His investigations had spooked those responsible for killing and covering up the young boy's death and so the hitman had been ordered. Kate was sure Cooper had information that would have incriminated Dickson in this. It was no coincidence that Tom was ordered to murder Cooper the very morning she had been due to meet him. Tom's disappearance was a severe blow.

'I warned you this might happen. You've been shilly-shallying about and now he's gone. That bastard Dickson probably got to him.'

The anger in his voice wasn't because Dickson might have silenced the prison guard, rather that Bradley hadn't been allowed to. Kate had promised justice for his best friend, Cooper, and he'd agreed that, in exchange for it, he and his ex-SAS colleagues wouldn't end Tom Champion's days. Bradley had played along with her, waiting for her to find further evidence against the man they knew was behind Cooper's death. She hadn't fulfilled her part in the agreement. It hadn't been for want of trying.

'It's been complicated,' she said. She'd spent four long months hunting for another underage sex-worker, Rosa, who'd been with Dickson in the room adjacent to the one in which the boy had been murdered. Rosa had additional information about Dickson that would, combined with what Tom had to say, bring him down.

'It isn't any more. You've kissed goodbye to any chance of bringing Dickson down.'

'You might be wrong. Tom could be alive.'

He shook his head. 'Somebody got to him and spirited him away. He took off without his wife and kids. There's no way he'd have left without them.'

'How did this happen? Weren't you watching him?'

His nostrils flared. 'He seemed happy hiding out in Devon, away from us, from his old life. Remember, we put the fear of God into him after we tortured him. There was no way he was going anywhere. We kept a watch on him as requested. Yesterday morning, he went for a jog along the south-west coastal path as usual. He didn't return to the car park.'

'Your man didn't follow him?'

A muscle flexed in his jaw. 'No. Champion took that route every single morning. Normally, they'd wait in the car park until he returned. The only other explanation is he jumped off the cliff. Topped himself before anyone got to him. My money's on Dickson. That son-of-a-bitch found him.'

Kate made no further comment. This was on her. She'd asked a group of ex-servicemen to watch over a murderer. She hadn't followed protocol and couldn't blame anybody but herself for the outcome. What had she been thinking when she'd involved Bradley and his friends?

'What do you suggest we do now?' she asked.

'Me? I don't suggest anything. I've been led by you on this. If I'd had it my way, I'd have dealt with Champion a long time ago, like he dealt with Cooper. However, you assured me your way was the right way, that Champion and Dickson would get what they deserved, so I did what you advised. I pushed for a second post-mortem on Cooper's body, which, instead of proving he was killed, only supported the initial theory he took his own life. A theory that is utter rubbish. Now we've lost Champion, along with any chance of nailing the bastard who paid him to murder my friend. I don't have any suggestions. Judging by the way yours have panned out, I don't think you should bother coming up with any new ones either. I thought you had this. I was wrong. I doubt you'll ever get one over on Dickson. He's way ahead of you.'

He gripped the door handle, nostrils flaring again. 'I think we're done here, DI Young.'

The door flew open. He was gone in a flash, rapid strides back to his car. Kate's chest rose and fell quickly. She'd failed. Badly. Some detective she'd turned out to be.

◆ ◆ ◆

The small tube glided over the white powder with practised ease. Ben inhaled the almost floral scent with a rapid snort, eyes closed, relishing the instant burn in his nostrils. The anticipated high was slower in coming but nevertheless arrived as expected, lifting him from the mental slump that threatened to swallow him.

He sat back in his armchair. On the television screen, a presenter was holding up a plant, the flowers an intense orange, the petals seeming to glow and dance like flames in 3D, becoming larger until they began to grow out of the screen.

'Better?' said Lisa.

'Yes. I had to take it.'

'I understand. It's been difficult for you. The first was always going to be the hardest. We knew that.'

Ben closed his eyes again, tried not to recall the look of surprise on the girl's face. Even in the darkness he had seen first confusion, then surprise, then terror. He'd seen the look on others' faces during his tours in Afghanistan. The difference was that, back then, he hadn't always been the one to inflict the fear.

'At least it passed off as we expected.' Lisa's voice was gentle. He imagined her talking to their baby son, soothing him, singing to him. The perfect mother.

The coke was doing its stuff now. He felt more energised, positive. Even though he knew he was becoming too reliant on it, he couldn't stop taking it. The last few months had been the worst in his life. The doctors had wanted to put him on a cocktail of medication, and he had refused, preferring to take the pain and heartache he deserved rather than numb it. Now he needed help, and at least a bump wasn't going to dull his senses. He was on a mission and the sort of pills the so-called experts would insist he took would prevent him from planning what he had to do. Planning was paramount.

Lisa spoke again. 'Where have you hidden the gun?'

His tongue was beginning to numb, his response indistinct. 'In your gym bag.'

'Oh, right.'

'It seemed the best place.'

'Sure. Why not? I'm not likely to use it.'

As the colours in the room glowed brighter, her features receded and became lost to him. He was sure she was looking at him and smiled at her.

11

'Ah, a smile. You're definitely feeling better. While you're in this good a mood, we need to plan the next move.'

'I know where's next. The railway station.'

She appeared to nod an approval. 'Rowena would like that.'

His attention was drawn to the daytime programme once again, the camera panning over plants so vibrant they made him squint at the screen. The confidence was back. Now he could do this. He'd wait at the station for as long as necessary, until the opportunity arose. Then he would be ready, stun gun to hand. If nobody appeared, he would return the next day and the one after.

That was the plan.

It was down to fate who lived and who died.

Back home, Kate hurled the smiley stress ball against the office wall with all the force she could muster. Four wasted months. Four useless, frustrating, pointless months! An increasingly desperate Kate had bulldozed her way around Stoke and Manchester, cajoling, bribing and even threatening those who might have been able to lead her to Rosa. But still she had been unable to find the sexworker. The squidgy ball rebounded to land on the carpet, face up, its grin mocking her. She emitted a low growl, stepped forward and booted it with a well-aimed kick; sent it spinning across the office floor, where it ricocheted against the desk legs before boomeranging back to halt right by her feet.

This had been her dead husband's space. The room where Chris, hunched over his keyboard, would type eye-opening newspaper articles, exposing secrets and broaching usually taboo subjects – hard-hitting pieces that had won him the coveted Journalist of the Year Award. This was where she usually felt his presence most keenly. She'd kept it exactly as he had, nothing out of place, as if this room where he had been at his most creative and happiest could somehow drag his spirit back and anchor it here. And yet, in spite of all her efforts, including spraying the chair with his favourite aftershave, his ghost had finally slipped away.

She couldn't work out why he had disappeared. She needed him. She was doing what she could to find justice for him. She could only deduce it was because she was too slow. Bradley was right. She had shilly-shallied. All because she'd wanted more on Dickson. She'd wanted him held accountable for more than one death. More than that, she'd wanted proof he had been behind the hiring of the hitman who had killed her husband.

She sighed. She had already given it everything she could. Juggling her work, all the while trying to ensure Dickson wasn't becoming suspicious about her activities, then using every spare moment to single-handedly track down Rosa, while again trying not to alert Dickson to what she was doing, was taking its toll. She had no social life. She'd made excuses, taken rain checks and turned down invitations from colleagues and friends to meet up. She kept odd hours, cramming her private investigation into what precious free time she possessed. She couldn't push this along any faster, not without help. The only person she could trust was Bradley Chapman. His methods were unorthodox yet effective. Now he was no longer watching over Tom Champion, maybe he and his friends could help her find Rosa.

It had been over a year since Chris's death, an anniversary she'd refused to acknowledge, mainly because she'd uncovered nothing new in her quest to topple the man she suspected was responsible for his murder. To mark the actual date of his murder was to accept it and accepting it meant losing him forever. She couldn't do that.

Her therapist would tell her she was in the final stages of the Kübler-Ross model for the five stages of grief: denial, anger, bargaining, depression and acceptance. And yet she didn't want to reach the final stage.

For several months, denial had kept Chris alive to her, ensuring she could converse with him, albeit make-believe. She'd slipped through the anger phase, her fury directed at Dickson, and had spent hours wishing and wondering what she could have done to have prevented that fateful day. She'd been trying to keep that phase alive through her efforts to bring down Dickson. Yet somehow, she'd entered the period of depression, exacerbated by the knowledge that unless she came up with a solution soon, she would only be left with memories which too would fade in time. If only she could keep stoking the anger, she'd rekindle those first few months when Chris's memory had felt as real to her as he had done before the train incident.

She stared at the A4 sheet she'd created; a smaller version of the whiteboard method she usually employed when heading an investigation. This was what had kept the flames of anger stoked. At its centre was a box containing the words *Maddox Club*. Chris had been looking into the place because it offered an underage escort service to its clients. Fearful her husband would stumble across the murder of a young, male sex-worker at the Maddox Club, the guilty parties had taken extreme measures. Chris had been shot on a train while returning home from London.

The Maddox Club was the key to her private investigation into Dickson. What had happened since had been due to what occurred there. There were several arrows leading from the box, the first linking it to the three men who had been at the club on the night of the lad's murder. Two of them, Alex Corby and Ian Wentworth, were now dead, leaving only one – Dickson. They had taken advantage of what had been called the Gold Service, offered by the club. All three had slept with sex-workers provided for them and although Dickson had claimed he had not slept with an underage girl, Kate had since discovered otherwise. He had spent the night with fourteen-year-old Rosa.

A second arrow pointed towards four names: Rosa, the murdered boy, and a third underage sex-worker, Stanka. The last, Farai, was the name of the pimp who had sent the youngsters to the Maddox Club.

Another arrow led to the man who'd helped cover up the boy's murder: Cooper Monroe, who was, thanks to Dickson and Tom Champion, also dead.

A thick red line joined the Maddox Club box to a second one marked *Operation Agouti*. This was a secret inquiry run by Dickson, set up, supposedly, to investigate underage sex-workers. Kate knew two of the officers who'd been part of the covert operation and was certain Operation Agouti was little more than a front to track down Farai, Rosa and Stanka. Beside this box were the names of two of the officers who'd taken part in it – DC Jamie Webster, who now worked on Kate's team, and Heather Gault, a civilian investigation officer, who had also been killed.

Heather had found Rosa. The day after meeting her, Heather had been murdered. It was too strong a coincidence for Kate to ignore.

Every person on her chart was connected by more red lines to a name – Dickson. Dickson was cleaning up after himself, ensuring anybody who could possibly link him to the boy's murder was eliminated. Tom Champion had been the latest victim, severing any connection between Dickson and Cooper. Next to die would be Rosa, Stanka and Farai. That was, if he hadn't already located them.

There was one final, extra-thick line, joining the superintendent's name to her husband's. With many of those who could have helped put Dickson behind bars for decades now dead, it was increasingly unlikely she could do anything further to avenge her husband. It also explained why Chris was no longer talking to her.

'You know I've tried,' she said. 'There hasn't been a single day I haven't looked for Farai and the girls.' The room swallowed her words and she let out a lengthy sigh.

For a long time after Chris had died, she'd held imaginary conversations with him. Driven by the need to discover the truth behind his murder, she'd felt close to him for many months. Until recently. Along with her dwindling resolve to avenge his death came an inevitable fading-away of the man she'd loved. Like her, he'd given up hope in her ever uncovering Dickson's role in the shooting. He had fallen silent, once and for all.

It pained her. Without make-believe Chris as a crutch, everything was harder, life greyer and increasingly unbearable. She couldn't accept he was no longer available to her, even if it was in an imaginary capacity, and every day that passed was one more when another piece of him seemed to vanish forever.

'There isn't anyone left to ask about them. Nobody at Farai's usual haunts will admit to knowing where he is or get a message to him on my behalf. None of my contacts, none of the other street-walkers will even talk to me about the trio! I've tried everything.' She winced at a sudden memory . . .

◆　◆　◆

The woman looks Kate up and down and sneers. 'Fuck off, copper.'

'I'm not here as a police officer. This is important, Cerise. Her life is in danger.'

Cerise is in her thirties, her black hair is shaved almost to her scalp and heavy eyeliner makes her eyes goth-like. Her face, however, is youthful. She puts both hands on her hips and juts her chin. 'You don't give a shit about people like us. So, fuck off. Go on, sling your hook before I call somebody to sort you out.'

'She's only a kid,' Kate persists, hoping to appeal to some maternal instinct in the hard-faced woman. The woman spits. The slimy glob hits Kate square in the eye. The woman laughs and walks away. Riled by the lack of concern for a young girl, fuelled by tiredness and desperation, Kate pursues her, puts a hand on her shoulder to stop her. She has been assured Cerise knows where Rosa is. The woman turns around quickly and slaps Kate hard. Without thinking, Kate thumps her in the face. Cerise yelps.

'You fucking bitch.' She yanks on Kate's hair. Kate is quicker, more experienced and trained in self-defence. She grabs Cerise's hand, works the wrist so it is bent backwards until she releases her grip. Then she twists and turns and pushes Cerise hard against the wall, where she presses her forearm against the woman's windpipe.

'She's only a kid. I must find her before somebody else does. What part of "her life is in danger" do you not get? Tell me where she is, and I'll walk away. If you don't, I'll kill you. What's it to be?'

The woman's eyes have become even larger, her pupils so enormous Kate can almost see her own angry reflection in them. She presses against Cerise's throat, cutting off the air supply and gradually crushing her windpipe. Cerise makes a gagging noise. Kate maintains the pressure.

'I . . . don't . . . know.'

Kate intensifies the hold. Cerise's eyes are bulging now. She won't release her. Not until she finds out where Rosa is.

'I . . . no.'

Kate cocks her head. 'Come on, Cerise. You can do better than that.'

Her eyelids begin to flicker. 'No.'

She is barely audible. She is losing consciousness.

Kate lets go and Cerise slides to the pavement, where she grabs her throat as she coughs and splutters.

Kate stands in front of her and waits for the noise to subside.

17

'Bitch.'

'What are you going to do? Report me?' says Kate.

'I don't know where Rosa went. They left Manchester. That's all I know. Rosa. Stanka. Farai. Gone. You attacked me for no good reason. You nearly killed me, you mad bitch.'

Kate stares at the woman, who is now getting to her feet. She turns on her heel without a word and marches away. It has been another fruitless evening.

◆　◆　◆

'What am I supposed to do, Chris? I can't get any answers! I can't do this on my own. My only recourse is to take what little I have to the chief constable, and yet where would that get me? At best, they'd look into my accusations, and at worst Dickson would be exonerated and might even file charges against me for wild accusations, make my life impossible, and I'd lose credibility, friends and most likely my job.'

Up until now, Chris would come back with his thoughts, which echoed her own or offered a different way of tackling the situation, but today, like many of the days prior to this one, there was no response. She slumped on to his chair, shut her eyes and repositioned the pieces of the by now familiar puzzle in her mind. No matter how she juggled it, it always spelled out Dickson.

She opened her eyes and stood up again. 'Chris?'

The only response was the sound of her beating heart. Where was he? Was she unable to hear him because she was finally accepting he was gone? The grieving process was carrying her along against her will. She didn't want to acknowledge he was dead. She didn't want to heal. She wanted to be able to talk to him.

The ball grinned at her and she snatched it up, shoved it into the top drawer, where Chris had kept it, and stomped out of the office. *What more can I do?* It was the same question that had been keeping her awake, night after night. It was a question she couldn't answer; one that burrowed into her mind and soul and threatened to destabilise her again. She was still on dodgy ground as far as the police force was concerned. Although she'd proven herself since Chris's death, her colleagues still studied her with wary eyes, and she continued to be held back by the very man she was determined to expose.

Her repeated request to return to former duties had been rejected. Dickson had somehow managed to convince the higher authorities that Kate was ideally placed in charge of a small team – a special-crimes unit – of only three individuals. She trusted two of her officers with her life but was certain DC Jamie Webster was a mole, planted by Dickson. She kept that knowledge to herself; as Chris had always told her, 'Know your enemies.' In spite of the fact that Jamie might well be reporting back to Dickson, he was an enthusiastic officer and a decent addition to the team. He was also a potential ace up her sleeve.

If she could win him over, he might help her bring down Dickson. She had a recording of CCTV footage from Stoke-on-Trent railway station revealing the meeting that had taken place between Heather Gault and Rosa. It also placed Jamie there, in the shadows, rather than where he'd claimed that day, and it didn't take a great mind leap to work out who had sent him there. She was so lost in thought she almost didn't hear her mobile.

All thoughts of Dickson vanished once she heard DCI William Chase's urgent voice – she was needed at a crime scene.

Blythe Bridge was only an eight-minute drive from police head-quarters, but even with the siren and blue lights, it took Kate a good twenty minutes from her house. She was waved through police barricades and directed on to a builders' merchants' car park. She emerged from her car in time to hear deep growling and witness the arrival of a two-seater sports car, driven by DS Emma Donaldson. The Nissan 370Z was polar-white with neon-orange decal stripes running along the sides. Emma pulled up beside Kate's Audi, jumped out and winced an apology.

'It belongs to Greg. Mine's in the garage. Failed its MOT. It needs some new brake discs.' Greg was one of Emma's seven brothers and ran a martial-arts training school where Emma trained almost every day.

Kate ran an eye over the sporty vehicle and nodded her approval. 'That one suits you,' she said as she pulled on her white suit.

Emma scuffled about in the boot, pulled out her own protective clothing and began suiting up. 'Better than my trusty, rusty, ancient Citroën C1? Surely not? The guys at the gym are always drooling over it. They say it's a babe magnet. Personally, I don't think so. It's too flash for my liking. It is damn quick, though. I see the others are already here,' she said, pointing out DS Morgan Meredith's Jeep and DC Jamie Webster's Saab. She pulled on shoe protectors and reached for latex gloves before aiming the key fob at the car, which locked with a noisy *blip*. 'I don't think I'd get away with performing any covert ops in this little beauty.'

'Probably not. Are you familiar with Blythe Bridge?' asked Kate.

'Not really. I pass through it a fair bit,' said Emma, in a matter-of-fact tone.

They stopped at a barricade erected in front of the level crossing, where they showed the officer their ID cards and waited for him to note down their names in the logbook. It was only a few paces to a turning, signposted for Blythe Bridge station. The pedestrian path was flanked by dark foliage that had grown too large and now crept out to overhang the way. They emerged on to the platform, where three men stood in a huddle under temporary lighting near a makeshift crime-scene tent: the first, Morgan, distinguishable thanks to his unmistakable height and broad shoulders, was talking to a lithe, silver-haired figure. Disguised as he was in his white paper suit, Ervin Saunders seemed rather ordinary this evening. Kate was pleased the head of forensics had arrived ahead of her. There was something about his manner that gave her confidence and helped ease her into an investigation. The conversation didn't reach her ears but the third man, Jamie, raked a hand through his copper-brown hair and shook his head.

'What's the story here then?' she said as she approached, making the men's heads turn as one.

'A shooting,' said Morgan. 'No witnesses. Once, in the forehead.'

They made for the makeshift tent a few metres ahead, where Morgan opened the flap, and Kate and Emma moved inside. A young man was lying on his back, dark eyes open in surprise, his forehead a mess of dark red matter and rivulets of blood down both smooth cheeks. His arms were wide, palms facing upwards. There was no wedding ring.

Ervin eased past them and crouched beside the body, where he pointed to the entry wound. 'I was explaining that it's unlikely a bullet caused this damage. There's a symmetrical circle, eleven millimetres in diameter, of what looks like powder soot deposits from the weapon's muzzle, caused by pressing what I assume to be a captive bolt pistol against the head. Harvey confirmed there is no exit wound and supports my theory. I came across something very similar to this about ten years ago.'

'Where is Harvey?' Kate asked. Harvey Fuller was a pathologist she'd worked with on several cases.

'Been and gone,' said Ervin. 'His best guess was that the deceased was killed less than a couple of hours ago. Rigor is only just setting in.'

'A captive bolt pistol,' repeated Emma. 'To stun animals?'

'Some guns render the animal unconscious and others kill. This one was a slaughterer's gun,' said Ervin. 'They're used by vets and butchers to kill large animals in a humane way, although I'm not sure how humane they are,' he added with a roll of his eyes. Ervin had been a vegan for as long as Kate could remember. He'd told her a spell working in a local abattoir during his university days had put him off eating meat for life. He waved his hands as if to dispel the thoughts and stood up. 'The deceased doesn't appear to have been injured in any other way, no fighting, no struggling, and no obvious defence wounds. It would appear he was surprised by his attacker.'

The illuminated tent emphasised the gory nature of the attack, making the reds and browns more vivid against the young man's pale skin. She turned around, spotted Morgan holding the flap open.

'Did he have any ID on him?'

Jamie's face appeared at the entrance. 'Yes, guv. His name is Tobias Abrahams, aged twenty-two. Address is local. Sutherland Crescent. His driving licence and wallet were in his jacket pocket. There's a mobile too. It was found further along the platform.'

She recalled the small marker possibly indicating where the phone had been found. 'Not a robbery then. No witnesses, you said?'

'None so far.'

Kate studied the man again: dark-blue chinos, pale-blue shirt and patterned tie, together with a dog-tooth blazer, gave off an air of maturity at odds with his youthful face. The gleaming burgundy shoes looked to be a recent purchase. Ervin spotted her looking at them. 'I have a similar pair I usually wear with my poppy and cedar plaid trousers.' Kate recalled the outfit, usually teamed with a white shirt, a matching red and green waistcoat and a large bow tie in the same soft green velvet as his jacket.

'They're what are known as brown derbys, a versatile brogue that goes with any outfit and a very decent make – Barker. Would have set him back around two hundred pounds or so. Mine did.'

Kate stepped back outside on to the platform. Emma was right behind her.

'He was out to make an impression.'

'Interview, or maybe a date?' Emma said.

'Both are possible. Jamie, would you find out what you can about him and why he might have been here on the platform. Has anybody any idea of train times? There don't seem to be any noticeboards here.' The station consisted of only two platforms, either side of the lines, and little else. The electronic sign next to the shelter suggested the next train to arrive at platform one was the Crewe train due in at 19.45 hours, fifteen minutes from now.

'Tobias might have been expecting to meet somebody travelling here,' said Emma as she inputted a timetable query into her mobile and read out the information. 'There's a train every hour and several stops between here and Crewe where he might have embarked – Kidsgrove, Longport, Stoke-on-Trent and Longton.'

'What about arrivals on the opposite platform?' asked Kate.

Emma scrolled through the screen. 'Same thing. One train from Derby every hour, arriving at twenty-two minutes past the hour.'

'I suppose he could have got off either train,' said Morgan.

'And crossed the lines to reach this platform?' asked Jamie. 'That's dangerous. Why would he do that?'

Morgan threw his hands up in the air. 'I don't know. A moment of madness. Maybe he saw somebody he knew over on this platform and rather than walk all the way down to the road, over the level crossing then back in, he hopped over the lines.'

Kate interjected. 'He might not have disembarked from any train and simply arranged to meet somebody here. Whatever happened, we need to narrow down the timing of the assault. Who found him?'

Morgan checked his notebook again. 'Yasmine Sheraf. She lives on the housing estate opposite. She was on the 18.22 train from Derby, along with her little boy. It was eighteen minutes late thanks to a signal failure outside Derby. She was the only person to get off. She didn't see the victim at first, because she was busy putting on the child's coat. It was only after the train pulled away she spotted Tobias on the platform. She thought he'd fallen or something. She sensibly didn't cross over the lines. She came via the road and level crossing, which took a few minutes. She rang emergency services straight away at . . . six forty-nine. She was shaken and the little one was crying when I spoke to her, so I sent an officer home with her and said we'd be round to talk later.'

Kate looked towards Ervin, who had rejoined them. 'Is there anything else you can tell us, Ervin?'

'Not at this stage. There was no ticket in his wallet or pockets. If he purchased his fare online, there's every chance we'll find evidence on his mobile. However, it's password protected, so until the tech team can crack that, it'll be of no help.'

It was nothing less than she expected. Two-factor security on mobile devices was the norm. 'Then we'll wait. Thanks, Ervin. Could you arrange for the deceased to be taken away now?'

'Sure. And once the area's clear, we'll begin a thorough search. Who knows? We might strike lucky and discover a fat, juicy clue as to the killer's identity.'

Emma suppressed a chuckle. 'That's very optimistic of you.'

'Irony, my dear Emma. I was being ironic. I didn't spot any-thing obvious when I walked the grid. Still, I am one of the best forensic scientists on the force, so if anyone can find anything, it'll be me.'

'Modest too. Or was that more irony?' said Morgan. Ervin threw him a pained look before heading off to issue instructions for the body to be removed.

Kate shook her head. Ervin was irrepressible. In spite of the horrendous hours and the difficulties he faced at times, he always tackled his job with zest. It was his life and his passion.

'We'll start by talking to Tobias's next-of-kin. They might be able to shed some light on the matter. Jamie, would you organ-ise canvassing in the area? Emma, I'd like you to interview Mrs Sheraf, and Morgan, I want you to come with me to break the bad news.'

Although it was only a ten-minute walk to Sutherland Crescent, they took her car and soon arrived outside a sandstone building with a front porch that extended over a garage, one of the only properties along the road where the garage had not been con-verted into accommodation. She parked on the road rather than the smart bricked driveway. Getting out, she caught sight of an anxious face peering from the downstairs window. She steeled herself for what was to come, silently grateful for Morgan's solid presence. He flanked her as she stood by the door, which opened without her having to knock. The woman wore a look of concern. It was hard to determine her age; however, with silver hair tied back and clear olive skin, it was not difficult to see she was related to Tobias.

'Hello?' The voice was wary.

Kate held up her ID. 'Mrs Abrahams?'

The woman's eyes widened a fraction and she nodded.

'I'm DI Kate Young and this is DS Morgan Meredith. Could we come in?'

The woman's dark eyes flitted from Kate to Morgan as her hand tightened on the door edge. 'Has something serious happened?'

'It would be better if we could talk about it inside.'

'It is something serious, isn't it? I knew it. As soon as I saw you get out of the car. I could tell. It was the way you looked – your faces. So solemn.'

'Mrs Abrahams, we really need to come inside.'

She shook her head. 'No. You can't. If you can't come in, you can't tell me. Then whatever it is won't have happened.' The woman's irrational thought process needed to be quelled. Kate had come across all sorts of resistance in her time as a police officer, families unwilling or unable to comprehend that the loved ones they had seen only a short while beforehand were never going to return. She took a pace forward, placed her hand over the woman's.

'Mrs Abrahams, you know that isn't true. Please, let's all go inside.'

'It's Tobias, isn't it? Something's happened.'

Kate manoeuvred her through the hall, into the sitting room, which was first on the right. A hefty white rabbit on the carpet chewed a leaf, unaware of the drama about to play out. Kate's eyes fell immediately to the framed picture of Tobias in graduation regalia. Next to it, a smaller, silver-framed photograph of him in the same outfit alongside his mother, decked out in a red coat and matching floppy hat. His framed university diploma hung on the wall, along with several other pictures of him through the ages. More photographs were dotted around the room on occasional tables, shelves. The room was almost a shrine to the boy.

Kate steered the woman to the chair next to a table on which lay some cross-stitching – a pattern of an emerald-winged butterfly settling on yellow and dusky-pink flowers. The rabbit loped across and was scooped into its owner's arms.

There was no way of telling this mother the truth about her son without bringing her world crashing down. Kate spoke with sincerity when she expressed her regret at having to bring such bad news. 'Mrs Abrahams, I'm very sorry to tell you that Tobias is dead.'

There was silence. Tobias's mother seemed transfixed, rabbit in arms, when a tiny sob that seemed to stick in her throat transformed into a guttural sound, half squeal, half howl. 'I've had a bad feeling all day. I couldn't shake it. It started when he went to the office. I knew something terrible was going to happen, but I didn't expect it to happen to him. Not to . . . my boy.' Her voice faded to a whisper.

'Is there anybody we can contact for you?' asked Kate.

'My sister, Elise. She lives nearby.'

Morgan asked for the details and left the room to make the call. Kate crouched before the chair. 'Can I get you anything? Maybe a cup of tea?'

'No. Nothing. I—' The words stuck in her throat, and she shook her head as her eyes filled with tears. She buried her face in the animal's fur and sobbed quietly. Kate gave her hand a gentle squeeze and let her cry. It was some time before she lifted her head, eyes bloodshot and her cheeks blotchy red.

'What happened to him?'

'I'm afraid he was shot.'

The intake of breath seemed to last an eternity. 'Did he . . . Did he suffer?'

'It was quick.' Kate watched the clouds of confusion and sorrow darken the woman's face.

'I don't understand. Was it a random attack?'

'We'll be investigating that angle. It happened at Blythe Bridge railway station. Could you tell me why Tobias might have been there?'

'He caught the lunchtime train to Stoke-on-Trent. He works for CRT Accountancy. Tobias has always been crazy about numbers, even as a child. He has a gift – his brain is a mental calculator.' She stifled another sob. 'He can perform all sorts of maths: any multiplication, any division in seconds.'

Her eyes filled again. Kate urged her gently. 'Did he contact you today?'

'No. He went to Stoke to attend an important buyout meeting. He told me it might go on a long time, that maybe there would be celebratory drinks afterwards. I wasn't to worry if he was late home.' A flicker of pride shone in her damp eyes before vanishing as quickly as it had appeared. She continued, 'He only started working there six months ago, so it was a big deal to be involved in this. He's been talking about it all week.'

'He hadn't planned on catching a particular train then?' asked Morgan, who'd returned to the room and was now taking notes.

She shook her head.

'Did he usually go to the office by train?' said Kate.

'Oh no. He usually cycles, but the forecast was for rain, so he took the train instead. He wanted to create a good impression.' She paused, eyes glazing again. 'He was on a fast track to be the youngest-ever partner in the firm. He looked so smart this morning when he left for work. My handsome boy—'

The tears began again, and she lowered the rabbit on to the carpet to blow her nose. The doorbell pealed and Morgan got up to answer it.

'Where is she?'

A whirlwind of orange and bergamot flew into the room and hurled herself at the figure in the chair. 'Chrissy, I'm so sorry. So terribly sorry.'

Morgan headed to the kitchen to make tea for the two women. To give them a few moments of privacy, Kate asked permission to look at Tobias's bedroom.

The walls were painted in pale teal, apart from one; a feature wall of geometric patterned turquoise blue behind the bed. She inhaled the scent of freshly laundered linen and took in the navy duvet cover, ironed to perfection, with not one crease visible. The plain roller blind that adorned the window was up. Watery light fell across a glass table where a line of Faber-Castell brown pencils, all sharpened to a point, lay in a row, each seemingly equidistant from its neighbour.

Kate slid on disposable gloves to open a black A4 Moleskine notebook which was on the desk. On the first page was a sequence of numbers and a baffling equation. Maths had never been her strong point. The neatly written numbers conveyed no meaning. She took out her mobile to snap a couple of photos of the pages. Somebody in the tech team would not only decipher the writing, but determine if it was significant. She ran a finger over the glass. It was dust free.

Standing up, her eye was drawn to a violin case, a foldable music stand, and a black wooden box that on opening revealed a pile of sheet music. In a wardrobe, trousers and jeans were folded neatly over hangers and pressed shirts hung with their collars buttoned up. Peering into a set of drawers, she found further examples of the order that permeated his life: his socks were rolled and lined up according to colour, his underwear folded. Tobias was a neat-freak. Another cupboard door hid a workstation where the 27-inch screen of a new desktop iMac filled the space. She pressed keys only to discover the computer was password protected.

She shut the door and descended the stairs. The women were more composed. Elise clutched a mug between her hands. Chrissy was stroking the rabbit again.

'I see Tobias played the violin,' Kate said.

'And the oboe,' said Elise. 'He was accomplished at both – a talented boy. We were both so proud of him.'

'He got his ability for maths and music from our father,' said Chrissy. 'So did Elise.'

Her sister shook her head. 'I'm not as good as either of them. Tobias was a far better musician and mathematician than me. You know, Detective, the two abilities go hand in hand. For two thousand years, music was regarded as a mathematical science and, in more recent times, many mathematicians have written on musical matters. Some great mathematicians also played instruments. The Russian astronomer and mathematician Friedrich T. Schubert played not only the piano but the flute, and violin. Oh, forgive me. I'm rambling. I do that sometimes.'

Kate continued, 'What about Tobias's father?' Even though she was pretty certain there was no Mr Abrahams, the question had to be asked.

It was Elise who answered. 'He left when Tobias was only four. We haven't heard from him since.'

'Then you don't know how I might contact him?'

'Not a clue and, if I were you, I wouldn't bother to track him down. He hasn't made contact since he left Chrissy, or paid a penny towards the boy's upbringing.'

It was as she suspected. 'Mrs Abrahams, do you mind if I call you Chrissy?'

'No. I don't mind.'

'Chrissy, what can you tell me about your son?'

Her hand rested on the rabbit's fur. 'What do you need to know? Hard-working.' The words became punctuated with sniffs. 'Decent. Kind. A good . . . son—'

As the sniffs took over, Elise jumped in with, 'He was such a lovely boy. An absolute darling boy. Never got into trouble. Everyone liked him.'

In Kate's opinion that wasn't always the case. People managed to rub others up the wrong way without knowing it. Maybe Tobias had unwittingly gained an enemy. 'He didn't give you any reason to suspect he was having trouble with anyone?'

'Trouble? Not Tobias.' His aunt patted her sister's hand. 'Chrissy, what about Ashleigh? She needs to be told.'

'Oh, goodness! Yes.' Her lips began to tremble.

Morgan spoke up. 'Is Ashleigh a relative?'

'His girlfriend. They met at work. Ashleigh Baker. They've only been seeing each other for four months, but we thought it was getting serious. Tobias seemed keen on her,' said Elise.

'Have you got a number or address for her?'

'No,' said Chrissy. 'His phone. It'll be on . . . on his mobile.'

'We'll speak to Ashleigh,' said Kate, before Chrissy burst into tears again.

Morgan caught Kate's eye. 'I think I heard a car pull up outside.'

Kate got to her feet, glanced out of the window and spotted somebody she knew getting out of a Ford Focus. The FLO, Richard Pilkington, known as Rich, was in his mid-forties with straw-blond hair and a face weathered by weekends spent climbing mountains.

'We're going to leave you now in the hands of the family liaison officer,' Kate said, 'but this is my card and, if you want to speak to me at any time, ring me.' She placed the card on the table and withdrew. 'I really am most sorry.'

She had a few words with Richard at the door. Reaching the end of the path, she let out a sigh. 'Jeez, the poor woman. Tobias was her life.'

Morgan cleared his throat. 'I don't want to be mean, but I think he was a mummy's boy. And maybe even a bit of a bragger if he thought he could swing becoming a partner in a top accountancy firm. So, I'm not sure what sort of bloke he was. I suppose he could have got up somebody's nose.'

'I wonder why he settled on a firm in Stoke. If he was as ambitious as we've been led to believe, why didn't he head to London to one of the top firms there?'

'As I said, mummy's boy. He didn't want to stray far from home.'

'We'll let Rich do his job and see if he can shed any light on the situation. I'd like to talk to some of Tobias's co-workers and Ashleigh this evening. Ring Jamie and see if he can get any contact numbers and addresses for us.'

She got back into the driving seat with a sense of confusion. Tobias struck her as odd. His bedroom had seemed staged rather than lived in. There was little sense of who he really was, unless what she'd been looking at encapsulated his essence – a young man, lost in a world of numbers and music. Somewhat of a misfit. Maybe that was the sole reason he'd been targeted, yet she thought there was something else. She couldn't put her finger on what exactly was niggling her other than the fact that Tobias seemed relatively inoffensive and harmless. He was ambitious, a hard worker, a 'good son'. There was no logical reason for anyone to kill him. So why had they? Was Tobias really the intended target? She felt for the answer, couldn't reach it before deciding it was the random nature of the act that was troubling her. It didn't sit right, and it gave Kate a sense of foreboding.

CHAPTER TWO

The offices of CRT Accountancy and Tax Planning were inside a one-storey modern sandstone structure with large-paned darkened glass windows, each covered by blinds. A wide, light-grey-painted strip, bearing the name Princes House, ran below the roof, which sloped only to one side. It was one of several identical buildings in this small business park. Architecturally it was the polar opposite of the yet-to-be-converted site on the opposite side of the road, where danger signs mounted on wire fencing protected the hillocks of red brick from a half-demolished factory. Morgan pointed out the Jaguar F-Pace parked outside.

'Jamie was right. The boss man is working late.'

Unable to contact the man on his mobile, Jamie had rung his home phone and spoken to Charles Trent's wife, who'd told him the MD was undoubtedly still in a meeting.

At the front entrance, Morgan pressed the button marked CRT. There was no response.

'Try again,' said Kate.

Morgan left his finger on the buzzer for several seconds until a peeved voice came over the intercom. 'We're closed. Call the office to make an appointment.'

'This is DI Kate Young and DS Morgan Meredith from Stoke-on-Trent police station, sir. We'd like a few words with you.'

The tone changed. 'Come in.'

The door unlocked with a loud click. Kate led the way into a dark, musty foyer. Everything about the place was unwelcoming, from the unmanned reception desk with its huge Perspex screen to a pair of functional brown chairs beside a table with a circular display of tax-planning leaflets. A door behind the reception desk opened.

'How can I help you, Officers?' The man was bordering on cadaverous. With thick white eyebrows and jet-black hair and a stoop, Kate thought he seemed better suited to the role of under-taker than accountant.

She strode towards him. 'Mr Charles Trent?'

'The very same. What's this about?'

'I'm afraid I have some bad news for you, sir.'

The bushy eyebrows tugged together. 'You'd better come through.'

They followed him into a long room, made gloomy by drawn blinds and a lack of lighting. Charles led them past individual workstations, separated by free-standing transparent screen divid-ers. Kate's boots were silent against the thin grey carpet tiles. The place felt almost melancholy, a far cry from her own small but lively office. Charles led them through another door where a table for twelve filled the room. Document files and sheets of paper were scattered over one end, along with an open laptop.

'You were lucky to catch me here at this time. I was just sorting through some paperwork after a long meeting,' he said, sweeping the documents together and sitting down. 'Take a seat.'

They did as bid.

'Well, what is this about?'

Kate broke the news. 'I'm sorry to inform you that one of your employees, Tobias Abrahams, was killed during an attack earlier this evening, at Blythe Bridge station.'

'You must be mistaken . . . He was here . . . until . . .' The man pressed long fingers against his forehead. 'Oh, heavens . . . I . . . I don't know what to say.'

'We'd appreciate your assistance in tracing his movements.'

He pulled himself upright to meet her eye. 'Of course.'

'We understand he came in today, for a meeting. Was that the same meeting that you referred to, a few moments ago?'

'Erm, yes.'

'But he didn't stay for the whole meeting?'

'No.'

'Why not?'

'Sorry. I'm not being very clear. This is quite a shock. Only a few hours ago, he was sitting two seats away from me.'

'Take your time.'

He cleared his throat. 'Erm. What I mean is . . . yes, he came in for that meeting. Like many companies, our staff now work flexi-hours. By and large, they all work from home except when we need to speak to clients face to face. Today, we were advising one of our companies on a management buyout. It's been in the pipeline for some time. We had to thrash out quite a few complex details, especially the tax implications. Tobias hasn't been with us very long. He's . . . I mean, he was very keen to become more involved. He asked if he could attend as an observer. The clients agreed, so we let him sit in on the meeting.'

'We?'

The other senior partner – Nilesh Gupta. We prefer to deal with our high-profile clients personally. You missed Nilesh by about ten minutes.'

'What time did Tobias leave?'

'Er.' Charles ran a finger around the collar of his shirt before replying. 'The meeting began at two and we broke at around five o'clock for refreshments. That's when I asked him to go home.'

35

'Why did you do that?'

'He'd interrupted proceedings a few times with what he imagined were useful proposals but were, to be frank, muddying the waters. Although Tobias was very astute and had an incredible memory for numbers, he wasn't experienced enough to offer advice or indeed challenge what we were suggesting. It was a complex deal. Tobias was in danger of jeopardising our hard work. Both Nilesh and I decided it was best he went.'

'Was he okay about that?' asked Morgan.

'Not really. He couldn't understand why we weren't open to his ideas. He has . . . had a very high opinion of himself. He wasn't able to accept he was out of line.'

Morgan spoke again. 'He wasn't angry or upset then?'

'Not in the least. More . . . disdainful than upset.'

Tobias sounded like a stroppy teenager to Kate. 'Was this normal behaviour from him?'

'I'm afraid so, but I took it for an exuberance of enthusiasm and self-belief. There's nothing wrong in being confident. Tobias was extremely good at what he did. How can I phrase this without being too damning? His *arrogance* had been commented on.'

'Yet you let him attend and interrupt an important meeting?' said Morgan.

He steepled his fingers and gave Morgan a serious look. 'I was young once. If I'm honest, cocky too. If I'd been blessed with the same ability Tobias had, I'd have been even more arrogant. He had the makings of an excellent accountant and, combined with ardour, which he had in spades, combined with greater experience, would have done very well here. We were lucky to have him.'

'His mother told us he was hoping to make partner soon,' said Kate.

A tired smile flicked over his lips. 'He had quite a few rungs of the ladder to climb before we'd have considered that prospect.

This is an example of what I meant by his attitude. Although he had grand aspirations, he lacked the wisdom and experience to bring them to fruition. That aside, he would eventually have made partner. Probably in ten years or so from now.'

'Did he get along with his colleagues?' Kate asked.

'With the current work rota system in place, he hasn't had many opportunities to see them in person. He was, as I recall, rather opinionated during Zoom meetings and was shouted down once or twice by his manager. However, I don't think he was disliked as such, because he was able and willing to take on others' work when they were overburdened.'

'Can you think of any reason somebody might have murdered Tobias?'

He shook his head. 'None. You might glean more from Donna Cuthbert. She was his manager. I'll give you her details.'

He logged on to his laptop and copied the information on to a notepad, tearing off the sheet.

'Could you also give us contact details for Ashleigh Baker? We were led to believe they were an item.'

His eyebrows lifted. 'Ashleigh! I had no idea they were together. She's a lovely girl. She'll be devastated by this news. Oh dear. Poor Ashleigh. I'll get her details for you.' He clicked a few keys on his laptop and scribbled down the information on the same sheet of paper and hesitated before handing it to Morgan. 'I wonder—'

'Sir?'

'I wonder if he'd still be alive if I hadn't been so hard on him today and sent him packing. Maybe if I'd asked him to be more of an observer and less vociferous instead, he could have stayed for the duration of the meeting and this . . . this wouldn't have happened. That's right, isn't it? I played a part in this.'

'We don't know if the attack was random or premeditated, so I wouldn't blame yourself, sir,' said Morgan.

'No. I feel I'm responsible in some way. I'll talk to his mother. Maybe the firm could send some flowers, make a donation to a charity of her choice—'

'Whatever you feel is appropriate,' Kate replied. She was met with a small nod. 'If you think of anything that might help us, please would you give us a call? I'll leave my card.'

He didn't reply but stood up to see them out. At the door, he said, 'I'm sorry. I didn't ask what happened to him. You said he was attacked, but how did he die?'

'He was shot,' said Morgan.

Charles seemed to shrink a couple of inches. 'Poor lad. I do wish I hadn't sent him home.'

His words set off again the disquiet Kate had experienced earlier. Would Tobias be alive now if he had not caught that train?

◆ ◆ ◆

It was coming up to half past nine by the time they drew up on Ashford Street, where Tobias's girlfriend Ashleigh lived. Morgan killed the engine and studied the boarded-up shop outside which they'd parked. His stomach rumbled loudly. He rubbed it with a frown.

'It's a pity that takeaway has closed down. I could really go for a chicken shish kebab. Or two. With chips.'

She couldn't help but smile. Just because she could go for hours without eating didn't mean her officers could do the same. On top of which, Morgan loved his food. 'As soon as we've spoken to Ashleigh, we'll find one that is open. There'll be one somewhere nearby. My treat. Whatever you fancy. As much as you want.'

His handsome face brightened. 'Cheers. Although you might regret saying that. I could eat a scabby horse.'

She threw open the door and stepped on to the pavement. Large drops fell from the darkened sky, pattering noisily on the corrugated roofs of run-down garages. The drumming intensified as they strode beside the row of red-brick dwellings, fat drops bouncing off the dustbins lined up outside each property awaiting the morning collection. Cars were jammed, one behind the other, with no available parking spots in front of any of the houses.

Morgan rang the doorbell. Kate shook off drops that clung to her hair and straightened her shoulders.

'Hi.' It was difficult to pin an age on the girl who answered. Her face, with elaborate eye shadow, heavily applied eyeliner and shining lip gloss, suggested late teens, her polar-white onesie and koala furry boots suggested younger.

Kate gave a small smile. 'Hi. We're police officers. We'd like to talk to Ashleigh Baker, please.'

The girl remained rooted to the spot for a moment. 'Police?'

'Could we come in?' Kate held up her ID for the girl to see.

'I guess so.' She slipped through another door, a burst of siren sounds escaping before she shut it.

There was barely enough room for both of them in the narrow entrance, and Kate stood against a radiator, trying not to elbow Morgan for a long minute before the door opened again and a voice called, 'Come in.'

The young girl who'd let them in sat on an arm of a chair, next to an older version of herself. Ashleigh blew on her fingernails and wriggled freshly painted candy-pink toes. 'Sorry, I was doing my nails. Is this about George? We're not together any more, so I don't know where he is.'

'No, it isn't about George. I'm afraid we've got some bad news.'

'Jeez, it's not Mum, is it?' The girl's face turned white.

'It's Tobias.'

'Tobias?'

'Tobias was involved in an incident earlier today. He was attacked and, I'm very sorry, but he was badly hurt and died at the scene. Again, I'm sorry to give you such terrible news.'

Ashleigh stared at her nails, then at her sister. Her lips parted and a small noise, a cross between a squeal and a strangled cry, burst from them. The younger girl put her arms around her.

Ashleigh spoke between sobs. 'What . . . happened . . . to . . . him? Where?'

'He was attacked at Blythe Bridge station.'

Ashleigh struggled for control, sniffed back tears. 'Station? I don't . . . understand. Why was he . . . at the station?'

'He was on his way back from the office. He'd been to a meeting there.'

'Had he? He didn't . . . mention it to me.' She wiped her face with the sleeve of her zip-up top.

'You okay?' Her sister's voice was hesitant.

'Yeah. I'm okay, babe.' She held and squeezed her sister's hand and spoke again. 'Shit! This is . . . awful. Poor Tobias.'

'I understand this is a very difficult time for you, but anything you tell us now might help us find the person responsible.'

'Yeah. Sure. I'll try.'

'You met Tobias at work, didn't you?'

'That's right. I'm a receptionist there.'

'How did he get on with everyone?' It was a question Kate had asked Donna, Tobias's manager only five minutes earlier, while they'd been driving to Ashleigh's. Donna had been polite about the young man but hinted he might have rubbed some of the other accountants up the wrong way. Kate was hoping Ashleigh had an ear to the ground and knew who they might be. It appeared not.

'People liked him. I never heard anyone badmouthing him.' Ashleigh's bottom lip trembled.

'How long have you been going out together?' asked Morgan.

'Four months tomorrow. Only four months but—' Her eyes became glassy again.

Kate didn't want to lose the girl to tears, so she quickly moved on. 'Did Tobias mention a falling-out with anyone? An old friend maybe?'

She shook her head. 'He didn't have any friends around here. He had a few from university. One or two of them live in London. I haven't met any of them. We planned to. We were going to head to London for a weekend. We just . . . hadn't . . . got . . . around . . . to it.' Her shoulders started to shake as the sobs began. This time in earnest.

'Oh, babe. It's okay,' said her sister, opening her arms again and embracing her.

'Ashleigh, when we first came in, you mentioned George? Who's George?'

'Her dick-arse ex,' said the sister when Ashleigh couldn't speak.

'Has he been in trouble with the police before?'

She pulled a face. 'Er, yeah.'

'Ashleigh, when did you and George split up?'

The girl sobbed against her sister's shoulders. The younger girl answered on her behalf. 'Four months ago. The day Tobias asked her out.'

Ashleigh lifted her head. Sooty mascara marks had ringed her eyes and streaked her cheeks. She spluttered, 'George wouldn't . . . have . . . hurt . . . him.' The sentence died away, drowned by lengthy hiccoughing cries of sorrow. The girls hugged each other, the younger soothing the older.

Kate decided to leave. Ashleigh wasn't in a fit state for further questioning. They'd have to find out about George for themselves.

CHAPTER THREE

DAY TWO – WEDNESDAY

Sweat flew from Emma's face and landed on the punchbag. She didn't give up. Relentless jabs followed by a volley of cross punches and hooks. The bag swung wildly as she slammed her fists into it. She wouldn't stop until she'd caused such muscle fatigue she couldn't raise her arms.

She grunted loudly. Her gloved fists smacked against the leather with impetus. Each punch not aimed at somebody but at a memory, one that had come to the fore and troubled her. She went through the same thing every year at this time. Her brother, Greg, who owned the gym, understood. It was one of the reasons he had given her a key, so she could come and go as she pleased. He wasn't as deeply affected by what had happened ten years ago. Then again, he hadn't been the one who had found her.

Energy drained from her arms, draining the fury with it. She took a step back, panting with the effort before pulling off her soaking gloves. The bag creaked on its chain until it came to rest in its usual spot.

Her brother's gym was silent, only her there alone, as she had been almost every morning for the last month. The workouts weren't as beneficial as usual. The memories weren't being exorcised. She reached for her towel and rubbed it over her hot face. She'd come back later. Try a martial-arts routine. It would be the only way she could cope until *the day*.

◆ ◆ ◆

The images were higgledy-piggledy; Chris was being pulled under a strong current, his hand above the waterline, face underneath, eyes pleading for assistance. When she reached for her husband, his face morphed into her stepsister Tilly's. Before she could speak a large red hole appeared in Tilly's forehead, the blood mingling with the water as she was sucked down into the murky depths of the reservoir. Kate woke with a jolt and threw the duvet back before she'd fully regained consciousness. She required focus. She needed to get on with the day in hand.

It wouldn't take a trip to a therapist to work out what was troubling her. And as for the dream, it wasn't about Chris or Tilly. Her subconscious mind had been working while she slept, ruminating over her problems and fears and translating them into dreams for her conscious mind to recognise. She was the person who was really drowning. Her failed attempts to find further evidence to bring down Dickson, combined with keeping up the pretence of normality, all the while keeping a watchful eye on Jamie and ensuring nobody suspected her of being anything than a hard-working detective, were getting to her. If only she could conjure up Chris's imaginary presence as she had after his death, it would help. His silence troubled and puzzled her. She had thought it was because she was acting too slowly to nail Dickson. But the dream gave her another idea. Was it because of Tilly?

Ever since Tilly had come back into her life, Chris had faded further into the recesses of her memory. Although her stepsister had returned to Australia, she remained in regular contact and was due to Skype that day. Much as Kate enjoyed talking to her and her nephew Daniel, she wasn't sure if she could keep paying the price of losing Chris.

'Chris, please, come back. I haven't given up on finding the truth. Don't give up on me.' The words stuck in her throat. There was no reply. How could there be? Chris was dead.

'Chris! Please!'

She yanked open the drawers and rummaged through the clothes, pulling out a top and running shorts. Fresh air and a workout would clear her head. More importantly, she had to reconnect with Chris. She made a quick stop at the bathroom to brush her teeth and pull her hair into a ponytail, then bounded downstairs, stopping only to pull on her trainers. It was then she spotted the time – 4.30 a.m. She paused by the door before deciding it didn't matter how early it was, she would still go. For the last four months, she'd made the daily thirty-minute car journey to Blithfield Reservoir to jog through the woodlands around the water. Even though there were parks and routes closer to home, she'd always felt more connected to Chris in this place and, today, she needed him more than ever.

◆　◆　◆

Parking as she always did by the edge of the reservoir, she gazed over the coal-black waters, as smooth as glass. There was no sound and she questioned her sanity: what was she doing running through dark woodlands before dawn? Truth be told, she wasn't sure she was sane. Sometimes, she felt she was enveloped in a whirlwind of confusion and couldn't fight her way free. Something had to give and at the moment that something was Kate. The faint rumble of an engine announced the arrival of another vehicle, somebody else up as early as her. Headlights appeared at the top of the hill, their bright beams picking out the causeway.

She couldn't fully understand why she was constantly drawn to this spot. When he was alive, Chris had only visited here once or twice, yet she now associated it with him, as if his ghost lived here. Soon after his death, she had chosen to jog the routes around the reservoir, and discovered he had been beside her, stride for stride, speaking to her, helping her chew over the details of her investigation into a murder close by. The idea that he was with her had been so vivid she had returned, even though it was some distance from her home. She had pounded along the pathways of the shaded woods, feeling his presence and gaining a sense of somehow being even closer to him than when he'd been alive.

Light fell on to a pair of swans asleep beside the water's edge, only their white plumage visible, heads bowed under broad wings, and the sorrow in her heart eased fractionally. They were together in sleep. They'd been here every day she had visited; soulmates for life. She couldn't explain why she felt such affection for the birds. Their unity had burrowed into her and, watching them, she was reminded of what she and Chris had shared. Not love. More than that – a connection that made them one whole being.

Standing in the darkness, she waited for the car to pass by and, when the growling ebbed and its tail lights disappeared from view, she turned on her headtorch. Choosing the longer route beside the lake which would eventually take her into the woods, she set off across the causeway before slipping over the fence and into the field and on to dewy grass. She soon fell into a rhythm and tried to imagine Chris running beside her, his breath heavier than hers. They'd often run together, matching each other's pace. Chris was faster than her, but she had more stamina and could always outdistance him.

The air cooled her cheeks. She inhaled the freshness and a light fragrance of meadow grass. These fields had been planted with flowers to attract increased numbers of insects and bees. She stuck rigidly to the designated route so as not to crush any of them, her thoughts untangling themselves as she ran.

The lake shimmered darkly beside her, gentle splashes from awakened wildfowl as they sought refuge from the stranger running along the shore. A pang went off in her chest. She couldn't sense Chris's presence at all. A movement startled her as a barn owl swooped low beside her, its wings outstretched. She stumbled on a rut, caught herself in time before she fell. *Concentrate. You'll break something if you don't pay attention.*

She abandoned her thoughts and ran up the slope into the woods, where tree roots twisted their way above ground and low branches attempted to capture her as she sped past. Startled calls from disturbed birds accompanied her movements. She was crazy to be out at this time.

'Chris, you're still there, aren't you?'

Twigs snapped, dry leaves rustled, but no voice was forthcoming. Career or not, if she gave up searching for Rosa, the final piece in the Dickson puzzle, Chris would never return.

◆ ◆ ◆

Kate was saved from having to knock on Superintendent John Dickson's door. He was striding through the foyer when she arrived for work.

'Sir, I'd like a moment of your time, please.'

'Make it quick. I have to be somewhere.'

'I'd like to request some assistance for our current investigation – the young man who was shot at the station,' she added when he frowned.

'I know which case you're referring to.'

Kate was slightly taken aback. Dickson could often be cold with her, but today there was something else in his manner; a sense of urgency, as if he didn't want to talk to her at all. Was it to do with Tom Champion? Dickson had prevented Cooper from talking to her, removed Tom from the equation. Now he could drop the mask, be as rude or difficult as he liked, in the knowledge that there was nothing Kate could pin on him. This idea grew, further inflated by the dark look on his face. He didn't speak. The silence became awkward. Then: 'Can't you and your team manage this?'

'We might manage it quicker if we had extra hands.' She wasn't going to back down on this. Dickson had blocked her requests to lead her old unit; he surely wouldn't dare deny her assistance on a murder inquiry. 'The sooner we do so, the better it looks for the station.'

'At present, we're extremely stretched.' He drilled her with a look. 'A liaison and a technical officer. That's all I can agree to. You'll have to manage.'

'We shall. Thank you, sir.'

He marched away without a goodbye, or a word of encouragement. He turned back as he slipped through the doors. The derisory look he fired in her direction chilled her bones. Dickson was no longer concerned he would get caught out. His dislike for her was evident. The gloves were off. Kate would have to be ultra-careful. Furthermore, she would have to get a speedy result. If it dragged on, she would become toast.

◆ ◆ ◆

Kate commandeered the meeting room on the top floor for a briefing.

'Our victim is the only child of Chrissy Abrahams. He obtained a first from Bristol University in Applied Maths eighteen months ago, and his CIMA accountancy qualification online. Four months ago, he took up a junior position at CRT Accountancy and Tax

Planning. He was a maths genius, a skill inherited from his grand-father. He was also an accomplished musician and as a teenager played with the North Staffs Symphony Orchestra. Rich, have you anything you can add?'

The liaison officer spoke with a soft Brummie accent. 'Like you said, he was a bit of a whiz-kid. He was into online quizzes, chess, music and maths. Big time. He even did equations for fun. Never got in any trouble. Had a handful of friends from university but they all lived in London. He was a keen advocate of saving the planet and mostly cycled, although he had a driving licence and occasionally drove his mother to the shops . . . in her electric Mini.

'He was very close to his mum and his aunt, Elise. They brought him up after his father walked out on them. Chrissy won't discuss his father, but he's named on Tobias's birth certificate as David Abrahams. They've had no contact with him since he vanished and have no address for him, nor do they want him to be notified. They seem to be a tight-knit, small family. The aunt lives nearby and often pops round at weekends. They didn't have a bad word to say about Tobias.' He punctuated the end of his sentence and thoughts with a small shrug.

Morgan was first to speak. 'They couldn't think of any reason for him being targeted?'

'None at all.'

'Didn't owe any money?'

'Nope. He worked at a pub while he was at Bristol to help fund his studies. His aunt gifted him six grand a year to help with the maintenance costs. To their knowledge he's never been in debt, taken drugs or smoked, and was teetotal. He had big plans to make partner at CRT Accountancy and Tax Planning as quickly as possi-ble and then set up his own firm.'

Kate maintained a poker face, even though her heart was beat-ing quicker than usual. Dickson had put the wind up her. She'd spoken to him about finding this young man's killer more confidently than she'd felt. Now she felt even less assured. 'Jamie. What have you found out?'

Jamie's head shot up and he blinked several times as if bringing himself to. 'Er . . . yeah. Erm . . . Financial records confirm Tobias has never been in debt. There are no odd movements in his current account. His savings account contains almost ten thousand pounds. From what I can gather, he didn't have much in the way of expenditure. Presumably his mother doesn't charge him rent and pays all the household bills.'

Richard nodded. 'That's correct. She's a pharmacist. Works in Hafton's Pharmacy in Stoke-on-Trent. It's only a seven-minute drive from her house.'

Jamie looked at his notes again, picked up from where he'd left off. 'His university professor said he was a confident student, a little arrogant at times and an excellent quizzer. He'd fully expected Tobias to stay on at Bristol after he graduated and take up a master's degree and was surprised when he opted to return home and study for his accountancy exams online. He hasn't been in contact with Tobias since he left university but pointed me in the direction of a couple of fellow students. Both of them suggested Tobias wasn't the easiest person to get on with and suffered from a big ego. The actual phrase one of them used was, "Tobias was up himself and eventually got on everyone's tits."' Although he lifted his hand to cover his mouth, it wasn't quite in time to conceal a yawn.

'Are we keeping you awake?' said Morgan.

Jamie waved away the comment airily.

'Only, we could put up a camp bed for you to have a snooze, if you need it.'

'Fuck off,' said Jamie with a grin.

Kate dragged them back to business. 'Ashleigh Baker was Tobias's current girlfriend. She didn't have a lot to tell us and didn't

49

even know about the meeting he was attending that day, however, we picked up on one thing; Ashleigh broke off a relationship with a lad called George Fox to start one with Tobias. Morgan, what do you have?'

'George is something of a hothead. He was cautioned ten months ago for dangerous driving. He maintained it was a one-off and he'd had a bout of road rage after somebody cut him up on the roundabout and smashed his wing mirror off. That said, there were a couple of other instances, suggesting he has a temper. He was charged but subsequently released, following fights in Hanley Park. In both instances, the victims didn't press charges, claiming they couldn't identify their attacker. We don't know for sure if there was bad blood between Tobias and George, so we'll follow it up today and ascertain his whereabouts for yesterday afternoon.'

'Which brings us on to the time of the murder,' said Kate, 'which we believe occurred between 17.45, when he disembarked at Blythe Bridge station, and 18.40, when Mrs Sheraf spotted his body.'

Jamie sat back, rested his hands on his head, fingers interlocked. 'Most likely closer to 17.45. He isn't likely to hang around on the platform doing nothing for a whole hour, is he? Somebody must have been waiting for him to get off the train and shot him then.'

'Plenty of guesswork going on there, Jamie,' said Morgan.

'Okay. Then he might have arranged to meet somebody on the platform. They got into a massive argument, which led to him being shot.'

Morgan shook his head. 'Mate, we're getting ahead of ourselves here.'

'Yeah. Fair enough.'

Kate began to speak. 'Tobias was dead by the time the Derby train pulled in.'

Jamie yawned again, shifted position, started to fiddle with a pencil on his desk.

'It's plausible—'

'We haven't talked about the train Tobias caught. Did nobody else get off at Blythe Bridge?' Jamie blurted.

'I was getting on to that,' Kate snapped. She didn't appreciate his interruption. But her irritation wasn't because he'd jumped in while she was talking or because he wasn't on the ball today. She didn't trust Jamie. If he was acting as a mole and keeping Dickson fully informed, she wanted to ensure she did everything by the book. Especially now. 'It's plausible he arranged to meet somebody who turned on him. However, we have learned that two passengers disembarked at Blythe Bridge. One was Tobias and the other was a man in his forties, wearing a high-vis vest.'

'Okay. Then this man might have been a witness or his attacker,' said Jamie. He flicked the pencil, sending it into a spin.

'Could you stop messing about with that, Jamie? It's distracting.'

'Oh, yeah. Sorry.' He folded his arms, concentrated instead on Kate.

'We need to contact passengers who were on both trains, however, this person should be our priority. Make sure appeal boards are erected at Blythe Bridge station and the surrounding area. I'll request media assistance in drumming up witnesses. Right, what else do we have? Emma?'

'I've got nothing. Mrs Sheraf doesn't recollect anything that might help us. She was fixated on getting help for Tobias, then on calming her crying child. I've interviewed residents who live opposite the station. None of them spotted anyone acting suspiciously or saw anything untoward until the emergency services appeared. There are no surveillance cameras on any of the properties, and none at the three access areas: the pathway, the platform opposite, or the level crossing. There are some CCTV cameras further along Uttoxeter Road, aren't there, Krishna?'

The dark-haired man opposite her nodded. 'There are several surveillance cameras along the length of the road. The tech team is already searching for pedestrians who were in the area around that time. We'll also compile a list of vehicles on Uttoxeter Road for the times in question. As you can appreciate, it's a mammoth task, especially as it's a busy road and, from what we can gather, there are numerous side streets branching off from it. The perpetrator could have vanished down any of them.'

Krishna adjusted the large-framed spectacles that added gravitas to his already serious demeanour. Kate was pleased to have been seconded him. He was one of the best in the technical department. 'Also from our side, we've unlocked Tobias's mobile phone and checked out his social media. Although he wasn't on Facebook or Twitter, he was on WhatsApp and a member of several quiz groups. Nothing has leapt out so far, but we're on it. This is more interesting. The call log reveals he was rung by a pay-as-you-go number at five forty-seven, around the time he disembarked from the train. The number isn't in his contacts list, yet he has rung it every day for the last two weeks.' He handed Kate a printout.

She glanced at it, then, tapping it with a forefinger, said, 'We need to find out who this number belongs to. Jamie, can you work on getting a triangulation for this call? Jamie!'

Jamie was stifling yet another yawn. 'Sorry. Didn't get much sleep last night. The little one was playing up. Sure. I'll do that.'

Kate resisted the urge to call him out there and then. His child might have woken him, but his wife, knowing he was working on an important investigation, would surely have stepped in to deal with the situation, leaving Jamie to rest. She couldn't help but wonder what he had really been doing to make him so tired.

She held up the photograph of Tobias in his graduation outfit. 'Finally, several of his acquaintances referred to Tobias as arrogant and extremely self-assured. There's a chance he might have pressed somebody's buttons enough for them to flip – maybe a friend or somebody he only knows casually. Morgan and I have already contacted and ruled out all his work colleagues. They have alibis for the evening, and none was in the Blythe Bridge vicinity.

'At the moment, there seems little motive to kill this young man. Don't forget, he shouldn't have been on board that train. He only caught it because he was sent home unexpectedly. Which means we must establish whether he was an intended victim or if he was in the wrong place at the wrong time. We need to dig deeper, people.'

The team set off to work, leaving her alone in the meeting room, the photograph of Tobias Abrahams in front of her. They had so little to go on – a phone number and perhaps a jealous ex-boyfriend.

A tap made her look up. DCI William Chase peered around the door. 'How's it going?'

'Nothing yet. There's something about the location that bothers me. It's not as if Tobias used the station regularly. He didn't. He cycled everywhere. Even supposing the killer knew he had caught the train to work, how could they know which train Tobias would catch home? He shouldn't even have been on that train. Had he not been sent home early, he'd have been on a later train. It isn't making any sense, William.'

William came into the room, pulled out a chair and dropped on to it. Kate had always had an affinity with her mentor, the man who'd been her father's work partner and best friend. The last few months, it had been strained between them. She'd kept him at a distance, citing work when he'd invited her over for a meal, film or chat. Chris's file had cast doubt on his character and a shadow over their relationship. Although she trusted Chris's instincts and admired his ability to unearth the darkest secrets, she struggled to believe that this craggy-faced, gentle man, who'd almost replaced her father in her affections, could be anything other than straight. His eyes crinkled.

'All investigations start out the same way. They're a jumble of puzzle pieces waiting for the right person to sort through them and slot them together. You're your father's daughter. You'll work it out.'

She studied Tobias's photograph – a young man full of fortitude and hope. The weight of determining who had killed him rested squarely on her shoulders. 'Did Dad ever get it wrong?'

'Never.' He sat back, folded his arms. 'Mitch never let go. Worried every clue like a dog worries a bone. You're exactly like him. I see the same single-minded look in your eyes, the same set of the jaw, and I know you'll work it out, like he used to. You should consider promotion.'

'Wow! That came out of the blue.'

'No, I've been wanting to talk to you about it for some time. I think you're ready to move upwards.'

'I doubt the super would approve any application.'

He gave a soundless laugh. 'Don't be put off. There are others who far outrank him who will agree with me. You've been noticed again, Kate. And for all the right reasons. Give it some thought. As you know, I'm retiring in a couple of weeks, and I'd like to think you had a bright future to look forward to in the force.'

'I'm not so sure.'

'You've fought back, had some seriously good results in recent months. I believe the time is right.' He stood up. 'Mitch would have wanted you to. And, it goes without saying, I'll back you wholeheartedly if you do.'

Kate was taken aback. William couldn't be oblivious to the tension between her and Dickson, could he? Had Dickson played him by pretending there were no issues between him and Kate? She racked her brains to work out if she had ever bad-mouthed Dickson to William. The answer was she hadn't. She'd played her cards close to her chest because Chris had left behind two legacies: a journal containing information about a paedophile ring he had been researching and an online document containing names of potentially corrupt officers. Among the latter were two names she knew well: Superintendent John Dickson and her mentor and friend, DCI William Chase.

Ever since the list had come to light, she'd had trouble processing it. How Chris had concluded that these people were bent baffled her. She couldn't be sure any others were guilty of corruption. Apart from Dickson, whose card was well and truly marked. Though Kate couldn't bring herself to believe William was crooked, she had never voiced her doubts to him about Dickson. She'd been masterminding her own game, apparently as successfully as Dickson. She wondered if she should come clean, tell William what she suspected about Dickson, then a warning bell sounded in her mind. She had kept this to herself for so long she dared not entrust it to anyone until she was certain of their loyalties and intent.

'Thanks, William. That means a lot to me.'

Even with William's backing, Dickson would be sure to block any opportunity for her promotion, yet the idea she would ruffle his feathers by putting herself forward appealed. Dickson wanted her out, not rising through the ranks. He would try to put more pressure on her and maybe, just maybe, he would trip up.

He gave a small smile. 'Don't take too long to decide. There's not much time left before they put me out to grass.'

'How will you cope without all of this? Your job? The daily buzz?'

'Better than you would, my dear.'

The talk with William had stirred a myriad of emotions, the desire to crush Dickson outweighing the investigation. She wondered if, despite his recent anger towards her, Bradley Chapman had gone on the hunt for Tom Champion. It was the sort of thing he would do. He wasn't a man to give up and he wanted Dickson to be brought to justice. She typed out a brief text message to Bradley, asking the question. She then resolved to search again for Rosa and Stanka as soon as she could, maybe even later today, if she could leave her team to work the case without her.

Promotion! She gave a brief, satisfied huff. She would love to be a fly on the wall when Dickson saw her application.

◆ ◆ ◆

Kate shifted in the passenger seat, settling into a fresh position in the Jeep. She'd taken part in more stakeouts than she cared to remember. It was mind-numbing work yet sometimes produced results. Ashleigh's ex-boyfriend, George, wasn't at his flat or answering his phone. His mother seemed to think the lad would reappear at some point but was vague about timings. Unwilling to run the risk that George would get wind of their presence and decide to abscond, they'd decided to wait it out until he appeared, especially as he was currently their only suspect.

Morgan released a sigh. 'I spy—'

'Don't you dare!'

He waved his phone at her. 'What do you suggest? I've eaten all the Jaffa cakes, levelled up on all my games and I'm now officially bored.'

'You're like a difficult teenager.'

'Aren't all teenagers difficult? It's a prerequisite of being a teenager.'

Kate tried not to smile. She enjoyed Morgan's company. He was easy to talk to and from nowhere came the urge to tell him about Tom Champion, Rosa and all her concerns about Dickson. She pressed her lips together tightly until they hurt. She couldn't tell anyone. Not even affable Morgan. She had no idea who she could trust. Although she wanted to share her fears and thoughts with him, and with Emma, she couldn't take the risk. Her mind flip-flopped as she weighed up whether she should at least test the waters and see where Morgan stood with regards to Dickson. Did he even like the man? Her phone vibrated and she pulled it out to read the brief message from Bradley.

You guessed right
No news
You?

She had judged Bradley correctly. He was still looking for Tom Champion. That he had replied to her apologetic text indicated he was no longer furious with her. There was hope they could continue to work together to bring down Dickson. For a fraction of a second, she thought she heard a sharp tone – Chris?

'You'd work with Bradley even if he took matters into his own hands and killed somebody?'

'Oh, wait a sec,' said Morgan, stiffening. 'What's that?'

Morgan's words flushed Chris's voice from her mind.

The motorbike pulled up outside the block of flats and the passenger dismounted, removed his helmet and handed it to the driver, who hung it over their arm before driving off.

Morgan checked the photograph he'd printed out from the police database. 'It's him.' He flung open the car door and bounded towards the path. 'George!'

George stopped in his tracks, then darted away from the flats.

'Police! We only want to talk to you.' Kate's words were carried by the wind and the young man continued racing away at breakneck speed, Morgan on his heels. She gave chase, pushing hard to gain on the pair as they turned down an alleyway beyond the flats. The youth was quick-footed, familiar with the local area, but Morgan was an ex-rugby player and in better physical condition. Kate rounded the wall, charged down the alleyway in time to hear loud swearing and a kerfuffle as a bin was kicked over. By the time she reached them, Morgan had a firm grip on George.

'We only wanted to ask you a couple of questions,' she repeated.

The lad glowered at her. 'Oh yeah?'

'Why did you run?'

He shrugged.

'Have you got something to hide?' Morgan asked.

George maintained his silence.

Kate moved in front of the lad, looked him square in the eyes. 'Listen, George, we can do this here, or at home in front of your mother, or we can take you down the station. Which is it to be?'

'What is this about?'

'Tobias Abrahams.'

He spat on the ground. 'What's that fucking weasel been saying about me?'

'Do you have a problem with Tobias?'

'No. He has a problem with me.' George wriggled, trying to escape Morgan's firm grasp, then gave up with a prolonged sigh.

Kate caught his eyes again. 'Will you talk to us about Tobias?'

'Not if he's accused me of something.'

'He hasn't.'

His face relaxed. The sneer disappeared. 'In that case, I'll talk to you.'

Kate gave the instruction to release George's arms and he rubbed at them.

'Police brutality—'

'Don't start that crap,' said Morgan with a growl.

'He was only restraining you. There's no damage done,' said Kate.

George scowled again.

'George, where were you yesterday evening?'

'Why?'

'I asked you a question. I'm not in the mood to be messed about. I'd be quite happy to let DS Meredith cuff you and leave you in a cell until you feel like chatting to us. But I'll give you another chance to be civil. Where were you yesterday evening?'

'I was out and about.'

'Who with?'

'Nobody in particular.'

'Come on, George, you can do better than that. Where were you?'

'I went into town. On my own. Chilled for a bit, did some shopping.'

'You're still not helping yourself, George. I'm rapidly losing my patience.'

'Look, I don't remember my movements exactly. I was drifting about, you know?'

'Okay, that's enough pissing about. Come with us,' said Morgan, taking him by the arm again.

'Are you arresting me?'

'We might if we don't get any sensible answers from us. For now, you're going to be helping us with our enquiries.'

'Enquiries into what?'

'Into the death of Tobias Abrahams.'

'Hang on. He's dead?' He tugged his arm free and stepped away from Morgan.

'He was shot yesterday evening, at Blythe Bridge station.'

He took another step back and raised his palms to them. 'Fucking hell! Whoa! That changes things, man. Shit! I didn't kill him.'

'Given you and he had history regarding Ashleigh Baker, we need to establish your whereabouts at the time,' said Kate.

He dropped his hands, pointed a finger at her. 'No way! I had nothing to do with it.'

'Then tell us where you were so we can eliminate you.'

'I was in town, like I told you. I went to Hanley Park. I hang out there sometimes.'

In the past, Hanley Park had suffered a bad reputation with gangs of teenagers intimidating visitors, but in recent years the council had invested a serious amount of money into returning it to its former Victorian splendour.

'You like jogging there, do you?' said Morgan. 'Or maybe you're an amateur photographer and like taking pictures of the ducks!'

'Fuck off!' Spittle landed at Morgan's feet.

'You'll have to come up with a better alibi than that.'

'I *was* there.'

'All evening?'

'Nah, for an hour. I was supposed to meet somebody, but she didn't show.'

Morgan puffed out his cheeks. 'Go on then. I'll play along. What time?'

The young man slouched, shoved his hands into the front pockets of his well-worn jeans and stared at the ground. 'Six. We were supposed to meet up at six o' clock, okay?'

'And who is this enigmatic woman?'

Morgan's question earned a look of contempt. 'Fuck me! Enig—? Whatever. Becky. Don't know her full name.'

'Got a contact number for Becky No Surname?'

He kicked at a small stone, sent it skidding across the road. 'No. I met her in town. We were in a queue for a takeaway. Got chatting and made arrangements to meet up the following day.'

'And you expect us to believe that crap?' said Morgan.

'You can't prove I *wasn't* there.'

Kate stared hard at him. He didn't buckle under her gaze. 'Which takeaway?'

'The Costa in Tunstall. The one opposite the retail park.'

Tunstall, once a village, was one of the original six towns that had federated to make the city of Stoke-on-Trent rich, and was the northernmost. The café he mentioned was the larger of two in town and, given that Costa coffee shops had surveillance cameras, she could probably obtain footage that might or might not substantiate his claim. 'What time were you there?'

'Mid-morning.' He dropped his gaze and scuffed at a pile of loose gravel with the toe of a grubby trainer.

'On Monday?'

'Yeah.' Another stone was sent pinging across the road.

She kept the enquiries short and quick. 'Describe Becky to me.'

He turned his attention from the pavement and faced her, head cocked to one side. 'My height. Short dark hair. Nice smile.'

'Anything else?'

'Not really.'

'What was she wearing?'

'I didn't pay much attention to her clothes.'

'What did you find out about her?'

'She's into Ariana Grande and Billie Eilish and watches *The Masked Singer*.'

Morgan tutted. 'Don't piss us about. Useful details, like where she lives, what she does as a job.'

'We were in a queue for a takeaway, not a bleeding job interview,' George replied with a semi-satisfied smile.

'Did she drop into conversation anything that might help us identify her?' said Kate, drilling George with another cold look.

'Okay. She mentioned she was a nanny. Looks after a little kid for a couple who work at the hospital.'

'How come you invited her to meet you at the park the following day?'

'She invited *me*. Said she'd be finished with work around then and asked if I fancied hanging out with her for a while. Really! I'm not making this up. I thought she was into me, but she blew me off. It was kind of annoying.'

'I'm sure it was. Maybe if you'd exchanged numbers, she could have told you she couldn't make the date.'

'It wasn't a *date*. Just a loose arrangement.' His shoulders slumped again, and a practised, bored expression changed his features.

'I see,' said Kate.

'When did you last see Tobias?' asked Morgan.

George's lips curled. 'That prick! A couple of months ago, I suppose.'

'Tell us more, George. Did you speak to him then?'

He dragged his hands from his pockets, swept strands of dark fringe across his face before answering. 'No. He was with Ashleigh. Going overboard on the PDAs.'

'Public displays of affection?' said Morgan, earning another look of contempt.

'Course. PDA. What else? It was all a fucking charade to show me what I was missing out on.'

'You believe that?'

'Yeah. The fucker eyeballed me and then put the moves on her right in front of me. He mugged me off.'

'I expect that pissed you off,' said Morgan.

He shrugged. The sparks that flashed in his eyes gave away his true response.

'Bet it came as a shock, Ashleigh dumping you for him.' Morgan's taunt found its mark. The young man's fists tightened into balls.

'We were sound until he came along. I'd have kicked his head in if Ashleigh hadn't asked me to back off.'

'And is that what you did? Backed off?'

He stuck out his jaw. 'Yeah. And you know why? Because I figured she'd eventually work out what a total wanker he really was and come back to me, so there wasn't any point in blowing my chances completely with her.'

'Did you contact Tobias at all, by phone, email, go and pay him a visit alone?'

'No. He'd have bleated to Ashleigh and she'd have thought I was the prick, not him. I played it cool.'

'Have you set eyes on him since that chance meeting?'

'No.'

'Whereabouts in the park did you arrange to meet Becky?' asked Kate, hoping to throw him off-balance.

He faltered before saying, 'On the bandstand steps.'

Kate knew exactly where he meant. The bandstand was only a short distance from the restored Pavilion café. She had jogged around the park numerous times and was fairly certain there were no surveillance cameras there. It would be difficult to confirm his alibi. He looked at her from under heavy lids.

'Can I go now? I've told you everything.'

'For the time being. We'll be back to talk to you again if we have any more questions.'

He slouched off.

'What do you think?' said Kate as he turned the corner.

'I think it's odd that any girl would arrange to meet a total stranger after only talking to him for a few minutes in a queue. After all, he's hardly Mr Charming.'

'It's certainly a bit odd. I'll ask Krishna to check out surveillance cameras at Hanley Park and, in the meantime, we'll see if anyone at the Costa remembers seeing either of them on Monday.'

CHAPTER FOUR

Kate slid on to Chris's office chair, ready for her arranged video call with Tilly. She was happy to have her stepsister back in her life. Although Tilly had left for Australia with Kate's ex-fiancé, Jordan, and had been out of contact for many years, they had recently rebuilt bridges.

Tilly had visited last year, bringing her five-year-old son, Daniel, with her and reminding Kate there were others in her life who would love and care about her. Kate had been working on a horrendous rape and murder case, one that had brought back memories for her stepsister, who had been raped at a young age. The investigation had proven to be closer to home than Kate could ever have expected but had also brought the sisters together. With Chris no longer able to advise her, Kate wondered if she could use Tilly as a sounding board. She glanced at the A4 sheet in front of her with its lines linking all the victims and Dickson back to the Maddox Club.

Chris and Dickson. If she concentrated on catching the man who was somehow mixed up in Chris's death, would she be able to reconnect with her husband, hear his voice again, and converse with him? Maybe she could ask Bradley for help in finding Rosa. Surely, with Tom no longer around, Bradley wouldn't turn his back on another opportunity to get even with Dickson. 'See, Chris. I'm still on it.'

For a brief second, she felt as if he might answer and then the moment vanished. She switched on the computer and waited for the incoming ringtone. How could she even begin to tell Tilly what she was trying to do? She rehearsed a few ways, each sounding bizarre, even to her own ears. Tilly knew so little about what Kate had been doing, it would be a huge revelation.

Tilly was looking tanned and relaxed. It was evening there and, judging by Tilly's strapless T-shirt, warm.

'Hey,' she said with a big smile.

Kate couldn't help but emulate it. 'Hey yourself. How's tricks?'

'Ah, good. Jordan's taken Daniel out so you've only got me today.'

'That's fine. I can't chat too long anyway. We were assigned a major investigation yesterday and I shouldn't really be away from the office.'

Tilly's thin eyebrows lifted. 'A murder?'

'I'm afraid so. Young guy got shot at a railway station.'

'That's lousy. There's way too much violence these days. You hear about stuff like this all the time on the news.'

Kate preferred not to get involved in a deep discussion about the wrongs in the world. Time with Tilly was precious. 'I didn't want to cancel our call. I'd like your advice on something.'

'Sure, sis. What?'

'Well, there are a couple of things. The first is about an investigation I'm running. It's a personal one.'

Tilly leant forward on her elbows. 'Oh, exciting. I get to play detective.'

'Not play—' Kate bit her tongue. She didn't want to alienate her stepsister. She moved on smoothly. 'I'm pretty certain a police officer was involved in Chris's death, and I've been trying to get something on him to prove it.'

Tilly's mouth dropped open. 'Get on!'

Kate continued, all the while wondering if this was a good idea. Tilly was no Chris. Chris had journalistic skills, a keen mind and a nose for trouble. Tilly's offerings would be more limited. She was down to earth, direct and had common sense. Was it enough?

'I had a witness who I was protecting but he's gone AWOL and now I have to redouble my efforts to locate an underage sex-worker who knows something vital about this officer, something that another officer discovered but she was killed before she could reveal it.' She licked her suddenly dry lips. Tilly's brow was furrowed.

'Jeez, Kate, are you sure you're not overdoing things? This all sounds a bit weird to me.'

'Yes. I know it does, but bear with me. It's all true.' She thought of CIO Heather Gault's body, lying broken in a skip. Dickson had had her silenced after her meeting with Rosa. The young sex-worker had been at the Maddox Club on the night of the boy's murder. She must have had some proof to connect Dickson to it. The idea fizzed in her head like a firework about to explode. Whatever Rosa knew had not only cost Heather her life but had sent the girl scurrying underground. It had to be dynamite. 'The last time I met the girl's pimp was at a café in Manchester. I've been back there, but the owner denies knowing this guy's whereabouts and I . . . I need to put pressure on the man to get him to crack – play dirty, drum up a bogus charge, anything to scare the man.'

Tilly's mouth fell open. 'Whoa! Slow down, Kate. Can't you launch an official investigation into this?'

'No. I can't let this officer know I'm on to him.'

'You're doing this single-handedly?'

'I've got some help from an outside source. An ex-SAS officer and some of his old team.'

Tilly made a tsk-tsk noise. 'Kate! This is bonkers.'

'I know it is, and I don't know which way to turn. The only way I'm going to make any headway is to cross a few lines.'

'But it's also dangerous. If an officer was killed because she found out whatever this sex-worker knows, the same thing could happen to you.'

'Not if I box clever.'

'And how do you propose to do that?'

'I don't know. I hoped I could talk to you. Maybe you could tell me if I'm on the right track.'

'Track? You sound like you've come off the rails altogether. Listen, I love you, but this is mental.'

'Really, it isn't, Tilly. You know me. I wouldn't be chasing after this if I didn't have reason to. This officer is connected to four deaths I know about. He's covered his tracks so well; I've not been able to prove how immoral he is. I have one last shot – find the sex-worker and listen to what she has to say. Tilly, this could help me find out the whole truth about Chris.'

'He was killed by a hitman.' Tilly's voice fell flat. 'And the man who hired the hitman was murdered in a revenge attack.'

'It's more complicated than that. Believe me. I've been working on it for months.'

The whiny voice she had as a teenager was back, and Kate winced at its grating tone. 'Why isn't this officer under police investigation?'

'Because he'll wriggle out of any investigation. He's crooked, Tilly.'

'Okay. I get it.' Tilly looked away, revealing a drawing of a family on the beach pinned to the fridge door. Kate took in the two taller stick people, a smaller one with a bucket in its hand. There they were. All that was left of her family.

Tilly sighed. 'Okay. You know the ins and outs. This is understandably mad, but go on. Run it past me. You think this pimp can lead you to a sex-worker who will spill the beans on your bent officer?'

'I think so.'

'You *think* so! With what you're planning, you'd better pray she can.'

Kate ignored the slight hysteria in her voice. All she had to do was find Farai and he would lead her to Rosa. She would do whatever necessary to force him to give the girl up.

'You could get in all sorts of shit doing this,' said Tilly.

'Uh-huh.' Each word Tilly spoke brought doubts. She was kidding herself.

'How do you intend getting some café owner to give up the pimp's whereabouts? You planning on a few trumped-up charges? Good luck with that. He'll probably pull a baseball bat on you and flatten you.' She paused, then her face took on the look of somebody watching a horror movie. 'You weren't planning on shooting anybody, were you?'

'No. Of course not!'

'But you have a gun. You must have thought about using it to threaten somebody. How else would you get them to talk?'

It was true. Kate would resort to any available desperate measures. Tilly's next sentence threw her even further.

'And how are you going to prevent any of these people you talk to telling the officer you are after?'

She didn't wish to discuss it any longer. Tilly was treating it like she'd watch a drama unfold on television, criticising the detective's methods but with no suggestions of her own as to how to go about hunting down the criminal. 'You're right. I ought to give it more thought.'

'Yes, you bloody well should. Or give up the idea altogether.'

'I think I will.'

'Really?'

'Yes.'

'Phew! That's a relief.'

'Thanks for making me see sense. I'll leave it for now.'

Tilly seemed satisfied she'd given sound advice and dissuaded her stepsister from pursuing dangerous avenues. 'Well, if you need me for any more help, you ring. Any time. Don't do anything stupid. Promise?'

'Promise.'

'What was the other thing you wanted to talk about?'

She was keen to get off the subject of Dickson. It was clear Tilly couldn't help her. What Kate really needed was Chris's input. 'William says I should put in for promotion. He's offered his full backing and I'm sure that, with his support, I'll get it. I've been really lucky having him as my mentor and boss.'

Tilly's reaction wasn't what she expected. Her mouth pulled down.

'Judging by your expression, you think it's a bad idea,' said Kate.

Tilly's expression changed, her eyes widening. 'Not at all. I think you should go for it. It's . . . William. I can imagine why he's offering his support.'

'What?'

'Kate, far be it from me to slag off your boss, but you know I always speak my mind and I don't trust him.'

'But you hardly know him. You haven't seen him since you were a kid.'

'Mum didn't like or trust him. She and I had some really big heart-to-hearts after we left. She wanted me to understand why she'd left Mitch and taken me away from you both. She told me so many things. One of them was that William was a bad influence. A really bad influence. It isn't him, is it? This officer you're after?'

'No!' Kate couldn't believe her ears. William and her father had been best friends and had had each other's backs for years, way before Tilly's mother, Ellen, came on the scene. Ellen was most likely jealous of their relationship. 'I don't buy that.'

'I don't expect you to. You saw him through your dad's eyes and your dad thought he was the bee's knees. He always went on about his best buddy. William was hardly ever out of the house. Mum saw a side to William that your dad simply couldn't or wouldn't see. She told me about everything that happened, and how William played his part in the break up.'

'Oh, come on! That's rubbish.' Even as she said it, she couldn't help wondering if there was some truth in Tilly's words. Chris must have had some doubts about William to have included him in his list of potentially corrupt officers. Chris hadn't left anything other than a photograph of William in his files. Whereas others had also been named in his journal, linked to child prostitution, or mentioned in a document about the Maddox Club, there'd been nothing else about William except that picture. Therefore, she'd not acted on it, having chosen instead to focus on Dickson, who'd appeared on the list, in the document and in the journal.

She'd chosen to believe the list was merely that – a list. It only proved that Chris suspected the officers named on it might have been immoral. And, without knowing how Chris had obtained his information, she couldn't take it at more than face value.

Who was she kidding? She'd chosen to chase after Dickson and leave her mentor alone. If Chris had his voice, he'd be telling her not to turn a blind eye, that the photo was there for a reason. Yet Chris wasn't speaking to her. Tilly, however, was. An itching began on her arms. The fact that William might not be the man she believed him to be was worrying. Was he pushing her to put herself forward for some nefarious reason, rather than because of his friendship with her father?

Tilly's face grew serious. 'I don't want to argue with you, Kate. Especially over something in the past. Sorry if I've been blunt. You understand what I'm like – big mouth and big opinions, and I don't want there to be any secrets between us. We've lost enough time.'

Kate only half heard her stepsister. Her brain was whirring. Several instances of William backing Dickson instead of her popped into her head. At the time, she hadn't questioned his judgement, but now the same memories made her think twice. The possibility her mentor and friend might be dishonest was too awful to contemplate, yet she had to face the reality of the situation. Her overwhelming desire to chase after Dickson had blinkered her to William. And there was Jamie, a plant in her office! He could be reporting to the pair of them. He could still be in Dickson's thrall. The itching intensified. She dropped her tone, aimed for sincere. 'No. Go on, please. I want to know what you think. Really, I do. It might be important.'

'I've said too much. It'll only upset you. Sorry. I open my mouth and shit comes out before I have a chance to think about what I'm saying.'

'Tilly, I won't blow up at you. If this affects me, I have a right to know.'

Tilly rubbed her lips together before speaking. 'Okay. You sure you want to hear this?'

'Yes.'

'Your dad and William used to go out to clubs and bars together.'

'Yes, I know. They were friends. That's what friends do.'

'They didn't go out for a friendly drink. They went out on the hunt – for women.'

Kate didn't know what to say. It was crazy talk.

'They picked up women at bars. They went to brothels too. And then it spilled over into work. Mitch got into some trouble over it.'

'Now you must be kidding me.'

'No, Kate.' She gave her a sad smile. 'In the end, that's why Mum left him.'

'Ellen left because she found somebody else,' said Kate.

'That was a story Mitch made up to save himself face. Mum walked out because Mitch cheated on her, and not once or even twice. She couldn't keep forgiving him. Your father was a womaniser.'

Kate choked back a laugh. It was ludicrous.

'If you don't believe me, check his work records. Do you remember when he took extended leave and said it was so he could do house repairs and spend time with us and Mum? Well, it was a lie. He was actually suspended for suspected sexual misconduct.'

'Bullshit!'

'Check his records.'

'It's not true.'

'I understand this is difficult for you but, trust me, I'm telling you the truth. I wouldn't make up something like this and Mum had no reason to lie to me. You didn't live with the fallout after she left.'

'Dad suffered, too. I had to be there for him.'

Tilly gave a small nod. 'I'm sure he did. But, Kate, Mum suffered way more. She cried herself to sleep every night for weeks and declined to the point where she even stopped dressing on a morning and sat about the house all day in a daze. She lost so much weight; I was terrified she'd die. She took it badly. Too badly for her to have fabricated what she told me.'

Kate remembered the quiet talks with her father, the tears soon after Ellen and Tilly had gone and the undeniable knowledge that she'd been thankful to have her father all to herself once more and enjoy a stronger-than-ever bond with him. She didn't contradict Tilly because although Mitch had been upset, he hadn't stayed down for too long. William had made sure of that. He became a regular visitor, bringing takeaways, presents, beer. There'd been offers to take his friend out for a night on the town. Invitations to both Mitch and Kate to join him for weekends away. William had filled the void Ellen and Tilly had left behind them. If this was true, William had never been the friend she had believed him to be. Why had he mentored Kate, guided her, supported her and been like an uncle to her? Guilt? Or something more sinister? She thought for an instant about how she had almost opened up to him after the briefing when he'd suggested she go for promotion. It would have been a huge mistake to have done so.

'Mum fell to bits, and it was down to me to help her find her feet again. It took a long time, a lot of persuasion and therapy for her to gain any confidence again.'

'I'm sorry. I had no idea what was happening between them. I thought they were happy.'

'You couldn't have known. I certainly didn't have a clue at the time either. She concealed the truth from us both. It was some time before she admitted she put up with his infidelities for *our* sake. We'd both lost parents and suffered heartache. She didn't want to add to it. She really tried to make it work. She didn't leave because *she'd* found another bloke. She left because he broke her heart. Over and over again.'

Numbness replaced the itching, and crept up her arms and face. Was her father capable of such cruelty? She unglued her lips. 'I can't believe this.'

Tilly's voice softened. 'Look, it's a lot to take in and I know how much you loved your dad and, to be honest, he wasn't entirely to blame. Which is how this conversation started. I wanted to explain why I'm not surprised William has offered to back your promotion. You see, William put your dad up to all the transgressions, the bad behaviour, the trysts or whatever you want to call them. Mum had her suspicions about him from the off, knew William was Mitch's closest friend, but had no idea how close. William warned her off on a couple of occasions, told her she could never live up to your mum. Of course, she ignored him. She loved your dad. At the time, she hadn't understood what a huge influence William had over Mitch. He was the instigator of all the drunken nights out and, as a result, for breaking up their marriage. And for what it's worth, I suspect he now feels guilty and is trying to right a wrong. After all, he's due for retirement soon, isn't he?'

'Yes. A couple of weeks.' She tried to concentrate on the conversation, her brain screaming confusion. William wasn't to be trusted. She could never tell him anything.

'There you are. After holding back Mitch for so many years, he wants to see Mitch's daughter make a success of herself.'

'What do you mean, *holding him back*?'

'Your dad was up for promotion to DCI but the whole sexual allegation thing put paid to that.'

Again, this was something Kate had not been aware of. Her mind flashed back to almost forgotten times of William appearing out of the blue, as they were about to eat or were watching television together as a family, claiming he and her father were needed at a crime scene, or the office, or on a stakeout. A vague memory of the conspiratorial look on William's face as they spoke in hushed voices and her father's weak protestations followed by more urgent, angry whispering. Had she been so blinkered she hadn't seen what was happening? More memory bubbles ascended: Ellen crying in the kitchen and, when young Kate asked if she was okay, claiming she was fine, 'just that time of the month'; of Ellen clinging on to Mitch's hand, pleading quietly with him to not go with William, who waited confidently by the front door. Some part of her must have known what was going on. Tilly's voice brought her back to the present.

'You should go for the promotion. You'll get it on your own merit. You don't need William to put in a word for you. You can do this by yourself.'

'I'll think about it some more.'

'Just do it. And when you get promoted, as you will, you must book a flight and come and celebrate with us. Have a well-deserved holiday.'

Although Kate had promised she would visit, she'd yet to do so. She'd been far too busy running in circles after Dickson to make any firm travel plans. And there was a concern that if she went to Australia, she'd further endanger or completely sever her connection to Chris. She couldn't afford for that to happen. She wasn't going to put hundreds of miles between them. Instead, she was going to reconnect with her deceased husband, and if that meant going to the reservoir, day after day, in the hope that his voice would once again come to her, then that's what she'd do. In the meantime, she'd make every effort with her stepsister. For the first time in months, Kate was in new, uncharted waters. These revelations had destabilised her and now, the only person she could fully trust lived thousands of miles away but was willing to help. Regardless of her shortcomings, Tilly was her stepsister, and Kate had to keep trying to cement their relationship. She smiled at Tilly. 'As soon as I can find the time.' Her words would be enough to appease her stepsister.

'You work too hard, Kate.'

Kate waved away her concern. 'Enough about me. Tell me about what you've been doing.'

Tilly launched into a more relaxed chat mode and regaled Kate with anecdotes about Daniel and life in Sydney until Kate called an end to the conversation. She really had to get back to the investigation. Tilly left with smiles and blew her several kisses before the screen went blank. Kate rested her arms on the desk. Her chest throbbed with sorrow. William and her father. Two men she idolised. Both potentially corrupt.

Even though she ought to return to the office, she had to look into Tilly's allegations. Her father's personal effects were in the attic. 'Chris, I wish you could tell me why you included William's photo in that document.'

'You can work it out, Kate.' The voice was so quiet she almost couldn't hear it, yet her veins fizzed. Chris was still with her for now. She had to ensure she didn't push him away forever.

'I shall. I'll get on to it immediately.'

◆ ◆ ◆

Surrounded by cardboard boxes, Kate finally landed on mementos relating to her father's time on the force. She pulled out a handful of photographs. There were numerous faces she didn't recognise. She paused at one depicting a fresh-faced Mitch in his early twenties, standing proudly in his uniform. The job had meant everything to him. He wouldn't have jeopardised his career. If he had cheated on Ellen, it suggested he might also have been unfaithful to Kate's mother, and Kate couldn't believe that was possible. She flicked through more pictures and was about to call it a day when she lighted on a photograph taken in a pub, the men holding up their pints of beer in celebration.

Her father was unmistakable, with his sparkling azure eyes and wide smile. The man next to him, with a thick thatch of black hair and even then the same serious look on his face that he wore today, was William Chase. It had been taken when she was a teenager; when Ellen and Tilly had been in their lives and presumably around the same time Tilly had been discussing on the Skype call. She studied the faces and caught her breath. John Dickson was with them. So he had been part of or had led their unit. How had she not known that? She couldn't work out the significance of this new information. All she knew was that it had to be relevant.

She shoved the other photos and bits and pieces back into the box, setting the last picture to one side. This was something she ought to tackle William about. A glance at the clock forced her to abandon the box. The time had passed without her realising it.

◆　◆　◆

'Any idea where the guv is?' asked Jamie.

Emma glanced up from her computer screen. 'She's most likely checking on something. You know what she's like; gets her hands dirty like the rest of us.'

'Yeah. It's just a bit odd, what with this being the start of an investigation.'

Morgan piped up with, 'Leave it, Jamie. She isn't skiving, if that's what you're hinting at.'

'No, mate. Not at all. Only an observation. Hope she isn't ill or anything.' He lowered his head and got on with his work.

Emma caught the look Morgan gave her. Kate was an enigma and, over the last few months, had been becoming increasingly secretive and withdrawn. Emma didn't think there was any dark reason behind it. Kate was still reeling from the aftermath of revelations regarding Chris's death. Consequently, she was submerging herself in work and exercise – both coping strategies. Emma understood this behaviour, especially as she'd been guilty of doing the same. It was a miracle Kate hadn't lost her mind. Although there'd been a point when Emma had begun to be seriously concerned about her boss, she was now of the opinion that Kate was managing. She was no longer pill-popping or muttering to herself and she always got results, whatever the investigation. Knowing Kate, she'd probably returned to the crime scene to try and make sense of it.

'Morgan, I'm going to check out the Costa at Tunstall in case anyone remembers seeing Ashleigh's ex-boyfriend, George, or the woman he met there in the queue Monday mid-morning. It might go some way to confirming his alibi that he was at the park with Becky at the time of Tobias's murder.'

'Nothing back from Krishna yet?'

'No. Poor bloke is right up to his eyeballs. We could do with some more technical help. I wonder if the super will cave in and let us have it.'

'He's more likely to growl darkly about cutbacks. Bring me back a cappuccino and a chocolate or a banana muffin, would you?'

'I'm going on business, not a flipping coffee run.'

Morgan pouted and emitted an exaggerated sigh. 'I missed breakfast to get into work early. You know how grouchy I become when I have a sugar dip. Pur-lease.'

Morgan always cracked her up. 'Oh, go on then! Jamie, do you want anything?'

'Tea, please, with soya milk. No, make that a double espresso. I need something to keep me alert.'

'What? Again?'

'Yeah. Wifey's having a rough time with this baby. Can't get comfortable at night and makes sure I know about it. And Master Webster decided to get up three times again last night.'

'Not sure how I'd cope with that,' said Morgan.

'You'd probably bugger off out with the lads and leave your poor missus at home to sort it out,' said Emma.

'Emma! As if I would. Could I have two muffins, please?'

'No. Only one. You'll put on weight if you keep eating unhealthy food.'

Morgan tossed a small rubber basketball at her. She caught it with one hand and hurled it back. It caught on the mini basketball hoop attached to the side of the desk but didn't fall through.

'And she shoots . . . and misses,' he said.

'You're lucky I didn't aim it at your head. Idiot!'

Emma left them to it. She'd become accustomed to working with a small team and was especially fond of Morgan, but as she strode past one of the larger offices, a small pang went off in her chest when she spotted her colleagues gathered in a semi-circle listening to DI Khatri, who had taken over Kate's old team. She'd expected to have been back working with them, with Kate at the helm again by now. Maybe the reason they weren't was because her superiors had also noticed Kate's aloofness. As far as Emma could see there was no other reason to have kept her in the shadows. The team had already solved two major murder investigations; if they could get a handle on this one quickly, there would surely be no excuse not to increase the size of the unit.

Coming out of the ladies' washroom she observed Superintendent Dickson talking to Jamie in the corridor. Neither man noticed her as she left the building, wondering why Jamie wasn't in the office and why he was in conversation with the super. He was always very keen. Maybe he was simply toadying in the hope he'd be promoted. Or Dickson had stopped him to ask him something. *Or, he's dropping Kate in it.*

She dismissed the latter. He had no reason to do that, had he?

◆ ◆ ◆

It was early afternoon when Kate bustled back into the office, barking questions as she shrugged off her jacket. 'Jamie, did you get a triangulation on the pay-as-you-go that rang Tobias's number just after he disembarked the train?'

'No, guv. Still working on it. I got hold of his call log, though. He was on the phone to a London number for most of the train journey. It turned out to be one of his old university chums. He said Tobias rang for a catch-up and to arrange to visit at the weekend. He reckoned Tobias was bragging about getting early promotion and how he'd helped sort out finances for a management buyout. The rest was general chit-chat. He rang another mate in Oxford straight afterwards. Similar conversation but not so long. Apparently, that friend wasn't in the mood for Tobias's self-important conversation.'

'Sounds like Tobias was prone to exaggeration.'

Morgan looked up from his screen. 'Emma rang about ten minutes ago, from the Costa where George claimed he met Becky. She's having no joy in finding witnesses, and no luck with the cameras.'

Kate tutted. 'We might need to question that young man again. I've just spoken to Harvey, who's sending over the pathology report any time now. He confirmed what we already suspected; that the weapon used *was* a captive bolt pistol. The version we're looking for is known as a penetrating pistol. This type has a cartridge or pointed bolt which is propelled by pressurised air, a spring mechanism, or a blank cartridge to penetrate the skull. The one we're searching for has a spring mechanism. Forensics haven't found it yet and are looking further afield.'

'We ought to contact local and online suppliers of humane slaughter guns,' said Morgan.

'I agree. One snag, we don't know which make or model we're searching for.'

'Might make it trickier. Especially with the online stuff.'

Kate had to agree that it would make their task more difficult, and cost them time as well as money. Dickson's sneering face came to the fore again. He would love for there to be hold-ups. 'Start with local suppliers and cross your fingers it wasn't bought online.'

Jamie asked, 'Do you think we could be looking for somebody who works in a slaughterhouse?'

'I'm not ruling out any possibility at this stage. Has George Fox ever worked at one?'

'I'll look into it. He's currently unemployed.'

Kate headed to her computer, checked the emails and found the report from Harvey.

The internal injuries had been extensive. The bolt had lacerated the right frontal lobe, torn apart the optic nerve and destroyed the right corpus striatum. In brief, it had ripped through Tobias's skull, destroying blood vessels and structures. Blood had been found in the trachea and bronchial tree and in his lungs. Such catastrophic damage would have resulted in immediate death. She sipped from a bottle of water and read the rest of the detailed report, the office full of background noise that didn't filter through until she heard her name being spoken more urgently.

'Kate, I've got a witness on the line.' Morgan had covered the phone mouthpiece.

The report was forgotten. 'What?'

'Gordon Haskins. He was travelling in the same carriage as Tobias. Do you want to talk to him?'

She leapt up, took the phone from him. 'Mr Haskins, this is DI Kate Young. Thank you for calling us.'

'I thought I ought to, although I don't know if what I have to say will help or hinder you.' His stuttering, slow speech led Kate to assume he was an elderly gentleman. She wondered how observant he might have been or whether he was one of those people who wanted to help but didn't have a great deal of information.

'I'm sure it will be of help and we're grateful to you for ringing us,' she said smoothly.

'Yes. Well, as I explained to your officer, I was travelling in a carriage with two men who got out at Blythe Bridge. I don't know how relevant it is to your murder inquiry, but they had a disagreement on the train.'

It sounded hopeful. 'Can you tell me what you noticed, never mind how small the detail?' From the sound of his voice, she semi-regretted saying the last bit.

'Yes. I boarded at Crewe behind a chap. He was in work clothes. I can't tell you if he was in jeans or trousers. I think they were dark-coloured. He was wearing a high-vis vest over a dark jacket. At first, I thought he was a railway worker, but afterwards I wasn't so sure.'

He was a talker. She would have to sift the relevant parts of his conversation.

'He sat in one of two seats behind a screen, by the doors. I sat further down the carriage, in a seat facing him, so I saw him quite clearly. He shut his eyes and rested his head against the window. There weren't many other passengers in the carriage, and all was quiet until we reached Stoke-on-Trent, when more people got on and shuffled off down the carriage, and a young man boarded. He sat in the aisle opposite the workman.'

Tempted as she was to ask him to speed up, she let him continue. There might be significant details littered throughout the monologue. His words were ponderous, and she could imagine he'd watched many a television murder mystery and was trying to create as much of a picture for her as possible. Morgan looked up at her. She made a winding motion with her free hand, as if cranking a handle, and he returned her a knowing nod.

'He was one of those irritating passengers who holds loud conversations on their mobiles and ended almost every sentence with a laugh. It clearly annoyed the other fellow, who asked him to dial it down. The lad ignored him and even made a comment to whoever he was talking to, something along the lines of people needing to get a life. After a few more minutes, he let rip with another raucous laugh and, when I looked up, the workman had got to his feet and was leaning across the aisle. "If you don't pipe down, I'll shove your phone right where the sun doesn't shine."'

He paused. Kate gave him an encouraging, 'Go on. What did he say?' If he'd been sitting opposite her, she might have been able to urge him along more quickly with gestures. As it was, the anonymity of the telephone was making this drawn out.

'I didn't catch the retort, but I thought it was going to result in a fight. Anyway, the younger man ended his call and the chap in the yellow vest backed off and returned to his seat. Then, less than a minute later, the lad was at it again, to somebody else, another similar conversation with more laughter. I glanced up and the workman was clearly infuriated. He was staring at the lad, but the train slowed and pulled into the station, and the young man got off without so much as a look at the man who followed him off the train.

'I admit I kept an eye on them, in case there was a scuffle, but the lad headed towards the shelter, still on the phone. The other man waited by the fence, head down, searching for something in his pockets. The train drew away and that was the last I saw of them both. Was it one of them who was killed?'

It was slightly disappointing there'd been no witness to the altercation, or the actual murder. 'I'm afraid the young man was. You described what the workman was wearing. Was there anything else about him you noticed?'

'He was carrying a plain black bag. The sort workmen carry tools in.'

And large enough to secrete a stun gun. 'How old do you think he was?'

'Thirties or forties. He had dark hair. No signs of grey. Not like me,' he added with a small chuckle.

'Was he tall?'

'Average height and average size – not a big man.'

'Any defining marks – tattoos?'

'None I noticed.'

'Is there anything else you can think of that might help us find this man?'

There was a sucking of teeth and a lengthy, 'No-o. Sorry, no. I was reading a report at the time. I only glanced up a few times.'

'Would you be able to come to the station after work to make a statement repeating what you've told me?'

'Yes. I can do that. I could be there about three, three thirty?'

'Thank you. Do you need directions here?'

'No, I'll take a taxi.' He seemed to hesitate, as if he had more to say, but ended with, 'There, I've written it down, so I don't forget.'

'I'll let the duty officer on the desk know you're coming, and they'll sort you out.'

Kate replaced the receiver. 'It appears we have another possible suspect. The man in the high-vis.' She relayed the brief description Gordon had given of the man.

Jamie rubbed at his chin, lips pursed. 'What I don't get is why a killer would wear an item of clothing that would make them stand out. That's plain stupid. Like sticking a target on his back.'

Morgan was quick to reply. 'If it was a spur-of-the-moment decision to kill Tobias, he wouldn't have planned his outfit for the day.'

'I'm just saying—'

'That's enough.' Kate's sharp tone was addressed at Jamie. This wasn't the time for him to try and score points off Morgan. 'Let's assume, if this is our man, he removed the vest soon after killing Tobias, so as not to draw attention to himself.'

Jamie nodded. 'Yeah. That make sense.'

'Krishna's looking for a man in a yellow high-vis on CCTV. He ought to be hunting for a man wearing dark clothing and carrying a black canvas bag. Morgan, nip upstairs and update him, would you?'

She returned to the pathology report she'd been reading. Gordon had reminded her momentarily of her father and the notepad and pen he'd kept by the phone for message-taking. She could still picture his lazy scrawl, his handwriting indecipherable to anyone but himself.

Her thoughts were interrupted by Jamie. 'Erm, guv? George Fox has had several jobs, including a brief stint as a farm labourer at a dairy farm near Rugeley.'

'When?'

'Two years ago.'

Kate pulled a face. 'That's quite a while ago and it doesn't necessarily follow that he'd have had access to, or have used, a slaughterer's gun.' She caught his disappointed look. She'd already pulled him up earlier, and she knew that if Morgan had approached her with this idea, she probably wouldn't have been so quick to discount it. 'I don't like clutching at straws when what we really need is some evidence. But that isn't going to be handed to us on a plate, so go ahead. Look into it to make sure.'

'Yes, guv.'

Regardless of her concerns about him, he seemed to be doing his bit. And in her experience, good policing usually won out.

Abandoning the pathology report, she allowed her thoughts to turn again to the passenger in the high-vis vest. If he'd acted impulsively, the gun he used was likely to be connected to his profession. It could certainly have been in the black bag he'd been carrying.

Jamie was by the door. 'Nobody's answering the phone so I'm heading to Bright's Farm. See if anyone there remembers George. There's a gun dealer on the way. I'll check with them to see if they've sold any stun guns.'

'Good idea. And they don't have to have been sold recently. If the perpetrator is the man from the train, he could have owned a gun for a while.'

He acknowledged her words with a small, weary salute.

She noted the dark circles under his eyes. He'd been like this for three weeks and she had put it down to his family life. She couldn't help but wonder if there was another reason; if Dickson had him working on some other mission. Could he even be looking for Rosa? The thought horrified her. Kate was certain Jamie had also been part of Operation Agouti. What if Dickson was still using him, out of hours? Her heart beat a little faster. She needed to reason through this. Not jump to conclusions. Despite other commitments, Jamie put work first, was always on time, followed instructions, seemed keen and respectful. Was he an innocent patsy?

She could argue he was, other than the fact that he'd been standing on the same platform when Heather and Rosa had met. Moreover, he had lied to Kate, told her he was elsewhere, when all the while he had been at Stoke station. That Dickson had placed Jamie on her small team was further proof her officer was untrustworthy. No, she shouldn't trust Jamie. Dickson had eyes on her. Of that she was sure. And there was a good possibility those eyes belonged to Jamie.

She removed a sticky notelet from her computer where she'd placed it, tiny scribbles where she'd attempted to piece her ideas together, and again thought of the notepad beside the phone. Her father had been a big note-taker, not just phone messages. His desk at home had been littered with squares of paper from notepads and, on the rare occasions he had taken her to work with him, his computer screen had been covered with sticky notes.

She reached into her bag for the photo of her father with William and looked at it again. Her father had been in with a chance of promotion too but had blown it, thanks to an allegation of sexual misconduct. It was such an alien idea that, had it not come from Tilly, she'd have been certain it was a manufactured fib. One person could clear it up. While her team were out and occupied, she could tackle her boss about it. And learn what? That her father wasn't the man she'd admired, that William was a home-wrecker, and that her enemy, Dickson, had been one of their close friends? She gazed at the picture as if it might yield an answer: her father smiling at the camera; William's eyes not on the photographer but on Dickson, who was giving a satisfied smile. Her brain fizzed as she worked through more pieces of a puzzle that seemed to keep growing. During the Maddox Club investigation, William had been quick to transport Dickson to a safe house, out of harm's way, and had tried to prevent Kate questioning him. Was he, like Jamie, part of Dickson's circle? *William. Jamie.* Both reporting back to Dickson. Both protecting him. Her mind jumped to Chris's file about corruption within the force. How far had the rot set in, and had her father been another bad apple? She would search for his work records and see if there was any truth to Tilly's claim.

'You busy?'

Kate jumped at Emma's voice. 'Sodding hell! What do you want?' The words came out far more sharply than intended.

'Bad time?'

'Yes . . . No. I just didn't hear you come in.' She shoved the photo back in her bag. This would have to wait.

CHAPTER FIVE

The afternoon dragged into early evening with no breakthroughs, until Jamie rang in. Kate put him on speakerphone.

'The farmer, Harry Bright, owns a captive bolt pistol with a spring mechanism. He recalls George watching him shoot some cattle. Said the guy was morbidly fascinated by it and the whole killing process, and even asked where he could find a gun like it.'

'Did George use it on any animals?' Kate asked.

'No. Although George asked if he could "have a go" and picked up the gun when Harry laid it down to deal with the dead animals, treating it like it was a toy, even aiming it at the farm dog.'

Emma wrinkled her nose. 'Ew, that's sick.'

'Was that why George quit the job?' Kate asked.

'He didn't quit. He was fired. He didn't pull his weight. This was the final straw. Harry said he wouldn't have him back, even if he came gift-wrapped and free of charge.'

'Didn't like him then?' said Morgan.

'To be honest, I don't think Farmer Harry is much of a people-person. He's a bit of a grumpy bloke. It took all my excellent people skills to get him to divulge as much as he did.'

Morgan gave a light guffaw. 'People skills! Yeah, right. I assume he hasn't seen George since then?'

'Spot on. There's no way George sneaked back here to get his hands on the gun. It's kept in a locked cupboard inside the house and when we looked it was still there. Still, we know George is familiar with this type of weapon and he might have purchased one himself.'

'Did Harry tell him where he got his?'

'Yeah. The internet. I took down the name of the website.'

'Any joy at the local gun dealer?' asked Kate.

'No. He's never sold any bolt guns. He gave me the names of another couple of dealers who might stock and sell them. One of them isn't too far away. Want me to try them? I might get there before they shut.'

She thought about his earlier tired appearance. He could do with some rest, or he'd be no use to her. Plus, his presence was distracting her. She needed to breathe, feel the investigation, not watch her back all the time, worried every word and action would be reported back to Dickson. 'Yes, and then get off home. I don't want you half asleep tomorrow.' She hoped he'd heed her words and not use the time to carry out any further business for Dickson.

'Cheers, guv. I appreciate that. If I come up trumps, I'll call you.'

No sooner had he rung off than Krishna appeared at the door. 'I thought you'd like to know where we're at.'

'Anything?'

'Not a great deal. We can't find George Fox on any local surveillance cameras in or around Hanley Park yesterday evening.'

'He might simply have avoided them and come in a different way,' said Emma.

Krishna nodded. 'True. There are other ways of getting into the park, not covered by cameras. I've more bad news. There's no surveillance equipment overlooking the bandstand. If he'd arranged to meet anyone at the Pavilion Café, I might have found him, but as it is, nothing.' His heavy dark eyebrows rose in apology.

Kate wasn't surprised. 'We'll have another word with George. See if we can narrow down which route he took to the park.'

'Good. The better news is that Felicity has given you a couple of junior technicians to help hunt down the guy in the high-vis. So far, there's no sign of him on the main road and we're checking cameras throughout the vicinity. I have to warn you, though, if he caught a lift with somebody, we might be snookered.'

Felicity Jolly was in charge of the technical department and Kate made a mental note to thank her for the extra support.

'Oh, and there's something else. I was talking to a colleague who let slip there was a shooting on Monday. I think somebody over at Hanley precinct is looking into it. Thought you might like to know.' Krishna removed his glasses, revealing sunken eyes. 'Anyway, I'm off duty now. Rachid's working the late shift. He has instructions to ring you if he finds anything.' He raised a hand in farewell and disappeared.

Kate tapped prayer hands against her lips before addressing the others. 'Have either of you got any contacts at Hanley?'

'No. I'll check it out, though,' said Morgan. 'It's probably an ordinary shooting. We'd have heard if it was connected to this case, wouldn't we?'

'Not necessarily.' Kate was aware communications between stations sometimes broke down and information didn't get passed along as swiftly as it should. 'We'll stick with what we have for now. Even though George's alibi is vague, I'm struggling to place him at the scene of the crime. Tobias was sent home early from the office, and it's unlikely George could have known that, unless somebody told him. I'm also not convinced he has motive enough to kill Tobias. This isn't adding up.'

Morgan rested his arms on the desk, brows low. 'If we discount George, we'll only be left with the passenger in the high-vis.'

'And let's face it, you don't normally shoot somebody for talking loudly on a mobile,' said Emma.

'Currently, they're our only two persons of interest, so we'll have to work with what we've got and, at the very least, eliminate them.' Kate began gathering her belongings. 'Which one of you fancies a trip out to interview George again?'

'I'll come,' said Emma.

Morgan blew Emma a kiss, which she caught in her hand.

'Morgan, you struck lucky. Try Hanley police station. There might still be someone there at this time.'

'They shut at five.'

'Try anyway. Then you can take off,' said Kate. 'Get some rest and, hopefully, we'll make progress tomorrow.' She reached for her phone. With everything that had been happening, she hadn't had the chance to message Bradley to ask if he would help her find Rosa. She sent a vague message asking him if he was free for another job, then rattled her keys.

'My car or yours?'

'I gave the Nissan back to Greg, so let's take yours.'

◆ ◆ ◆

Crouching on his haunches, secreted in bushes beside the car park, Ben could see any comings and goings to the Premier Inn. So far, only a handful of travellers had passed by and checked in. Nobody had emerged. It wasn't their time to die.

The Trentham Estate was huge, with its famous gardens, monkey forest and treetop adventure park. He had avoided those, choosing instead to settle close to the shopping village.

'It's almost like you don't want to go through with this at all,' said Lisa. He shifted uncomfortably at her words. She knew him too well. The other attractions were where he'd almost certainly find children and he couldn't bring himself to face that challenge.

She continued, her words barbs in his heart. 'If you don't face up to it, this plan of ours won't work.'

The cocaine he'd taken before he left home was wearing off. He wouldn't have long before his will weakened and he found himself back in the bad place, hiding in his bedroom, wishing the world would swallow him up. If he failed today, he would be obligated to return tomorrow and, in between, Lisa would go on and on, wheedling and pressing him to lurk by the gardens or the monkey forest.

Ben focused on the captive bolt pistol, feeling its familiar weight in his hand. The spring was loaded. It wouldn't require much time to line it up and fire. Despite his reluctance to follow through with his promise, once he aimed he thought no more about the why, only the execution. One press of the trigger and it was over. Quick. Painless. Efficient. He had excelled at weapons training during military training. After he had passed out and joined his regiment, he had spent many a night on sniper duty. Some skills were never lost.

The weapon had been purchased from the internet the day he and Lisa had come up with the plan. It had been her idea. Somehow it seemed more fitting than an ordinary gun. He sat motionless. Another skill he had picked up from his time in the army. He hoped he would not have to wait much longer. Patient as he was, he was coming down fast. He needed more coke.

'You should have brought a top-up with you,' she said, reading his mind.

Another car, a Volvo, drove into the car park. It didn't stop. Instead, it pulled up outside the Premier Inn. A man got out, reached into the boot for a backpack and a laptop. The lid dropped with a bang. The man headed inside.

Lisa sighed. 'I don't think much of your location. Nobody is going to use this car park. The shopping village closed at four and

93

those people visiting the garden centre have parked closer to it. This is a waste of time. Why did you choose here?'

'Because it felt right. You told me to follow my gut. It led me here.'

He didn't want to argue with her. The truth was, if she told him to move, he would. He'd do anything she asked of him. She was his world.

A woman appeared at the end of a path from the direction of the shopping village. He stiffened as she pulled out her phone to make a call, her voice drifting towards him.

'Hi, Sarah. Sorry. The delivery was late. I've only just left work. Are the girls okay?'

She began to walk in his direction, pausing every now and again to converse with the person on the other end of the line.

'You're the best auntie ever.'

She took another two steps then said, 'Hello, sweetie. You got what? A gold star? Wow! I'll be able to see your lovely picture when I pick you up from nursery tomorrow. Yes. Be good for Auntie Sarah. Put Ivy on.'

His hands became clammy. He couldn't kill her while she was on the phone. It sounded as if she was talking to her children.

'Fate,' whispered Lisa.

'Hi, Ivy. Yes. I'll sort it out tomorrow. Don't forget to take your gym kit to school. Love you.'

'I can't,' he said. 'Not while she's talking to her children.'

'Don't be silly. Fate decides when. Death happens while you're shopping, speaking to your neighbour across a hedge or making love in bed. She's the one.'

He wiped his hands on his trousers, one after the other.

'I've got a bottle of wine chilling, bath bubbles and some candles from work. Thanks again for looking after them.'

The woman slipped the phone back into her pocket. Her car keys jangled as she yanked them out. She was five paces from the Honda, close to where he was hiding.

Lisa had heard the keys too. 'This is her car. It's her destiny. Act now.'

His grip tightened around the pistol. He eased stealthily from his hiding place and drew himself to his full height. Her face registered first surprise then horror as her eyes dropped to the weapon in his hand. The plastic bag she'd been carrying landed on the tarmac with a soft *thunk*. He gave her no time to scream or run. Using the rabbit-caught-in-the-headlights moment, he crossed the short distance between them, rested the cool barrel against her forehead, and pulled the trigger.

He turned before her body had hit the ground. He knew what death looked like. He now had a brief window to make good his escape. Lisa said nothing, which meant she was proud of him. He bundled the gun back under his jacket and moved as fast as he dared.

◆ ◆ ◆

The Foxes' flat smelt of blossom-fresh washing. George's mother had set up an ironing board in the living room, where crisp, folded sheets lay in a pile on the settee and those yet to be tackled were heaped on a chair. George sat in the only free armchair, mobile in his hand, while a television drama played out on the set in the corner of the room.

'We've got a few more questions for you, regarding your whereabouts yesterday,' said Kate.

George gave her a cold stare. 'I told you where I was.'

'We'd like some specific details, such as the route you took to the park and which entrance you used to place you there.'

A smile teased the corners of his mouth. 'You having trouble proving I was there?'

His mother looked up, her face blank. 'If he said he was at the park, then that's where he was.'

'Which entrance did you use, George?'

'I didn't use any entrance. I jumped over the fence along College Road. It's not my problem if you can't prove I was there.'

'Well, it might be your problem if you can't help us eliminate you from our enquiries,' said Kate calmly. 'Can you tell us some more about Becky?'

'She didn't turn up to the park and I don't have her phone number so, no, I can't.'

Emma spoke up. 'It's odd that nobody at the Costa remembers either you or Becky being there on Monday.'

'I couldn't have talked to her if she hadn't been there, could I?' A lazy smirk spread across his face. 'I bought a bottle of Coke and a ham sandwich, if that helps. Becky had some sort of smoothie thing. Maybe the staff will remember that.'

He was playing with them. He needed shaking up a little.

'Have you ever used a gun?' Kate asked. The smirk remained fixed.

'A mate and I shot some rabbits once with an air rifle.'

'What about a captive bolt pistol?'

'I don't know what one of those is.'

'A farmer in Rugeley says you do. You worked for him as a labourer for a short while before he let you go. Does that ring any bells?'

'Oh, yeah. I remember old Harry. You're talking about the stun gun, aren't you?'

'That's right. Harry told us you were keen to have a go at killing an animal; in fact, he told us that you picked up the gun and aimed it at his dog.'

He snorted a laugh, but the cavalier attitude shifted. 'He's exaggerating. I didn't aim it at anything. He was a bit upset about killing the first cow. I offered to take over, that's all. Thought I'd be helping him out.'

'That's not the version he told us.'

'Yeah, well, he never liked me. And he's past it. He's probably forgotten what really happened.'

'He told us you were morbidly fascinated by the whole process.'

'Whatever.'

'So, have you ever used a captive bolt pistol?'

'No!' His mobile lit up with a text message. His eyes strayed briefly to it and he covered it with his hand, not before Kate had spotted who it was from.

'I see you're in touch with Ashleigh.'

He feigned indifference. 'Yes, she's cut up about Tobias. Needs a friend to talk to.' He slid the phone into his jeans pocket.

'Have you stayed in contact with her while she's been going out with Tobias?'

'Sort of.'

'We can check phone records if we have to.'

'Alright. She's messaged me a few times. Might have had the odd call from her too. She was getting fed up with Tobias's attitude.'

'Yet she still went out with him.'

'It would have come to an end, eventually.' He looked away at the drama unfolding on the television set.

'What do you mean exactly?'

He didn't reply.

This was getting them nowhere. She was wasting valuable time. Mindful of Dickson waiting for her to stumble, she urged, 'George, we need some cooperation from you. We're talking about the murder of somebody who you disliked so much you'd have "kicked his head in". You told us that, *didn't you?*'

The iron released a lengthy hiss of steam and his mother put it down and pointed a finger at Kate. 'That'll do. Just because my boy's been in a little bother in the past, it doesn't give you the right to come here upsetting him again about Ashleigh and suggesting he'd be capable of killing somebody. The farmer was a miserable so-and-so and, like George said, probably can't remember what happened that day. George has told you where he was yesterday evening, so, if you've finished your questions, you can both leave before my husband gets home. He won't take kindly at all to you being here pestering the lad.'

'Mrs Fox, we're investigating a murder of a young man—'

'I said you can leave. You've nothing on George and you know it.'

'Thank you for your time. We'll be back if we have any more questions.' Kate gave a polite smile even though inside she was screaming with frustration. It would be much easier if George could give them a concrete alibi.

The landing was empty, the only noise some hip-hop music emanating from one of the flats closest to the staircase. Emma's face was rigid. She said nothing as she clattered down the stairs.

Reaching the entrance, Kate stopped her for a second. 'I feel the same way. If he was involved, we'll nail him.'

'Cocky little shit. He knows we haven't got anything on him, and he's right, we can't disprove he wasn't at the Costa or the park. We don't even know if Becky is real or fabricated.' Emma pushed the front door open with both hands and stomped down the path. 'He's laughing at us, Kate. And I hate that.'

'We'll get to the bottom of it. We'll check Ashleigh's and George's phone records to see how often they were in contact. Don't forget we have another person of interest to locate.'

'I haven't forgotten. It's just there's something shifty about George. I can feel it.'

Kate unlocked the car and got in, strapping on her seatbelt. It was early days. They'd find out exactly what George had been up to. And she'd lay money on the table it wasn't to do with anyone called Becky.

◆　◆　◆

As soon as she got home, Kate headed straight for the fridge, drained the contents of an open bottle of rosé into her glass, picked up a box of rice crackers and settled on to the settee. She flicked on the television for company, trawled through endless channels to settle on a rerun of *Fleabag*. It seemed a lifetime since she'd been able to lie down full length on the settee, propped against her husband's muscular body, where they would rest in companionable silence, listening to music.

Chris's days, like hers, had been punishing and fraught, and both had treated home as a refuge from the craziness they endured during the day. Their house seemed to sense his loss too and, where it had once felt happy, it was now an extension of her own emptiness; a place where she ate, slept and brooded. She'd long since given up the idea of cooking for herself and, although she kept the place spotless, it lacked something. Or rather someone – Chris.

She shoved a half-eaten rice cake back into the packet, snapped off the television. Ignoring her father's boxes, still waiting to be returned to the attic, she made for the kitchen again. There'd been no opportunity to talk to William about her father or check out his work records and it was yet another piece of the gigantic, messed-up puzzle she had to resolve. She gulped down the wine, turned on the tap and stood, hands on the sink, while the cold water ran. Tilly had to be wrong about her father; after all, Ellen might have twisted the truth or conjured it up. Maybe Ellen was the jealous one, envious of her father's close bond with William. A part of her couldn't accept that scenario. She cupped her hands under the icy water and splashed it on to her face, letting the drips trickle down her chin and land in the steel basin. She remembered her father's impromptu holiday. He'd told them he'd taken leave to spend some time with them all . . .

◆ ◆ ◆

Kate grabs her swimming costume from the bottom drawer. She can't remember the last time she wore it. Tilly is carefully applying mascara to her already lengthy eyelashes.

'That'll come off in the swimming pool,' says Kate.

'It's waterproof,' says Tilly in a bored tone, and continues to sweep the brush in upward strokes until she's satisfied with the result. 'I don't see what all the fuss is about. It's only a couple of days away at Center Parcs.'

'Exactly. It's a couple of days away, all of us.'

'But we see each other every day.'

'Not Dad. He's always at work.'

'I suppose.' Tilly opens her wardrobe door. 'Reckon we'll meet any boys there?'

'I dunno.'

'We'd better. I'm not wasting a whole weekend.' She pulls out a short black dress that Kate has seen her wear before. It fits and flatters her tiny frame perfectly. Tilly bundles it into a sports bag before searching her drawers for more items – tights, knickers and tops – dragging them out with little care or interest before stuffing them in the bag. 'Why's it such a big deal to spend time with him? I wouldn't care if I didn't see Mum as much as I do.'

Kate grimaces. She'd love to see her mum one more time, even if it was only for a few minutes. Kate's mother, Kathleen, was a nurse, originally from Scotland, with the same wide-set silver-grey eyes Kate had inherited. She calls Ellen by her name, not Mum, just as Tilly calls her dad by his name, Mitch.

'It makes a nice change, that's all,' Kate replies. She doesn't want to discuss it. She's hardly seen anything of her father since Ellen and Tilly arrived. In fact, he seems to be even busier than ever and out at all hours.

◆ ◆ ◆

Kate and her father had been devoted to one another. He would have told her if there'd been any false accusations about sexual misconduct. If not soon after it happened, then certainly in the wake of Ellen's departure, when he had been at his lowest ebb and needed all of Kate's compassion and love. Yet she had her doubts. Why would Tilly lie?

She made her way to Chris's office as if it would somehow help her think more clearly. She dropped on to the chair, rubbed her hands over the soft leather, searching for a residue of Chris.

'I wish you could actually tell me why William's name was on your list and why my father's wasn't.'

She reached for a gyroscope that sat on the desk and spun it. She observed the optical illusion of a continuously flowing helix until it came to a stop, and then she rang William's number.

'Kate, is everything alright?' She could imagine his rugged face, grey eyebrows lifted, his expression concern personified. She hadn't reached out to him in such a long time that it was natural to assume she was in some sort of trouble or distress to be ringing him after 10 p.m.

'Tilly told me something awful about Dad and now I need you to be honest with me. Was he ever suspended for suspected sexual misconduct?'

She heard the sharp intake and noted the lengthy hesitation before he was able to answer her. 'It was a long time ago.'

'I know when it was. I remember him being off work at the time. I have to know the truth.'

'Mitch was a wonderful father and a good man.'

'I know he was, and nothing you say will change how I feel about him. I only want to know if Tilly is right or wrong. If she is, then it's only fair you tell me.'

William's voice was steady. 'She's right, and he was extremely ashamed about the whole thing, even though the allegations were unfounded and he was subsequently cleared.'

'Then why didn't he talk to me about it? Tilly and Ellen knew. Why keep me in the dark?'

'Listen, I don't know how Ellen found out. To my knowledge, your father didn't tell her anything about it. But she was the only one who could have told Tilly. Your father was gutted by the accusations. He didn't want any of his family, especially you, to find out about them and, afterwards, when it was over, he just wanted to forget about the whole terrible episode and move on. He wanted to be a father you looked up to and respected. You've no idea how important you were to him.' The sadness in his voice seemed genuine and she couldn't deny she felt considerable relief that it had been a false accusation.

'Who accused him?' she asked, then wished she'd asked William to his face.

He was floundering. 'It's . . . it's not important. Let it go.'

'You won't tell me?'

'It's really not important now, is it? Tilly is right, but it was an allegation, not a conviction. There's a difference. Now, get some sleep. I don't need to remind you that you're heading up an important case.'

Call over, she switched off the light, found her way out of the room now plunged in darkness and into the hallway, lit only by moonlight coming in from the small pane of glass in the front door.

'Should I believe him, Chris?'

She waited for a full minute for an answer that didn't come, then padded upstairs.

CHAPTER SIX

DAY THREE – THURSDAY

A symphony of birdsong accompanied her as she jogged the final stage of the yellow route around the reservoir. She was no ornithologist and couldn't recognise the variety of calls but today the full orchestra of trills and chirps, harmonised with lower, more powerful notes, was creating musical bedlam.

She emerged from the woodlands, down the slope towards the water. Black-faced sheep observed her with mild curiosity, their jaws working as they lifted their faces to watch her power past them. The water was ice-blue with a flock of white gulls bobbing on the surface like plastic ducks at a funfair. She caught sight of a pair of swans ahead, standing out with their white feathers and elongated curved necks bowed as they glided effortlessly side by side. She could identify with them; keeping calm on the surface, and yet paddling like crazy underneath.

Chris, who had an ability to store huge amounts of trivia, not only told her that swans lived to be twenty or thirty years old and mated for life, but that they were very intelligent and could remember people who were kind to them and those who were not. She stopped for a moment to watch the by now familiar pair. Their beauty was breathtaking and their devotion to each other magical. She shouted out a hello to them. Told them they were magnificent and wished them well. They seemed to respond with slight bends of their heads, which warmed her soul. She hoped they'd be together for the duration of their lives, not bereft like her. Yet even the sight of the swans didn't revive Chris's imagined voice or his presence. Why was she blocked like this?

She ran on, the causeway only a few hundred metres away. She would come again tomorrow, or however long it would take until she could speak to Chris again.

◆ ◆ ◆

The police station was beginning to bustle with life: raised voices in the corridor and doors banging. She greeted a couple of colleagues and, taking the stairs two at a time, prepared to confront her father's best friend.

'Kate?' A look of paternal concern flashed across William's features, the same one he'd worn when her father had finally drifted into peaceful oblivion and replicated when he'd stood by her side at the grave, a plot adjacent to her mother's. It was an expression that spoke volumes and reminded Kate that William had been the only one of her father's colleagues who'd visited him in the care home, throughout his illness, even when his closest friend had no longer recognised him. It brought back recollections of evenings spent with him and Chris at their home, where he'd filled the role of a favourite uncle, confidant, ally, friend – a time when she'd trusted him wholeheartedly. The file on Chris's computer had cast doubt on him and on their relationship, yet seeing William's face, knowing he genuinely cared, stirred her feelings.

She laid the photograph from her father's box flat on the desk, so it was facing William, and pointed to Dickson, standing with him and her father. 'Was it him? Was he the one who accused my father?'

William ran a hand over his chin, pushing loose skin over his cheekbones. The gesture gave her the answer she sought and, until his eyes abruptly emptied, she thought he'd confess. An invisible switch that controlled his emotions had been flipped and his voice held a note of menace.

'This is ridiculous. You're in charge of a serious investigation and yet you're wasting time, rooting about in the past – a past that can't be changed. There's no point to all of this.'

'You haven't answered my question,' she replied.

He pushed the photo back in her direction. 'And I've no intention of answering it.'

'Because Superintendent Dickson *was* the person responsible?'

He placed his hands together and pressed his fingertips to his lips. Footsteps rattled up the corridor, muffled voices accompanied by laughter lifted through the door and reached her ears. She ignored the background noises, eyes fixed forward. She could play the waiting game.

On a shelf behind his head stood a photograph of a younger, dark-haired William in full regalia, shaking hands with the deputy constable. William had lived alone for many years; his sole companions were two Burmese cats and his bees. Kate had little recollection of his wife, a woman who'd favoured the outdoors and who'd played the piano with soulful intent and a soft smile on her lips. She'd died in childbirth, along with William's baby daughter. The tragedy was never discussed, but he and her father shared a common sense of loss that had cemented their friendship.

'There have been many here who didn't believe you could make a comeback after Chris was killed. I wasn't one of them. I've supported you and spoken up for you when others have doubted your abilities because I believed in you and wanted you to have the chance to show everyone you were still the same DI Kate Young who was head and shoulders above many others and who would, given the opportunities, shine again. And although you've been getting results, you still have your doubters, people who continue to voice concerns regarding your mental health. When I leave the force, you won't have anyone to shout on your behalf and you've got critics who are biding their time, waiting for you to slip up. I promised your father I would never abandon you, and I haven't. I've been there even when you've thought you haven't needed me. I've lived up to my promise and I shall never let you or Mitch down. However, if you continue to pursue this matter rather than concentrate on the investigation into the death of Tobias Abrahams, I shall be forced to change sides and join the dissenting voices.'

'I would never lose sight of what's important. Tobias deserves justice and I'm doing my utmost to ensure he gets it.'

'Good. Then stick at what you're best at – investigate this crime and uncover the perpetrator. Make me proud. Make your father proud. You have to, because once I retire, you'll be on your own.'

She took her father's photograph from the desk without saying a word.

◆　◆　◆

'Morning, guv. Lovely day, isn't it?' Jamie's overly bright greeting grated on her already frayed nerves. Ever since she'd deduced that he was working for Dickson, she'd had to box clever and was once again reminded of the swans she'd seen earlier – on the surface gliding with ease yet, underwater, scrabbling frantically. She couldn't afford for Jamie to get an inkling she was on to him. In the fullness of time, she'd use him to her advantage.

'Morning, everyone. How's Sophie doing, Jamie?'

'The doctor says she needs to rest more. He's talking out of his arse. I bet he hasn't got any kids, let alone a hyperactive toddler who thinks it's great fun to bounce on his parents' bed at two o'clock in the morning. I doubt either of us will get any rest for the next five years.'

'Make that twenty-five years,' said Emma. 'My brothers were a pain right up until they left home and, given how difficult it is to get on the property ladder, I reckon you'll be saddled for a good while yet.' Emma had moved out from home to live with her grandmother when she was a teenager. Kate had never really got to the bottom of why she had and, on the rare occasions they'd broached the subject, Emma had clammed up, or casually claimed she'd left because seven brothers were seven more than she could handle. Her eyes told a different story and Kate half expected it was more to do with her stepfather than her siblings.

Jamie blew out his cheeks. 'You reckon?'

'Don't listen to her,' said Morgan. 'She's in a mood. George Fox wound her up last night.'

'That little shit is definitely keeping something back from us. And I'm not in a mood. I'm concentrating on doing my job.' She tapped her pile of paperwork to make her point.

'You rung Hanley police station yet, Morgan?'

'Got a young officer who knew nothing about the shooting. He advised me to ring back later.'

'Right, we'll have to follow up on George, then. Check his phone records and see if he and Ashleigh were, as he suggested, in contact with the odd message, or whether he was stalking her. I have a feeling he was more hung up on her than he's willing to admit, and I have doubts about this so-called Becky. I can't work out if he's being shifty for a different reason or because he's somehow involved in Tobias's death. I'm tempted to talk to Ashleigh again.' Kate let the thought hang before shaking her head. 'No, let's wait for his phone records first. Any news from the tech team?'

'Nothing. Or from Forensics. We still have no weapon, no suspect, other than a bloke in a high-vis and no proper motive for

Tobias's murder.' Morgan sat back in his chair and rubbed at his chin. 'Where do we go from here?'

For a moment, Kate couldn't reply. She was as stumped as them. Then she spotted Jamie tensing and looked over her shoulder to discover Superintendent John Dickson at the door.

'Sir?'

'A word, Kate.'

She went into the corridor, heart thumping.

He lowered his voice. 'Emergency services got a call ten minutes ago. A woman's been found dead in the Premier Inn car park on the Trentham Estate. The word is, she's been shot in the forehead. I understand you are dealing with something similar.'

'Yes, sir. Our victim was shot with a captive bolt pistol.'

He gave a grave nod. 'I think it might be wise if you headed over there immediately. Take your team and establish what happened. If it's unconnected, I'll pass it over.'

'Sir.'

'And Kate?'

'Yes.'

'I don't need to tell you to keep a lid on this until we know what we're dealing with.'

'Understood.'

His eyes rested on her for the longest moment. His face was a blank. Then he turned on his heel and strode away. She knew what he was up to. The hard stare was a ploy to unnerve her. This could even be a wild-goose chase to slow her own investigation. But whatever he was up to, she still had to obey orders.

◆ ◆ ◆

They took two vehicles for the ten-minute drive, pulling off the roundabout with its sign thanking them for visiting the Trentham

Estate on to a side road that led to the Premier Inn. The emergency services were present. With fellow officers arriving to assist, she left Jamie and Morgan to arrange barricades and to ensure witnesses were detained. It was her role to assess the situation. Getting out of the car, she quickly ascertained there was one vehicle, a white Honda, parked under trees and another, a silver Volvo, several metres away, parked at a haphazard angle.

'We'll cordon off from here.' She secured the crime-scene tape to a bollard and they unwound it to form a rough circle around the scene, anchoring it to more bollards as they did so. It fluttered in the breeze as they pulled on their paper overalls.

Emma had gone quiet.

'You okay?'

'I'm fine. It's just, she looks so . . . I don't know. She looks discarded. Like a bag of old clothes. Yet she's important to somebody.' She stopped herself.

Kate wriggled her hands into her latex gloves. Emma wasn't usually as affected as this at a crime scene. Something was off with her.

'It's never easy, Emma. Our job is to track down who did this and at least give her family closure. I find it helps to focus solely on that.'

'Yeah. Just having a *moment*.'

'If you'd rather, I can film the scene alone. Or you could swap duties with Morgan and send him out.' Although an official police photographer would arrive shortly, a video of the crime scene was essential.

'No. Really, I'm fine to do the filming.' She picked up her work-issue phone and checked the battery level. 'It's good to go. So am I.'

'Wait a sec.'

An officer was walking in their direction, a clipboard under his arm. He came to a solemn halt near them.

'I've been sent to record the logbook, ma'am.'

She gave him a nod of thanks. 'Go ahead. Okay, let's begin, Emma.'

They ducked under the tape. Emma lifted the phone and turned slowly so all the immediate surroundings could be captured, before walking towards the body.

The small figure wearing black trousers, ankle boots and a cream blouse lay a metre away from the Honda. As they moved closer, Kate noticed the gold chain around her neck, a gold letter H dangling from it. Her face was framed by deep-auburn hair, so mingled with dark blood it was difficult to determine its real colour. Kate grimaced at the sight. The woman's forehead had completely caved in, crushed by the force of a bullet or a spring bolt.

'Victim is female, Caucasian, possibly in her twenties.' Kate knelt beside her as she spoke, patted the woman's trouser pocket gently and pulled out a mobile phone. She held it up for Emma to film.

'It's a Samsung Galaxy with a rose-gold protective case.' She pressed keys to no avail. 'Discovered in left-hand trouser pocket. Password protected.' Placing it in an evidence bag, she left it beside the body for Forensics. She patted the other pocket. 'No ID, wallet or purse.' From there she rose and began a spiral search, one of the common patterns used for outdoor crime scenes. She started from the epicentre and walked a helix, searching for any obvious clues, followed by Emma, who continued to record. She crouched down beside a plastic bag and pointed out the pink writing on it.

'A plastic shopping bag from Nina's,' she said loudly. She opened it a fraction to spy an array of scented tealights. Probing deeper, she shook her head. 'Contains coloured tealights but no handbag or purse. Might belong to victim.'

She continued walking the area methodically until she reached the cordon's edge. Emma checked the footage. 'What do you reckon?'

'Between you and me?'

'Yes.'

'I think she was killed with a captive bolt pistol. I couldn't see any gunshot residue or spent cartridges. I might not be a forensic expert, but her head wounds looked horribly like Tobias's.'

'Then the cases are connected.'

'Better wait for the experts to confirm. For what it's worth, I think they are.'

Emma gave a small nod. 'Incoming,' she said. Morgan was striding in their direction.

'The driver of that Volvo – he's the one who found the body – has asked to speak to the lead officer,' he said.

'He wouldn't talk to you?'

'Not really. He wasn't in a fit state to be interviewed. He got flustered and then asked if he could talk to you. I think he's in shock.'

It wasn't usual for witnesses to request a senior officer.

'What's he like?'

'Nervy.'

'Well, if it'll help him to talk, I suppose so. Emma, can you stay here and wait for the teams to arrive?'

'Sure.'

Kate signed off on her documentation then strode across the tarmac and into the hotel lobby.

The small man was in his mid-to-late fifties, his face as white as the walls behind him. He sat on the edge of a small settee, chin resting on clasped hands.

'Are you okay, sir?' she asked.

He dropped his hands to his lap and lifted his head. His eyes behind their thick lenses were like small globes. 'Sort of. Oliver Perkins,' he said without any prompting.

'I'm DI Young. Is there anything we can get you, Mr Perkins?'

'I've got some water.' He nodded at the plastic bottle on the floor beside him.

She got straight to business. 'I understand you wanted to speak to me.'

'I . . . Yes. I . . .' He slid a look at Morgan. Kate got it in a flash. Oliver felt intimidated by her officer. Nevertheless, she wasn't going to send Morgan away on a spurious task. The man could say whatever he had to in front of them both. She adopted a friendly tone as the man was clearly nervous. 'Can you talk me through how you came to find the deceased?'

'Er, yes. I spent the night here.' He rummaged in his trouser pocket, bringing out a wallet. 'I've got a business card,' he said, fingers fumbling as he searched. He found one, tugged it free and handed it to Kate. His name and position as a salesman were above a logo of a pharmaceutical company based in Newcastle upon Tyne.

He tried to put the wallet back in his pocket, got to his feet, jammed it in and fell back on to the chair.

'And why were you here, sir?' Kate asked.

The man looked disorientated. 'Oh, yes. Sorry. Meetings. I had meetings down south yesterday and the day before. I'm making my way back up to Newcastle today. More meetings.' He reached for the bottle of water, fumbled with the cap, gave up and put it back down. He ran a hand over his balding head and left it resting there. 'Sorry, forgive me. It's a bit of a shock. Erm. You need to know more, don't you?'

'Anything you can recall might help, sir,' said Kate.

'Yes. Right. Erm. I checked out at eight thirty. I didn't notice anything at first. It was only after I left the small car park outside the motel and drove across the adjoining car park, I spotted some-body lying on the ground. I stopped to see if there was anything I could do to help. I thought at first somebody had taken a tumble and injured themselves . . .'

He reached for the water again, his hands sliding around the screw top. Morgan stooped low and took it from him with an 'Allow me', and undid it for the man.

Oliver took it back with thanks and gulped down the liquid, wiping his mouth on the back of his hand. 'It was only when I got closer that I saw what had really happened.'

'Did you touch or move the deceased at all?'

He covered his mouth with his hand and shook his head. His skin seemed to sag. The mumbled words were barely audible. 'Her brain . . . was hanging out of her skull—'

'You didn't spot a handbag or wallet, did you?' Kate asked.

'No. I took one look at her and backed right off, made the call and stood as far away as possible.'

'Thank you. That helps us greatly when we're examining the body for traces of DNA,' she explained in soothing tones. Oliver rubbed his eyes, as if to erase the memory of what he had seen.

'Did you happen to notice anybody else in the car park at the time?'

'No.'

'But there were other cars around?'

'Only in the car park where I parked, right outside.'

'And what time did you arrive last night?'

'Around five.' He swallowed hard, took another sip of water. 'I drove past the car, the Honda on my way in. She . . . the deceased . . . wasn't there then. I'm sure I'd have seen her if she had been.'

'Did you go back out at all, Mr Perkins?'

'No. I had sandwiches from a petrol station and stayed in my room, working on some notes for today. Then I watched a film and had an early night.'

'I don't suppose you heard or saw anything out of the ordinary? A fracas? Raised voices?'

He shook his head and covered his mouth again.

'Are you feeling all right, sir?' asked Morgan.

'Give me a minute.'

They waited for him to speak again. He apologised again. 'Bit nauseous. No. I didn't hear anything. I didn't hear any gunshot,' he added.

Kate didn't tell him that would have been unlikely if the woman had been killed by a slaughterer's gun. She gave him a gentle smile.

'Thank you for your time. I think that'll be everything for the moment. If you can think of anything else, please let us know. We'll keep your card in case we need to get in touch again.'

He nodded, his eyes unfocused.

'Maybe you should cancel your meetings and head home,' she said.

'I think I might.'

Walking back outside, she noticed more vehicles had drawn up, including the pathologist's car. Harvey Fuller was already crouching beside the body, his silver hair catching the sunlight as he moved. She didn't return to the spot, instead choosing to walk down the nearest path, which took her into an avenue of shops. She turned left and found Nina's, a shop selling candles and diffusers, only four doors down. The sign on the door showed opening times – ten until four. If the victim had bought tealights here, it must have been prior to closing time. Wandering back, she noticed all the shops had the same opening hours. The victim wasn't by her car when Oliver Perkins drove in, so where did she go after four o'clock when the shops shut? The answer came to her quickly – the nearby garden centre.

Staff had been detained in its tearoom, where Jamie and another officer were in the process of interviewing them. Jamie broke away to update her.

'Nobody I've spoken to so far has spotted any unusual activity in the car park either yesterday or today.'

'Can I have a word?' she asked.

'Sure.'

'Ladies and gentlemen,' she said loudly. Heads snapped up and the light buzz of conversation abated. 'Thank you for your patience. You may have heard that there's been an incident in the car park adjacent to the Premier Inn. We're trying to work out the movements of a young woman in her twenties with long, deep-auburn hair who might have been here yesterday afternoon after four o'clock. Did you see or serve such a person?'

She was met with headshakes and concerned looks and then a woman put up her hand. 'I might have done.'

Kate scooted over to talk to the potential witness. 'Thank you. When did you see her?'

'I was outside the centre, helping Jackie move pots. It was just after closing time. Jackie, did you see her?'

The woman, in the same green and yellow outfit as her co-worker, gave a blank look. 'I didn't see her.'

'Well, I did, cos I thought at the time it was a bit late to be at the shops. They all shut at four.'

'Did you see anyone else?'

'Only her.'

'And this was about sixish?'

'That's right. We finished up soon after, didn't we, Jackie?'

'And you didn't drive past the Premier Inn car park on your way home?'

'No. We use the staff spaces in the garden centre car park.'

She noted the wedding ring tight on the woman's podgy finger. 'Thank you for your time, Mrs . . . ?'

'Partridge.'

'If you think of anything else, Mrs Partridge, have a word with one of the officers, will you?'

The woman dropped her voice, leant forward conspiratorially. 'Detective, the rumour is, there's somebody dead in the Premier Inn car park.'

'I'm sorry, but I can't discuss the situation yet. I'm sure you understand.'

The woman nudged her friend. It didn't matter what Kate said, the tongue-wagging had already begun. Kate collared Jamie on her way out.

'Once you're done here, would you head back to the station? We need an identification quickly.'

'One of them just told me. A woman with auburn hair, works at Nina's.'

'That's useful to know. See if you can get a name.'

Kate hastened to join Harvey, who was taking samples from underneath the victim's fingernails.

'This is another nasty one,' he commented. 'The assailant held the pistol against her forehead before firing. The frontal damage was undoubtedly caused by the impact, however, some of the injuries to the rear of the skull will have come from falling backwards on to the tarmac with force.'

'It was the same type of captive bolt pistol as used against Tobias, wasn't it?'

'For certain. Body temperature and rigor mortis suggests she's been dead over twelve hours.'

'I think she might have been killed around six last evening. She was seen headed this way about then.'

'That adds up.' A small sigh escaped his lips as he turned the body over and caught sight of the mess beneath the skull. 'Very nasty indeed.'

Emma appeared, notepad in hand. 'We got a name and address from her car registration – Mrs Helen Doherty, aged twenty-seven. She lived in Burslem. Nobody's reported her missing and she isn't wearing a wedding ring. Could be divorced.'

'And she probably works at Nina's. See if you can track down Mr Doherty or any other relatives.'

More cars were arriving, and it wouldn't surprise Kate if one or two of them contained members of the press. It was time for her to disappear. A decent journalist, spotting her at this crime scene, would quickly put two and two together and guess the two deaths were connected. Dickson had made it clear he didn't want any information to leak before the press office issued statements. She signalled for Emma to join her.

CHAPTER SEVEN

Some three hours later, Kate briefed the team. They'd established an approximate time of death. Helen Doherty had been working at Nina's and had made a phone call to her sister from the car park at ten past six.

'We've got the full cooperation of the technical team, who are giving us priority, so footage from every surveillance camera on the Trentham Estate is being examined. Emma and I have spoken to everyone who was working at Trentham Shopping Village yesterday. Not one of them stayed later than four thirty. The only person who spotted Helen was a garden centre worker who was also late leaving. She and another member of staff were outside moving pots around when Helen walked past. Neither saw anyone else hanging around or following her.'

Emma picked up the thread. 'Helen was a single mother with two girls, both under the age of six. They're being looked after by her sister, Sarah. Her ex-husband has been notified and is travelling up with his current wife to collect the children. Rich is working solely as our FLO on this. He should be with Helen's family by now.'

'Those poor little kiddies,' muttered Jamie.

Two photographs had been adhered to a board that took up valuable space but to Kate was essential. They needed to keep the victims in mind. Nothing did that better than a photograph of them, reminding every one of the team that these people were like them, ordinary, hard-working individuals with families and loved ones who would miss them. Kate pointed to Tobias in his graduation outfit and then to Helen, in a simple patterned top, her hair clipped back from her oval face, smiling sweetly for the camera.

'First things first, Helen was killed with a captive bolt pistol. It's safe to assume we're looking for the same perpetrator who killed Tobias Abrahams. What we need to ask ourselves is why were they targeted? Is there anything else to connect these victims?'

'We should interview our persons of interest. They might have known both victims,' said Jamie.

Morgan gave a slow handclap. 'See you caught up on the sleep last night. There's one problem. We only have one person of interest we can interview.'

Jamie threw his hands in the air. 'I'm only putting it out there. You wait until you have kids who keep you up all night and see how quick-witted you are then.'

Morgan made an 'Oo-ooh' noise before throwing Jamie a wink.

'Personally, I can't fathom why he'd kill a mother of two. He might have had a motive to attack Tobias because he nicked his girlfriend, but why kill Helen?' said Emma.

'Should I check his alibi . . . you know, just in case?' Jamie's eyebrows were drawn together. Kate had already decided they would follow up on George. It was sensible procedure. If Jamie was hoping to run to Dickson and accuse her of not pursuing every avenue, he'd be disappointed.

Her phone flashed. She reached for it, noted the message was from Bradley, then casually slid it out of view. She turned back to Jamie, fully aware he might have seen the mobile light up. She couldn't read the message in front of him. Dickson's mole would report it back. She had to pretend it wasn't important.

'Yes, please,' she said. 'There may be some connection we don't know about.'

'Guv,' said Jamie, 'if the bloke in the yellow vest killed Tobias because he was mad at him for talking loudly on the phone, there's a chance he also killed Helen. She also made a call around the time she was killed. She was on the phone for a few minutes, talking to her children.'

'Firing on all cylinders today, aren't you, Jamie-Boy? That would suggest our killer walks around Stoke with a captive bolt pistol, waiting to shoot anyone who uses their mobile in public. It's a bit of a leap of imagination to expect that to be the case.'

Jamie stood up and rested his palms on his desk, preparing to do battle with Morgan. 'We've encountered killers with odd patterns of behaviour before. What about the killer who raped then carved the word MINE into his victims last year, or the one who choked victims to death using a medieval torture device? Some killers don't require a great deal of motivation to vent their anger. They go off like a firework over the smallest thing. Anger isn't a primary emotion. It's a product of negative emotions and more killings are committed spontaneously in anger rather than premeditated.'

'Whoa, Professor Jamie, wind your neck in.' Morgan held up his hands in a submissive gesture.

Kate had to admit Jamie had a point. Had things gone to plan, had Tobias left after the meeting at CRT Accountancy and had Helen not been held up with the late delivery, they might not have met their fate. However, Jamie's theory implied the killer was patrolling the streets of Stoke-on-Trent acting only when somebody riled them enough to turn anger to rage. A woman talking to her children on a mobile seemed an unlikely trigger. Although it might suggest a killer out of control. She looked directly at each of the officers in the room, holding their gaze momentarily as she spoke slowly. 'We *have* to establish a connection between Helen and Tobias, because if we don't, and Jamie is right, we can't possibly know who the killer will target next.'

◆ ◆ ◆

After assigning tasks to the rest of the team, Kate made for the washrooms, where she picked up the message from Bradley. It was only two words: 'Ring me.'

He picked up immediately. 'Your contact in Manchester has moved.'

If Farai had left the area, she'd never track him down. 'Shit! Any idea where he has gone?'

'The café owner reckons Lancashire but can't be more explicit. Believe me, we were as persuasive as we could be.'

'You haven't hurt him, have you?'

'Only a little. His café's a bit of a mess, though. Might need a glazier to fix his windows and cabinets. He wasn't as tough as you thought.'

She winced. Bradley's methods were unorthodox and risky. If the café owner reported him or somehow let Dickson know they were looking for Farai, it could all blow up in her face.

'What did you say to him?'

'Don't get your knickers in a twist. I let him believe I was a disgruntled client who had a bone to pick with Dickson. He won't have had a clue I was working for you.'

Cold fingers walked down her spine. It had come to this. She was overseeing a bunch of ex-servicemen who did her bidding but didn't care what methods they employed to get results.

'Okay, thanks. Are you able to continue looking?' Bradley and his friends would have jobs and families. They couldn't spend all their time hunting for Farai and his girls.

'We can try. It might take a while. We don't have anything else to go on other than a county.'

'They must be in a city or town.'

'Not necessarily. Sex-workers operate in rural locations too,' he said.

'I'll see what I can find out and send you details of the hotspots where you're most likely to locate him.'

'As for our recent lost property. It's looking increasingly likely it won't turn up.'

The lost property in question was Tom Champion. She wasn't surprised by this news. Dickson had got to the ex-prison guard. She could feel it in her bones.

Bradley dropped his voice. 'I'll wait for your message.'

The phone went dead, leaving Kate staring at her reflection in the mirror. She looked different. A leaner, harder, colder version of herself. She was still the same officer she'd always been, wasn't she? The damp handset suggested otherwise. She had joined forces with people unafraid to operate outside of rules. She might resemble the old Kate, but inside she was somebody she didn't recognise.

'Chris?'

She didn't wait for an answer. There wouldn't be one. Chris didn't recognise her any longer either.

Leaving headquarters, she set off for Church Leigh, one of ten hamlets that made up the straggling parish of Leigh, closer to Uttoxeter than to Stoke, and set in rural Staffordshire. The area was steeped in history, none of which appealed to Kate. She vaguely recalled her father mentioning Nordic influences and monks who farmed the land, but teenager Kate had not shared the same passion for history as her father. She did, however, appreciate the beauty of nature and every time she left Stoke and drove back into the countryside a tangible sense of calm washed over her. It was for that reason she chose the slightly longer, more scenic road over the ever-busy arterial route.

She'd lived in these parts almost all her life and never grew tired of seeing herds of cows or hedgerows or fields of crops, or quaint villages with pubs and stores, populated by people who'd grown up here and worked locally for decades. She felt anchored here, as rooted as the wide-trunked oaks planted on verdant, undulating land, and like the migrating birds who returned to the reservoir and lakes in the region she could never imagine herself leaving. If only Chris could be with her, her world would be complete.

'I miss you every hour of every day. I want the torment to stop. I need something to cling to and prevent me from drowning. I think I know why you won't talk to me. You don't approve of my methods, do you? I have to do it this way. I'm up against somebody who doesn't play by the rules. If I want to catch him, I have to do the same.'

Her heart burned a hole behind her ribcage, and she attempted to distract herself by concentrating on her surroundings, taking in the scenery along the lanes. The trees were not yet in leaf, their branches dark and twisted, affording glimpses of the fields and farmhouses secreted behind them. Clumps of snowdrops, the hopeful signs of spring, provided relief from the damp, brown foliage. They reminded her that it had been over a year since Chris's death and yet, if anything, she felt worse now than she had then. If time was a healer, then it had bypassed her.

The trees gave way to arable land, deep brown in colour thanks to freshly spilled manure where enormous flocks of land gulls swooped and screeched after the tractor churning the land. At last, signs of village life appeared. She traversed the low bridge over the River Blithe and rounded the bend, where white cottages with frontages adorned with wisteria yet to flower stood opposite a grass triangle. Protected by a white chain fence, trumpeting daffodils surrounded a traditional black and white signpost.

Larger houses dominated the edge of the village, to be replaced by bungalows, then a group of four terraced houses, all with views over fields. Pulling up on the roadside outside the end one, she spotted Rich's Ford Focus. The fact that the FLO was here was comforting. It was bad enough talking to bereaved adults, but when children were involved it could be heartbreaking.

The driveway could easily accommodate two average-sized vehicles, leaving enough space for a garden. Painted metal butter-flies had been erected on thin posts the length of the borders to give the appearance of hovering over the herbaceous perennials. Waxy-leafed shining ferns stood among tricolour sage with its edges bordered in patchy splodges of white and interiors splashed with shades of pink and purple, while tiny hyacinths and delicate yellow and purple crocuses punctuated the various shades of green. She took a deep breath and rang the doorbell. Rich's face appeared at the window and within moments he was at the door.

'Hi. How's it going?' she asked, sotto voce.

He shook his head. 'Kids were hysterical. The youngest has cried herself to sleep. The older one, Ivy, is watching a film in the bedroom.'

He took her into a bright room, and her eye was drawn to a large canvas picture of a field of sunflowers. Under it sat a woman with deep-auburn hair, the same shade as her sister's, and the same neat nose. She snuffled a greeting, her hand clamping a ball of tissues.

'I'm very sorry for your loss.'

Sarah choked back a reply.

'I'm Kate. Can I call you by your first name?'

She nodded.

'Thank you. Sarah, I'm heading the investigation into your sister's death. I was hoping you'd be able to tell me about Helen but, before that, is there anything you want to ask me?'

'No. Rich has been very helpful. I know what's happening.'

Kate gave the man a smile. He motioned to a chair. 'You sit down, Kate. I was about to make us a cup of tea. Would you like one?'

'I'm fine, thank you.' She sat on the edge of the seat, facing Sarah.

'He's very kind,' said Sarah after he'd gone.

'He is.'

'He was so good with the girls. I didn't know what to say to them. He did.'

'I understand their father is on his way?'

'Yes. They should be here in the next hour. It's a long trip from Somerset. They were on a minibreak. Neil lives in Leek.'

'Then the girls will still be able to come and visit you?'

'I guess so. It'll be different, though. I'm used to seeing them regularly.'

'You were close to Helen?'

'Yes.' She sniffed hard, lips trembling.

Kate offered a sympathetic smile. Even though she and Tilly were stepsisters, she understood the bond Sarah and Helen would have shared. 'Was there any special reason the girls stayed over with you last, or was it normal for them to stay over?'

'Helen asked if I could have them because she was working late.'

'Was that because she'd made plans with somebody?'

'I don't think so. She was looking forward to a long soak in the bath with a glass of wine.' She sniffed again.

'Was Helen seeing anybody?'

126

'She was on Tinder, and she dated guys, but she wasn't looking for a long-term relationship, not with the little ones to consider.'

'Did she talk to you about the dates she went on?'

'Uh-huh. She didn't spare the details.' She gave a wan smile. 'She didn't go out a lot. I don't want you to think she was a tart or anything. She wasn't.'

'I don't think that at all. Did any of these men give her cause for concern?'

Her forehead wrinkled. 'In what way?'

'The date was pushy, rude, aggressive?'

'They all seemed okay; some boring, some not what she expected, but okay.'

'Did she see any of them for second or third dates?'

She rubbed the ball of tissues under her nose. 'A couple of them. Noah was the longest relationship she had. She saw him for six months before he decided he wasn't cut out to play father. I don't understand how this is helping.'

'Anything you can tell me might help us find the person responsible for her death.' She gave her another smile. 'You're being most helpful. Did Helen ever mention anyone called Tobias?'

Her auburn locks shook. 'Never.'

'What else can you tell me about your sister?'

Sarah's eyes filled again. Kate grasped the extent of the pain she was going through. A sororal relationship was special. 'She was a great mother and sister. She wasn't into anything that might have got her into trouble – no drugs or anything like that. She always put her children first.'

'Had she been divorced long?'

'Fourteen months. She and Neil are still friends. It just didn't work out between them.'

'Does he have the children to stay over?'

'Every other weekend.'

'And did you and Helen go out together when they were with their father?'

'Now and again. I'm married, so she'd drop around here and share a bottle of wine with me while my husband went out with his mates. We're both at home a lot.'

'Has she had any concerns recently, about any individuals?'

'Nothing springs to mind.'

'What about work?'

'She loved that job. It fitted in with school hours and she had a thing about candles. She was considering setting up her own business selling from home. She didn't have them in the house in case one of the girls accidentally knocked it over but if a special one arrived in the shop she'd buy it for me.' Her eyes filled at the thought. Rich chose the moment to appear with two mugs of tea. Spotting the shaking shoulders, he sat beside her.

'Here you go. Drink it while it's warm.'

She obeyed, cupping hands around the mug.

Kate caught Rich's eye, and with a nod got to her feet.

Emma stared out of the window at the passing traffic below, plastic cup in her hand. The machine coffee was weak and flavourless, but she didn't care. She'd needed an excuse to get out of the office for a few minutes. Finding Helen's body had not only changed the direction of the investigation, it had also affected Emma on a personal level far more than she wanted to admit to Kate, or anyone.

The woman had children. Moreover, she'd been on the phone to them minutes before she was shot. It sucked big time. Two little girls who wouldn't have their mother. She knew how bad that felt.

She tightened her grip and felt the plastic give.

'Hey!'

Morgan nodded at her cup. 'You know it makes your hair fall out, don't you?'

'This?'

'Yeah. That's the real reason why everyone avoids this machine. You obviously didn't get the memo.' He gave a small smile that lit his eyes.

Emma knew what he was doing. Dragging her out of her low mood in typical, daft Morgan fashion.

'And as for the chocolate bars, well, I can't even tell you what they do to a person.' His eyebrows danced.

'Enough. I get it.' She threw the contents into the machine overfill tray and tossed the cup into the bin. 'You are now going to have to do a coffee run to replace that.'

'I was rather hoping I could persuade you to do one. I fancy a latte and pastry.'

'On your bike!'

'Damn. It means I'll have to get off my nice comfortable chair.'

'You're already off it.'

'Fair point. What do you fancy?'

'I don't mind. Choose for me.'

'Double hot chocolate with extra sprinkles and a chocolate brownie it is. I'll only be ten minutes. Don't let me catch you lurking by this machine again. I can't imagine you bald. Although you'd probably carry off the look with your usual flair.'

She watched him bound down the flight of stairs. It had taken only a silly exchange to lift her mood. She owed Morgan, and not just for the drink and cake he was about to buy her.

◆ ◆ ◆

The technical department in a separate building, next to where Kate worked, was locked and accessed only by a keypad. Kate entered the code to find herself in a room reminiscent of days spent in school science laboratories, with benches set beside long tables. Instead of Bunsen burners and tripods, there were electronic devices attached to mobile phones and open laptops downloading software. There were two further rooms, one with a door marked 'Tech 1' where technicians like Krishna and Rachid would be searching through surveillance footage on large screens, and a glass-fronted office where a woman in a lab coat with steel-grey hair, bright, orange-framed spectacles and a bemused smile was watching her. Felicity Jolly beckoned her and spoke as soon as Kate entered the room.

'The answer is no. So far, our hunt for a man in a yellow high-vis, or dark clothing, is proving fruitless and, to be honest, it's doing my head in. I don't see how he can have evaded all the surveillance along the road and on the streets. We've pulled footage from local firms, individual houses, not to mention the numerous road cameras, and the man doesn't appear on any of them.'

'Then he must have taken a route that avoided them.'

Felicity's eyebrows arched. 'Have you ever tried to avoid surveillance? It's downright impossible. There are cameras everywhere, especially on major thoroughfares like the A50 that runs through Blythe Bridge. I have my own theory.'

'Which is?'

'He's a ninja,' said Felicity, straight-faced. Her eyebrows waggled. Only when Kate grinned did her face crack.

'You've been playing too many of Bev's computer games.'

While Felicity's partner of over thirty years was a comic-book illustrator who'd moved into designing characters for computer games, Felicity was averse to spending any more time with technology than necessary, preferring a book, a crossword or easy conversation to gaming.

'Touché!' She got to her feet and made for the door. 'We have *some* news for you. Rachid has been working on the mobile device

130

found on the Trentham Estate and, in accordance with your earlier request, we've been trying to ascertain if the victims were in contact with each other. Follow me.'

Felicity marched across the lab with the authority of a school-marm and rapped on the door, opening it almost immediately as she did so.

'Rachid, did you pull anything else off that iPhone?'

Kate caught a glimpse of two desks, back to back, each filled with computer screens. A bearded technician faced the door.

'No. Nothing further to report. I've been through all the contact details, call and text logs, and social media on both devices. I can't find anything else to link the pair other than the dating app. Although I'm still working on WhatsApp.'

Felicity turned around. 'They were both on Tinder,' she explained.

'You don't know if they connected on there, do you?' asked Kate.

Rachid shook his head. 'There's no way of knowing without contacting the website hosts and that could take days . . . even longer.'

'Thanks anyway,' said Kate. 'It's something we can look into.'

Felicity shut the door again and looked Kate straight in the eye. She hesitated briefly before asking, 'There wasn't any other reason for dropping by in person, was there?'

'Yes. To thank you for giving our case priority and putting extra officers on it.'

'No need. You're heading a murder investigation. And now, a double-murder investigation. You should have as much support as you require. I'm only surprised the superintendent didn't request extra assistance himself.'

The look she gave Kate spoke more than words. Even though Kate was certain she could trust Felicity, she wasn't going to

131

badmouth Dickson. Walls had ears and she couldn't afford for her act to be exposed. She gave a small shrug instead and, in spite of holding her gaze for several seconds, Felicity said no more on the subject. She made to move then stopped and put a reassuring hand on Kate's shoulder.

'If there's anything to be found, we'll find it. I've got my best men working on this for you.' She gave a light squeeze before pulling away.

'I appreciate that.'

She left with a sense that Felicity had wanted to say more about Dickson. If she hadn't been leading this investigation, she'd have stayed to find out what.

CHAPTER EIGHT

The afternoon saw the team discussing what they'd so far uncovered. Although Jamie still had no information regarding the mobile that rang Tobias as he was getting off the train, he was spouting his latest theory – that the call was from a woman, maybe even Helen.

'It's possible. They might have matched on Tinder and hit it off. Tobias had a girlfriend and didn't want her to know about Helen, so they purchased a pay-as-you-go so she could ring him without arousing suspicions.'

'I'll grant you it's possible, but who are you pinning this double murder on?' said Morgan.

'George and Ashleigh, in cahoots.'

Kate put away her mobile. There were no messages from Bradley. She hadn't had a chance to investigate red-light districts in Lancashire and hoped he was on it. She half listened quietly while Jamie pontificated. It wasn't the maddest supposition she'd encountered. Morgan clearly didn't feel the same way.

'Jeez, you really have overdosed on the caffeine. I think I preferred it when you were yawning your head off. Why don't you do your job and find out who the fuck owns the mobile rather than coming out with all this bullshit?'

Jamie wasn't fazed. 'This team is unique, not only because it's small and made up of, quite frankly, superb officers, but because those officers share ideas and mull them over.'

Emma rolled her eyes. 'Calm down, you two. We get it. Morgan's right in that we need proof and evidence. Jamie's right in as much as we are all superb officers who pool ideas.'

Kate set aside her thoughts about finding Rosa, forcing her mind to remain anchored to the investigation. Once again, justice for Chris would have to take a back seat. Her mind blipped. Chris had been assassinated by a gunman hired from the dark web. Was it possible someone, connected to these two killings, had done similar? 'While we're on the whole sharing thing, what are your thoughts on the killer being somebody else completely, maybe even a hitman?' The final word almost made her gag. It was one thing coming up with this theory and another voicing it. She tried to quell the tide of emotion threatening to wash over her.

Jamie was quick to agree. It struck Kate that whereas Morgan and Emma were more selective and sometimes took convincing, Jamie was almost always enthusiastic about her suggestions. Like he was sucking up to her. She questioned whether it was genuine or part of an act to disarm her, deciding firmly on the latter.

'Yes. The callous shooting. The direct shot to the head. That makes sense,' he said.

She tried not to scowl at the man. If Dickson's plant wanted to tell him anything, he could tell him Kate was doing her job. She continued with her theory. 'If you remember, the pathologist's report for Tobias stated that the residue, caused by sooting, was confined to a circle, eleven millimetres in diameter. That suggests to me that there was no tremor, no hesitation. The killer placed the barrel against his forehead and shot him in cold blood.'

'Definitely sounds like a pro shot him,' Jamie said.

'What about Mr Angry on the train, Kate?' asked Emma. 'He's done a great vanishing act for somebody wearing a high-vis.'

'I've been thinking about him too. He either is incredibly smart and managed to avoid all the surveillance cameras in the vicinity, or he was just an ordinary bloke who got off at the right stop. The witness, Mr Haskins, said he didn't leave the platform straight away. He was standing, searching in his pockets. He might have been looking for his phone to ring somebody for a lift or pick up a text message from somebody who was already there waiting to meet him. There are no cameras directly outside the station, which means he could easily have been met and, if he removed his vest when he got into the car, there's no way the techies could have spotted him.'

Morgan ran a hand over his head. 'Fuck. If that's the case, we're back to square one. No person of interest.'

'Apart from George, or an unknown assassin,' said Jamie, earning a frown from the big man.

Emma shook her head. 'How would a hitman have known Tobias was on that train? And how could they have known Helen would be late leaving work?'

Kate had already thought that through. 'Well, if we wish to speculate further, such a person could have been tailing them for a while and struck when the moment presented itself.'

'Nobody else got off that train,' said Emma.

'They didn't have to *catch* the train. If they were watching the accountancy offices and saw Tobias leave, they'd be able to guess which train he'd be on. It takes the same length of time to drive from Stoke station to Blythe Bridge as it does to travel the distance by train, give or take a few minutes, depending on traffic. However, there's only one train every hour and Tobias left the CRT Accountancy and Tax Planning offices at around five. A taxi to the station would take about six to eight minutes, in time for Tobias to catch that train. The killer could have waited at Blythe Bridge station and seized their moment when they saw Tobias alone on the platform. Or, another possibility might be that the killer rang Tobias and arranged to meet him there.'

Jamie drummed a beat on the desk with his fingers. 'The pay-as-you-go that rang him as he disembarked the train! That's a good call, guv.'

Kate stood up. 'Not really. It's total guesswork. I'm chucking it out there for you to consider and hear your thoughts.'

'If the killer had also been stalking Helen, they could simply have waited close to her car until she came to collect it,' said Jamie.

'Uh-huh.' Kate studied the photographs. 'Although why they'd wait there until six, when they could have shot her in the shop without running any risk of being seen, is another mystery. And we have one major, unsolvable question – who would want them both dead?'

Jamie was the first to fire back an answer. 'Somebody who was jealous because they met on Tinder and were in a relationship.'

Kate shrugged. 'Then we should discount George. He wanted Ashleigh back in his life, so Tobias having an affair with another woman was the answer to his prayers. As for Helen, she was single, had an amicable relationship with her ex-husband. It didn't matter who she was dating.' Helen's face smiled out at her from the board. The room fell silent until Emma spoke.

'Which brings us back to the idea of a random killer, enraged by people on mobiles.'

Kate pondered the idea. 'Phone rage? Yes, it's possible. There might be another connection, though. Has anyone spoken to anyone else who worked at Nina's? Was Tobias one of their customers?'

Morgan picked up a worn notebook, flicked the pages until he found the information and shook his head. 'The shop is named after the owner, Nina. She didn't recognise his photograph, but admitted she has a terrible memory for faces and doesn't serve in the shop very often. She's never used CRT Accountancy and instead has her own bookkeeper. She also confirmed Helen was a model employee and unlikely to have angered anyone. Nobody else works there.' He threw the book on to his desk and got to his feet, stretching his arms with another weary sigh.

Kate gritted her teeth and stared at the photographs. They could follow the path of phone rage, but her gut said there was another reason the victims had been chosen.

'I spoke to Tobias's mother again. She only repeated what she told us a couple of days ago. She's struggling to come to terms with what's happened. She didn't recognise either Helen Doherty's name or her photo,' said Emma.

'And George. Have you spoken to him yet?'

'He's not answering his mobile,' said Morgan.

'What about Tobias's girlfriend, Ashleigh?'

Emma spoke. 'She didn't pick up either or return my call, and she wasn't at home when I dropped by.'

'Try her again. Let's see if we can join the dots up and work out what is going on between her and George. Morgan, find the elusive George Fox. Question him about his whereabouts yesterday evening and see if either he or his mother knows Helen. Jamie, I want to know who owns that pay-as-you-go that rang Tobias. Pronto!'

With that, she left the room. Her stomach was in knots. She could do with some fresh air. The investigation was stalling. If they didn't get leverage soon, it could go on for weeks, or even months, sweeping away any hope of promotion. With that thought came the realisation that she wanted to make DCI. William's words had struck home. She would put herself forward. The higher up the ladder she climbed, the more secure her mask. If Dickson believed she was career-minded, he might assume she had lost interest in pursuing the idea that somebody else had been involved in the murder of her husband. She would take a few steps around the block and then inform William of her decision. It could be a very good move.

Discarded pizza boxes were heaped on a filing cabinet by the door, and the aroma of warm basil and baked dough hung in the stale air. Kate washed down the last of her margherita with the sparkling water, bubbles bouncing on her tongue, cleansing her palate. She wiped greasy residue from the melted cheese on to the napkin provided by the Pizza Parlour and was about to address the others when Morgan stomped into the office and announced, 'George's mother hasn't heard of Helen and didn't recognise her from the photo. She also hasn't a clue where George is. I'm starting to wonder if he's deliberately hiding from us.'

Kate threw the napkin into the bin. 'We'll have to track his mobile and get a location.'

Emma handed Morgan a box. 'Here, big guy. I figured you'd be hungry. I got you pepperoni, but it's gone cold.'

'Great. I don't mind if it's cold. I'm famished. Thanks.' He lifted the lid and ripped away a slice, rolling it and ramming it into his mouth.

Emma continued. 'Coincidentally, Ashleigh's also not answering her phone.'

'I still think they could be in this together,' said Jamie.

It was beginning to look as if the pair were up to something. Kate digested the information yet still couldn't accept they'd kill Helen. So far, they had no evidence linking Helen to them. Morgan shrugged.

'It makes little sense to me. I can just about accept George might want Tobias out of the way, the rest—'

Jamie interrupted with a triumphant, 'Yes! At last. The network provider has given us the information on the pay-as-you-go.'

He shifted closer to his keyboard, scanning the information on the screen. 'It's a 2019 Nokia 105, purchased two months ago at Buy-A-Phone in Hanley.' His face fell. 'Purchased by Tobias Abrahams. Shit!'

'No, we're not done yet. We'll see if there's any CCTV at the store or if the owner recognised Tobias. If he bought it and gave it to somebody, that person might have been with him at the time.'

Jamie still looked downcast. 'It hasn't been operational since it rang Tobias, two days ago, so we can't triangulate it unless it comes back online.'

'Contact the network again and request they inform us if it does. In the meantime, Morgan and I will head to the shop. Emma, try Ashleigh again, please. I'm beginning to wonder what the heck she's playing at.'

CHAPTER NINE

Kate was lost in thought again. She wanted to find out where most sex-workers worked in Lancashire so she could task Bradley with hunting down Farai, yet hadn't had a moment to do so. Now she was in Morgan's Jeep, him at the wheel, headed for the phone shop with no opportunity to even make a Google search.

As usual, he didn't bother her. He was accustomed to her silences and would no doubt put them down to the investigation. She glanced at his pleasant, open face.

'You ever been to Lancashire?' she asked.

He gave a half-laugh. 'Not a question I expected. Once. Went to Morecambe on a stag do a couple of years ago.'

'What was Morecambe like?'

'Huge beach, sand, bars, beers. We wanted to go to Blackpool but had left it too late and couldn't get any accommodation. Morecambe was sound. We started drinking on Friday evening and finished sometime Sunday afternoon.' He gave an enigmatic smile.

'No nightlife?'

'Sure. Bars, clubs . . .'

'Red-light district?'

His eyes crinkled. 'We weren't there for that sort of nightlife. Besides, Morecambe's too genteel. Full of elderly couples and families, as I recall.'

She stopped herself asking any more leading questions, before Morgan cottoned on that she was fishing, not merely chatting amiably. 'I've never been. Thought I might go to Blackpool. See the tower.'

Morgan nodded. 'Why not? Hey, you could arrange a team-building exercise for us at the Pleasure Beach.'

She chuckled. 'I can see that working out well.'

'Choose a day when Jamie isn't half asleep. Hopefully, he'll be more on his game after the next sprog is born.'

She let the conversation drop. There were at least four or five large towns in the county where Farai could be hiding. Numerous places where his girls could be working. Sex-workers operated in all areas, genteel or otherwise. She would have to wait until she got home before she could consider where would be best to send Bradley.

They pulled on to a run-down street. Morgan stared at the tacky, cherry-red Buy-A-Phone sign over the shop and the windows plastered in graphics displaying devices and an array of potential purchases and services.

'They cover everything here, don't they? "Unlocking, unblocking, repairing, refurbs, batteries, chargers". Oh, and check out the catchy slogan, "If your phone is sick? We will fix!" I wonder if they also provide under-the-counter services like stolen mobiles, trackers or bugging devices.'

'Today, I don't care what they're up to as long as they remember Tobias.' She swung her legs out of the vehicle and wrinkled her nose at the fog of bad smells she identified with urban decay: the stench of neglect, blocked drains and vomit combined with a musty aroma. Many of the houses on the street were boarded up, rubbish left outside front doors, the bags torn apart, the contents spilt on to the pavement.

'Shit location for a shop,' said Morgan, following closely behind. 'There's hardly a line of customers beating a path to it. Still, I expect the rent is cheap.'

The door required a heave and shuddered open with enough noise to make any doorbell redundant. There were devices either locked in glass cabinets or secured to brackets, as in many other shops, only more pictures of what might be purchased here. Morgan stood in front of a handwritten notice advertising the latest iPhone. 'Wonder what the uptake is on one of these.'

Kate shouted, 'Anyone here?'

A barely audible voice answered. Within moments, a man shuffled behind the counter. Kate held up her ID. 'We're investigating the recent murder of a young man and would appreciate your cooperation.'

'Murder?' The man tugged the neck of his baggy sweatshirt, the logo, ZZ Top Recycler Tour, almost faded to the same shade of grey as the top.

'We believe this man purchased a Nokia 105 phone from this shop two weeks ago.' Kate showed him the photograph of Tobias. Recognition flashed immediately in his pale eyes, as faded as his shirt. He scratched at the side of a bulbous nose.

'He did. It was a good phone. A new one.'

'We're not interested in the provenance of the mobile,' said Morgan, lending his height and stature to the proceedings. 'Do you have any CCTV?'

'Not in the shop.'

'I'm surprised. Nothing to ensure your valuable phones are protected?'

'Oh, you're a funny one, aren't you? I keep them locked upstairs, in my flat.'

'Okay, then do you remember if he came in here alone?' Morgan asked.

'Yes, he did come in alone. He was in a rush. Asked me for a pay-as-you-go phone. He didn't care which make or model it was.'

'And you sold him the Nokia?' said Kate.

'That's right. He didn't seem bothered by price, so I sold him one of my better models. I have to make a living, you know?'

'Is there anything else you can tell us about him?'

'He paid in cash. He was in a hurry. And that's about it.'

Tobias had travelled a fair distance to this street to purchase a phone. Kate could understand him wanting anonymity, yet to come here when he could have bought a mobile online or at any store closer to where he lived or worked struck her as odd. What made it more peculiar was that he rarely drove.

'This might seem an odd question, but was he wearing cycling gear? Did he come here on a bike?' she asked.

'No. He came by car. Somebody was waiting for him outside.'

'Did you get a look at that person?'

'Not really. I can only tell you it was a woman and I only saw her face briefly. To be honest, I wasn't that interested in either of them. I was looking at the car.'

'Was it an electric Mini?'

'No. It was one of those fancy sports cars – a Jaguar. You don't see many around here.'

◆ ◆ ◆

Ashleigh finally answered Emma's calls and agreed to meet her at home. She looked washed out, her hair lacklustre, along with her demeanour. Her shoulders were hunched, and she sloped to a throw-covered settee, where she sat with her bare feet curled under her and her chin lowered.

'Are you alone?' asked Emma.

'Yeah. Little sis is out with friends. Mum's at work.'

'I have to ask you some questions about George,' said Emma.

The shoulder shrug was weary, like the girl herself. Emma was a little concerned for her. 'Are you okay?'

'Not really. What do you expect?'

'I understand. Tobias's death has been a huge shock to you.'

The girl opened her mouth to speak, changed her mind and said, 'Yeah.'

'Do you know where George is?'

'Haven't a clue.'

'He told us you've been staying in touch with him since Tobias's death.' Emma brushed away a strand of black hair and looked keenly at the girl, hoping she'd look up. She didn't.

'That's right. He knows me better than anyone. He's been looking out for me.'

'You need support at a time like this.' Emma kept up the gentle tone, trying to win the girl's confidence. 'I know they were rivals for your attention. George admitted as much and how he felt about him. He also said you were growing tired of Tobias. Is that right?'

She lifted her head, caught Emma's eye, and sighed. 'It was . . . complicated.'

'Tell me about it.'

'What's to tell? George was my boyfriend. Tobias came along. I realised I didn't want to be with George any more, so I dumped him to go out with Tobias. Now he's dead.'

There was more to it. The girl's voice had cracked as she spoke, and she was now running one thumbnail under the other, cleaning out invisible dirt.

Emma shifted forward on her chair, lowered her tone and tried once more. 'Were you in love with Tobias?'

She swallowed hard, opened her mouth again and whispered, 'Yes.'

'Then I understand how difficult this is for you. Losing somebody you love is very painful.'

'Have you lost anyone?' asked Ashleigh.

'Yes.' Emma didn't elaborate. It was fine if Ashleigh assumed Emma was talking about a boyfriend when she was actually alluding to two people: her grandmother, who'd looked after her and whom she'd adored; and the poor, sick cow who'd been her mother.

The revelation extracted Ashleigh further from her shell. 'I wasn't getting tired of him. He was getting tired of me. I'd already lost him before this happened.'

Emma didn't say anything. A brief nod was enough to encourage the girl further.

'He was cheating on me.'

'How could you be sure?'

'I had a weird feeling, a hunch, he was seeing somebody. It was George who found out what was going on. I asked him to spy on Tobias for me. I needed to know if I was right.'

'And George was happy to do this?'

'Yeah. Of course. He wanted us to break up, so he was keen to find out the truth.'

'It must have been tricky for him to follow Tobias at times, especially as Tobias knew George.'

'George's cleverer than you think. He bought a tiny tracking device off the net and stuck it on Tobias's bicycle so we could trace where he went. He visited the same place frequently, an address in Barlaston. Josiah Drive, to be exact. He'd stay there one or two hours, sometimes longer.'

The street, just outside the city boundary and next to the famed Waterford Wedgwood factory, had recently been listed in the local newspaper as one of the most affluent in the Stoke-on-Trent area.

'I challenged Tobias. Said I knew he was seeing somebody else. He lied to my face, told me I was fantasising. Swore there was

145

absolutely nobody else in his life. I didn't mention the tracking device or that I knew where he went. I wanted to believe him. I even thought there'd be a reasonable explanation for all the trips to Josiah Drive. I decided to let it drop and wait for him to end whatever it was. George had other ideas. I should have guessed he'd make it all about him. He went to the house, spoke to the woman who lived there.' She paused before raising damp eyes. 'Believe me, I didn't know anything about it until he told me earlier!'

Emma's heart thudded a little faster. 'Told you what, Ashleigh?'

'He blackmailed the woman. She's called Joanna Roberts. She's married with a little boy. Tobias was having an affair with a married woman. George demanded five thousand pounds to keep her affair secret from her husband. She paid him!' She began to sob.

Emma scooted across and put an arm around her. 'Hey. It's okay. It's better to get it off your chest.'

'I thought George was being a friend, that he still had feelings for me and respected me, but he's just a greedy bastard. He did all that snooping on Tobias for himself, not for me. He intended blackmailing her all along.'

'Do you know when he met Joanna?'

'Tuesday at six. She couldn't get away from work before then and had to pick her kid up from the nanny at half past six.'

'Where did George and Joanna meet for her to hand over the money?'

The girl snivelled. 'He mentioned something about Wedgwood Cricket Club. By then I was too shocked, upset and angry to listen to what he was saying. All I could think of was how fucked up it all was. Tobias using me. George using me. He wanted to give me half the money! Can you believe that? I told him to poke it. I didn't want any part of it. I ran off. Tried to work out what I should do next. I was going to ring you back. I was going to tell you about the blackmailing. I just needed some time to—'

Ashleigh choked back tears and Emma soothed her again. 'It's okay. You've spoken to me now.'

The girl's eyes shone. 'I sat in the park all afternoon, wondering what to do for the best. I turned off my phone because he kept messaging me, asking me to forgive him, and I can't. I never want to see him again.'

Even though this revelation certainly cleared up a lot of things, it also complicated the investigation further. If George had been with Joanna at the time of Tobias's murder, then he wasn't responsible for the death. With George out of the frame, they now had no idea who they were hunting for. She had to confirm this story and make sure there were no holes in what would turn out to be George's alibi. 'Ashleigh, can you give me Joanna's exact address?'

The girl nodded and Emma wrote it down. 'I have to pass this information on to my boss, who will want me to talk to Joanna. Will you be okay if I leave you?'

Ashleigh nodded. 'My sister will be home soon. Will you arrest George?'

'It depends on what Joanna tells us.'

'I don't really care what happens to him. Not now.' She wiped a stray tear away.

Emma gave her a half-smile of encouragement. Ashleigh had gone through a lot of emotional distress, but she was young and would overcome it. Emma knew all about coping. She had more than a lifetime's experience.

Speaking to Ashleigh had sent Emma spiralling back to a time when she had cowered in her room feeling there was nobody she could confide in, certainly none of her brothers or her mother, too weak-willed and bowed down to even listen to her only daughter's fears about the man who she'd brought into their home.

Her situation had been different to Ashleigh's, yet she still recognised the fear, the uncertainty and utter bewilderment the girl was experiencing. Ashleigh had lost a boyfriend and a friend. Emma had lost her world the day her worst fears were realised.

She pulled out her phone before any images could surface and drag her back to the pain she had carefully put behind her. She reflected that it was strange how both she and Kate had undergone emotional traumas. Emma had buried hers and moved on. Kate was still struggling. That much was clear to Emma. Kate never went out, had refused on several occasions to join the team for a drink after work. Before Chris had died, she'd often been the one to instigate such occasions; now, she packed up her bag and shuffled away, sometimes without even a goodbye. She'd not heard her when Emma had come back from the Costa, even though Emma had made plenty of noise. She'd been edgy and nervous and had almost jumped down Emma's throat, embarrassed because she'd been caught out looking at a photograph, most likely of Chris, rather than working. Emma wished she'd been open about it rather than stuffing the photo away. There was no shame in grieving. Maybe she should have said something to Kate. After all, she understood what Kate was going through. Chris hadn't just died. He'd been murdered. And so had Emma's mother.

She rang Kate. If the opportunity arose later, after she'd spoken to this woman who was being blackmailed, she'd take it. It might be therapeutic for them both.

◆ ◆ ◆

Morgan turned to Kate. 'Oh, holy crap! I've just remembered. I'm really sorry. I didn't get back to Hanley police station. We got called out to the Trentham Estate, and it completely slipped my mind.'

Kate clicked her tongue. 'I suppose it's too late to get hold of them today?'

'I'll try.' He flicked through his call history, found the number he had rung first thing that morning and dialled it. It rang continually.

Kate sighed. 'Try again tomorrow.'

'I'm sorry.'

'I know you are. There's been a lot going on, though.'

She understood how the call had been forgotten. They'd been whizzing about all day, ever since Dickson had sent her to the crime scene. A sudden thought struck her. Dickson had said he wasn't sure if the Trentham death was connected to their investigation, yet he obviously had an idea that it was. Why else would he have sent her so quickly to the scene? Or was it that he didn't know but was deliberately trying to keep her buried in work so she had no time to find Rosa? The more she thought about it, the more likely the second explanation became. She glanced at Morgan, who looked crestfallen. He rarely slipped up.

'Don't beat yourself up about it.'

'You say that, but I will. Can't help it. I don't like screwing up.'

'None of us do. It happens.'

They fell silent again and Kate lifted her mobile. Morgan was too preoccupied to see what she was doing. She ran a search on Lancashire and identified the main towns in the region. Rosa was in one of them. She had to reach her before Dickson did.

The house in Josiah Drive was way above Emma's pay grade. Mrs Roberts clearly favoured a contemporary look that bordered on sterile, and Emma found herself in a spotlessly clean kitchen with white cupboards and even a white oven, staring at an enormous white clock over a white radiator cover while she waited for Joanna to settle her little boy in front of the television in the adjacent room. The only relief, splashes of bright green, came from a handful of potted ferns dotted around the room which Emma was certain were artificial.

'It's really his bedtime, but he should be fine for a while,' said Joanna, pulling out a white leather stool and sitting down on it.

'Thank you for seeing me.'

'Rest assured I wouldn't have let you in if my husband had been at home. I don't want any of this to get back to him.'

'Well, I can't guarantee—'

'If you don't promise me that he'll not be told about this, then I won't talk to you.'

'I shan't mention anything to him,' said Emma. Whether or not Kate did would be a different matter. 'I'm sorry to give you such bad news.'

She'd already told Joanna about Tobias's death. Joanna had appeared to take the news well, but Emma could see she wasn't as composed as she tried to make out. Her eyes had filled with unshed tears.

'Shot, you said?'

'That's right.'

The woman hunted in her pockets, pulled out a tissue and blew her nose. Then, staring at her hands, she said, 'Do you have any idea who might be responsible?'

'We're following a number of leads.'

'It wasn't my husband, if that's what you're thinking. He had no idea about my relationship with Tobias.'

'Are you sure of that?'

She bit her bottom lip and nodded. 'I'm certain. We were incredibly discreet. I . . . I couldn't afford for him to find out.'

Emma weighed up Joanna's reaction. Her tightened hands were now clenching the tissue. Each nail with its French polish was perfectly shaped, her hands white and smooth. Joanna didn't strike her as the homely type. She was a woman who enjoyed a comfortable lifestyle and, judging by her comment, would not have wanted to throw any of it away.

'He didn't know. I swear. I didn't give him any reason to suspect I was—' She looked away, wiped her eyes. 'Oh, Lord. This is horrible. I should never have let myself get swept away like this. It's not like me.'

That she had made it about her rather than Tobias served to complete the picture for Emma. Joanna was selfish and egocentric. She wasn't going to make it easy for her. 'Where was your husband on Tuesday afternoon?'

'Daniel? He's on business, in Switzerland.'

'And who does he work for?'

Joanna's voice rose slightly. Panic creeping in. 'You don't need to know that, do you? I told you. He couldn't have killed Tobias. He didn't know about him. He wasn't here. He wasn't even in the same country.'

Emma watched the tissue now being destroyed, twisted in the woman's hands. She couldn't be sure if Joanna was anxious because she was fearful her husband had killed Tobias or scared that he would find out about the affair. She repeated her question.

'A major pharmaceutical company. He's not due back home until tomorrow.' Emma noted the name of the company. The hysteria in Joanna's voice increased. 'You won't check up on him, will you? Please don't. If he hears you've been making enquiries, he'll become suspicious and then—' A tear broke free. Emma watched it trickle down Joanna's face, followed by another and another. Were they for Tobias or for herself?

Emma suspected they were the latter. Joanna was terrified of her husband finding out about the affair. It wasn't her call to make. If Kate deemed it necessary to double-check the man's whereabouts at the time, they would, regardless of the impact it could have. Joanna dabbed at her eyes again.

'I have to ask you about your relationship with Tobias. We're talking to everyone who knew him.'

She sniffed away more tears and nodded dumbly.

'Is the Jaguar on the driveway yours?'

'Yes.'

'And did you and Tobias drive to Buy-A-Phone two weeks ago to purchase a Nokia 105?'

Another nod. 'Yes. It was Tobias's idea. I'd started to get cold feet and told him I wanted to call off the affair before we made a foolish mistake. I said Daniel could easily pick up a message or read a text he shouldn't and we'd get caught. Tobias talked me round. He suggested I used a burner phone if it would help alleviate my concerns.'

'Does your husband often check your phone?' asked Emma.

'No. Never. He's not the suspicious type. Quite the opposite. I got it into my head he might . . . if he became suspicious.' She released a long, painful sigh. 'I was behaving recklessly, putting my marriage in jeopardy. I was guilty about what I was doing and with the guilt came fear. I was paranoid he'd find out.'

'You rang Tobias on Tuesday afternoon, didn't you?'

'Yes.'

'Why did you call him then?'

Her voice cracked. 'I . . . I was having serious second thoughts about him and what we were doing. Everything. It had to stop, I couldn't put it off again. You see . . . I was being blackmailed. I got scared. Really scared. I decided to pay off the blackmailer and end it with Tobias at the same time. It brought it home to me – how much I was going to lose by hanging on to Tobias. When it came to it, I couldn't bring myself to do it over the phone. Instead, I

152

arranged to meet him. We were due to meet tomorrow afternoon, before Daniel's plane landed.'

Emma studied Joanna's face, wondering if she was capable of killing the young man who could ruin her marriage, or arranging for somebody else to dispose of him. It seemed a dramatic way to end a relationship when all she had to do was break up with Tobias. She had, though, already confessed how difficult it was to break up with Tobias. He might have been horribly manipulative. Her stepfather had been. Her mother had been forced to do all sorts of things she would never have agreed to, to perform perverse sexual acts. She blinked away the image of leather handcuffs, plastic bag, long screws. And what if Tobias had threatened to expose the affair afterwards? Reveal everything to Joanna's husband. It was worth considering. Many murders were love- or hate-related.

Her mother's had been.

'We know about the blackmail,' she said.

'You do? How?'

'Tobias's girlfriend. She knows the blackmailer and he confessed everything to her. She told us.'

'Girlfriend? Tobias had a girlfriend?'

'Yes.'

Her eyebrows knitted together. 'I didn't know that. He never said.'

'They'd been together four months.'

Joanna shook her head slowly. 'That's mad. Totally mad. Tobias was playing me! I thought he was head over heels. He swore I was the only person he'd ever felt that way about.'

Emma held her tongue. The woman put her head in her hands and groaned. 'Did he play me from the start? Was his girlfriend involved in the blackmail? Did they cook it up among themselves?'

'No, she had no idea it was happening. She only found out about it today.'

Joanna lifted her head, her jaw jutting. 'Who was this black-mailer, then?'

'He was her ex-boyfriend. His name is George Fox.'

'George Fox,' she repeated flatly.

'Can you tell me exactly what happened? When did he contact you?'

She twisted her wedding ring around her finger. 'Last Friday. Daniel had just left for work and the doorbell rang. I thought it was him, that he'd forgotten something. It was another young man who stood on the doorstep. He had a big smirk on his face. He called me by my name, said he knew all about my relationship with Tobias. He told me if I didn't pay him off, he'd make sure, the next time he rang the doorbell, Daniel would be at home. He wanted five thousand pounds to keep quiet.'

The unconscious hand movements became more frantic, the ring now going around and around her finger without stopping. 'I told him I needed some time to get my hands on such a large amount of money. I knew Daniel was going to be away from Monday, that I could take out some savings then and he'd be none the wiser. I agreed I'd get the cash by Tuesday, only if he promised to never bother me again. We arranged to meet on Tuesday evening.'

The ring stopped spinning. Joanna dropped her head before whimpering, 'I had to pay him off. I didn't want to lose Daniel.'

'Mrs Roberts, in light of what I've told you about Tobias, would you like to press charges against George Fox?'

She shook her head again, her voice feeble. 'No. Absolutely not. I want that horrid man *out* of my life. He can keep the money. I just want all of this to go away. I should never have got involved with Tobias. It was a terrible mistake.'

'Mrs Roberts, I'm not here to judge you. I'm simply gathering facts so we can find out who murdered Tobias.'

'Of course.' The eyes filled again. 'Poor Tobias. What's happened is dreadful.'

'Can you confirm the time and place where you arranged to meet George Fox to hand over the money?'

'Outside Wedgwood Cricket Club . . . Six o'clock . . . Tuesday evening.' The sobs began.

'I'm sorry to ask you this, but have you any proof you withdrew this amount of money?'

'I took cash out of my personal building society account. I need my laptop. I'll be a moment.'

Emma waited for her to return. From the room next door, she could make out light chuckling from the cute toddler. Her eyes fell on to a large black and white family photograph of Joanna, her son and a good-looking man, no doubt her husband. She questioned why a woman with apparently so much would be willing to jeopardise it all. It made Emma glad her life wasn't complicated. She had good friends, the odd date and the freedom to do whatever she wanted. It was a lot simpler. Joanna returned and handed over the laptop, open on the account page. She'd withdrawn the money Tuesday afternoon.

'The stupid thing is, I wasn't even in love with Tobias. I enjoyed the attention more than anything. He was intelligent, sweet and charming and made me feel . . . young and desired. I knew all along it couldn't last and as soon as that man turned up and threatened my marriage I wanted it to end there and then. But not this way. Not with Tobias dead.'

Emma replied with, 'Thank you for being so frank with me.'

'What happens now?'

'I'd like you to drop by the station and make a statement going back over what you've told me.'

'And what about George Fox? Will he be charged?'

'Not if you don't want him to be.'

'I really don't.'

Emma reached into her pocket, pulled out a business-card holder and passed one of the cards to Joanna. 'My details are on this. If you could come by at your convenience tomorrow, somebody will take your statement.'

Joanna took the card with a small nod.

'I've one last question. Do you know the name Helen Doherty?'

'It doesn't ring any bells.'

Emma brought up Helen's picture on her mobile and showed it to Joanna, who peered hard at the face. 'I haven't seen her before.'

'Well, thank you again for your time.'

Emma was glad to be back out in the street. The house had lacked warmth and homeliness and there was something else. It had felt sad.

◆ ◆ ◆

'Joanna Roberts confirmed she was being blackmailed by George Fox, and that she arranged to meet him outside Wedgwood Cricket Club at six o'clock Tuesday evening, to hand over five thousand pounds.' Kate threw the file on to her desk with an exasperated, 'And that is that! We only have one person of interest. One! Some bloke wearing a high-vis who we can't trace.'

She leant on the desk, her palms slightly sticky against the coolness of the top. Jamie's head was lowered, the only sign he was listening a steady *click, click, click* as he repeatedly pressed the top of his pen. Morgan, who ordinarily would be the first to tell Jamie to stop it, was silent, arms folded, chin down.

'There's nothing for it,' said Kate. 'We'll have to return to the beginning. Which means trawling through statements again and canvassing on the streets, anything that might give us some bloody idea of who we are searching for. Tomorrow, we'll talk to Helen's relatives. We must have overlooked some connection between the victims. Somebody knows both Helen and Tobias. Once we can link them, we can move forward. Right, pep talk over. Try and get some rest. I'd like to make an early start, if that's okay.'

There were mumbles of assent and the clattering of furniture as they cleared out of the office. The day had taken its toll on them all. Kate felt unravelled. If her hunch was wrong and the killer was somebody who lost the plot thanks to phone rage, it would be almost impossible to track them down. The man in the high-vis had completely disappeared and Kate had nothing else to go on. If she didn't crack this case, she could kiss goodbye to any promotional prospects. She really wanted to stick it to Dickson. The supercilious bastard was waiting for her to fail.

On top of all this, of course, she still had to work out where Farai might be without Dickson getting wind of what she was up to. She picked up her jacket. That was something she fully intended doing in the privacy of her home.

◆ ◆ ◆

The lake stretched in front of him, yet all he saw was a kaleidoscope of colours, a medley of greens at the side of shimmering, silver-blue waters. The more he strained to see the colours, the brighter they became until they shifted into smaller sections, mercury grey, polar white, peacock blue. Each piece of the lake leapt from the picture to exchange places with others, as if he were enlarging a photograph and the pixelation was growing out of all proportion.

He turned his back on it. The lake was becoming so large it would soon swallow him up.

'Lisa.'

'Yes, love.'

'I've overdone the coke.'

'Sit down on the bench for a moment. Take deep breaths. Remind yourself why we're here.'

Ben fumbled for the wooden seat, collapsed on to it and shut his eyes. There were few cars parked here at this time of the day. The café had closed and the place was given over to dog-walkers, nature-lovers and joggers. He inhaled, allowing the air to swell his lungs. He held his breath for a count of ten before releasing it slowly between pursed lips. He repeated the act ten times, flexed his fingers a further ten times and stilled his mind, as he had been taught years ago. Snipers had their own individual methods of controlling their bodies and emotions. His were second nature to him, coke or not. As long as he didn't stare at the lake, he'd be alright.

He rose to cross the shady car park towards the playground. From here he could see anybody coming back to their cars. At present, there were people walking around the lake who would return in dribs and drabs. Some would come alone. When fate dictated, he would take advantage of their isolation in this quiet area to take them down. The pistol was primed and ready for use. He placed it under his jacket and rested his fingers loosely on it. It would take only a fraction of time to pull it out, aim and shoot.

'Look at me! Mummy. Watch me!'

He turned towards the shouts. Thanks to the distraction of the lake, he hadn't spotted the child, or his mother hidden in the gloomy corner of the playground. The boy was at the top of the slide, his mother head down, texting. She looked up briefly and the boy slid down with a loud 'Whee!'

'Well done, Billy.'

'Perfect,' whispered Lisa.

'No. His mother is there.' The boy was scrabbling up the rungs, an eager expression on his face.

'She isn't paying any attention. You could shoot him at the top of the slide. She wouldn't have a clue.'

'No. She called him by his name. Billy. I can't kill him now I know his name.' His calm evaporated. Lisa was asking too much of him.

'It makes no difference. Destiny has put him within your grasp.'

He marched away, back to his car, Lisa still talking.

'You have to face up to it sometime. You can't pick and choose adults every time. The idea is you take whoever is thrown in your path. That boy is there for a reason.'

Ben paced up and down, head lowered so he didn't become distracted by the lake. This was too great a burden for him. He couldn't take the child's life. He half heard the boy's mother shouting that it was time to leave.

Lisa wasn't letting up. 'You still have a chance to do this. Turn back and shoot him. He's dragging behind his mother. She won't realise until it's too late.'

The enormity of what was being asked of him hit him square on. He began to cry.

'No.'

'And what about our plan?'

'Don't make me do it!' He marched back to his car, threw himself into the driver's seat and released the flood of emotions. The sobs racked his body. He didn't want to kill a child.

Lisa shushed him. 'It's okay, baby. It's okay. It wasn't meant to be. Let's get back on track. Come on, pull yourself together. We're here now and there are others out there. Why don't we wait and see what fate sends us?'

The pain eased slightly. Lisa understood. He didn't have to kill the child. They were back on track. 'Okay.'

'Good. I love you, you know?'

'I know.'

'More than anything in the world. You've got this.'

Her soft voice reassured him some more and eventually he got out of the car again. The colours had muddied. The water was normal, reflecting the colours of the sky. The trees were subdued hues of green and brown.

'I'm with you. Remember that. No matter what you do, I'll always be by your side.'

His nerve had been restored. He blinked. A sole jogger was headed in his direction, a dark-haired, middle-aged man. He took a step back into the shadows.

'Fate has decided,' said Lisa.

CHAPTER TEN

Kate stared from her kitchen window at the garden. In the fading light, she made out a sparrow pecking at the bird feeder before darting away with its supper. It was right to be cautious. The neighbourhood cats had identified this as a hotspot for birds and, recently, she'd chased away two who'd been prowling under the bushes. This time of the year, when birds were pairing up and preparing nests, always made her anxious for the offspring, some of whom would not reach adulthood.

The bird feeder had been Chris's addition to the makeover. It had been Chris's suggestion that she tape the USB stick, containing all information about Dickson, underneath the top of the feeder, where, so far. it had remained hidden. She could really do with more help from him now. She'd spent the last hour running searches on red-light areas in Lancashire. It would require a huge amount of time and manpower to cover all the areas she'd identified. Neither of which she had. She wanted Dickson outed. He was a thorn in her side and, while he was in office, she would never feel safe, not in her job or in her life.

The momentum caused by the sparrow subsided and the feeder came to rest. Her eyes grazed over the bench and memories of happier times unfurled, of when she and Chris had sat beside the fire pit, swaddled under a blanket against the cold, planning their future in their new home.

Damn! She was thinking of Chris in the past again.

The light was fading rapidly and the garden was merging into a hazy darkness. The nebulosity of her thoughts prevented her from stirring into action and moving away from the window. She should eat but had no appetite. Her current saturnine temperament was part of the grieving process and she couldn't shake it off. She needed motivation, rage, direction, and none of them were currently residing inside her. Promotion might save her from herself. She stared ahead at the empty love seat. When it came down to it, she didn't care as much about her job as she should. By allowing Bradley and his crew to get involved, she had somehow changed. Worryingly, she'd become something akin to Dickson. She'd turned a blind eye to Bradley using torture, smashing up people's business premises and heaven knows what else, all in the name of justice. She might not want to end up as rotten as Dickson or the others Chris had named; however, if she continued on this path, she was as bad as them. And the only thing that would halt this descent would be to take Dickson down by whatever means necessary, right or wrong. Only then would she be able to put it behind her, return to her duties and continue as she always had.

Dusk turned into night and Kate made it no further than the kitchen table, where she sat with her head in her hands. Thoughts about the investigation replaced those of Chris and Dickson. She had no idea how to proceed other than to involve the media big time, make public appeals and pray for witnesses to step forward. This wasn't the way to earn promotion. She'd put herself forward too eagerly and too soon. Had William deliberately set a trap for her to walk into? The idea bounced about in her mind, filling the space until there was nothing other than suspicion and doubt in there. She ought to have bided her time and seen how the investigation played out before throwing her hat into the ring. If she ruined this opportunity, she wasn't sure she'd try again. There and again, if she blew this, Dickson wouldn't let her try again.

The kitchen clock ticked steadily behind her and still she sat, unaware of the moving hands, lost in a fog of thought until the sound of her ringtone forced her into action; if it was Ervin inviting her round, she'd come up with an excuse. She didn't feel in the mood for company. In the event, it was William.

'Bad news, Kate. We have a third victim.'

◆　◆　◆

The teams were in place and emergency lighting and a tent had been erected beside Westport Lake. She shoved the car door open and emerged into the cool evening. She stood for a moment, allowing the breeze to caress her cheeks, and stared across the inky waters. A sound like wild laughter, a low *ha, ha, ha, ha, ha-ah*, reached her ears, the alarm call of a duck.

'Ready, Kate?' Emma's voice jolted her back to the present and she moved towards the car boot, where she kept her protective clothing. Three murders. Three separate locations. Their worst fears were being realised.

Suited up and names handed to a serious-faced officer, they joined Ervin.

'I was going to say that we should stop meeting like this, but it didn't feel appropriate,' said Ervin.

Kate couldn't raise a smile. 'Please tell me you've found something.'

'Only a hand towel, an open boot of a car and a body.'

'What about witnesses?'

'You might be in luck there. Five people saw the deceased jogging around the lake between five and six o'clock. Morgan's interviewing them over by the visitor centre. It's not open but there are some benches outside for people to sit on.'

'Okay, let's do this. Is Harvey here?'

'In the tent. It's the same MO. There's one difference. The victim wasn't using his phone. It was switched off and in the car glove box.'

Kate's stomach sank further. If the killer wasn't enraged by people using mobiles, then what was triggering these attacks?

She traipsed after the forensic officer, who bounced briskly towards the tent.

Emma was by her side. 'It's making no sense.' Emma's voice echoed the same concern she felt.

'You ready?' asked Ervin.

'Go ahead.'

He held open the tent flap. Kate stared inside at another ruined face. The man had been in good physical condition, with muscular arms and a narrow waist. Only the pale-blue veins raised on the back of his hands gave a clue as to his age. The wedding band on his finger caused her heart to sink further. She didn't want to look at him for long. Her inability to work quickly enough had allowed this to happen. They'd run around in circles, and this was the result. Another victim, and when would it stop? After another three people had been murdered? Another thirty? She spun on her heel and trudged past Ervin without a word, away from everyone, to stand by the lake, in search of calm.

A sliver of moonlight appeared from behind a cloud, a giant silver sword cutting a swathe through the waters, urging her to scoop it up and use it against the army of bad guys she was pursuing. She scoffed at her own thoughts. She was only a police officer doing her best and, at present, it wasn't good enough. The clouds blossomed again, and the imaginary sword faded away, much like her memories of Chris.

She questioned whether her depression over Chris was affecting her judgement and weakening her. Since his voice had faded, her usual instincts had been letting her down. Her self-belief was waning, chiselled away by her inability to find further proof that Dickson was shady. She was being ground down and it was spilling over into her work life. Dickson was winning.

Dickson's sneering face once again surfaced in her mind. With it came a small spark of anger which she fuelled with more self-berating. If she allowed Dickson to permeate every aspect of her life, she would have nothing. He would take it all and leave her an empty husk. It was what he wanted. He'd been working on her for months. All the sighs and sad looks when he talked to her, as if he were doing her a favour keeping her on. The anger grew, warming her insides and bringing back confidence in her abilities. William still believed in her. Her dad would have wanted her to fight on. The victims' loved ones needed her to bring this perpetrator to justice. She'd surmounted hurdles before. She allowed the deliberations to stream into her consciousness. Then, with determined strides, she made her way to the visitor centre.

Jamie was crouching beside two women on a bench, notebook in hand. Morgan, who had finished talking to a middle-aged man, approached her.

'What can you tell me about the victim so far?' she asked.

'His name is Asif Baqui. Aged forty-seven. The next-of-kin is his wife, Inaya Baqui. Lives in Tunstall. He was found dead by another jogger who had spotted him earlier running around the lake, doing fast laps. That's the man I was just speaking to.' Kate had noticed the running apparel. 'It's not looking promising. The victim's vehicle was hidden from view. Not one of them saw what happened.'

She raised her face to the sky and let out an exasperated sigh.

'I know. I feel the same way. Everybody we've spoken to was walking around the lake at the time of the attack and knew nothing

165

about it until they returned to the car-parking area. Their stories tally. We have nothing, Kate. Not a fucking thing.'

She pointed at the children's playground. 'Somebody standing over there would have been able to see Asif's car.'

'None of those people were there, though.'

'Do they have any recollection of who else was here at the time or of other vehicles parked near their own?'

'That's what we're trying to establish.'

'Aren't there any surveillance cameras around here?'

'There don't appear to be any. The assailant might even have made their escape via the canal. We'll head there after we've finished interviewing.'

'For crying out loud! Somebody must have seen something.' She shut her eyes and breathed deeply, ordering her thoughts. Opening them again, she said, 'Right, we'll do whatever we can. Check out the canal. Run a background check on those witnesses you spoke to, on the off-chance one of them followed Asif back to the car park and attacked him. And find out if there are any surveillance cameras in the vicinity. I'll catch up with you all at the station. I'm going to talk to William, see if we can approach this a different way.'

'You got it.'

She stepped back out to the cordoned area, removed the protective gear and hurled it in the disposal bin. She returned to the Audi, slammed the door and remained motionless until the interior light extinguished. If she didn't get her act together, this case was going to be her undoing. 'Chris, I bloody well need you.'

When no reply came, she pounded the steering wheel until her hands throbbed.

◆ ◆ ◆

William's grey eyebrows were low on his brow as he considered the options. His meaty forefinger tapped a slow rhythm against his chin. Kate had shared her concerns. What she wanted was action.

'I'd like to put a profiler on it. We'll continue to follow procedure, attempt to connect the three victims and follow up on any CCTV footage, but what we're lacking is an idea of who the killer is. We don't know what's triggering the attacks and, until we have that vital piece of information, we're shooting in the wind.'

'It might be time to put a bigger team in place,' he said.

'Led by me?'

'I can't guarantee that.'

'Why? Because almost a year ago, while still grieving for my husband, whose body I stumbled over at a bloodbath of a crime scene, I made one error – one!' Kate had almost attacked an innocent man on a train, believing him to be wielding a weapon. It was a mistake that still haunted her. 'Since then, I've headed two murder investigations, one at Superintendent Dickson's behest, and still there are those who don't think I'm good enough to manage more than three officers.' She steadied her heart, kept the fury from her voice.

'No, Kate. Because I don't get to choose who leads the investigation. There are other DIs who are equally qualified, and who have had more recent involvement with larger teams. DI Khatri, for one. At best, you might find yourself collaborating.'

'William, I don't want to risk being removed from this investigation. I'm too heavily invested in it. You know how damaging a career move it can be if another officer steps in to take over. It suggests the original officer was incompetent. We've already got the technical team on board. Much of the legwork is being done by them. My team is dedicated and smart. They're among the best, if not *the* best. We simply require a nudge in the right direction.'

'The super isn't keen on profilers—'

'Superintendent Dickson needs us to find this perpetrator before any more lives are lost, before hysteria takes over the streets of Stoke-on-Trent. As lead officer, I'm best placed to say what might or might not work, and I believe we need a profiler.' She kept her chin lifted, hands loose by her sides, fully aware that her body language spoke confidence. It was part of the act that convinced everyone she was in control, even when she felt she wasn't. *Like the reservoir swans.* William's reluctance bothered her. She couldn't determine if he was on her side or if she was being manipulated. She ought not to have confided in him so readily earlier. What if he was hand in glove with Dickson? Or if he had unwittingly passed information on to Dickson and her investigation was being interfered with.

The silence seemed to go on forever until William grunted. 'You can have your profiler.'

'Thank you. I'll get on to it immediately.'

◆ ◆ ◆

The team was back in the office by ten that night. When they trooped in, a lanky man with jet-black hair and trimmed facial hair jumped to his feet, immediately knocking a plastic cup of leftover coffee on to the carpet. 'Oh, shit! Sorry!'

'Don't worry about it,' said Emma, snatching a piece of A4 from her desk to dab the stain. 'I wouldn't like to imagine what else has been dropped on it in the past. You might even have done us a favour and we'll get the replacement carpet we've been after for months. Eh, Kate?'

'We'll need more than a few coffee stains before they'll sanction that. Everyone, this is Samuel Links. He has kindly agreed to be our profiler on this investigation.'

Samuel held up a hand as large as a garden trowel. 'Hi.'

'Hey, Sam,' said Jamie. 'You got any ideas about who we're looking for yet?'

'Erm, if you don't mind, I prefer Samuel to Sam, and I've only been here fifteen minutes.' He aimed a half-smile at Jamie, who squeezed past him to his desk without responding.

'That's Jamie, our resident Duracell bunny. I'm Morgan. Good to have you aboard.'

'And you've met Emma,' said Kate. Emma gave a small wave.

'Samuel needs access to the files, so he'll be working here for the next few hours.'

'You won't notice I'm here,' he said.

Jamie rubbed a finger under his nose and muttered, 'Somehow, I doubt that.'

Kate called them to attention. 'Can we quickly discuss our most recent victim, Mr Asif Baqui, please? I've got a few scant details on him. He's worked for the same company, Grunning Tech Solutions, at The Towers for the last ten years. Having spoken to the company owner, Mr Grunning, it seems Asif worked mostly from home and was a well-liked employee. I had a quick call with Rich, who informed me Asif went to the lake every evening, at around the same time, when it was less busy. His wife is in too great a state of shock to tell Rich much more at this stage. As far as he can gather, the couple had no financial difficulties, no enemies, and Asif was very much a family man. What have you found out? Morgan?'

'I'm afraid we've not got much to add. The victim wasn't known to any of the witnesses, although the jogger who found him recognised him as a regular visitor. Nobody noticed any suspicious activity. We've yet to check them out, but my feeling is none of them was responsible for Asif's death.

'Escape on foot would have been fairly easy thanks to the canal, which runs close to the lake. We spoke to all the boat residents and found somebody who was on deck, mending his pump, around

the time of the attack. He saw no one besides a dog walker he recognised as a regular along the towpath while he was working. He
left the deck a couple of times to fetch tools, so there is a possibility
somebody slipped by then. There's also a chance the perpetrator
headed in the opposite direction, towards the centre of town. We
checked and found there were no boats moored on that section. In
short, we have zippo, I'm afraid.'

'Plus, there are no surveillance cameras down by the canal,'
added Jamie. 'It would be possible for a person to follow the towpath to Canal Street, then flee in that direction or take off through
one of the industrial estates, without being spotted.'

'Or, they could have simply driven away,' said Morgan with
an air of resignation. 'In any event, we've got a team of officers out
canvassing nearby streets. I'm not holding my breath.'

Jamie bounced his fingertips together. 'Here's an idea, guv. Do
you think they're stalking their victims?'

It was a notion she'd considered and not given a huge amount
of credence. It would require excellent covert skills. 'I suppose it's
possible. The killer's exit strategies have been well thought through.'

Emma leant against her desk with her arms folded. 'These killings. They remind me of executions. That's what they are, aren't
they? Maybe all the victims were members of a group or held a
belief that the perpetrator disagrees with.'

Samuel nodded. 'That's logical. From what you've told me,
DI Young, I agree these are considered executions. There will be a
reason Mr Baqui was targeted today and I suggest you are dealing
with somebody who has a plan, not simply acting on impulse.'

'It's a man, right?' said Jamie.

'Er. Not necessarily.'

'But what about the bloke in the high-vis, guv? It's well weird
he's vanished into thin air. It could be him.'

'I'm still considering the possibility he's responsible.'

Samuel gave a small cough. 'Erm, can I interject again? A person leaving no trace at a crime scene, who has targeted victims in public places, is unlikely to draw attention to themselves by wearing a high-vis vest. This killer is more chameleon-like.' He folded his arms, knocking his elbow against a cupboard.

Morgan let out a long sigh. 'Then how are we going to catch our perp?'

'Through good old-fashioned police work,' said Kate. 'Which will begin first thing in the morning. Samuel, you can take Emma's desk. The rest of you can go. I'd like to see you fresh and ready for action in the morning.'

When the last footsteps had died away and Samuel was settled, she logged on to her computer. She wasn't tired. She believed what she'd told her team: methodical investigation would win out. She'd progressed as far in her career as she had by being orderly and not letting anything escape her attention, no matter how trifling it might seem. She drew up a map of the local area and on a notepad jotted down the times and locations of the murders. There had to be some sense to all of this. If not, the investigation was doomed.

CHAPTER ELEVEN

DAY FOUR – FRIDAY

Ben hugged Lisa's soft body more tightly, spooning against her back. He was spiralling again, in need of regular fixes to stop him from falling into the canyon of despair. The plan was the plan, and yet carrying it out was far harder than he could have ever imagined. Lisa had gone through it with him step by step and, even then, he had almost faltered at the last minute.

'I can't do this again,' he whispered.

'You have to, my love. You've started this. It can't stop now. We're all depending on you.'

'But not children. Lisa. Not children.'

'If fate dictates—'

'It isn't really fate that decides. It's me. I have a choice.'

Her voice was sharp. 'No. You don't have a choice. None of us has a choice.'

He released her and rolled on to his back. She'd fallen silent, annoyed at his weakness. If he pulled out now, those people who had already lost their lives would have died in vain. Lisa was right. There was no other option. He had committed to this and had to see it through. He rested his arms behind his head. There were no noises outside and the only light came from a plug-in nightlight on the landing which lit the way to the bathroom. He stared at the ceiling until a movement caught his eye and a pitiful voice made him sit up.

'Uncle Ben? Uncle Ben?'

'What's the matter, Gracie?'

'I can't sleep. Will you come and read me a story?'

'I'm not sure. It's late.'

'But I can't sleep.'

He sighed. The same thing had happened every night for the last two weeks.

'Go back to bed, sweetie. Try to sleep. I'm too tired to read any stories.'

'But I won't be able to sleep.' There was a pause. He knew what was coming next. 'And it's all your fault.'

He squeezed his eyes shut. Lisa was right. None of them had a choice.

◆ ◆ ◆

Kate's mobile woke her from a dreamless sleep. She reached for it, mumbled a greeting.

'DI Young, you should talk to your colleagues in Burnley. They found a body.'

The distinctive voice roused her in an instant. This was the man she and Bradley had been looking for. Rosa's pimp, Farai, who might lead them to her and help bring down Dickson.

'Farai?'

'Talk to them.'

'Who is it? Farai? Who's dead?'

Silence.

'Where are you? I have to speak to you.'

The phone went dead. Caller ID had been withheld and she knew Farai would have already removed and destroyed the burner phone SIM card. Her screen displayed the time – 5.15. What the heck was going on? Farai wouldn't have contacted her unless it was something to do with Rosa or Stanka. Which could only mean one thing – one of the girls was dead. Farai was giving her the heads up.

It was too early to ring Burnley station, and there was no way she would get back to sleep. Her head buzzed with the news. Damn Farai. Why couldn't he have contacted her sooner? He knew Rosa had information about Dickson and had tried to keep her out of Dickson's reach. He ought to have let Kate at least speak to the girl to find out whatever it was she knew. She'd believed Farai had wanted Dickson brought down as much as she did. In reality, however, Farai was all about self-preservation. He knew too much and was fearful that Dickson would locate him and have him killed.

She kicked off the bedcovers. She needed to talk to somebody badly. She needed Chris. She threw herself out of bed. There was no other option. It would be afternoon in Sydney. She punched out Tilly's number.

'What's up?' said Tilly, with no preamble.

'I needed to talk to somebody.'

'You all right?'

'I'm not ill, if that's what you mean. Do you remember what we were talking about when we last Skyped?'

'Yes. Hang on. I'm in the office and it's a bit crowded. Let me go outside.'

Tilly worked in a centre for abused women. Kate heard background voices, Tilly telling somebody she'd be five minutes, a child crying, then silence and, finally, Tilly.

'I thought you were going to drop the idea,' she said.

'Something's happened to make me change my mind. I think the girl I was looking for has been killed.'

'And that your bent copper has killed her?'

'Him, or somebody carrying out his orders. Yes, Tilly, I believe he has.'

'But you don't know for sure. You don't know if she's dead. You don't know if he killed her. Kate! Come on. You're living in fantasy land. I'm worried about you.'

'No, Tilly. I feel it! I know how he works. Listen, this is compli-cated. I don't expect you to understand how, but I *know* she's dead.'

There was a silence. Then, 'Where do I come in, in this?'

'I can't work out how he found her when I couldn't.'

'He had guys looking for her. If he's as corrupt as you think, he'll be able to pull as many people as he wants to track down someone.'

It triggered a thought, one so obvious it made Kate catch her breath. 'That's right. He ran a covert operation to track down underage sex-workers, except it was a front. He was only ever after one, the girl I've been looking for. The girl who could have brought him down. I bet after his operation folded, he started another, or maybe it never folded. Maybe it has been going on all this time, under a new name.'

Operation Agouti had come to light only after CIO Heather Gault's murder, when, against orders, Head of Technology Felicity Jolly had given Kate's team access to Heather's computer and they'd uncovered emails from Dickson to Heather regarding the opera-tion. Kate's heart beat faster. It was making sense. Tilly was helping. Kate felt reassured by being able to bounce ideas off her.

'One of the officers who worked on the operation was mur-dered too – the one who found the girl and spoke to her.'

175

Tilly sounded wary again. 'Kate, I think you might be out of your depth. Too many people have got killed. If I were you, I'd back away.'

Her concern broke the spell. Kate needed encouragement, not hindrance.

'If he's been using his resources to find the girl, he'll use them to stop you too.'

'I've kept under his radar, played everything close to my chest. If anything, he'll have suspected I was trying to find out more about Chris's death. Now he's eliminated almost everyone who could spill the beans, he'll be more confident. He won't suspect me.'

'Why don't you wait until you get promoted? You'll have more power then,' said Tilly.

Promotion! The word set off another chain of confused thoughts. Had putting herself forward for promotion made Dickson extra wary? It demonstrated she had regained confidence in her abilities. He wouldn't like that. So far, she hadn't fallen foul of him because, primarily, she hadn't challenged him and, secondly, he didn't think Kate capable of uncovering all his dirty secrets. So far, she hadn't represented a threat. Now, however, he would be watching her even more carefully. By encouraging her to go for promotion, William had allowed her to walk into a trap. She would have to be even cleverer if she was to survive.

Tilly was talking. 'Now the girl is dead, I guess you're stumped for evidence against him. You'll have to drop it, Kate.'

Tilly couldn't understand the situation. Not like Chris would have. Nor could she offer any solutions. She had, however, allowed Kate to gain focus.

'No, you are absolutely right, Tilly. Thank you again.'

'You will drop it this time, won't you?'

'Yes.'

'Kate, you worry me.'

'I don't mean to.'

'Then stop whatever this is, concentrate on your career and take a holiday.'

'I'll do that.'

'I'm here whenever you need me.'

'Same here. Whenever.'

The call had made some things clearer. She had to really watch her back now. She left the phone on the bed and went in search of her running kit. Chris might be able to better advise her what to do.

◆ ◆ ◆

At the reservoir a gentle mist fell against her skin, spritzing it and coating her hair in a fine spray that clung to the ends. Combined with the morning air, it was refreshing and invigorating, lending impetus to her movements as she jogged the familiar route over a field towards the woodlands. She spoke to Chris. 'It's either Rosa or Stanka that they've found dead. I have to wait for confirmation of identity, but what should I do once that happens?'

She rounded a gnarled trunk carbuncled with time, its roots and lower trunk mossy and its branches misshapen and twisted, some mere stumps, broken off in hard-fought attacks from the weather to emerge battle-scarred but victorious.

'Chris, I need you more now than ever. You can't desert me, not while this is going on. I know I should have made sure Tom Champion was in a more secure safe house or forced him to make a full confession of his own free will sooner. I should have found Rosa before Dickson. And I didn't do any of those things because I didn't want Dickson to suspect me. I thought I had more time. I ought to have hired a PI to find Rosa, or asked Bradley and his ex-SAS contacts to track her down sooner, or find Farai again, but I didn't, alright?'

'No.'

She came to a sudden halt under a tree, strained for further acknowledgement, hearing only mournful cooing from distant wood pigeons. The low, sad sounds seemed to speak to her, sympathise with her plight, and compounded the enlightenment. *No.* It wasn't because she hadn't acted swiftly enough, rather *how* she had acted that was keeping Chris silent.

She took off again. 'Chris, I had no option. How else would I have got Tom Champion to confess? How would I have found out Farai was in Lancashire? I can't do this by the book! Dickson has eyes and ears everywhere. I can't move without him knowing about it. I have Jamie watching me in the office and the house was broken into, months ago. That was down to Dickson. He wanted to know if I had anything on him. I've had to behave as if I suspect nothing or, even if I do, I'm unwilling to follow it up. It goes against everything I stand for. I want to catch him out and, if that means crossing a few lines, then I don't see what other option I have.'

She ran on, trees and pathway now one continuous blur.

'Listen, as soon as I get something, anything, I'll use it this time. I won't squirrel it away to build a case. If we find Tom or Farai, I'll persuade them to talk. I won't let this slip away from me. You'll speak to me then, won't you? Once Dickson is facing charges? You'll forgive me and . . . Chris! Please speak to me. I can't handle your silence and anger, on top of this and the investigation. I can't juggle all these balls at the same time. I'm watching my back every hour and . . . I can't . . . cope!' She drew to a halt, face to the sky, and as the rain caressed her, it mingled with tears.

Emma was kicking seven bells out of a punchbag, pursuing a sequence of roundhouse kicks, front and side kicks, until her dark hair was flat to her head and her pale, pixie-like face pink through exertion. There were the usual early birds at Greg's gym, keen martial-arts followers, mostly men, who grunted and yelled as they followed their own personal routine. The outcry, or Kihap, emitted while executing a manoeuvre helped with breathing and power, a sharp, quick yell from the diaphragm. It also helped with technique and to intimidate an opponent. The Kihaps echoed around her, spurring her on.

This was where Emma felt most at home, among others who shared her passion and who treated her like an equal.

The case was frustrating and, unless the profiler could conjure up a magical formula for them to identify the killer, they all knew they were stuffed. Kate wasn't herself. Although she was going through the motions, Emma could see her boss was distracted. There'd not only been the episode with the photograph, when she'd snapped at Emma, but also the way she kept checking her phone, as if expecting a call or a message. Something odd was going on.

When Kate had first come back to work, after a leave of absence, she'd acted very strangely, thanks to a cocktail of medication and grief. But this was different. It was like she was keeping something from the team and, surprisingly, that hurt. Emma thought a great deal of Kate. Morgan had often joked she fangirled her, but it wasn't that. It was more. Kate was not only the police officer Emma wanted to become but the closest to a female role model she had. She hated to use the word, yet Kate was a better, stronger-willed, more resilient and independent *mother figure* than her own mother had been.

She balanced on one foot and aimed a perfect front kick at the bag. It was one of the hardest kicks to master and one of the deadliest, and Emma had perfected the art of delivery. Although she'd been invited to perform at competition level, Emma had never taken up the opportunity. She trained for personal reasons, not to defend herself should she find herself in a sticky situation but to dispel the rage that flared inside her from time to time. It was worse the closer she got to the anniversary of her mother's death. She hated this time of the year. It brought back memories she usually suppressed.

'Hya!' The yell came from deep within her to obliterate the past but, even as she threw herself into the kick, the memory surfaced, as always: her mother's naked body, handcuffed to the bed, a plastic bag over her head, and her stepfather on his knees in tears. She squeezed her eyes tightly shut, willed it away and, when it had gone, opened them again. She tucked her hair behind her ears and, with another yell, kicked the bag with another well-aimed kick, knowing she would never be able to fully erase that sight, no matter how hard she tried.

◆ ◆ ◆

Kate finished her tea and washed the mug up in warm, soapy water, letting the suds slide and fall into the sink before placing it in the rack. She pulled the plug, watched the swirling water attempt to suck down the soapy residue. *Drowning*. She reached for the tea towel and wiped it around the mug, the smiley-faced sheep on the cloth disappearing and reappearing time after time until she deemed the mug dry enough to return to the cupboard and folded the towel into three, smoothing it flat before hanging it over the oven-door handle, then adjusting it until the sheep smiled out at her in regular formation. Then, picking up her mobile and keys, she headed out to work, the only sound the steady tick of the kitchen clock.

She climbed into her car, parked as always on the drive, in front of the wide garage that they'd only ever used for storage. She glanced at the perfect white house with its neat frontage and post and chain fence. On the surface, it was the perfect idyll for a young couple, a chocolate-box cottage among equally enchanting houses on Cherry Lane, named after the three trees that grew on a grassy triangle at the bottom of her road. And it had been their forever home, one they hadn't had time to enjoy together. Now she was the sole custodian and the joy it had once brought had vanished along with her husband. She pulled away, numb.

The drive up the motorway afforded her time to collect her thoughts for the day. She'd stayed with Samuel until almost midnight, when he'd declared he needed to turn in to allow his brain to assimilate what he'd read. While Samuel had been trying to get into the killer's head, she'd been doing some deducing of her own and had a theory she needed to run past the team. First, she had to learn if a body had been discovered in Burnley without Dickson finding out. She'd devised a plan, taking into account that, if Jamie was in league with Dickson, he too might be aware of the body that had recently been uncovered there.

The solid, red-brick building was her second home, as it had been her father's before her. It had evaded modernisation to become an annex to the purpose-built headquarters next door. Kate was glad it had escaped. She'd worked here for four years and, as she shouldered the faded blue door that welcomed her with its usual groan, she became enveloped in familiarity. Her boots squeaked across the tiled entrance and, as always, she greeted the desk sergeant seated behind the waist-high desk in the drab waiting room. She couldn't count the number of times she'd performed this same routine. Every notice and photograph, the six chairs lined against the wall, reminiscent of those outside her old headmaster's office, and the smell unique to this building that she'd once described to Chris as 'warmed experience', were part of her soul. The door behind the desk opened into the corridor leading to a narrow wooden staircase and, with each creak of the stairs, she became more determined to pull this off. She would investigate the situation right under Dickson's nose.

She stopped at the first landing, straightened her shoulders and made for the office with all the confidence she could muster. The team was already in place. Emma, propped against the wall, smiled a greeting.

'Morning, everyone.'

'Morning, guv.' As usual, Jamie's voice was the loudest. Kate had initially thought it was down to enthusiasm, now she was sure it was a show. He was always the first to volunteer for tasks, often turned up early to work and rarely left on time. Today, Kate couldn't look at his smiling face without thinking he was faking everything, all the while watching her.

She put on her own game face. She had work to do even though she really wanted to find out whose body had been uncovered in Burnley. She placed her mobile on the desk, checking first there were no messages from Bradley. She caught Emma watching her. She glanced around. Jamie was moving his chair. Morgan, cup in hand, was reading something on his screen. Why was she so edgy? There was nothing abnormal about this scene. Her every movement wasn't being scrutinised. Emma often made eye contact. Jamie was invariably loud.

Kate placed her bag on her desk and extracted the photocopies she'd made the night before. 'Samuel should get back to us sometime this morning. In the meantime, I want us to see if there have been any similar attacks in other regions. The pathology reports we've had so far reveal there were no hesitation marks, that is to say, no smudged soot deposits, no smears where the killer might have nervously placed the pistol against their victim's head, or where the victim moved. This suggests speed and accuracy. That takes either an extremely callous and assured individual, or somebody with experience. Samuel and I discussed this last night. He agrees there's a strong possibility Tobias was not the killer's first victim. I want you to ring around regional serious-crime squads and see if there have been any similar cases, recently or historically.'

She had laid down the first part of her plan. She rubbed a hand over her drying lips. She had to keep up the pretence. She was going to be the one who rang Burnley. It was the only way she would be able to establish whether Rosa was the dead girl, without Jamie getting wind of her plan. She was going to use his enthusiasm, fake or otherwise, to make him part of it. *Keep your friends close and your enemies closer.*

'I also want to consider something else. I've been looking at the locations and times that the three murders took place and I believe I've uncovered a pattern of sorts.'

She stuck the photocopied map on the board, under the photographs. Asif Baqui's had been added, his dark hair shining and his white teeth on display. The map contained three red circles. She pointed at the first. 'Blythe Bridge station, where we believe the victim was killed between quarter to six and twenty to seven. Next, Trentham Gardens, where the victim was also killed around six o'clock, and, finally, Westport Lake. Another killing around the same time. Each attack took place in a public space where there were other comings and goings. In spite of the possibility of being spotted, the perpetrator chose these locations, and all the murders took place between quarter to six and quarter to seven.' She wrote down the times on the board.

Emma was first to realise what Kate was getting at. 'You think the timings are relevant?'

'I do. It's only a hunch, but I wonder if the killer chooses a specific time to arrive at the location they've chosen and waits there until a suitable victim appears. By suitable, I mean the situation is right – the victim is alone and there are no witnesses.'

'That's certainly food for thought,' Morgan said.

'It seems to fit with what little we know about the killer – their methodical planning. It seems the location and escape strategies are well planned, so it would follow the killer is going to ensure they'll only pick off targets when they are certain they won't be seen.'

Emma nodded. 'I get where you're coming from.'

'See, guv, you don't need any profiler. You can do the job yourself.'

Coming from Jamie, the praise sounded hollow. The idea that he was the office spy governed how she felt about him. That he might be an innocent patsy didn't sit right with her. He was a joker at times, generally upbeat and, on the surface, a grafter, yet the fact that he'd lied about being at the station the day Heather and Rosa met there was a major negative for Kate. She couldn't accept he was anything other than Dickson's ears and eyes. 'I'd prefer to have somebody trained in psychology looking into that side of things. I'm only looking at it logically. I could be way off. There's another detail which might or might not be relevant. The Trentham Estate is about twelve kilometres from Blythe Bridge station via the main road and Westport Lake is roughly twelve kilometres from the Trentham Estate. It could mean the next place the killer will strike is approximately twelve kilometres away from the lake.'

She stuck a map with its encircled locations on the board.

'I realise this assumption is highly speculative and I'm reluctant to waste valuable resources on testing my theory out. However, we have a killer on the loose and I, for one, don't want any more photographs going up on this board.'

It was time to carry out her plan. She kept her voice level and her face neutral. 'Jamie, I'd like you to start by checking in with regional units and see if they've come across any similar instances of attacks with captive bolt pistols. I'll give you a hand with that. Morgan, please list all the potential visitor attractions you can find that are approximately twelve kilometres away from Westport Lake, and Emma, can you continue looking into Asif's background, and the possibility that the three victims were members of the same groups or organisations, as you suggested last night? See if we've missed anything else that might connect these victims.'

'Sure.'

'How do you want to divide up the regions? North and south?' asked Jamie.

She was prepared for his question. She pulled out lists containing contact details of the regional squads and pretended to divide them equally, handing half to him, all the while keeping the one containing details about Burnley for herself. He took them with the usual gusto he exhibited when set a task. She picked up her bag again. 'Give me a shout when Samuel arrives. I'll be in the briefing room. It's impossible to be heard when we're all on the phone.'

Outside the room, she exhaled slowly. She'd got away with it and now all she had to do was ring Burnley police station and ascertain what they'd uncovered. Two birds with one stone. Chris would have been impressed by her subterfuge.

She couldn't get through to start with, so tried various other stations under Lancashire Constabulary, before she finally got hold of an active number for the station. Cutbacks and closures had meant the station was often not manned. Half an hour passed before she finally got hold of somebody. She introduced herself and asked to be put through to a senior officer. She sat in silence, fingers drumming against the top while the phone remained silent. Then, finally, when she was beginning to wonder if her call had been forgotten, there was a scraping as the receiver was picked up and a voice. 'Hello.'

'Hello. Yes, I'm DI Kate Young from Staffordshire—'

The knock at the door gave her a start. The door opened and Jamie's face appeared. She held up a hand to make him wait and spoke into her phone. 'Could you bear with me a minute.'

'Sorry. I'm having trouble getting hold of information out of Newcastle. Can you try? They said they'd rather talk to somebody senior.' His eyebrows knitted together, face a picture of innocence.

'Sure. I'll speak to them.'

'Thanks. Sorry for the interruption.' He backed away and the door shut. She didn't restart the conversation in case he was listening at the door. She couldn't risk it. She got to her feet, made for the door, calculated how long it would take him to walk down the corridor and disappear, then opened the door. Had he been there, she would have asked if he had the details for Newcastle. As it was, she let out her breath. There was no sign of him. Putting the phone to her ear, she spoke.

'Sorry, are you still there?'

The person had hung up.

She redialled, explained she had been cut off and waited again for somebody to speak to her.

'DI Jackson.' The voice was querulous.

'Hi. This is DI Kate Young again. I'm sorry our conversation got interrupted. You know what it's like. You're never off duty and don't get five minutes to yourself,' she said, hoping to appeal to the fellow officer. She relayed the registration number required to get information via the phone from other police forces.

'How can I help you, DI Young?'

She kept her response deliberately vague. 'I'm heading an investigation into some recent murders and we're trying to establish if they're connected to any in other counties. Have you dealt with any murders or unusual deaths in the last couple of weeks?'

'No murders.'

'What about unusual deaths?'

'No.'

She closed her eyes. Shit! How could she get him to tell her about the dead girl?

'So, there have been no suspicious deaths in the last few days?'

'Not suspicious.'

The tone of his voice was enough. Her eyes flew open. It was an in.

'But you thought it might be?'

'At the time. The pathology report suggested it was an overdose.'

'Oh crap. We have our fair share of that here too. What was it? Heroin?'

'No. It was ketamine. Poor kid couldn't have had a clue what she was using. She injected it into her veins.'

She. He'd admitted it was a girl.

'That's a bad mistake for a junkie to make.'

'There weren't any other needle marks so we're guessing it was her first time.'

The sigh he gave suggested empathy with the victim.

'You got kids?' she asked.

'Yes, two teenagers about the same age as the victim. And I haven't any clue what they get up to when I'm out at work. It's a wonder I sleep some nights.'

'I'm sure they're sensible, what with their dad on the force and all that.'

He let out a small snort. 'Like they'd listen to their old man!'

'What about the girl? How did her parents take the news?'

'Don't know. She was a Jane Doe up until we got an anonymous phone call yesterday, telling us her name was Rosa. No surname. So now she's a Rosa Doe.'

Rosa. *Damn!* It was Rosa. Kate's heart sank. Up until then, she had been holding out hope it had been Rosa's friend, Stanka. That bastard Dickson had finally caught up with the girl and silenced her. He'd tied up all his loose ends. Kate would never be able to bring him down now. She wanted to get off the phone and howl in despair. But then it struck her: DI Jackson had mentioned ketamine. A thought began to bubble up in her mind.

'Not the easiest case to solve,' she said, her mind elsewhere.

'All in a day's work. What are you dealing with?'

'Shootings.'

'Gang-related?'

'We don't think so. The attacks are with a stun gun. Victims are shot in the forehead. Have you had any historic cases that sound similar?'

'That's unusual. I've not come across anything like that before. At least, not during the twenty years I've been here.'

'Listen, thanks for your time. Let me know if you unearth anything that might be useful and good luck finding Rosa's parents.'

'Thanks. Good luck too.'

She stared at the blank screen. Ketamine. A few months earlier, Ervin had divulged that Heather Gault had secretly asked him to identify a substance linked to Operation Agouti, which turned out to be ketamine. A popular date-rape drug because of its speedy paralysis effect, it was usually taken orally, or through snorting 'bumps'. Some users injected it intramuscularly but rarely intravenously. Because it was so fast-acting, there was every chance it would render the user unconscious before they'd even removed the needle. Therefore, it was highly unlikely Rosa would have injected herself with ketamine. This had been no accidental overdose. It was murder.

Farai must have made the anonymous call to the station to tell them her name. Or it had come from one of Rosa's friends. Stanka, maybe? However, Kate now had a clearer picture of what had transpired. Dickson had set up Operation Agouti to flush out Rosa with the intention of killing her, by using ketamine. When Heather had stumbled across the substance and tested it, she could not have guessed it was going to be used for murder. Kate thought she now understood why Dickson had removed Heather from the operation. And, as for the CIO's death . . .

She rested her head in her hands. She'd fucked up. It didn't matter that the pieces slotted into place. She could prove none of it. Stanka and Farai would have bolted again, and Kate would struggle to locate either of them, even with Bradley on side. She massaged her forehead, yet no amount of rubbing could ease the mental strain. She sat back, limbs suddenly weary. This was over. She couldn't keep chasing around hunting for those people who might know something about Dickson that could bring him down. She was one woman. He had heaven knows how many at his beck and call.

She shuffled the A4 printouts into a tidy pile. Work was the only anchor left in her life. She abandoned all thoughts of Rosa and dialled a number from the list in front of her. Policework involved time-consuming tasks like this that sometimes yielded results and often didn't. Yet this was what made her a good police officer. Kate held the phone to her ear again. This time she really did want to know if there had been any historic cases of somebody using a captive bolt pistol.

There was another knock at the door. Expecting Jamie again, she barked a loud, 'Yes. Come in!'

It was Morgan who appeared.

'I've just got off the phone to a DS at Hanley.' One look at his face told her what was coming next. 'Their investigation sounds like it's linked to ours. A young woman, a snowboarding instructor, was shot dead with a captive pistol.'

'When?'

'The day before our first victim. Monday evening. Around six o'clock. Sounds like our perpetrator is on a killing spree.'

CHAPTER TWELVE

Kate stood in front of Dickson's desk, almost shoulder to shoulder with William. Dickson gave a nod.

'There are certainly grounds for believing that the death of this snowboarding instructor, Harriet Parkinson, is connected to your investigation. I'll ensure the case is transferred from Hanley.'

'This should have reached us before now. Had we not heard a rumour—'

Dickson fixed her with a gimlet eye. 'Mistakes happen, Kate. When a case is assigned to one station, it does not necessarily follow there will be a transfer of information.'

'We are supposed to be a special-crimes unit. We should have been sent in as soon as it was established it was murder.'

'As I said, mistakes happen.' His voice dripped ice. 'What's more important is how we handle this information. I'm inclined to hand it over to a larger team.'

Her heart sank. A result in this investigation might secure a promotion. Moreover, there was her unit's morale to consider. They wanted this as much as she did. She didn't need to debate the issue.

William, who had insisted on joining her for this meeting, spoke. 'I'd like to point out that our other teams and departments are already stretched to the limit. To take them off an operation and have them start at the beginning when we have a ticking-bomb situation wouldn't be wise. We suspect the perpetrator is hell-bent on killing a person every day.'

'All the more reason to bring in more officers and hunt them down.'

William stood firm. 'I disagree. If necessary, I'll take my recommendation to the chief constable because I firmly believe we have the best-placed team on the case. It wouldn't take much to spook the perpetrator, who could not only go into hiding but leave the area to continue their killing spree elsewhere. We don't want this to spill out into other regions, involve a huge multi-regional task force, scare the public and draw bad publicity to ourselves. The way we are handling it, almost covertly, is going to work. I have the utmost confidence in Kate. You can't deny she's caught some slippery, devious criminals over the last few months. In record time, I should add. Her results speak for themselves. Let her prove she is worthy of becoming a DCI.'

Kate couldn't believe her ears. William was sticking up for her, his voice unwavering. He matched Dickson's stern look.

Dickson was the first to break eye contact. 'I'll give you a window to prove yourself. After that, I hand it over.'

'Thank you, sir.'

'It's not me you should thank,' he replied. 'You are dismissed. DCI Chase and I still have matters to discuss.'

She left the office with mixed feelings. That William had stuck his neck out for her buoyed her up. However, now everything was on the line there was no option other than to succeed. And on top of that, Dickson had pissed her off big time. He must have been feeling supremely confident now Rosa was dead. That only left Farai and Stanka. Even though Kate didn't know if they would be able to help her in her quest, she was going to find them. To that end, she rang Bradley not only to update him but to ask him to hunt down the pair.

◆ ◆ ◆

By mid-morning Kate's mouth was dry through talking. As she crossed the last station off her list, Jamie showed up.

'Nothing, guv. Any other cases, outside of Stoke, involving a stun gun or captive bolt pistol have been resolved and the assailants sentenced. I made a list of those in case you wanted to cross-ref them with victims.'

'Thanks.' Like him, she'd discovered there had been incidents involving stun guns but only one fatality, a husband who'd shot his wife. The only one left to examine was that of Harriet Parkinson, a snowboarding instructor, killed outside the ski school in Stoke where she worked. Until they received the documentation, they still had only scant details about her death.

'And *Sam-u-hell* is here, waiting for a briefing.' He gave a chuckle. 'Sorry. I can't help myself. Sophie says I'm a right clown at times. I've always been the same. Too late to change, eh?'

It was rare for Jamie to be so forthcoming and, playing along, she gave him a smile. 'Never too late. If you want to change.'

'Well, maybe, what with another kid on the way. I might make more of an effort, you know, look to the future and all that.'

She stored this information. Jamie could be considering his own career advancement, which in turn might mean working with her, rather than against her. He had a lot to prove before that ever happened.

Samuel, in a turtleneck cable-stitched jumper and jeans, looked refreshed. He smelt good too, of woods and spices, ginger and something else, reminiscent of a cosy, firelit night.

'Morning, Samuel. Shall I hand the floor straight over to you?'

'Yes. Erm. Right. I correlated all the information available to me, along with what DI Young and I discussed last night. I've come up with the following.' He gave a nervous cough into his fist.

'The person you're looking for is intelligent and efficient. They've demonstrated the capability to avoid surveillance cameras, handle a firearm and shoot to kill without any qualms. This suggests they are trained in weaponry as well as in evading-capture techniques. They might have seen action in war zones. That suggests they are ex-armed forces, ex-police or are currently employed in those professions.' He looked up briefly. When no comment or question was forthcoming, he continued, 'It's difficult to pin an age on this individual. Given there is little to indicate any of the victims attempted to flee or put up a struggle, the perpetrator either has a commanding physical presence or quick reflexes, enabling them to surprise their victims. Which in turn suggests you are looking for somebody younger. I say suggests, because there are many older people who are equally capable of demonstrating speed and strength.'

Kate immediately thought of Bradley Chapman. Maybe the killer was also ex-SAS or, like him, trained in martial arts.

'There is one factor which is important – the timing of the killings. The killer strikes at around the same time. So far, the killings have all taken place between quarter to six and quarter to seven in the evening. It would make more sense for the perpetrator to target his victims under complete cover of darkness, rather than when it is dusk going into night. This leads me to conclude that this time slot is significant for our killer. Whether that's the only time the perpetrator is free to kill, or it holds a relevance for them, I can't say. If we combine the fact that they strike during this period of time and apparently choose random victims, it leads me to question if the killer might not have also been a victim of a random attack, one that has left them traumatised.'

Kate knew all about trauma. A thought sprung to mind. They might have something on file to help them. 'Sorry to interrupt. Jamie, when we're done here, would you drag up local, historic investigations? See if there are any that might relate to what Samuel is telling us.'

'What sort of cases?'

Samuel raised a hand and cleared his throat. 'A fire, accident, an attack, something grave. Something serious. If I'm right, it would have been something major to cause this sort of PTSD.'

'Oh, okay.'

'I'm sorry I can't be more specific.' He looked up again. 'Any questions?'

'I've got one,' said Jamie. 'Earlier, the guv suggested the killer might have a starting point. That from a certain time, presumably at or close to quarter to six, they begin their vigil, waiting for the right victim to come along. What do you think about her suggestion?'

'I say it's a good hypothesis. One that also suggests the perpetrator might strike later in the evening than they hitherto have.' Samuel gave Kate a nod of recognition.

'You didn't mention it, though, did you?' Jamie's face was a mask.

'I admit I hadn't considered it,' Samuel replied.

Kate was about to deflect the conversation when Emma spoke. 'Can you give us an idea of where the perpetrator might live?'

Samuel's face relaxed again. 'Ah, yes. I have given *that* consideration. Based on the locations of the attacks and the killer's excellent local knowledge, they must live or have lived in this area. Many – dare I use the term? – serial killers operate locally. They often require familiarity. Your perpetrator is striking in this area for a reason. I can't be sure what that might be. Obviously, that's for you to determine. I, er, just create a bit of a picture for you.'

Emma beamed at him, causing his neck to flush.

Jamie was at it again. 'When you say they're striking for a reason, that isn't really saying anything, is it? Obviously, they're attacking people here for a reason or they'd be doing it elsewhere. Can you be more specific?'

'This area might be where they experienced a traumatic event or lost somebody close to them. It might be where they were fired from a job, or where they grew up and they want to be on home turf to carry out their acts of violence. It could be for any number of reasons. What is evident is that Stoke-on-Trent is significant. Is that clearer?'

'As mud. Have you considered the possibility that this individual is angry about something in their childhood and something in their victims triggers that rage?'

'Jamie, I've considered a whole range of scenarios and I don't have all the answers. I can only paint a picture for you of who I think is behind the attacks. Like you, I have a limited amount of information to hand and, if you give me more, I'll be able to tell you more.'

'Sure, Samuel.' He laboured over the name. 'I understand.'

Kate gave Jamie a sharp look. He was bordering on being obnoxious. Giving Samuel a silly nickname was one thing, being rude was another. What was his problem? Had Dickson asked him to play up and make the investigation stutter along? Although she agreed it wasn't a huge amount to go on or as helpful as she'd hoped, what Samuel had said had given her an idea of who she was up against. A member or ex-member of the armed forces or the police would make a formidable opponent. Her task had just become more onerous. A trained individual could evade capture for weeks, months, even longer. And what of the victims? Four seemingly unrelated individuals. There had to be a reason the killer had chosen them. Could the killer be sending a message that wasn't about the individuals themselves?

She gave Samuel what scant details they had about Harriet, the snowboarding instructor, who had been shot on Monday evening.

'We can't work out what is attracting the killer to their victims. They don't share any physical features, beliefs or interests, they are not members of the same groups, or even religions. They don't even fall into the same age category. Why might that be?' she asked.

Samuel rested calm, grey eyes on her. 'I was afraid you'd ask me that. I don't have an answer on this.' He tore his gaze away, found Emma and smiled at her. 'I wish I could tell you more.'

'Me too,' grumbled Jamie.

Kate told Samuel about her latest hypothesis, regarding the distance between each location. 'I was toying with the idea that the perpetrator is choosing locations that are around twelve to thirteen kilometres of each other. I wasn't sure until we heard about Harriet. She was killed at a ski school that is 12.87 kilometres away from Blythe Bridge station. There is a pattern of sorts there.'

Samuel nodded. 'It would confirm that the killer has a clinical mind. Choosing locations within a certain distance of each other might appeal to this individual's sense of logic. Or those specific locations may simply hold some sort of significance.'

Jamie sighed. 'That's like saying something might be square or round.'

'Not really,' said Samuel.

'Can we get back to the important stuff, please?' Kate looked at Jamie as she spoke. He grunted. 'How have you been getting on determining potential locations, Morgan?' Kate asked.

'Surprisingly, there are loads of places that distance from where the killer last struck at the Trentham Estate,' said Morgan. He reeled off a list. 'Whitfield Nature Reserve, Bathpool Park, in fact several smaller parks. Alsager Golf Club, Wetley Moor Common and Biddulph Grange Country Park, for starters.'

Kate glanced at her watch. 'Well, if the killer struck on Monday, Tuesday, Wednesday and Thursday, there's a chance they'll strike again this evening. I'll try to arrange for extra manpower to be sent out to at least some of those locations you mentioned and request another public appeal in case there were other witnesses who spotted something unusual yesterday at the lake. Morgan, speak to the DS at Hanley again. See if you can drag any more information about Harriet out of him before the official details are sent over. Samuel, thank you.'

'Would it be okay if I stayed for a while? I might be able to come up with something else as the case progresses.'

'Alright. Morgan, could you print me off a list of the places you've identified?'

'Sure.' He typed swiftly until a clicking and whirring began in the corner of the room as the printer sprang into action.

Kate collected the printout from the printer and raced off. Time was racing by and, if they hadn't got this right, somebody else could well die later today.

She rapped on William's door and, without waiting for a response, walked inside. She stopped in her tracks. Dickson, in full police regalia, was sitting in the visitor's chair. There was no sign of William.

'I was hoping to speak to DCI Chase, sir. It is urgent.'

Dickson levelled a cool regard in her direction. 'He'll be back shortly. What is it?'

She had no choice other than to lay out her request. 'We might have identified locations where the killer will strike next, and I require extra officers to police them.'

'I see. And how certain are you about this?'

'I have good reason to assume the perpetrator might head to one of these locations this evening and I believe it's better to be proactive and try to prevent another murder if we can.'

'You understand the cost implications of such an exercise, don't you?'

'I do, sir, and I've taken them into consideration.'

'How many locations do you intend patrolling?'

She stepped forward and handed him the list. He took it without looking at it. The paper dangled limply in his hand while he continued staring at her. 'Talk me through your reasoning behind this.'

She explained her theory, adding Samuel's thoughts to her own.

Dickson cocked his head to one side. 'This profiler. What do you know about him?'

'He has a first in Psychology from King's College, London, and an MSc in Criminology with Forensic Psychology from Middlesex. He's been working with young offenders for the last two years and comes highly recommended.'

He lifted the list, appeared to give it attention and, for a nanosecond, she thought he might agree to her request. Then a cruel look she'd seen before manifested on his features and his voice took on a patronising air. 'You must agree that your hypothesis is, at best, woolly. It's based on supposition rather than concrete facts. I can't action the release of officers who are currently on other investigations, or bring in extra manpower on the back of it.' The paper fell on to the desk like a leaf tumbling on a breeze.

He shrugged casually; a deliberate attempt to goad her.

'If somebody is murdered at one of these locations this evening, we'll have failed in our civic duty to protect citizens,' she said. She quelled the desire to raise her voice. She would not bend to his will.

'And if I agree to your request and nobody is attacked, we'll not only have wasted valuable resources but will have to answer to the higher authorities. I'd find it difficult to justify such a request based on a hunch. Consider the fallout if somebody is murdered at another location altogether. One your team hasn't identified. It wouldn't look good on your record. You wouldn't want to blemish that at this stage, would you?'

His eyes burrowed into hers as he spoke. He knew about the promotion. That was why he was refusing her request. He wanted to make the investigation as difficult as possible for her. The bastard. He'd messed up her father's chances of promotion, now it was her turn. She wouldn't let him beat her.

'No, sir.'

He picked up the sheet of paper by the corner as if it were contaminated and held it out to her; when she took it, he hung on to it for a fraction of time. 'I'm glad you understand. I don't like this any more than you do, but we're both governed and restricted by finances.' The sheet was released.

She maintained her composure. 'I have another, less costly request. In the absence of any CCTV footage, I'd like to put out an immediate public appeal for witnesses to last night's attack at Westport Lake.'

He rested his fingertips against his lips, then nodded. 'Agreed.'

'Thank you.'

William burst into the office with a surprised, 'Oh, Kate! What can I do for you?'

Kate couldn't determine if his reaction was real. Only a short while ago, William had stood up for her, then Dickson had kept him back after the meeting and now he was in William's office. Something was going on. Had he taken William to task, or had it all been a set-up, an act to disarm her, make her believe William was on her side so she'd let down her guard, maybe even confide in him? Once again, she was thrown into confusion.

'It's all sorted,' said Dickson smoothly. 'Isn't it, DI Young?'

She thrust out her jaw. The man had got under her skin again. Regardless of what was going on between these two, if she hadn't been so slow to react, Rosa might also be alive, and Dickson wouldn't be sitting there with a supercilious smile on his face. 'Yes, sir.'

'Keep up the good work. Don't let these hurdles set you back.' His words sounded as false as his smile; nevertheless, she thanked him and left, the paper held tightly in her fist.

◆ ◆ ◆

Emma couldn't help but smile back at Samuel. He had what could only be described as a kind face and there was something appealing about his clumsy, puppy-dog ways. She hadn't felt any strong attraction to anyone in a long time. Morgan was the closest she'd come to caring about a man. They'd known each other for many years, yet never tested any romantic waters. It wasn't that she didn't find him attractive, because what wasn't to like about the beefcake? Besides, he made her laugh, and he always had her back. That was the issue, they were too close. Any physical relationship would ruin what they shared. She'd hate for them to end up bitter or disliking each other if things went wrong. Samuel was refreshing. She'd dated other officers and guys from the gym, never a profiler.

Samuel looked up again, passed over a note. Assuming it was to do with the investigation, she took it, unfolded it. Her cheeks warmed without warning. He'd written down his phone number and a message: *Fancy a drink later?* She folded it back up, put it in her pocket and nodded in his direction.

It wouldn't hurt to go for a drink after work instead of heading to the gym as she usually did. It'd do her good, take her mind off things, especially with the anniversary of the death of her mother coming up. Things were looking up after all.

◆ ◆ ◆

Kate sat in the Audi, hands gripping the steering wheel. Instead of returning to the office, she'd left the building to make the brief trip to the university campus. She wasn't sure what she hoped to achieve by talking to Ervin. Once again, Dickson had needled her. Even though his refusal to consider her request to police locations where the killer might next strike was reasonable, the look he had given her had riled her. To her mind, he'd enjoyed refusing her assistance. Moreover, the phoney, morale-boosting advice he'd dispensed after William had turned up made her blood boil. She saw right through the fake sincerity. The man was a snake. Her unfulfilled promise to Chris twisted and turned inside her mind, blocking out the rational part of her brain that screamed she should be focusing on the investigation, until she had to get away from the office.

To that end, she'd taken off. She'd been toying with discussing Heather Gault with Ervin again. Now was that time. She watched as a small group of students tumbled from one of the many buildings here. There was an ease to their languid movements that provoked a sense of envy and a yearning for more innocent times. They weren't yet jaded by life's disappointments or sorrows.

She threw open the car door, still unsure of how best to broach the subject of Heather with Ervin. What more could he tell her that he hadn't already? She ought to be with her team, hunting for the killer. On the other hand, if Ervin could at least lend support to her cause against Dickson, she might find a way of getting Chris's voice back. With Chris in her life, she would be able to cope. Her mind would clear. She'd get back on top of the investigation. Decision made, she strode towards a white, rectangular building whose facade appeared to be constructed of a series of elongated blocks, with one strip of windows midway and a glass entrance reached by wide steps. She bounded up them into a brightly lit room, sterile and as silent as a library, her boots squeaking over the polished surface towards the security guard, who, after checking her pass, buzzed her through into the restricted area, used only by members of staff.

She paced along the corridor and stopped in front of the intercom.

'Yes?'

'DI Young. Here to see Ervin.'

The door opened with a soft click and Kate acknowledged the staff working at their desks. It had been a while since she'd visited the premises. As always, she was impressed by the abundance of light and the pristine cleanliness of the work surfaces.

'He's in the office,' said one of them. 'Just knock.'

'Thanks.'

She tapped on his door and waited for a soft 'Enter!'

Ervin pushed aside a thick document and sat back in his chair, smoothed a yellow cravat adorned with blue polka dots into position under a sky-blue waistcoat and commented, 'This is a pleasant surprise, unless you've come to ask how we're getting on with the investigation, because we have zip for you.' He curled elegant fingers into the shape of a zero. 'That said, the eternal optimist in me won't abandon hope yet.'

'Actually, I came for a chat.'

'How terribly cordial of you.' He flashed her a genuine smile and proffered a seat. 'Take a pew and then tell me what's on your mind, because you, my dear Kate, are not the sort of person to drop by for *a chat*.'

She gave a soft chuckle at his words. 'I didn't realise I was so transparent.'

'Not at all. It's more that I'm incredibly astute.' He brushed an invisible thread from the waistcoat with a flourish and replaced his hands on his lap. 'Go ahead. I'm all ears.'

'It's regarding a conversation we had a few months ago about Heather Gault.'

His nostrils twitched. 'Uh-huh.'

'Something about her death didn't quite add up at the time and her attacker is still insisting she was alive when he last saw her. I have a terrible feeling he might be telling the truth.'

'Kate, the poor woman was raped, beaten half to death and then dumped in a skip. There's every chance she died as a result of her injuries or shock or a combination of both, after he abandoned her.'

'I know. And yet—'

He gave her a warning look, but it came too late.

'I don't need to spell out where I'm going with this. Heather had concerns about a fellow police officer destroying evidence. She confided in you, asked you, off the record, to analyse a drug that turned out to be ketamine, and intended exposing the officer concerned. As far as I know, nobody was disciplined over it. Shortly afterwards, she was removed from the operation and warned you to keep schtum about it if you valued your job. Now that all sounds suspicious to me.'

'Suspicious, yes, but what you're hinting at is way off. I don't believe what she told me would be enough to get her killed.'

'You're right. It isn't enough. But Heather didn't back off. She continued with her own investigations and unearthed something else that would have had serious implications.'

'Kate, I'm not sure I need to hear this.'

'Do you want me to stop? Really? Heather came to you. Do you believe she was worried over nothing?' She gave him a long look until he gave a small sigh.

'No. I think she had valid concerns.'

'Me too, and I *know* that she came across something so important it might have got her killed. Ervin, I think after the attack she was still alive and was dumped in the skip, as her assailant claims, but somebody else got to her and ensured she died.'

Ervin didn't move a muscle. 'If I hadn't spoken to Heather and seen how concerned she was about the ketamine, I would say your hypothesis is too far-fetched. What exactly do you want from me?'

'Your support. I want to know where you stand on this.'

He held her gaze. It was several moments before he answered. 'I think highly of you, Kate. I respect you and I feel for you after what happened to Chris. As a *friend*, I'm telling you that nothing good will come of you probing into this. If you're right about Heather, and heaven knows how you'd even begin to prove it, you'll find yourself in deep water.' He smoothed his cravat, before folding his hands again. 'Heather warned me I could lose my job and worse if I ever let on about the ketamine. She was afraid of somebody, and I heeded her warning. Although I don't know who she told about it, I half suspect it was Dickson.' He paused to look Kate directly in the eye. 'I believe she was murdered by a vile rapist, the same person you and your team caught. However, there's a slim chance someone else murdered her. But Kate, whatever our suspicions, you will never prove she was murdered as part of a cover-up. All the forensic evidence suggested she fell foul of the same predator who attacked those other innocent women. The assailant confessed to attacking her and even though he was sure she was alive when he dumped her body it is almost certain she died of her injuries. Case closed.'

'*Almost* certain—'

His gentle gaze silenced her. 'Case closed. I'm here for you, Kate. I always will be; however, I can't take a risk on this. My job is me and I am it. Should anyone separate me from it, I'll be left floating in limbo. This is who I am.'

'Then you won't help me?'

'I didn't say that. I don't wish to stick my neck out, expose myself, so to speak. I shall, however, be happy to support you in a semi-undercover position. Should you have any suspicions or find-ings that require my assistance, I'll go through them for you. If you require any forensic assistance, you have it. And should you unearth corruption and require somebody to speak out on your behalf, I'm yours. On one condition. That your discoveries and accusations are airtight. There can be no wriggle room for Dickson or whomever to escape and resume duties. I won't jeopardise my safety or position for this. Moreover, I won't allow you to jeopardise yours.'

'And if I find further evidence, would you also be prepared to disclose what you know about Heather and her concerns?'

He studied her through half-closed lids, his lips pursed in thought. '*If* you find something concrete, then we can have this conversation again.'

'Thank you. That's what I needed to hear.' She got to her feet. Ervin didn't move.

'Be careful, Kate. You don't want to throw away your career or lose your friends. Or worse.'

She made for the door, her hand resting lightly on the handle. 'Me neither. I'll be on my guard.'

CHAPTER THIRTEEN

Samuel was still in the office when Kate returned. He was glued to a screen, long fingers poised over the keyboard like a pianist about to perform.

'Samuel, have you had any additional thoughts about our suspect?' she asked.

He blinked. 'Er, sorry. I was miles away.'

She repeated the question.

'No. Sorry. In fact, I have to head off. There's something I need to look into. Ring me if you have anything else to add to the picture.' He scrambled to his feet, knocking over a pile of folders stacked on the floor.

'It's fine. We'll sort them,' said Kate as he fumbled about on the floor, limbs sticking out at all angles.

'I'm terribly sorry.'

'It's fine. Chill.'

'Thank you. See you later then.' He tumbled out of the room.

'Has he been like that for long?' asked Kate.

'Like what?' said Jamie. 'Clumsy? Probably all his life.'

'No, vacant. Strange.'

'He was okay half an hour ago,' said Emma. 'Must have something on his mind.'

Morgan responded. 'Probably too much. It's got to be tough doing what he does. Imagine reading all those books about murderers and what goes on in their heads.'

'You don't need to worry about that,' chirped Emma. 'You're still struggling with Harry Potter, aren't you?'

'So much sauce,' he said.

Kate brought them up to speed on her brief meeting with William and Dickson.

'But we identified several potential locations. The killer could go to any of them,' said Jamie. 'Should we stake them out ourselves?'

If Jamie was reporting her actions to Dickson, there was no way she could go against orders. 'The superintendent correctly pointed out that if we made a wrong call and somebody else died at another location altogether it would reflect badly on us. We must have clear, solid motives as to why we've chosen these locations, rather than my woolly hypothesis.' She'd repeated Dickson's words and managed to make it sound as if she supported his reaction. Should Jamie be questioned by the man later, he would only be able to relay that information. Nevertheless, he seemed dejected.

'I thought it was a good shout,' he said. 'How else are we supposed to catch the killer if we don't take a chance? This is a quadruple murder, not a shoplifting offence. Everyone available should be seconded to the case.'

Morgan, slumped in his seat, grunted. 'It's testament to how highly he values our skills. We are a special-crimes unit, after all.'

A noise, half snort, half laugh, erupted from Emma. 'I'm with Jamie on this. We should be getting support.'

'Whatever you think, it's non-negotiable and, just so as you know, DCI Chase is considering merging us with a larger team. If you want me to push for it, I will. Or we can continue as we are.'

'I'm for carrying on and getting all the kudos when we nail the fucker.'

Morgan shrugged. 'For once, I agree with Jamie. We've worked alone and caught murderers before.'

Emma gave a nod in Kate's direction. For the time being, Kate would plough on with her unit. She'd meant it when she'd told William they were excellent officers. She couldn't really ask for better.

'Sunset is at 17.43 hours and it's now pouring down. If the rain continues, it'll turn darker earlier this evening and people will be less inclined to visit or stay late at visitor attractions, especially outdoors ones. The perpetrator might not even strike this evening,' said Jamie.

Kate didn't share his optimism. The killer had begun a cycle and, if they were as damaged as Samuel suggested, they'd be repeating the act regardless of the weather, ad infinitum, until they were stopped.

Even though Morgan had scoured the area for possible locations, she wanted to see if there were any he'd overlooked. The temptation to have her officers drive past each was great until she began looking at the numerous possibilities. If the killer intended choosing a spot where there'd be people, they had a multitude to choose from. Maybe it had been an over-ambitious theory after all. She shut her eyes, recalled the discarded list falling to the desk and the cold look in Dickson's eyes and decided it wasn't the craziest idea by far. It had been all she could offer.

By four o'clock, the stale atmosphere was permeating Kate's skin and coating her tongue.

Morgan threw himself into a full body stretch, accidentally kicking the back of Jamie's chair hard.

'Oy! Watch it.'

'My bad. I was seizing up.'

'Thought you'd gone all Samuel on me for a sec.' Jamie rubbed at strained eyes. 'Rain's stopped. I'm going outside for a few mins. Clear my head. All this screenwork is giving me a headache. Don't know how the tech boys manage it, day after day.'

'I'll come with you,' said Morgan. 'I need a leak.'

'Make sure you hold hands in the playground,' said Emma, without looking up.

Jamie called, 'Yes, miss,' in a high-pitched fashion.

Once they'd departed, Emma rested an elbow on the desk. 'Pair of idiots. I think they're getting on a lot better these days.'

Morgan and Jamie hadn't hit it off to begin with. The tension between them had been difficult to ignore. Kate had preferred it when Morgan had disliked Jamie. She cared about both Emma and Morgan, more than she ought to, and she didn't really like the idea of Jamie becoming chummy with either of them when he was such a snake in the grass. As tempting as it was, she couldn't reveal those thoughts to Emma. She had to maintain a harmonious balance in the team if she wanted them to work well together.

'Jamie's found somebody else to goad – Samuel. He's like the angry terrier my nan owned. He'd bark and snarl at strangers until he got to know them, then he was as good as gold and let them rub his tummy,' said Kate.

'Somehow I can't see Jamie letting Samuel rub his tummy.' The comment made them both smile.

'Kate, is everything okay?'

'What makes you ask?'

'You've been a bit . . . distracted.'

'The investigation, Emma. It's bugging the shit out of me.' She smiled. What else had Emma noticed? Kate thought she'd masked her concerns. The trouble was, Emma was perceptive, and she'd caught Kate staring at the photo of her father.

'Erm . . . you can tell me to butt out if you like—'

'No, go on.'

'You're not taking medication again, are you?'

'Gosh, no! I'm coping fine without.'

Emma looked relieved. 'I hope you don't mind me asking. I was concerned because I remember what happened when you were on it. You were . . . Well, there's no need to go back over it.'

'That was then. I was turmoiled. Things are better now. I can talk about Chris; even accept he has gone. It's just some days are harder than others. I take time out to do normal stuff, sort out the house, spend time visiting places we used to visit. It's all part of the healing process. My counsellor recommended I got out and about.'

'And are you going to visit your stepsister?'

'That's the plan once I get some leave. We Skype regularly.' The lies came easily. She couldn't tell Emma that every waking minute she'd not been on duty had been spent hunting for Farai and Rosa.

'That's nice. I wish I had a sister.'

'You have Greg.'

'As sweet as he is, I'd swap him for a sister.'

The sadness that swept across her open face tugged at Kate. She'd known Emma long enough to know she was hurting. Maybe her question hadn't been to draw out what was wrong with Kate, more to encourage Kate to ask after her.

She set aside her document. 'Want a girl chat?'

'I'm not great at that sort of thing.' Emma flushed.

'Me neither. I think that's what keeps us so focused on our careers. We have no time or ability to hang out with other girls.'

Emma's face brightened momentarily. 'I'm good, thanks.'

'Really?'

'Yeah. It's soon the anniversary of my mum's death, so I tend to get a little down this time of the year.'

'That's understandable. Have you got any photos of her?'

Emma shifted in her seat, stared at her screen then lifted her phone. She thumbed it and stood up.

The woman in the picture was raven-haired and could have been Emma's older sister. Her oval face was pale and, whereas Emma had striking deep-blue eyes, her mother's were the colour of pale cornflowers. She had an arm around a young man who Kate recognised to be Greg.

'It was taken years ago. It's Greg's photo. I don't have any actual photos of her.'

'Why not?'

'I burnt them.'

'Oh, Emma. Why?'

'Because I needed to forget her.' She swallowed. 'The trouble is, I can't.'

Kate put a hand on top of her colleague's and for a second there was an unspoken empathy and camaraderie, then the sound of pounding footsteps in the corridor sent Emma scurrying back to her desk.

Morgan raced back into the room.

'We've got a witness from the lake. She's downstairs.'

The floorboards in the interview room protested as Morgan marched across them and drew out a chair for himself, dropping down next to Kate. The woman was small-framed, brown hair a mess of curls that she fingered nervously.

'Jenny, isn't it?'

'That's right.'

'I'm DI Kate Young and this is DS Morgan Meredith.' They'd chosen the best of the three interview rooms, all equally stark, but at least this one had a window.

'Firstly, we'd like to thank you for coming to the station to help us with our enquiries. We appreciate it.'

The corners of Jenny's mouth twitched into a tiny smile. 'I've never been to a police station before. It's not how I imagined it to be. It's more *Heartbeat* than *Line of Duty* here, isn't it?'

'Yes. It has been mentioned that the place is lost in the 1960s. The washrooms certainly are. Still, we upgraded you to our five-star interview room. It's the only one with padded seats,' said Morgan.

The woman twisted her hair into a tight corkscrew and grinned nervously. 'What happens now? Do we record this interview, or is someone next door watching it on a monitor?' She glanced at the smoke detector in the ceiling.

Kate shook her head. 'No. We're simply going to have a chat about what you saw yesterday evening at Westport Lake. We'll have to take an official statement later, but you'll get to check it through before you sign it.'

'Oh. Okay.'

'Are you happy for us to begin?'

She released her hair, which bounced back to join the other curls. 'Yes.'

'Take your time.'

The woman wetted her lips. 'I took my little boy, Billy, to the lake after I picked him up from nursery. He was a bit hyper. He gets like that sometimes. Usually, when he's in that sort of mood, we stop off on the way home and take a walk around the lake, then play in the playground. It helps calm him down. Anyway, we were longer than usual because Billy found a friend to play with. Even after the kid went home, Billy wouldn't leave. I let him burn off some more energy. I don't know where he gets it from.' She paused and smiled at Kate, who nodded as if she understood all about young children.

'At half past five I insisted we left because he hadn't eaten tea. Besides, it was getting close to his bath and bedtime. He played up all the way to the car, sulking, dragging his heels, carrying on, so I didn't pay any attention to the man at first. He was walking up and down, talking loudly to himself. I figured he was on his phone so I ignored him. I already had my hands full with Billy, who played up big time when I tried to get him into the car. He wouldn't let me fasten his seatbelt.'

Kate resisted the increasing urge to bark at the woman that this wasn't some dull murder mystery drama and to get to the point. This circumlocution was serving no purpose other than to frustrate Kate. An image of Dickson's mocking face made her grit her teeth. He would love it if this investigation dragged on for months while the death count continued to rise. She'd never be allowed to lead her old team, let alone have the chance of promotion. She concentrated on the woman, who was nodding and smiling as if performing for the cameras.

'I gave up trying to buckle him in. I stood up to recover my breath and wait for him to calm down. By then, the man had stopped pacing, but he'd put both hands over his face. I'm sure he was sobbing. Proper big cries; wails, not sniffles. I thought about speaking to him, but you read about criminals distracting you and then kidnapping your child or stealing your car, and by then Billy had stopped messing about. So I crouched down again, strapped him in and, when I next stood up, the man was inside his car with the door open. He was leaning on the steering wheel, head in arms. I thought it was best to ignore him. I got in my car and drove off. I heard about the attack on the local news and thought I should come and speak to you.'

Kate digested the nub of the woman's revelation. There'd been a distressed man at the crime scene. The woman could have telephoned them with this news, instead of wasting their time. She considered leaving Morgan to continue the interview, then took stock of her emotions. She was frustrated because she wanted to make headway. She was irked because she knew Dickson was itching for her to fail. She was furious because she'd not got to Rosa in time. The irritation she felt was not solely due to the woman in front of her. She leant forward, hand resting on her chin. Morgan had taken the initiative.

'Jenny, where were you parked?' Morgan pushed forward a map of the car-parking area beside the lake.

'Here, along the roadside.' She pointed to a layby, opposite the visitor centre.

'And where was the man?'

'He was parked on the other side of the road, a couple of car lengths away from mine. In one of the disabled bays.' She moved her finger to a spot closer still to the centre.

Morgan nodded. 'Did you notice the colour, make or model of the car he was in?'

She nodded vigorously. 'It was a silver Ford Focus. My brother had one similar to it. I don't know what model it was, though. And I didn't look at the registration plate.'

'Was there anything distinctive about it, maybe something hanging from the rear-view mirror or a sticker in the window?' asked Morgan.

She shook her head slowly. 'No. It was a plain, silver Ford Focus. Quite ordinary.'

It was a lead, albeit a small and possibly insignificant one. Kate straightened up. 'Can you describe the man to us?'

'Average height, with dark hair and dark clothes – black jeans or trousers and a dark coat, maybe navy or black. I didn't really pay

215

him any attention until he began crying. By then, he'd covered his face with his hands.'

It sounded similar to the description of the man in the high-vis vest.

'Could you estimate how old he was?'

'Not got a clue. Sorry.'

Kate chewed on her lip. There had to be more. The woman had given chapter and verse about her offspring, down to the last detail of how he'd wriggled in his car seat. She must have spotted something else. She tried a technique she'd learnt from her therapist. She took the woman back to the moment she first spotted him. 'He was pacing up and down, right?'

'Yes.'

'Where?'

'Under the trees. Near the parking bay.'

'Okay. Did he walk away from you?'

'Yes. He had his head lowered.'

'And you were headed for your car?'

'Yes.'

'Why did you look up? Did he shout? Did he say something that made you notice him?'

Jenny's eyes narrowed. She fell silent. Just as Kate was about to repeat the question, she spoke. 'There was something that caught my attention. He said, "Don't make me do it" really loudly.'

'Are you sure that's what he said?'

'Pretty certain. Sorry, I'm not being very helpful, am I?'

'You're doing very well, Jenny,' said Morgan. 'Did you detect any accent when he spoke?'

She shrugged. 'I don't think so.'

Kate took over again. Jenny needed cajoling, and Morgan had helped by praising her. 'Later, when you looked up, he was back in his car.'

'Yes.'

'He was crying. Sobbing.'

'Yes.'

'With both hands over his face?'

'Uh-huh.'

'Can you think back to that moment and tell me, did you notice if he was wearing a wedding ring?'

Jenny shut her eyes for a few seconds and opened them with a nod. 'Yes, I think so.'

'How sure are you?'

'Fairly sure. I can picture his hands. They were large and covered all his face. There was a gold band on this finger.' She touched her ring finger.

'Good, thank you. And finally, did you see this man at all?'

Kate slid across a photograph of Asif Baqui.

'I don't remember seeing him there. Who is he?'

'I'm afraid that's the man who was killed.'

'Oh, wasn't it the man I saw?'

Kate was already on her feet. She'd spent enough time dragging minimal information from this witness. 'No, but he might have witnessed the attack, so we'll try and track him down. Thank you for your time, Jenny. We're going to leave you here for a few minutes while we find an officer to take your statement. Can I get you a coffee or tea, or water?'

'Tea, please,' she replied. 'No sugar.'

In the corridor outside, Kate asked Morgan for his thoughts. He shrugged.

'It could be something or nothing. This incident took place half an hour before Asif was killed. The guy in the Ford Focus could have taken off before Asif even went back to his car. Dark hair. Dark clothes. Sounds vaguely like the other train passenger who got off with Tobias, but that description could equally fit a number of men, including me and Samuel.'

'Pity Jenny didn't get a proper look at his face.'

Morgan folded his arms. 'I wonder if the crying was an act, so he could hide his face from her.'

'He'd have drawn less attention to himself if he'd turned his back on her rather than sobbing loudly.'

'Yeah. Guess so. Then all we've gleaned is that a man driving a silver Ford Focus and possibly wearing a wedding ring was in tears at the scene half an hour before Asif was attacked.'

Kate put her hands on her hips, shifted from one foot to the other. This was probably another dead end. 'I can't get excited about it. There simply isn't enough evidence to suggest this man was doing anything more than having a row over the phone with somebody.'

'I'm with you on that. Our killer is in control, a calm assassin who lies in wait for their victims. It's not likely that one minute he'd be bawling his eyes out, the next sneaking up on Asif to shoot him.'

'We're in agreement, then. Still, we'd better try to find him in case he witnessed the attack. If he's emotionally unstable, he might have seen what happened and been too terrified to come forward.'

'There was nobody matching his description at the scene when we began interviewing. No Ford Focus cars either, silver or otherwise, in any of the car-parking areas, so yes, we ought to pursue this.'

'Find someone to take her statement and see if you can track down this man. Maybe one of the witnesses you spoke to also spotted him or his car.'

She checked her watch: 4.35. If the perpetrator intended attacking again today, they'd probably be preparing around now. She was powerless to prevent them. Each death would become a strike against her record, a sign she was not up to the position and a victory for Dickson. If somebody died at one of the locations her team had identified, simply because of a lack of police funding and protocol, she'd take it right to the top and complain. Her team's reputation may have been at stake, but the human cost of screwing this up was even higher.

CHAPTER FOURTEEN

The minute hand on the office clock slid past the hour with an audible click. Kate wasn't sure how long she'd been eyeballing the timepiece. A glance about the office confirmed she wasn't the only person keeping watch on the time. Morgan's mobile was propped up on his desk, the display in large digital numbers. Emma's eyes were glued to the clock in the corner of her computer screen and Jamie had rolled up his shirtsleeves to expose the watch he was wearing.

'No news is good news, right?' said Jamie.

Morgan grunted an acknowledgement.

Jamie spoke again. 'We shouldn't be here doing nothing. We should have split up and covered the locations ourselves.'

'Our brief was to sit tight.' Kate hated saying it. She was as anxious as everyone else and had fought the urge to disobey instructions and send her team to stake out some of the tourist attractions at the very least.

Morgan chimed in. 'I loathe waiting around as much as anyone else here, but we aren't any closer to establishing who this crackpot is, and that's what we should be doing.'

Kate stirred herself. Her legs were going to sleep. 'Spot on, Morgan. Come on, folks, we're good at this. We have to keep ploughing on. Give it until seven and, if we've heard nothing by then, we'll go home.'

She headed to the washrooms and stared at her reflection. Her face had become more angular, cheekbones more prominent, over the last couple of months. And what was that she could see? She tugged at the white hair, yanked it out and rubbed the smarting area. Sighing, she tucked in her blouse, hand slipping easily behind the loose waistband. If she intended pushing on with promotion, she'd have to address her physical appearance. She was beginning to let herself go. She ran the tap and splashed water on to her face. Since Chris had slipped away from her again she had no appetite, and her lack of self-care was beginning to show. Little wonder Emma had expressed concern for her well-being.

Another officer came in, gave a quick 'Ma'am' and headed for the cubicle.

Kate smoothed her hair back off her face and clipped it into place. She already looked more groomed. She slicked on the lipstick she kept in her pocket and studied the result. Even though nothing could erase the dark circles or the sunken cheeks, she was presentable. If she'd been able to still communicate with Chris, things would be different. She stared at her reflection and demanded, 'Why won't you answer?'

'Hello? Are you speaking to me?' the officer called from the cubicle.

'No, sorry. I was on the phone.' The lie came naturally, and with it an epiphany. On the phone. Not on the phone. Talking to himself. How had Jenny described the man's distress? 'Proper big cries; wails, not sniffles.'

A memory flitted through her mind, of Dan the journalist handing her Chris's journal and of her sitting in the lounge, head in hands, wailing like an injured animal, howling uncontrollably, after finally understanding Chris was dead.

What if the sobbing man had been experiencing something similar to her own grief? Samuel's words came back to her: *'it leads me to question if the killer might not have also been a victim of a random attack, one that has left them traumatised.'*

She clung to the sink, heartbeat accelerating. What had he said? 'Don't make me do it.' It was possible he hadn't been holding a conversation on the phone at all but with somebody who was deceased, just like she had been talking to Chris.

It made sense to her. But she wasn't convinced her team would follow her logic. Without confessing that she'd been holding imaginary conversations with Chris, she wasn't in a position to explain. Samuel could. She searched for his number on her mobile and rang him.

'I have to speak to you. It's urgent.'

'Er, I'm a little tied up at the moment.'

'It can't wait.'

'Sorry, but I'm with some young offenders. I can't get away. I won't be free for another hour.'

'Okay. I'll meet you at your office then.'

She gave him no time to refuse.

◆　◆　◆

'Shh. It's fine.'

'Not today. Not today,' Ben repeated.

Gracie's toy unicorn with the pink mane lay on the bed. He picked it up and held it to his chest. The sobs wouldn't abate.

'Shh! Shh! That's enough now. I understand. You need a break. It's too much for you.'

'Yes.'

'Rest up. Sleep. You're tired.'

'We're all tired, Lisa.'

'Yes, but only you have the power to resolve that.'

Samuel wasn't at his office as arranged. Kate waited ten minutes and was about to ring him when he came rushing towards her. 'Sorry. It wasn't easy to get away.'

He unlocked the door and snapped on the lights. 'Make yourself at home.'

The room was basic, furnished only with a Formica table and two mismatched chairs. She glanced at a stack of books resting covers up on shelves, the one on the top written by one of the FBI's legendary criminal profilers; next to it were various books to do with mental-health issues and cognitive behaviour. Her eye was drawn to a copy of *Lost Connections: Why You're Depressed and How to Find Hope* by Johann Hari. The spine, unlike all the other books, was fractured in numerous places. She was about to select it from among the other undamaged books but stopped herself when she spotted a small furrow pulling his eyebrows together. He didn't want her to.

'I call it Scandi chic,' he said, sweeping his hand towards the table. 'Sit down. Make yourself comfortable. These are temporary premises. I was supposed to move into proper offices at the university, but there's been some hiccup and I'm waiting for it to be resolved.'

'You're working at the university?'

'I've taken up a position there, lecturing in Psychology. Profiling is only a part-time occupation for me. Fortunately, my services as a profiler aren't in huge demand and, well, it can be very . . . draining, so I need to do other things as well to keep a healthy balance and pay my bills.'

'How come you got into profiling?'

'I was interested in human nature. It grew from there. I'd offer you a drink but, as you can see, the catering facilities leave a lot to be desired.' He indicated the half-drunk bottle of water on the table. 'Right, what did you want to ask me?'

'You suggested the perpetrator might have been a victim of a random attack that had traumatised them.'

'That's right.'

'Could it also be possible they lost somebody, a loved one, during this attack?'

He unscrewed the lid of the bottle, took a sip as he appeared to consider her question, then returned the bottle to the table. 'Yes. That's also possible. Something serious happened to trigger a flurry of murders and this individual can't control their emotions or the situation. They could be fuelled by a deep anger, again possibly caused by the loss of somebody close to them.'

'In your professional opinion, could somebody traumatised in this fashion be unwilling to accept the situation?'

'I'm not sure I understand what you're suggesting.'

'I mean, could they be unwilling to accept their loved one was dead?'

'Denial is common, Kate. It's the first part of the whole grieving process.'

'I know.'

His face softened. 'Naturally, you do. I'm sorry. I didn't intend to sound condescending.'

She'd prepared what she was going to say next. She didn't want Samuel to guess the depths of her own struggle to accept Chris's death. She'd become accustomed to downplaying her feelings and hiding her emotions from her colleagues, and even from Tilly. It had become second nature to pretend everything was okay. She didn't want this stranger to be privy to them. Moreover, she didn't want him to see the weakness in her. If he spotted it, he might also see something more – her hunger for revenge.

'When I lost Chris, I unconsciously developed various coping mechanisms. Apart from the tears and being unable to accept he was gone, I used to speak to him, like he was still around. What I'm asking is, could somebody take that one step further? Could they actually believe they really *are* speaking to that person?'

He replaced the top on the bottle with slow movements before nodding. 'Bereavement reactions are associated with numerous physical and mental complications. I've come across atypical bereavement reactions in both my studies and my work. I read of a case of an eighty-year-old woman who believed her deceased son was alive, even though he'd died in his twenties. For decades, she kept his room ready for him. Whenever she heard an aeroplane overhead, she'd rush outside, convinced he was returning home on it. And there's the famous Canadian singer Céline Dion, who believed she could sense the presence of her dead husband, René, over a year after he passed away from cancer. During an interview, she confessed she used to talk to him and could hear him respond. It isn't uncommon. In light of how Chris died, it is certainly not unusual for you to experience this. You've done well, Kate, to fight back as you have and to continue your work. Especially such a stressful, demanding job.'

She waved away his comments. This wasn't about her, nor did she want it to be.

He continued. 'Sensing a deceased spouse happens more frequently than you may imagine. There's even a name for it – bereavement hallucinations. It's a normal, helpful way to cope with grief.'

'Then it wouldn't be out of the ordinary for our perpetrator to have experienced something similar to me and those other people you have mentioned. It wouldn't be strange for them to be acting on what they imagine to be their loved one's instructions, would it?'

He brought his hands together and rested his chin on the tips of his fingers. His eyelids fluttered before he resumed his original position and spoke again with the confidence of a pedant. 'It would be entirely possible. If someone is sufficiently distressed by an event, it could alter their normal reactions, tip them over the edge, so to speak.'

'Could it change them sufficiently to make them behave in a bizarre fashion – one moment distraught, the next a killing machine?'

'This isn't my field of expertise. That said, anger is another stage of grief. If the perpetrator of these crimes is grieving badly for a loved one, they could well flip from one emotion to the other quite easily.'

Kate nodded. It was hypothetical but lent credence to her theory that the driver of the Ford Focus might be the killer and therefore worthy of pursuit. 'Would you present this to the team tomorrow? It would make more sense coming from you.'

'What time would you like me to appear?'

'Is eight thirty all right?'

'I can manage that.'

'I hope I didn't mess up any plans for this evening,' she said.

'After I got the call to go to the young offenders' prison, I had to cancel them anyway.'

'It's not easy balancing life and work in this job, is it?'

'It is for me. Work always comes first,' he replied. 'It keeps me anchored. Can I ask you something?'

'It depends what it is.'

'How did you cope after your husband's death? Your occupation is incredibly demanding, and you must require steely focus at times.'

'I coped *because* of the job. I submerged myself in my work. It saved me from going under.' She wasn't prepared to say anything more on the subject. Samuel nodded, yet the way he maintained eye contact unnerved her slightly, as if he could see beyond the facade and into her soul.

◆ ◆ ◆

Kate checked in with the station to ensure there had been no emergency call-outs or fatalities and was relieved to learn there had been no reported instances of any shootings. She turned on the local radio station to listen to the late-evening show. Its mix of easy-listening music and its comforting presenter with a honeyed voice made the journey pass more quickly. Halos of headlights blurred past her until her eyes began to sting, causing her to blink several times to clear her tired vision. She wondered how much longer she could maintain the frantic pace that had become her life. She wasn't, like many, going home to rest and recuperate for the next day. She would worry the pieces of the enormous puzzle she was piecing together until she'd attached another section. At work, she was dealing with the investigation. At home, ways to outmanoeuvre Dickson.

She threw her head back, yawned loudly before winding down the window to suck at the incoming breeze. Fatigue had come on without warning. She gripped the steering wheel tighter, forcing herself to concentrate on the road ahead. The fresh air wasn't enough to revive her. Soon apathy accompanied the weariness and sudden lethargy. She'd been fighting for so long to get nowhere. Perhaps she would simply drive herself into the ground and join Chris in the afterlife. She fought back another yawn and wound the window down further. She wasn't done with the day yet. Or with Dickson. She still had one ace up her sleeve. Something Chris would approve of.

Cocooned inside her home, she set about returning her father's effects to the attic. This was one concern she was going to ignore.

William had assured her Mitch wasn't guilty of the sexual allegations. That Dickson might have been the person who raised them in the first instance was a different matter. She'd added it to her mental score sheet. It wasn't, however, something he could be punished for, at least not by the justice system. She shoved the boxes into place and climbed down the ladder, brushing cobwebs from her top, before taking a shower and setting up shop in the bedroom, rather than in Chris's study.

The contract for Chris's mobile had run out. Nevertheless, she'd bought a pay-as-you-go SIM card for it. She fitted it into the iPhone and fired it up. The screensaver of the pair of them on holiday in Italy was still in place, saved to the phone's memory, along with numerous selfies of them. She had similar pictures on her phone. All the same, she thumbed through them all before calling a number she'd committed to memory. It belonged to journalist Dan Corrance, who had worked closely with Chris at the *Gazette*.

'I was going through some of Chris's bits and pieces and stumbled across some stuff you might find useful. Thought we could meet for a quick coffee and let me drop them off with you.'

She hoped Dan understood the message she was trying to convey, that what she really wanted was a meeting. He did.

'I don't suppose you could drop by tomorrow morning, same place and time as last?'

'That'd be great. See you there.'

Dan Corrance had helped Chris on the paedophile case that led him to the club where the young sex-worker had been murdered, and was in possession of Chris's journal containing the names of eminent people connected to paedophile rings. Kate had given him the journal, but now she needed it back. Dickson's name was among others there and she was going to add it to her armoury.

She had something better to offer in exchange.

CHAPTER FIFTEEN

DAY FIVE – SATURDAY

Although the takeaway van was still outside the glass-fronted offices of the *Gazette*, the woman who owned it had been replaced by a young lad, wearing a pinstriped apron and a disposable mob cap. The offerings had changed. There were no tempting flapjacks or platters of sausage rolls that Chris had always raved about. Gone were the small, neatly written chalkboard signs advertising pasties and home-made quiche, to be replaced by a plate of cellophane-wrapped white rolls.

'What can I get you?'

'Just a white coffee, please.'

'Soya, oat, semi?' he asked, setting up the machine.

'Ordinary milk will be fine.'

She glanced behind her at the building where Chris had worked. She conjured a memory, a surprise drop-in to meet him for lunch and of him whisking her through the busy office, introducing her to the others on the same floor. It had been immense, with several workstations and journalists seated in rows, one behind the other. His desk had been close to the window. She picked out the pane of glass, tried to imagine him looking at her.

'One fifty, please.'

No sooner had she paid for it and sat down at one of the brightly coloured tables than Dan appeared. He made a beeline for her.

'Hey. It's been a while.'

'Not far off six months.'

He nodded. 'I thought about you. I wanted to contact you but . . . well, it seemed wiser not to.'

'Same here. That's why I didn't call you from my phone. In case anyone checked your call log history.'

'Isn't that a bit cloak and dagger?'

'I prefer to exercise caution. Especially in light of what happened to Chris.'

'Fair enough. I thought about you on the anniversary of his—'

She silenced him with a gesture. 'Thank you.'

He adjusted his coat, fiddled with the buttons. 'I tried, Kate. I took the journal to my editor, told him what I had planned, and it was all systems go. Then the *Gazette*'s lawyers swooped in, voicing concerns, shouting about legalities and potential court cases, and the newspaper's owners got cold feet. They vetoed my first article, an hour before it was due to go to print. So much for freedom of speech. I tried to take the story to other papers, but none of them would touch it either. They all claimed it was "too hot". Some of those people named in the journal wield a lot of power, enough to shut down a newspaper, and certainly enough to make sure somebody like me never works again.'

When the story hadn't appeared as she expected, Kate had guessed something like this had happened. To her mind, it was another reason why Chris had disappeared.

'I let you down. I let Chris down,' he said.

The only way the information in the journal could have been used was if it had been given to the appropriate police authorities. She'd chosen not to. They'd both failed her husband.

'You weren't the only one. I'd really like it back. Especially if you can't use it.'

'I haven't got it. I was forced to hand it over to the lawyers. I don't know where it is.'

'Didn't you make any copies?'

Dan glanced over his shoulder to make sure nobody was nearby. 'I didn't have time. It all happened very quickly. What do you need?' he said quietly.

'To be honest, I'm not sure. I'm scrabbling for proof. The journal would have helped me build a case, something that could be of interest to you.'

He thought for a moment. 'I've kept copies of private WhatsApp messages Chris sent me relating to our investigation into the paedophile ring. He was looking into the Maddox Club and their special service. There'll be dates at least of when he was investigating it and a few names.'

Kate already had information on the club found in Chris's filing cabinet. She'd photographed all the pages and uploaded the images on to the USB stick before destroying the files. However, anything Dan could offer her was welcome.

'Would you email them to me?'

He nodded.

'And I'll have something for you in return.'

'Go on.'

'An exposé.'

'Uh-huh.'

'I can't give you all the facts at the moment, but it will be an exclusive. Police corruption within the force.'

'Bent coppers?'

'Not just bent, dangerous.'

'Okay. I'm in.'

'Good. I'll be in contact. Send the info to Chris's email.'

'I'll do it this morning.'

'Thanks, Dan.'

He took her hand and pressed it in his own. 'Look after yourself.'

'You too.'

'You bet.' He gave her a wink and stood up.

She watched him saunter through the main doors. Nobody was in sight other than the lad in the van, who had his back to her. It wasn't a great deal to work with, but with Dan and Ervin on board, she might be able to topple Dickson yet.

Samuel was as good as his word and arrived at the office at eight thirty on the dot. He'd no sooner finished explaining about the way grief, especially trauma-related, affected some people, sometimes even triggering bereavement hallucinations, than William walked in, his face solemn.

'I have the information on the Harriet Parkinson case. The team at Hanley didn't have much. They suspected she'd been attacked by an ex-boyfriend, but he had a cast-iron alibi.'

'Then there's nothing we can take from their investigations?'

'Only the basic facts.' He dropped the files on to Kate's desk. 'I couldn't see anything of value. Maybe you'll spot something I didn't. I'll leave you to it.'

With that he was gone.

'That's a bastard. I was hoping there'd be some sort of lead or connection we could use,' said Jamie.

Kate flicked through the file. Her eyes fell to a photograph pinned to the front page. The victim was lying with her back slightly arched, her arms and legs splayed, reminding Kate of a floppy doll. Her old jeans were well worn and scuffed in parts. Her small hands were bare and her nails nude. Her pale-pink Superdry jacket was done up to the neck and the black straps under her armpits suggested she was resting on a backpack. Kate looked for jewellery, spotted none, only music buds in her ears, and couldn't help but wonder what the girl had been listening to in her dying moments. She held it up.

'Where was she killed?' asked Morgan. 'That looks like another car park to me.'

Kate confirmed his guess. 'It seems she was crossing the car park to reach the road. She doesn't live far from the ski centre. She was about eighty metres from the entrance.'

'Erm, it might help if I visited the crime scene, got an idea of what happened. I might pick up something fresh by being there,' said Samuel.

Kate nodded. It wouldn't hurt. 'It would be a good idea for one of you to accompany him. Any volunteers?'

'I'll go,' said Emma.

'See if you can talk to someone who knew the girl. If you get any fresh information, ring me. We could do with a breakthrough.'

◆ ◆ ◆

Samuel hardly spoke in the car. Emma tried and failed to engage him in general conversation. Considering he had asked her out for a drink then cancelled at the last minute, now would have been a good time for an explanation or to rearrange the date. She soon tired of his monosyllabic answers and switched on some music.

'Sorry, Emma, could you turn that off? I need to think. Sorry, I'm not being much of a conversationalist, am I? I have to prepare for this, you see?'

She didn't see. Nonetheless, she shut off the music and kept her eyes on the road. She wished she were going to the ski school with

Morgan instead. He was much easier to talk to. By now, they'd have been singing along to one of her favourite tracks or chatting about the case. Samuel was a poor substitute. He might be cute, even good-looking in his own way, but she couldn't do complicated. She'd had enough complications to last a lifetime.

Mercifully it was only a short drive and they soon turned off a wide road into Festival Park. Over the years it had been transformed from a park created to celebrate the National Garden Festival in 1986 into a huge leisure and retail park. With its numerous shops, businesses and hotels and an array of leisure facilities, it was a hugely popular destination for locals and visitors alike.

They turned off Festival Way, a wide and busy road running beside the ski centre, into the car park.

'Our killer doesn't seem to be afraid of being spotted,' said Emma. 'It's a fairly busy road. Waterworld is, what, a three- or four-minute walk away? And there's the large gym opposite. There'd be people travelling up and down here at any time. Could be the killer is hiding in plain sight. Samuel?'

The profiler was gazing around at the surroundings. 'Er, I'll get back to you on that.'

The slopes stood in front of an Alpine backdrop. They were divided into two runs, one longer and wider with a ski lift running beside it for ski enthusiasts, and the shorter used for tubing and beginners. A spectators' stand ran the length of both slopes.

They walked through the car park and stood in front of a windowless building with a padlocked door. Emma pointed to the main building.

'She must have come out of the door over there. If I were the killer, I'd wait somewhere I could keep an eye on the entrance/exit. Like here.'

Samuel's response was vague. His voice dropped; his eyes took on a faraway look. 'Yes. A good view of both the ski slopes from here. Can see who else is on the slopes. Dark clothing. Pressed up against this building. Invisible. Patient. Allow people to come and go until certain. Waiting. She emerges. Ear buds in. Music on. A perfect target. She won't know a thing until she is there . . . Then it's too late.'

Emma was fixated by the trance-like look on Samuel's face. It was unnerving. She could only assume it was how he got into the mind of the killer. She'd read of profilers like him before, just not realised this was one of the methods he employed.

She didn't speak until he looked directly at her. 'Shall we see if there's anybody inside to talk to?'

'That's more your area of expertise than mine. I'll stay here. I need to work some things out.' He pulled out Harriet's file, opened the first page and stared at the photograph of the girl.

She tried the door and found it open.

'Hello!' she shouted. 'Anyone here?'

'Hi!' A guy in his late twenties appeared.

'I'm DS Donaldson. We've taken over the investigation into Harriet's death. I wondered if you could tell me anything about her or what happened.'

'I'm Ant Deacon. I'm a snowboarding instructor. Like Harriet. I was here the night she was killed. I just didn't know about it until the following morning when I came in and found her body. I made a full statement.'

'We will have that in our files. I wanted to talk to somebody in person. Find out first-hand what they knew.'

'There's not a lot more I can tell you.' He rested against a drink-and snacks-dispensing machine, hands thrust deep into the pockets of thick camouflage trousers, his coat still on and buttoned up. Tall and lithe, with wavy blond hair and a healthy colour that came with spending a great deal of time outdoors, he blended in well with the images of fit young skiers adorning the blue-skied, Alpine posters stuck on the walls. 'I still can't get my head around this. I don't know who'd do such a thing. She wasn't even rostered for the day. She only came in to practise for a course. We have to take them every year to keep our qualifications current. She was also filming for her YouTube channel.'

'You knew her well?'

'Well enough. We've been working together the last two years. She was working abroad before that, but Covid happened and she returned to the UK.' He removed his hands from his pockets, made for the nearest chair. The very act of sitting seemed to sap his strength and will. He rested his head in his hands. 'She was lying in the car park. I'd left for work, in the dark, and didn't even notice her. Her face! I don't think I'll ever forget her face.'

Emma crouched beside him. 'It's okay, Ant. You will. In time.'

He looked up. 'You reckon?'

'Let's just say it will get easier. Trust me. I am an expert on that.'

He nodded. 'I hope you're right.'

She stood up again. 'Can you tell me anything about Harriet's movements that night?'

'I was teaching on the beginner slopes while she was filming herself doing tricks on the big slope.'

'And the slopes were floodlit?'

'Yes. We always put on the lights on dull days and around dusk on brighter days. It was around six o'clock when she packed it in for the night and shouted goodbye. That was the last I saw of her until the following morning when I came into work.'

'Did you notice anyone hanging about in the car park? Any vehicles coming and going?'

'I went through all of this in my statement.'

'Sorry, we only got the report an hour ago. I'd appreciate it if you could run through some of the answers again with me.' She gave him a smile.

'Sure. You can't see what is happening in the car park when the floodlights are on. They're so bright you can't see anything or anyone from the slopes, not even spectators when they come to watch.'

'Were there any lights on in the car park?'

'It was lit as usual. Not very brightly, though, and I turned off the lights from inside before I left.'

'Were there any other vehicles in the car park at that time?'

'No.'

It struck her the perpetrator might have checked out the place prior to striking. They would need knowledge of opening times, comings and goings, and whether there was any CCTV. 'Do you recall anyone hanging around outside the ski school, maybe watching your lessons, or somebody enquiring about lesson times?'

'There are usually people about in the stands watching us. We don't get many, if any, drop-ins, though. Almost all of our enquiries and bookings are made online or from phone calls.'

The killer could have easily blended in among spectators and obtained the information they needed, might even have had lessons with either Harriet or Ant.

'I really should lock up now, if you don't mind. I only came in to teach a private client. I'm supposed to take a few days off, you know, under the circumstances. I promised my girlfriend I wouldn't be late. She's been really upset about Harriet. They were friends.'

'I understand. Thank you for your time.'

She wandered back outside and spotted Samuel sitting on a low wall.

He shook his head. 'Something has been troubling me. In all of these cases, the killer doesn't appear to take away any trophies. Keeping a souvenir, a part of the victim, allows the assailant to preserve both the memory of the victim and the experience of his or her death. This individual holds no store by that. The victims are unimportant to them. What's important is the act itself, the one humane shot to the head. What matters to your perpetrator is the actual method of execution and timing. The deaths have to occur around a certain time.'

'Why?'

'I don't know. I can only tell you what I *think* is going on in this person's mind.'

He looked away, his features changing as he stared towards the slopes. 'You won't catch me,' he whispered.

'Sorry?'

He snapped back to reality. 'You're up against it. You aren't going to be able to catch this individual easily.'

'What do you mean?'

'You won't be able to catch them because *they* don't know who they're going to kill next.'

CHAPTER SIXTEEN

Emma was quick to report to Kate.

'Samuel said what?'

'Word for word, "You won't catch me." Then he explained we couldn't catch the killer because *they* don't know who they're going to kill next. He was in a weird mood. He started off by performing a sort of role play in which he played the part of the killer, then wanted me to leave him alone to think. When I returned from interviewing Ant, he talked about trophies and how the killer hadn't taken any.'

'That's true.'

'Samuel thinks that's significant. It means the perp doesn't place any value on what he's done. They don't want to remember the victims or what's happened to them. Samuel thinks what is more important is the act and the timing of it.'

'And where is Samuel?'

'He's gone to get some air. I've never met anyone like him, Kate.'

'Me neither. I hope all this isn't a charade.'

'I didn't get the feeling it was. It's creepy, but I think he's really into this.'

Kate digested what she'd learned. If Emma trusted Samuel, then she would give him the benefit of the doubt, even if what he had to say was chilling.

The day rolled into afternoon, a succession of interviews, discussions and policework that fatigued every one of them and culminated in the discovery that Kate would be addressing the press outside the station at four o'clock.

There was light knocking and a soft, 'Kate?' William's voice came from the other side of the washroom door. She ignored him and ran her wrists under cold water and tried the breathing technique she'd been taught in the wake of Chris's death to quell her angst, and still she could feel damp on the back of her neck and had an urge to throw up.

'DI Young, over here!'

'Kate, is it true your husband was one of the victims?'

'Did you know he'd be on that train?'

'How did you feel when you found out your husband was among the dead?'

William's hand on her arm, steering her through the crowds. The pop of a flashlight.

Kate had always shunned the limelight, but Chris's death had propelled her to the front of every tabloid. What could she possibly say to appease the press today? And what if they began firing questions about Chris again? She'd go to pieces. Dickson was throwing her to the lions.

'Kate?' William tapped on the washroom door for a second time then opened it. 'I came to see how you were.'

'How do you think?'

'Nervous, anxious, angry even that you've been put in this predicament.'

She rested one hand on the sink and faced him. 'Then why the hell am I the one speaking to the press? Shouldn't you or the superintendent do this?'

'It was my suggestion you took centre stage.'

'What? Are you mad? You know there's every chance I'll muck it up. They've only got to mention Chris and I'll blank.'

His face wrinkled into a fatherly smile. 'You won't. You know how this works. You say the minimum but reassure the maximum.'

'I'm not up to it.'

'If you want to make DCI, you'll face them.'

'Is that why you suggested I do it?'

'Ah, see, there's the clever detective I'm talking about.' His attempt at humour fell flat.

'I don't understand how speaking to the press will help my chances of promotion.'

'It shows everyone you've got over the events of last year and are prepared to step up to the mark. *When* you get promoted, you'll regularly face challenges like this. Jump in with both feet and get it over with.'

'I don't have a clue what to say.'

'You tell them that we are looking into a series of deaths we believe to be connected and, at this stage, are pursuing several lines of enquiry. That you are confident of a result soon and will speak to them again when you have more details. No more, no less. When they bombard you for more, which they will do, you hold up your hand and exit with a sense of purpose. It's not hard, Kate.'

'You've done lots of these.'

'And so will you. We all started somewhere. I was panicky too before my first.'

She let go of the basin. His words hit their mark. It was a hur-
dle she had to overcome.

'Want me to accompany you?'

'Yes, but only to present a united front.'

'See you in ten minutes.'

He slipped his hands into his pockets and wandered off.

She changed into her dress uniform, ensured her hair was
clipped back from her face, then checked her make-up and
smoothed her blouse. She checked her reflection one last time.
'Wish me luck, Chris.'

◆ ◆ ◆

Kate strode to the microphone. A sea of faces turned eagerly in
her direction, pencils poised, cyclopean lenses raised. She lifted
her chin.

'Thank you all for coming today. As you know, we are looking
into a series of deaths we believe to be connected.' Photographers
slid silently across her eyeline to capture her face from every angle.
Journalists stared, eyes hungry for information. 'Our thoughts are
with the families of the victims at this very difficult time, and I
hope you will give them the privacy they deserve to grieve for their
loved ones.'

She caught sight of Dan, a friendly face in a hostile crowd, and
locked eyes with him.

'At this stage, we are pursuing several lines of enquiry. We are
confident of a result soon. I shall speak to you again as soon as we
have further details. Thank you.'

The shouting began at once.

'Is it true the victims were all shot?'

'Are you searching for more than one killer?'

'Are our streets safe?'

'Have you any idea where the killer might strike next?'

That last question froze her to the spot. Samuel's chilling premise whispered in her head. *'You won't be able to catch them because they don't know who they're going to kill next.'*

She faced them once more. 'As you appreciate, this is an ongoing investigation, and I can't release any details which might jeopardise it. Please bear with us. Show patience. Thank you.'

She walked off to more shouts, a merging of voices into one nonsensical cloud, apart from one, distinct from the others.

'DI Young, can you confirm all the victims were killed at various tourist attractions in the area?'

Tourist attractions. An idea blossomed. Could this be the clue they'd been missing?

She marched into the office. 'Where's Samuel?'

'Gone outside for a smoke,' said Jamie.

'Okay. Listen, I've had a thought. The killer seems to be favouring popular tourist spots in and around the city. Can you drag me up a list of the main attractions in Stoke-on-Trent?'

'Bear with me.'

A couple of clicks later and she thought they had their answer. 'The Trentham Estate, Westport Lake and Stoke Ski Centre are all on the list. There's a chance the perpetrator is targeting top tourist attractions. I need to run this by Samuel. Could you fetch him, please?'

Morgan shot off.

'Guv, where does Blythe Bridge fit in? That isn't a tourist attraction. It's a tiny station, not even a main one like Stoke.'

'It's somehow relevant.' She placed a hand on the back of her neck, felt the muscles bunched up, pressed with firm fingertips to release the tension. Her gut said she was on the right track. In the absence of hard evidence, it was all she could rely on.

Jamie was voicing further doubts. 'I don't know if we should be putting so much faith in Samuel. Not that I'm knocking the bloke, but it feels strange to be heavily reliant on what he has to say. We're used to dealing with facts and leads, not guesswork.'

A flash of irritation went off like a firework in her head. Jamie was being deliberately obstructive. Dickson hadn't approved of the profiler either. She bet he'd asked Jamie to play up, question Samuel's every suggestion and try to confuse her judgement. If so, they could both think again. She was backing Samuel, even if he was a little odd. 'We don't have any other leads, Jamie. We can't find a shred of evidence to guide us to the perpetrator. We don't know who they'll target next. All we can do is second-guess their next move. I don't see what choice we have other than to take on board what Samuel has to offer.'

He looked her in the eye. 'You're the boss. I'll go along with whatever you decide.'

Kate folded her arms, breathed deeply through her nose to quell her annoyance. She didn't need any more obstacles in her way. The situation was serious enough, so bad it was beginning to make her feel nauseous with anxiety.

Quick footsteps pounding towards the office alerted her to Morgan's return. Samuel was with him, eyes bright, face keen. 'Morgan told me you have a theory about the killer,' he said.

'Take a seat and give me your honest opinion.' She put forward her idea that the killer was choosing popular tourist attractions.

He rubbed a hand backwards and forwards over his whiskers. 'I agree, but only in part. Blythe Bridge station is an anomaly, which means I'd need to give this further consideration before I could be one hundred per cent on board with it.'

She could see Jamie out of the corner of her eye. He lowered his head, she assumed, so she wouldn't see the I-told-you-so look on his face. Rather than dissuade her, it only served to make her determined to prove them both wrong.

'The profile you gave us is of a person who has undergone a traumatic experience and is repeating an act to rid themselves of the trauma. Might it not relate to an incident at one of these venues – an accident, a death? Something along those lines.'

'Unlikely. If that were the case, they'd stick to one location, the place where the event took place. This person is targeting innocents at a number of tourist attractions. You need to work out what significance these places hold for the killer in order to get closer to them.'

Damn! She saw the sense in what Samuel was saying.

But support for her theory came from an unlikely source. 'No. I think the guv is on to something. What if the assailant had visited these attractions at some point in the past, maybe with their spouse, loved one, or kids?' said Jamie flatly.

Samuel began to nod slowly. 'Let me weigh that up for a moment. Yes. That makes sense.' His eyes took on a faraway look. 'Yes. They could have spent happier times there with a loved one . . . or family.'

Kate didn't interrupt. It was as if he was going into a trance. He began wringing his hands slowly, as though washing them. Words tumbled from his lips. 'The loved one has gone. They've left . . . or they're dead. Something tragic has happened to them and now the perpetrator who's been left behind is upset. No. Not upset. They're *guilty*. Guilt is a more powerful emotion. A guilt-ridden person might question why they'd survived when those they loved had perished. Survivor guilt. Culpability makes them behave irrationally to try and rectify the situation. Rectify it in their minds. It is fitting that they should suffer too. They feel *responsible* for whatever took place. Consequently, they are destroying happy memories to eradicate the raw guilt. No. That's not it! It's something else.' He looked up from his monologue, eyes vacant. 'I must go. I need to work through this alone. I'll be back later.' With that, he made for the door, head lowered.

'And off he goes,' said Jamie. 'Just like that. Is he right in the head?'

Kate was as flabbergasted as her colleagues. Samuel was unlike any profiler she'd ever met before. His presentation was bizarre but, underneath the jumble of words, he had triggered something in Kate. The person he was describing was on a similar journey to her. They'd both lost somebody they cared about deeply, in terrible circumstances. She was reminded once more of the crying man, along with her notion that he had been conversing with the imagined voice of somebody he had lost. She and this man were following the same emotional trajectory. Which meant she understood what he was after. It was the same thing she was seeking – revenge.

Her pulse quickened as she considered the logic of her thoughts. It made perfect sense to her. She held Dickson partly responsible for Chris's death and had been attempting to exact retribution. The perpetrator, this crying man, could be following a similar path, seeking out whoever he considered accountable for the death of his loved one. Which, in turn, would suggest Tobias, Helen, Harriet and Asif were somehow culpable. She couldn't even fathom how. All she could count on was her instinct, which told her she had to hunt down the man at the lake. He could be their killer.

'We need to find out if the man spotted crying at the lake was anywhere near the other scenes around the times of the murders. Ask Krishna to trawl through CCTV footage again for a silver Ford Focus. Dig into the victims' pasts. See if they were involved in a tragic event, an accident, witnessed a killing, an attack, anything that might link them to the killer. Find out if anything dreadful took place at these locations: a drowning at the lake, a heart attack, an accident on the slopes. Absolutely anything where a person was seriously injured or died. I need to talk to DCI Chase.'

Armed with the list of tourist attractions, she headed to William's office to update him. He welcomed her with a smile.

'Good job earlier with the press. You handled it perfectly.'

'Thanks.'

'What can I do for you?'

'This isn't going to be easy for me to explain.'

'You want to sit down?'

She took the seat. William's office was comforting, a reminder of her father's study, where, after her mother died, she'd spent many hours curled up with a book, while he'd worked at his desk. William's desk was made of aged oak. When she'd been a junior officer, she'd once sat in this same chair and, while being read the riot act for not following procedure, had counted all the knots in it – twenty-two. Some were large and deep brown, others smaller and lighter, and on occasion she'd still run her fingertips over it, absorbing the residue of its energy. Unlike her father's, William's was tidy, a leather desk set and matching tray, a photograph of his late wife and a Caithness glass paperweight of a bee on a flower, a birthday gift from her old team to the keen apiarist.

'I know I discussed something similar with the super yesterday, but the situation has developed. We've got a clearer idea of where the perpetrator might strike next.' She passed him the list and explained her thinking.

He studied it for the longest time before placing it in front of him. 'You'll get the same response as yesterday. Superintendent Dickson won't approve this. And to be fair, it would be tricky to bring in extra support. We're ridiculously short of manpower.'

'Can't we at least try?'

'I can, but there's an anomaly here that will be jumped upon – Blythe Bridge station doesn't fit in with your theory. On top of which, your conjecture yesterday was inaccurate. There were no murders last night. I can't back speculation. To be honest, Kate, I'm surprised you are going down this route. It isn't your usual way of doing things. You've always stuck to procedure and won through.'

'William, I've never been faced with a situation like this. We have zero evidence. The strikes are random and frequent, with a likelihood of another happening this evening, and we have no witnesses. What else can I do?'

His forehead wrinkled and he tapped a finger against his chin, a gesture she was familiar with. Although she would have at one time sworn she could read William like the proverbial book, now she trod more carefully. As far as she was concerned, the jury was out on his relationship with Dickson. He might not be thick as thieves with him, yet she was damn sure he'd supported some of his actions in the past and certainly had, on occasion, allowed him to ride roughshod over her. However, he had at other times stuck up for her, notably recently. Moreover, it had been largely thanks to him that she had advanced as far as she had in this job. He had also been by her side through some of the toughest times in her life, and she couldn't forget that, no matter what he might have done. Truth be told, she would miss him more than she cared to admit when he retired.

'I won't request support. Only because I won't have you lose face if it goes wrong. You mess this up, and you'll blow any chance of a promotion. I don't want that for you. I tell you what I'll do. I'll meet you halfway. You can operate your own personal stakeout.'

'With four officers?'

'That's all I'm prepared to agree upon.' He cocked his head. 'Make it five officers. I'll join you.'

She took in the baggy-skinned neck that gave him the appearance of a tortoise and noted how old he was looking. Had her father still been alive, he might have aged similarly and, for a moment, she felt small flames of affection for the man who still backed her. 'Thank you. I'll let you know when we leave.'

She bounded back to the office. Five officers. They would have to choose their locations wisely.

CHAPTER SEVENTEEN

The team had decamped to the briefing room, chairs repositioned to face Kate, who stood behind a plinth. Using an iPad, she pulled up the list of the most popular attractions in Stoke-on-Trent, which appeared on the screen behind her.

'So far, we haven't found anything to suggest the victims witnessed or were involved in any accidents or tragic events. We're going to have to take a leap of faith and attempt to cover as many tourist attractions as possible, in the hope the perpetrator will show up this evening. As you can see from the list behind me, they have already targeted three of the top five locations. Trentham Monkey Park, Trentham Gardens and Trentham Shopping Village are listed as separate attractions. Please feel free to disagree with me but my feeling is, because they have already struck on the Trentham Estate, they're unlikely to return there. The Ski Centre is the eleventh most popular attraction, which leads me to believe all of the top twenty should be considered.' William, directly opposite her, gave an encouraging nod.

'Samuel believes the timing of the attacks is important and, to date, the killer appears to be striking after quarter to six. Because of our limited numbers we could rule out those attractions shutting their doors at four.'

Morgan raised a hand. 'Can I point out the shops at Trentham shut at four.'

'The garden centre was open until six, and the Premier Inn later still. I don't think the perpetrator was waiting for somebody who'd been shopping at the village per se, only somebody on the Trentham Estate. I think for the purposes of identifying potential areas of attack tonight, we'll have to discount those places that close early, where there will be fewer people to target. Agreed?'

There were nods and mumbles of accord.

'As for the Regent Theatre, there are currently no productions, therefore insufficient people for the killer to target. I propose we strike it from the list. That brings us on to Stoke-on-Trent railway station, which is a contender.' The list behind her scrolled down to the station, which became highlighted.

William cleared his throat. 'They have already killed at a railway station. And one that isn't on the list. If we apply the same logic to the stations as we just have with Trentham Estate, then I think the chances of them killing at another station are low.'

'I disagree with the DCI,' said Morgan. 'If the killer is hunting for targets, there's a lot of footfall at Stoke station and potential to attack somebody. It would be my choice if I were selecting places from this list.'

Kate rested her hands on the plinth. 'We must narrow this list down, folks. If we keep a watch on the station, we'll have to leave off another potential attraction. I have a question mark over Waterworld because it's close to the ski centre; I don't imagine the assailant will return to the same area tonight, especially as officers are still at the scene. This leaves us with three parks, Longton, Biddulph Grange Garden and Burslem.'

'Burslem Park is open twenty-four hours a day,' said Jamie. 'It's huge, about nine hectares, I think, and it has two pedestrian access points. One person couldn't possibly cover the whole area.'

'Well, with the exception of Blythe Bridge, the other executions have taken place close to or in a car park. I would hazard the perpetrator will continue following the same pattern, which would mean us covering car parks only. They seem to wait for their victims to emerge from the attraction rather than seeking them out inside. Unless they change their MO, of course.'

'Just an observation, but Biddulph Grange Garden closes at four thirty and it's owned by the National Trust. There are likely to be stricter entrance and exit controls, which might put off the perp,' said Emma.

'Okay. We'll cross that off the list. There haven't been any attacks at a museum and there's one on this list remaining open until five – the Potteries Museum and Art Gallery. What do we think?'

'It should be covered,' said Emma. 'There's a public car park opposite the museum. And, as you say, most of the killings have taken place in car parks.'

The discussion continued until Kate drew the altered list on to the screen. Those to be covered were now all highlighted. 'I suggest the following: Jamie, you stake out Burslem Park. William, Longton Park. Emma, you take the museum, Morgan, the station, and I'll go to the stadium. I don't think we can do a lot more, given our resources. Make sure you stay in your positions until at least seven o'clock, remain in contact, and report any suspicious activity. Keep an eye out for a silver Ford Focus like the one spotted at Westport Lake. Any questions?'

Jamie raised his head. 'Yes. Wasn't Samuel supposed to be coming back with some more thoughts on the killer?'

'I don't know where he is,' said Kate. 'I'm sure he'll appear in due course.' She turned off the iPad and dismissed the team. She was glad Samuel wasn't one of her officers. He was too unreliable.

Emma slumped as low as possible in her car seat, knees pressed against the steering wheel. The discomfort didn't trouble her. She wanted to capture this sick bastard so badly it almost burned a hole in her chest. He had destroyed lives, taken loved ones, left children bereft. He'd given no thought to those left behind, people who would forever be haunted by the memories of how their loved ones had died. They would live and relive those horrible moments, much like she did.

She shut her eyes, replayed the memory of a young, uncomprehending Emma tugging at the plastic bag until it pulled from her mother's wide-eyed face, sucking the loose skin as it came free in her hands. The scene played out, Emma trying to shake her mother awake, stroking her face, pleading with her to come round. All the while, her stepfather cried and cowered on the floor by the bed. Some things could never be forgotten.

She was glad she was no longer driving Greg's flashy motor. She preferred the anonymity of her Citroën, now stationed at the far side of the car park, away from the dozen cars scattered in various bays. From here, she had a good view of the vehicles, the car park entrance and the museum and art gallery. There was no sign of a silver Ford Focus, but should one come into view she'd be after it in a flash.

Kelly Clarkson's 'Stronger (What Doesn't Kill You)' was playing from a compilation Emma had put together and called her Angry List, containing uplifting songs to help her through the tough days. Today was one of those. She didn't mind that Samuel had cancelled their date. There'd been plenty of times her work had got in the way of her social life. She wasn't bothered that he hadn't rearranged it. What was irksome was his sudden weird attitude. One minute behaving normally, the next trance-like and vacant. The episode at the ski centre had clinched it for her. He'd behaved bizarrely and, if she was honest, she'd been a little alarmed by it. It was probably a good thing they hadn't met up for a drink after all. She didn't need any Jekyll and Hyde characters in her life. She'd moved on from those.

She absent-mindedly felt for the chain she wore under her blouse. Her fingers ran lightly over the delicate metal, gently embracing the links that made up the rope chain. It had belonged to her mother. On her death, as the only girl in the family, she'd been given it. It had been left in a drawer for years until recently, when she'd decided it was time to grow up and face up to what had occurred without bitterness and blame. Her mother's death had been a heartbreaking, sick accident. Her stepfather had paid the price for accidental manslaughter. In wearing the chain, she hoped to rekindle those earlier memories of her mum, before her father passed away and before her stepfather appeared on the scene. Most of all, she wanted to banish that last horrific image of her mother's lifeless body.

The music changed and No Doubt's 'Just a Girl' began playing.

Emma hummed along, eyes scanning for any signs of activity. A man in a long coat came into view, ambling down the road. He was middle-aged and dark-haired. She sank even lower as he entered the car park, making in her direction. His lips were moving, and icy fingers clawed their way up Emma's neck. He stopped only a hundred metres from her car, facing her as he talked. She turned down the music in case any of his words would reach her, but his voice was too soft. The Peugeot's indicator lights flashed as the car unlocked and he reached for the door handle. He got inside. When the engine didn't start immediately, Emma toyed with the possibility he was either on the phone or gearing himself up for another murder. As the car spluttered into life, exhaust rattling like pebbles in a tin can, she decided there was somebody who owned a car in worse condition than her own. She turned up her music and resumed her watch.

There was little movement. A few passers-by: a couple of kids in hooded tops and low-slung jeans slouched along the pavement, heads lowered over mobiles; a middle-aged couple emerged from the museum, each carrying a gift bag; individuals made for their vehicles and drove away. The street and pavement became deserted, leaving Emma only to contemplate the flat-roofed building in various shades of drab grey and beige and wonder if the same architects who designed these buildings furnished their own in such dreary colours.

More people strolled by. One of them, a man in dark clothing, halted by the wall, hands in pockets. She stopped humming. The witness on the train to Blythe Bridge had seen the man in the high-vis vest standing, fumbling in his pockets before the attack. The man lowered his head. Emma strained to see what he was doing until he drew a cigarette from a packet and lit it. He sucked on it a couple of times. Wisps of grey smoke rose in front of his face before evaporating above him. Then, jamming the packet back into his pocket, he moved on once more. Emma released the breath she'd unconsciously been holding.

Her digital display revealed the time was 5.40. The killer would surely be in position by now, waiting for a target. She couldn't spy anyone acting suspiciously. More tracks from her list played. Judging by the radio silence, the others were having as much luck as her. She considered leaving the car to stretch her legs and take a look around, check the other side of the museum. Then she spied movement as a tall figure appeared between the trees lining the pavement. She caught sight of him again. Dark clothing, head lowered. It was only when he drew level with the car park and looked directly at her car that her breath caught in her throat. *No!*

Samuel paced towards her, making directly for the passenger door, where he tapped on the window and smiled. 'Okay to come in?'

255

She waved him inside and he scrambled in quickly, bringing his shower-fresh scent with him. 'This is a nice surprise.'

'Samuel, what are you doing here?'

He gave her a puzzled look. 'What's the problem?'

'I'm on police business.'

'Here? Alone?'

She didn't reply. That he had turned up here made her nervous.

'Oh, I get it. You're hoping to trap the killer, aren't you? Are the others here too?' He glanced around. 'I can't see their cars.'

She turned on him. 'Why are you here?'

'I spotted your car, saw you in it and came to say hello. I felt bad about last night and I haven't really spoken to you about it, or rearranged our date.'

'Not why you're in my car. Why are you here? On this street.'

He grinned. 'Oh, sorry. Work.'

'I thought you worked on the other side of town.'

'Er, I do, but I also have to go out and about at times. I was at the YMCA a couple of streets away. I'm parked here.' He pointed out a black Vauxhall Corsa. 'A young offender I've been working with is staying there. I had to meet with them.'

'Why?'

The amiable grin vanished. 'That isn't any of your business. And why the sub-zero tone?'

'I'm busy, so if you don't like my tone you can jog on.'

He didn't move. His eyes sparked and the grin was back. 'Oh, I get it. You're on the lookout for the killer, see me and put two and two together to make five. Emma, I've nothing to do with the murders.' He held up his hands. 'Go on, frisk me. See if I'm carrying a weapon.'

'Shut up and get out.'

'You're pissed off with me about last night, aren't you? Listen, Kate wanted to speak to me urgently and I had to let you down. I didn't want to.'

'I don't give a shit about last night.'

'Sure you do. You've been let down by lots of people in the past. I see it in your eyes and the way you conduct yourself. You're feisty, bright and gorgeous, but you keep people at arm's length.'

'You know fuck all about me.'

'I know you're a damaged soul, Emma.'

She glared at him, caught the look of deep understanding in his eyes. He put a hand on her arm, halting her angry retort.

'Let me in. Let me help you.'

Jamie's voice came in through her earpiece. 'It's gone six and there's fuck all going on here. I've only seen one jogger all evening and a sodding dog has pissed over my front tyre.'

'I've got work to do,' she said.

'Then I'll stay with you,' Samuel said. 'Two heads, and all that.'

'I don't need a partner. I've got this. Clear off.'

◆　◆　◆

At the Bet365 Stadium, Kate had chosen to wait at car park West 1, which afforded her a view of the ticket office and club store. Although there were twenty cars scattered over the three car parks, she assumed that unless a private tour of the stadium was taking place, they belonged to staff. Although there was a red Ford Focus in sight, there wasn't a silver one and she wondered if she was barking up the wrong tree again in her quest to find it.

There was a dead-end road leading to the stadium, with no traffic on it. She'd passed several car dealerships along the way and, as she waited, she wondered if the killer might not target one of those instead. There was nobody in sight here, although she caught the occasional glimpse of movement inside the store.

The prospect of somebody else dying on her watch was intolerable. She was failing in her duty as a police officer. If Chris were here, he would contradict her, tell her she was doing what she could in the circumstances and that she couldn't save the world. As it was, she had only self-doubts and a gnawing in her stomach intensified by the knowledge that she hadn't found Rosa in time and that every opportunity to bring down Dickson had been lost. Bradley hadn't been in touch either. Although she knew he had other obligations, she couldn't help but feel frustrated. Should she call him, or would he take umbrage at being hassled?

In the end frustration won out. 'Hi. I hope I'm not disturbing you?'

'I've literally walked in from a driving lesson. I intended calling you today.'

'You have news?'

'We looked for your package in the Burnley depot and were redirected to Lancaster.'

Farai had done another bunk. It was inevitable.

'Are you able to send anyone to Lancaster to pick it up?'

'We're not sure what depot it might be in; however, we're headed up there tomorrow.'

'Thank you.'

'We'll update you, should we locate it.'

'I appreciate that.'

Bradley was doing what he could. It would have to do for now. She ended the call and turned her attention to a blue VW Tiguan, the driver invisible behind a heavily tinted windscreen. It turned into the same parking zone as her and drew up beside a pickup truck which obscured it from her sight. Nobody emerged.

Tempting as it was to accost the driver and demand to know what they were doing here, she couldn't. She'd only act if somebody came out of the stadium. Nothing happened. The doors to the stadium remained shut. The VW Tiguan remained in its bay. Jamie's voice interrupted the silence, and she half smiled at his complaint about a dog urinating on one of his tyres.

The store lights extinguished. A woman emerged and came to a halt on the pavement, where she rummaged in her bag. Kate rested her hand on the door handle, ready to act should a man appear. She craned her neck in search of somebody on foot and was taken by surprise when the Tiguan shot out of its space towards the store, where it drew to a halt. Kate bounded out, racing towards the vehicle with no thought other than saving the woman. She reached the pavement and car in time to see the woman's foot disappearing into the footwell. Both passenger and driver turned surprised faces. Only then did Kate realise she'd misread the situation. The thin-faced man in the tracksuit had only come to pick up the woman from work.

◆ ◆ ◆

'Mummy, can I go and look for some chewy sweets for the plane journey?' Grace had put on her pleading voice.

'Honey, we can get some at the airport.'

'But what if they don't have the kind I like, the little chewy bears? You promised I could have some of those to stop my ears popping when we take off.'

'I want some too,' said Archie.

'You don't mind if the kids go in and grab some sweets do you, while you fill up?'

'We're running tight, Rowena. If we get held up on the motorway—'

'*You're such a worrywart. It'll take you ages to fill up this old bus. I'll hustle them along. We'll be as long as it takes for you to refuel. Come on, kids.*'

The memory played out. Ben stared at the petrol station's glass windows, lit by the interior light. From here, in the parking bay, he could see who was inside the store. A man was by the magazine rack, another paying at the till. The last time he had been here, he'd watched Archie and Gracie emerge with beaming faces, waving family-sized bags of sweets. Tears dried on his cheeks. The pain never left him.

'If only we had left sooner.'

'Providence decided otherwise,' said Lisa.

He watched as a lorry driver emerged, a bottle of orange juice in one hand and a bag of crisps in the other. It was this man's lucky night. It wasn't time yet. He wouldn't begin his search for a victim until the digital display clicked on to 17.45, then it would be time to let fate decide.

CHAPTER EIGHTEEN

The exercise had been futile. Not one of the team had spotted any suspicious activity. Morgan had suggested it was because the killer had seen them first and abandoned their plans, but Kate knew he was only being upbeat to cheer her sour mood. After the debrief she'd sent the team home, apologised to William, who'd told her she'd done the right thing. He didn't say what they were both thinking, that it had been a wise decision not to involve extra staff or bring the stakeout to Dickson's attention.

She checked the bird feeder and carefully removed the USB stick, then took it and a glass of orange juice with her into Chris's study, where she slumped on to his chair and stared at the wall. The investigation was going badly. She was screwing things up, left, right and centre. She'd fucked up the whole Dickson fiasco. And because of that, Rosa had been killed and Tom Champion was most likely dead too. To boot, she was under the spotlight because she'd put herself forward for a promotion she wouldn't get.

She hadn't a clue which way to turn. Even if Bradley located Farai or Stanka, what good would they be to her? And then there was this mind-fuck of an investigation. Her last call had been way off. William had warned her not to work on supposition. Look where it had got them – nowhere!

She yanked out the drawer and grabbed the stress ball, squeezing it repeatedly until her hand ached. Police work, checking facts, going back over statements, footage. It would take forever to track down this perpetrator and how many would die before they slipped up, or her team got a breakthrough? Weeks? Months? Longer? She squeezed the ball one last time. Like it or not, it was how she was going to have to play it.

'Any bright ideas?' She took a drink from the orange juice, then set the glass back down with a thump. 'Clearly you haven't, because you're in a funk with me and won't answer me. You should try swapping places. It's so fucking hard to keep up appearances, do a good job and at the same time work out how to trip up Dickson. I'm exhausted, Chris.'

Her sharp words and frustration were due to the mess she was making of everything rather than the fact that she was unable to communicate with Chris.

'Are you ignoring me because I'm screwing up everywhere? You'd be right. I have made a monumental cock-up of how I've gone about bringing down Dickson. Now I'm going to do what I can to rectify that, even if it's too little too late.'

She sighed, then switched on the computer and logged on to Chris's email account. Dan had been true to his word. There was enough information which, when added to her narrative, would build a picture that would incriminate Dickson. She typed furiously, providing as much information as she could about the night the boy was murdered. This, together with a secret recording she'd made of a conversation with the youngster's pimp, would go some way to helping Dan write a damning article. She transferred all the information on to the stick before deleting it from the computer.

She waved the stick in the air. 'Further proof of Dickson's corruption. It's not enough, though. I really could do with your help, not all this silence. After all, I am trying to find out who was also responsible for *your* death. So, could you stop sulking and help me mull over some ideas?' When no answer came, she swore. Bullying tactics didn't work any better than pleas. She was on her own.

She would have remained in the study, puzzling over how best to track down Rosa's friend, Stanka, had her mobile not rung and taken her mind completely off the subject.

◆ ◆ ◆

Kate blinked her way through strobing blue lights. She ducked under the cordon strung across the brightly lit forecourt and walked to the far end of it, where a car was parked in the shadows, away from the pumps. A whiff of gasoline carried in the night air; the residue dripped from careless motorists' pumps. Morgan was already in situ and, catching sight of his grave face, she was unable to think of a single thing to say. Her chest rose and fell, her inbreath jagged. How could she have called this so badly?

The petrol station beside the M6 motorway didn't fall into the category of popular tourist attractions, nor was it situated approximately twelve to thirteen kilometres away from the location of the last murder. Kate had failed to identify any pattern, merely sent her officers on a wild-goose chase. While they'd all been sat in warm vehicles, pointlessly watching parks, museums and stadiums, fifty-eight-year-old Susanna Lopez had been murdered.

Kate edged closer, stuffed her hands into her pockets. The victim's head was lowered over her chest, cropped hair the colour of a frosty morning all that was visible. Her upper body, clad in a black dental tunic piped in pink, rested against the side of the Mercedes door, legs in boot-cut trousers and white clogs stuck out in front of her, one hand still clasping a takeaway cup.

'She runs a dental practice in the centre of town,' said Morgan. 'Lives in Sandbach. Dressed like that, I expect she was on her way home. She was found by a customer. The shop assistant remembers serving her at around seven. She only came in for flowers, coffee and a magazine. She seemed in a hurry, a bit jittery. She put in her PIN and got it wrong the first time, apologised and said it had been a long day. Because she wasn't parked beside a pump, the assistant didn't have a visual on her car and had no idea she hadn't left. As you can see, it's out of sight from the shop. The only surveillance camera is positioned over the front door.'

'Better check footage to see who went in before her. What time was the body found?'

'Not until twenty-five past seven. The assistant confirmed the busiest spell is between five thirty to six thirty, after that it falls off.'

'It was probably too busy for our perpetrator to act before then, without the risk of being spotted. They must have lain in wait, possibly even around this very spot where the victim parked. It's dark enough here to hang about without creating too much suspicion. People don't stay here long enough to wonder why somebody else is waiting.' Kate walked to the other side of the Mercedes and peered through the passenger window, where she spied a bunch of flowers on the seat and a magazine, *Animals and You*. 'She put her purchases into the car before she was killed. The killer must have been watching her from nearby. That looks like a children's magazine. She hasn't got kids, has she?'

'She's got a thirty-year-old son who lives in Manchester.'

'Married?'

'Yes.'

'Who's breaking the news to the husband?'

'Family Liaison. Rich is on it.'

Kate returned to the victim's side of the car and turned, trying to calculate where the shooter would have come from. Cars were parked around the station, some by the air pump, others close to the drive-through carwash. There were also spaces for those customers who only wanted to use the cashpoint or pick up shopping.

The killer could easily have hidden in plain sight. There was only one course of action open to Kate. They still hadn't identified the sobbing man and she was going to follow her gut on this.

'Pull the CCTV footage from this place and from every camera in the vicinity. Ask the tech team to hunt for a silver Ford Focus from five forty-five to seven twenty-five.'

'Sure. Do you want appeal notices to go up?'

She stood grounded to the spot, hands back in her pockets, fists clenching and unclenching as she spoke. 'Yes. And if there's any possibility of locating drivers who came through the station between those hours, I want them interviewed to find out if they saw any such vehicle.'

She walked off, mind tumbling over the facts. She'd been sure the killer was targeting tourist spots but now two locations didn't fit her theory: Blythe Bridge station and the petrol station next to the M6 motorway. Moreover, they'd found nothing to connect the victims to any incident. It would appear Samuel was right when he said the perpetrator was selecting targets at random. And not only targets; they were choosing locations at whim. She would never be able to outmanoeuvre somebody who had no strategy. The answer to this lay somewhere. A person didn't get up one morning and start killing off others at the rate of nearly one a day, at around the same time each day, without good reason. The only option left to her was to go back to the station, comb through everything they'd unearthed up to this point and try to look at it with fresh eyes.

'Kate!'

Emma was crossing towards her.

'Morgan will fill you in on the details,' said Kate. 'I'll meet you back at the station.'

'There's something I ought to tell you. I should have said some-thing earlier, but the idea was so ridiculous—'

'Go on.'

'I saw Samuel. Or rather, he saw me staking out the museum and art gallery. He got in my car. I challenged him about why he was there, and he gave a legitimate reason – he'd been to visit an ex-offender at the YMCA.'

'Emma! You should have told me, or at least brought it up at the debrief. What were you thinking?'

'I know. I . . . My head's not been in the right place. It's not an excuse. I've been struggling. You know. My mother. I shouldn't have let it get to me. It's just that it seemed such a mad idea that Samuel might be the killer. He doesn't fit the profile.'

'No, not the profile *he* gave us.' Kate stared hard at her junior. Emma never made bad judgement calls. Worse still, this might have been a costly one.

Emma pressed fingers against her temples and groaned. 'I didn't suspect him. He explained why he was there. It made sense at the time. It was only later when I thought about how weirdly he behaved at the ski centre, and again in the office, muttering and then taking off unexpectedly and not coming back, that I started to wonder if he could be the perp. Kate, I'm really sorry. I've fucked up, haven't I?'

Kate sighed. Emma's track record was impeccable. This was a bad mistake. Speaking up beforehand might have saved Susanna. However, Emma wasn't the only one to have made errors. Morgan had cocked up when he forgot to ring Hanley station and Kate had made the biggest blunders of all. 'No. You haven't. There's time to sort this. Chances are he has nothing to do with it and is no more than eccentric. We can't suspect him solely on that basis. We'd need stronger evidence. Don't get into a stew over this. It's highly unlikely Samuel had anything to do with it. Check with the YMCA first to put your mind at rest.'

Emma lifted her face to the night sky before looking Kate in the eye. 'That's why I'm telling you about him. I rang the

YMCA a few minutes ago. They haven't heard of Samuel, let alone seen him.'

Kate took a step back. 'Oh, no! No!'

Emma's face was pure concern. 'I should have told you sooner.'

Kate shook her head. What was done was done. It was how they handled it that mattered. 'Let's think about this logically. What time did you last see him?'

'Just after six. He left a minute or two after Jamie made that crack about the dog peeing up his tyre. It's only a ten-minute drive from there to here.'

Shit! Had the killer been under their noses all the time?

'What car was he driving?'

'A black Vauxhall Corsa.'

'Registration?'

Emma reeled it off.

'Speak to the tech team about this. Ask them to hunt for it.'

'I'm sorry, Kate.'

'Forget it. Make sure you check every detail. He's a potential suspect until we determine otherwise.'

Her Audi turned over with a low grumble, mirroring how she felt. If Samuel was their perpetrator, Dickson would have a field day. Even if he wasn't, there was every chance, now there'd been another victim, that Dickson would insist on the investigation being handed over to a bigger team, led by another DI. Either way, her reputation would be tarnished. She took off, lips pressed so tightly together they throbbed.

◆ ◆ ◆

Back in the office, she took a call from Emma.

'The car Samuel was driving belongs to a university colleague who isn't answering their phone. I've left a message for them.

It doesn't show up on any CCTV footage at the petrol station. Nobody we've spoken to recalls seeing a black Vauxhall Corsa, or a silver Ford Focus for that matter. Felicity's been helpful and put somebody straight on to hunting for signs of either car.'

'There's not a lot else we can do for the time being, other than question Samuel.' Kate weighed up the options: question him and risk upsetting him, or wait until they were more certain he was their perp.

'Want me to do that?'

'Let me do some digging on his background first.'

'All right. We're almost done here.'

Kate delved into Samuel's employment records, noting he had taken several months off for 'personal reasons' in 2018. She wondered what reasons they might have been – a death, perhaps? While she had come across all sorts of unlikely perpetrators in her career, she struggled to believe the goofy academic was responsible for the deaths they'd been investigating. The way he had spoken to her about loss and grief, the empathy she had experienced, didn't equate with somebody who would then shoot an innocent in cold blood. Her mind see-sawed between the facts. Samuel had also told them the killer was humane. Could he be that person? Her gut rarely let her down. That said, she had been way off once before. She'd befriended a killer, believing them to be nothing more than a work colleague. She lifted her mobile. She wouldn't repeat past errors of judgement. Until they determined otherwise, Samuel had made himself a suspect. She rang his number. There was no reply. Samuel, like his friend whose car he'd borrowed, wasn't answering his phone.

Ben's head is pounding. His tongue feels like it's licked an ashpan clean.

He dry-retches over the toilet basin.

That was the worst killing so far. He would have been focused, had he thought of the children. He hadn't been able to shake the memory of their laughter as they ran back to the car.

He blinks away the look of utter horror in the woman's eyes as he stood in front of her. He shouldn't have made eye contact with her. He shouldn't have seen her lips plead with him. He should have stuck to the task.

He heaves again, wipes the dribble of yellow bile from his mouth, and staggers to his feet.

Lisa has told him what he is to do next. There will be no getting out of it.

Even before he leaves the bathroom, he knows what will happen tonight.

They will all talk to him.

Kate rubbed her gritty eyes, and then stretched, catching the sour smell from under her armpits as she did so. She'd sent the others home shortly after midnight. She would have gone too, had she not been determined to plough through old investigations in the hope they would somehow link to her current one. The idea that the perpetrator was seeking revenge for the death of a loved one had burrowed into her mind. What troubled her about her theory was the random choice of victims with seemingly nothing connecting them. Her hunch they might all have been involved in one tragic incident was looking as weak as her theory that the perpetrator was targeting popular tourist attractions. For the first time in her career, she was floundering.

She mollified herself with the knowledge that there were still people who'd been at the petrol station they could interview when daylight came. She ought to turn in for an hour or two. Instead, she shut her eyes to rest them for ten minutes.

Her mobile ringtone brought her to.

It was Krishna.

'I might have found your Ford Focus.'

All fatigue vanished.

'I'll be with you in a sec.'

She charged down the corridor and out into the night, making the short walk to the technical building, where Krishna was already at the door. He beckoned her in, back into warmth, and took her through to the room where he'd been working alone. It was the opposite of the chaos she'd left behind. Clean, tidy and smelling of oranges, with only a high-energy drink can and a bag of caramels on the table near the computer screen. He dived into the bag, pulled one out.

'Fancy one?'

'I'm good, thanks.'

'I need the sugar to keep going,' he said. The screen was divided into two. On the left was a grainy image of a silver Ford Focus driving along a narrow street; on the right, a clearer picture of the rear of a similar car.

Krishna wriggled into position, sweat between his fingers.

'This image was captured on Tuesday evening at seven minutes past six, taken by a surveillance camera at a packaging company on Brammell Drive, which is only a six-minute walk from Blythe Bridge station.' She peered at the picture, trying hard to establish if the driver bore any resemblance to Samuel. It was too indistinct to make out who it might be, but she was sure the driver was shorter than Samuel.

'Go on.'

'The second image is also from a private surveillance camera, at a construction company on Festival Way, taken on Monday at six twenty. The building is a seven-minute walk from Stoke Ski Centre.'

'It looks like the perpetrator parks up and walks to the location where they select victims.'

'It would seem that way.'

'Apart from Westport Lake, when the car was spotted by a witness.'

'I've no idea why that would be the case.'

Kate couldn't explain the anomaly either. 'Can you get a registration for the vehicle?'

'I've struggled with that. The first image becomes too pixelated when I run it through our software. The car is at the wrong angle to make out the number plate or the driver. When I ran the second image through, I got a partial number plate and identified what used to be called local memory tags – the first two letters of the plate, denoting where the car was first registered. This one, BD 19, was registered in Birmingham in March 2019.'

There was every chance that by working their way through every silver Ford Focus on the database they could pinpoint who it belonged to.

'Is there no way we can get a clearer image of the driver?'

'Sadly not. I'm trying a new software to enhance the pictures and if I have any luck with it, I'll let you know.'

'Good work, Krishna.'

He unwrapped his sweet, popped it into his mouth, his cheek bulging immediately. 'You're welcome.'

Reinvigorated by the news, she headed back to the office and began searching for the vehicle. At last, they were one step closer.

CHAPTER NINETEEN

DAY SIX – SUNDAY

Emma arrived first, to find Kate asleep, head on her desk. She shook her gently. She woke, blinking. 'Shit. Must have dozed off. What time is it?'

'Ten to eight.'

'I'll freshen up.'

'Want me to grab you a coffee?'

'It's okay. I'll nip out and get one. I could do with some fresh air. By the way, we've made progress and I don't think we need to worry about Samuel being our perpetrator. A silver Ford Focus has appeared close to the crime scenes.' It was an enormous weight off her mind to know she hadn't misjudged someone she worked with again to such a huge extent. Relief wiped across Emma's features.

'Oh, thank goodness.'

'Yes, I felt the same way. We're going to concentrate on the Ford.' She brought Emma up to speed. 'There's an extremely lengthy list of Ford Focus cars beginning with BD. We're picking out all the silver ones and trying to match them with owners who live locally. Could you pick up where I left off?'

'Sure.'

Downstairs she washed and changed into fresh underwear and a blouse and applied make-up to mask her sickly pallor. At least she had something to appease Dickson with, should he start making a fuss about their lack of progress, and the team had plenty of follow-ups to handle in the coming hours. The breakthrough had been the tonic she needed. She might feel jaded but she also felt more positive. If only she could make strides in her quest to nail Dickson.

Small daffodils on the patch of grass outside the station gave her further optimism. The coffee house was a two-minute walk, long enough for her to gather her thoughts. She'd been floundering, but no more. Her phone rang and, thinking it might be Emma, she answered without checking the caller ID. It was Samuel.

Samuel sounded drugged up, his voice ponderous and slow. 'The person you are looking for is local and harbouring enormous remorse. They've lost somebody close to them, somebody who they converse with, who they listen to, and who is manipulating their actions. This individual has become deluded. They believe they must strike repeatedly to banish the guilt they are suffering. They're not out for revenge. Each killing is quick and humane, hence the use of the captive bolt pistol. The perpetrator wants the execution to be over with quickly. To that end, they surprise their victims, dispatch them and don't torture them. In my opinion, they're highly disturbed and incapable of rational thought. If the perpetrator is the crying man, his behaviour suggests he knows that what he's doing is wrong, yet he is powerless to stop. That's all I can tell you for now.'

'Thank you. It's very useful.'

His words unsettled her. She understood what was making the killer tick. Moreover, she was on a similar path. Except it was anger, not guilt, that had her gunning for Dickson. And Chris had been her voice of reason, not destructive. If Chris had been like that, would she have listened to him and obeyed his instructions? The answer was: possibly yes. She'd have done anything to maintain that bizarre connection she had with him. Even now, she was still doing

273

what she could for his imagined voice to return. Whereas their perpetrator was being manipulated by a vengeful loved one, Chris had become the opposite, Kate's conscience, disapproving rather than supportive of her actions. *That* was the reason he had fallen silent! The answer was clear now. Chris disapproved.

She dragged herself back to the here and now. Up until the discovery of the Ford Focus, Samuel had been a suspect.

'Samuel, why did you lie to Emma and tell her you were with a young offender at the YMCA when you weren't?'

'She was about to make the illogical assumption that I was the killer. I needed to tell her something credible that would assuage her fears.'

'Yet you didn't tell her the truth.'

'I felt my version was more plausible than the real reason I was there.'

'Which was?'

'I was checking out some of the attractions the assailant might have visited, trying to get inside their head. It's how I operate, Kate. I have to think like them and *become* the killer. I get into their mindset, see the streets and opportunities through their eyes. It's . . . effective but difficult. Not everyone understands my methods. It sounds random, weird, and even a little scary, but it seems to work. I've had several successes.'

'And you happened to be at the museum on Saturday?'

'I could equally have been at any of the main tourist hotspots. I was testing out your theory, Kate, that the perpetrator was targeting victims at tourist hotspots. I was trying to give you something to go on. I didn't expect your team to be staking them all out.'

She didn't reply. It seemed too mumbo jumbo for her and at the same time also conceivable, especially considering what Emma had told her about his behaviour at the ski centre. Samuel was an oddball. If they weren't searching for the Ford Focus driver, she might have been more inclined to quiz him further. As it was, she gave him the benefit of the doubt – for the moment.

◆ ◆ ◆

By the time she returned, revitalised by a brisk walk, warm coffee and an energy bar, the office was buzzing. Phone calls were being made and there was an air of productivity. It gave Kate further optimism that they'd crack the case.

Having handed over the task of trawling through the list of silver Ford Focus cars to Emma, she used the extra time to work out her next move. Samuel's words reverberated through her skull. He'd said the killer was trying to banish guilt. That this wasn't about revenge. She wasn't the same as this person. She didn't feel any guilt about Chris's death. She only wanted revenge. The words turned over in her mind and a quiet voice questioned her. Was she not feeling some guilt for being unable to give Chris the justice he deserved? The answer was yes. In her situation, guilt and revenge were intermingled. Whether that held true for the killer was another matter.

She shut her eyes to enable her to give more clarity to her deliberations until she thought she understood the killer's motives. For her, the trigger had been Chris's brutal murder. Had he passed away from illness or an accident, she was sure she wouldn't have reacted in the same way to his death. This person must have experienced something similar. Motivated by this, she decided to hunt through historical investigations in the hope they would unearth something. Maybe there had been a stabbing or shooting in recent months during which somebody had died, and their perpetrator was avenging that person. It was an hour later before she surfaced from staring at the screen, eyes already bleary. Jamie was by her side, notepad in hand.

'One of the petrol-station customers believes he saw a silver Ford Focus parked up in one of the bays. Said there was a man sitting in it but he didn't give him a second look. This was at ten to six.'

'If that's the killer, he waited over an hour before he attacked Susanna. Someone else must have seen the car too.'

Another twenty minutes passed, and Morgan struck lucky. 'We've got another sighting of the Ford Focus, parked in the furthest bay from the pumps. The witness didn't get a good look at the driver because the interior lights weren't on, but said it was a man, with his seat reclined. She figured he was waiting for somebody to come out of the shop. She clocked the registration too. She noticed it when her headlights fell on it. Apparently the last three letters were the same as her son's initials. I gave it to—'

'Found it!' shouted Emma. 'The registered owner is Mrs Charlene Leith, lives in Scarratt Drive, Forsbrook.'

'Where's that?' asked Kate.

Emma came back with the answer. 'Right by Blythe Bridge.'

'Whoa! This woman lives near Blythe Bridge railway station?' said Jamie.

'According to the map, less than a mile away.'

'That can't be a coincidence, can it?' said Jamie.

'No way,' Emma replied, reaching for her car keys and jangling them. 'Who do I take with me, Kate?'

Kate was going to tell Morgan to accompany her then changed her mind. She'd go with Emma. 'See what you can find out about Mrs Leith and update us en route, Jamie.'

Jamie, who'd been pulling at his bottom lip, said, 'Judging by what our witnesses told us, we're looking for a man, not a woman.'

'Let us know if there are any other named drivers on her insurance.'

Kate was out of the door and halfway down the stairs when she heard William call her name. She ignored him and raced on. She'd deal with whatever he wanted later. For now, they had the first important lead in this investigation and she wasn't stopping for anyone.

In the car she told Emma about what Samuel had had to say regarding his whereabouts the day before when he'd met her in the car park.

'And you believed him?' said Emma.

'I believe he would do something as bizarre as walking the walk of the killer.'

Emma kept her eyes on the road ahead. 'Yeah. I can see him doing that. Unless he's related to Mrs Leith, I suppose we'll have to take him at his word. I really don't know what to make of him.'

They left the city centre via the longer but quicker route, the Queensway, skirting around the city centre back to where the investigation had begun.

Emma spoke quietly. 'It's the anniversary of my mum's death today.'

'Today? How long has she been gone?'

'Ten years. I guess that's why it's been tougher than usual. Ten years seems such a long time.'

'Do you need some time off to visit her grave, or spend time with your brothers?'

'I'll go later, after we've got somewhere with the Ford Focus. She won't mind.'

Silence fell again until Kate spoke. 'You miss her?'

'In some ways, I miss my gran more. She gave me what my mum couldn't. But there's a large part of me that wishes Mum was still alive. After my stepfather moved in, we lost our mother–daughter connection. I believe, in time, we would have got it back. What hurts most is we never got that opportunity. I feel like I lost her twice. The first time, when she chose my stepfather over me, and then when she died.'

'I'm sorry, Emma. That's tough.'

'And knowing Helen Doherty's children will go through life without their mum got to me.'

'You should have told me. You could have taken time out from this, or I could have assigned you different duties, not thrown you into the thick of things by asking you to video the crime scene.'

'No. I'm better off working. Don't even consider it.'

Kate's mobile interrupted the conversation. She put it on speakerphone and said, 'Jamie, what do you have for us?'

'Charlene Leith is forty-five and widowed. Her husband died two years ago. I haven't any details about how he died yet. She works at a building society in Stoke. There are no penalties on her driving licence, and nothing has red-flagged on the database. But get this, she has two children, and one of them, Reece, has been in a young offenders' institute since 2017. He was released only a couple of months ago.'

'What was he convicted of?'

'Accessory to robbery with violence. I'll see what else I can find out.'

'Good job, Jamie.'

'Thanks, guv.'

'That's interesting. A car that matches our description and a lad with form.'

Emma spoke without facing her. 'Samuel works with young offenders.'

'I wouldn't jump to any conclusions. I've already demonstrated conjecture isn't the way forward.'

'You only did what you could. This is a tough gig, Kate. We all appreciate how difficult it is.'

They turned off the main road on to a street of semi-detached houses and then into a short street of semi-detached bungalows. Emma slowed down until they reached the property they were searching for, towards the end of the street. Rusty iron gates to the driveway were pegged open, weeds growing around the base of both. The blinds at the windows were down and, although the grass had been cut, the borders were overgrown.

There was no sign of a Ford Focus on the driveway, nevertheless Kate rang the bell and waited for an answer. When nobody came, she crossed to the drive next door and tried there. A woman in her late sixties answered. Kate explained who they were, showed her police ID and asked about Charlene.

'There's nobody at home. She's gone to her sister's place to recuperate from an operation.'

'What about her sons?'

'They don't live here.'

Kate felt her stomach lurch. Had they got this wrong? 'When did she leave?'

'A week ago. Her sister came by to collect stuff for her and left her sitting in the car. I nipped out and had a quick word with her. She looked very sickly to me. I didn't ask what was wrong or what she'd had done. I didn't want to appear nosy.'

There was a chance one of the sons had taken the car, or it had been stolen while Charlene was away. 'Then, the car is in the garage?'

The woman nodded. 'I assume so. She wasn't in any fit state to drive.'

'Of course not. Did she leave you a key to her house?'

'No. We're not close friends.'

'Do you have Charlene's mobile number?'

'No.'

'Do you know her sister's name?'

279

The woman shook her head. 'Sorry. Ben mentioned something about her living in Wales. Maybe he knows.'

'Who's Ben?'

'He's a maths teacher. He lives over there. Ben Hopkins.' She pointed out the small detached house on the corner of the street. 'He's been helping her out with odd jobs while she's not been well.'

'Have you seen anyone going in and out of the house while she's been away?'

'No. I can only see her driveway if I'm outside. Mr Wilson might be able to help you.' She waved at the house opposite Charlene's.

'I don't suppose you've heard or seen her car going out recently?'

Her thin eyebrows locked together. 'Why would I see her car when she isn't there to drive it?'

'We have reason to believe her car has been used recently. Anyway, thank you for your time. If you think of anything else, would you ring the station, please?'

The woman hesitated before replying then said, 'Have you tried her garage? I remember her saying, the day before she went into hospital, something about it not locking properly. Her car might have been stolen.'

'We'll take a look.'

Kate and Emma returned to Charlene's house. Anxiety was tying Kate's stomach in knots. They'd decided the car they were hunting for was Mrs Leith's when the car in question could have simply been on fake plates. She couldn't face more failure.

'The lock hasn't been renewed,' she said. She twisted the handle firmly. The up-and-over door opened with a whisper. A silver Ford Focus car filled the garage, which was otherwise empty apart from thick, dark cobwebs coating the far end of the ceiling.

Emma sidled into the garage and shuffled sideways along the wall to peer inside the vehicle. 'There doesn't appear to be any damage from hotwiring, and there's no key left in the ignition.' She felt under the arches and on top of the tyres. 'Nothing.'

Kate couldn't meet her eye. She'd got it wrong. This wasn't the perpetrator's vehicle. It belonged to an innocent woman who was recuperating at her sister's house. Her insides felt squelchy. She'd blown it again. She turned away. Emma would have reached the same conclusion and Kate wasn't prepared for her disappointment.

From this angle, the driveway appeared even more unkempt and the gates very rusted. She turned towards the house, took in the paint peeling off window frames and then back to the garage, where Emma stood under a small, cracked pane of glass covered by cobwebs. The garage door lock was broken, yet the door made no noise when it was raised. She ran a finger over one of the struts that lifted the door. It came away greasy. Somebody had oiled them recently.

'Emma, why would somebody oil the struts?'

'To make sure the garage opened quietly.'

'Exactly. The neighbour suggested the lock had only recently been broken, before Charlene went into hospital. I think we could be on the right tracks.'

Emma made her way out. Kate pulled down the door, which shut quietly. 'I suggest we talk to the neighbours first. They might have spotted somebody using her car while she's been away.'

'I'll try Ben Hopkins, although, if he teaches, he'll most likely be at work,' replied Emma, and made for the furthest house on the street.

Ben wasn't at home. However, his next-door neighbour, Mr Wilson, whose house was opposite Charlene's, was in. Although he admitted to being hard of hearing, he was certain he hadn't noticed any strange comings and goings opposite. Nor had he spotted her car being driven.

'Charlene's always kept herself to herself. Like most of the folk on this street. You know, I've lived here for forty years and I'm only really friends with one of the neighbours. One. And he's lived on this street for twenty-five years! I used to know everybody here, but people move on, new ones come in. They're not interested in their neighbours.' He gave a sigh. 'Charlene was a bit more friendly when they first moved here, her, Mick and the two boys. I used to see them cycling up and down the street. Then Reece, who was a bit of a tearaway, got into bother and was sent inside,' he said, looking around as if somebody might overhear. 'After that, they didn't mix with anyone. Embarrassed, I'd say. Not so long back, her husband, Mick, died and after that I hardly ever saw her. I doubt she gave a house key to anybody.'

'You haven't seen her boys out and about here, have you?'

'No. They never seem to visit.'

They tried everyone along the street without any luck. Nobody recalled seeing the car. Back by their own vehicle, Emma huffed. 'Great. The Ford Focus must have been driven down this road every day at around the same time, and not one person noticed.'

That somebody had succeeded in taking and returning the car from the garage daily without being spotted troubled Kate deeply. Driving Charlene's car in full view of the neighbours required either supreme confidence or ambivalence. The latter was of greater concern. Someone who didn't care if they were spotted might take greater risks, endanger other lives, even injure children. However, there might be another reason the car hadn't been seen.

'What if the car hasn't been moved every day? It only needed to be taken from the garage once, then it could have been left elsewhere. If it was driven away under cover of darkness, curtains would be closed and there'd be much less risk of being caught.'

'Then why is it back in the garage?'

'It's no longer needed.'

'Then why not burn it to get rid of any evidence?'

For a moment, she was floored. Then her gut kicked in. 'I don't have all the answers on this, only a feeling it has been returned to its owner. Destroying other people's property isn't part of our perpetrator's plan.'

'Does that mean this is over? That the killer has replaced the car, shut the door and walked away and they're not going to kill any more people?'

'That's a possibility. Or they've changed vehicles, as a precaution.'

Emma pulled a face. 'Shit! I hope not. This is our only lead.'

'We'll get a surveillance team set up here. If the killer comes back for it, we'll be ready for them.'

'But if they've changed vehicles, we've got nothing.' Dismay was etched on to Emma's forehead.

'We've discovered something: they knew Charlene was away, have a key to her car, and they're bold as brass. We have to keep pecking away at what we know.'

'What if it isn't enough, or they strike again?'

'I don't know, Emma. I really don't know.'

Kate got into their car. The truth was, she did know. She'd be sidelined. Somebody new would front the investigation and Kate's unblemished record would come to an end.

CHAPTER TWENTY

Kate parted company with Emma on the stairwell and went to face the music in William's office. In this instance, he took the news with no more than a small grunt. Kate had little choice but to lay her cards on the table and hope he was really on her side.

'I could be making a right balls-up of this. The Ford Focus captured on footage could even be on fake plates. I'd consider that possibility, were it not for the facts that her garage door lock is broken, the struts have been oiled so the door doesn't make a noise when it is opened, and she is currently away. It's too happenstance to ignore.'

William grunted again and she prepared herself for disappointment that was not forthcoming. 'I'm with you on that. Not the balls-up part. You haven't screwed up. You've more than likely traced the vehicle. We'll learn more once Forensics have examined it.'

'You can't send in a team yet. If the perpetrator finds out, they could do a runner, and we'll lose any chance of finding them.'

He nodded. 'Okay. What do you propose as your next move?'

'Contact Charlene Leith. See if she actually left her house keys with anyone. Find out if the car has been in for repairs or a service recently where somebody might have got a duplicate key made. I can't work out how else the vehicle could be taken and used. Jamie's trying to get hold of her sons. If it's not one of them, then it's somebody else who knows her well enough to know she'd be away for a while.'

William stood up, placed his hands behind his back and stared out of the window. Several tufts of grey hair curled over his shirt collar. 'I don't want our last investigation together to fail.'

'Nor do I.'

'I won't be able to stop Superintendent Dickson from stepping in. If the killer strikes again this evening, he'll insist on bringing in extra support and I'm half inclined to agree that's the best solution. It surprises me he hasn't already given orders for that to happen.'

Kate flexed her fingers. The bastard was probably waiting for there to be an outcry at her poor handling of the investigation, then he'd have an excuse to remove her altogether and quash promotional aspirations.

William sighed. 'The reality is, you can't continue to conduct such a major investigation with such limited manpower. I'm really sorry, Kate. I know you want this one for yourself, and your team, to earn the kudos you deserve. I want that for you too. But, you understand, we can't let any more people die.'

'I understand.'

Outside, heavy treads on threadbare carpets over aged wooden floorboards seemed to echo in the room. William turned and caught her gaze. His voice was heavy. 'Do what you can until the super makes that call.'

There was little time left before another victim would be chosen. The air in the office was stale, a mixture of warmth, body odour and coffee breath. Faces were screwed up in concentration. Sleeves were rolled up past elbows. Damp patches under armpits. Jamie cussed at his screen and Morgan rolled his desk basketball in tight circles under one palm as he held a phone conversation.

Emma was on her feet again. 'Charlene's next-door neighbour has rung. She spotted Ben's car outside his house and wondered if we'd like to ask him about the house keys. I'm going back. I'll check in on the surveillance team too.' She was gone almost before she'd finished speaking.

'Have you managed to speak to anyone who works with Charlene?' Kate directed her question at Jamie.

'No. I can't get hold of anyone at the building society. Business numbers and opening times only. Sundays it's shut. I'm still trying to get hold of her sons. I think the number I have for Reece is an old one. I keep getting a "number not in use" message and her other son is not picking up.'

'Okay. Stick at it.'

Kate picked up where she'd left off, going back over historic cases in which the victims had died in traumatic circumstances, hoping she would have a eureka moment. She kept one eye on the clock. The next few hours would not only decide somebody's fate, but they'd also decide her future.

◆ ◆ ◆

Emma retraced the route back to Scarratt Drive, where Charlene lived. The investigation was getting under her skin. This bastard was a slippery character who clearly had no qualms about whose life they extinguished.

The children's magazine on the passenger seat of the latest victim's car had upset Emma more than she cared to admit. It meant another child would grow up without that special love a mother or grandmother could give. It didn't help knowing she was being oversensitive because of the anniversary of her mother's death and because she was plagued by damn memories she couldn't block out. She wanted this case to be over, the perpetrator caught and for there to be no more murders. She didn't want anybody else to face what she faced year after year. She gripped the wheel harder, squeezing it as tightly as she could until her fingers cramped. They had to find the person responsible, and quickly.

She drew up outside the detached house at the end of the road. A man was bent over the bonnet of a white VW Golf, sponge in hand. The foamy suds ran down the side of the vehicle, dripping on to the ground, and he stopped cleaning when she got out of the car.

'Hi, I'm DS Emma Donaldson. Sorry to disturb you.'

He dropped the sponge into the bucket, wiped soap from his face with his sleeve. 'You're not. This is one of those Sunday jobs I have to do.'

'Are you Ben Hopkins?'

'I am.'

'I spoke to one of your neighbours earlier who said you've been helping out at number ten, Charlene's place.'

'Only a couple of times.' A slight furrow appeared between his eyebrows. 'Is Charlene okay?'

'We've been unable to contact her and wondered if she left any house keys with you?'

'Me? No.'

'Do you have Charlene's mobile number?'

'Sorry, I don't.'

'I understand you might know where Charlene has gone.'

'She mentioned she was going to head to Wales. To stay with a sister. I think the plan was for her to recuperate there, following surgery.'

'She never mentioned her sister's name or whereabouts in Wales she might be staying?'

'I'm afraid not. Can I ask, why are you questioning me?'

'We have reason to believe somebody has been using her car while she's been away.'

The furrow deepened. 'I doubt that. Isn't it in the garage?'

'It is now.'

'Then I don't want to appear rude, but it's not likely to have been her car.'

Emma didn't flinch. She had questions, and it didn't matter if he didn't understand why she was asking them. 'We have reason to believe it might be. You haven't noticed any strangers on the street recently, have you? Maybe a car you didn't recognise or somebody hanging around near her house?'

He started to shake his head then said, 'Wait a minute, come to think of it, there was a young man. That would have been Monday – no, I think it was Tuesday. I noticed him because I'd just got in from work and was at the kitchen window, waiting for the kettle to boil. He walked past Charlene's house, stopped, turned around and came back this way. At the time, I thought he'd taken a wrong turning. I spotted him a couple of days later, about the same time. Again, I didn't think anything of it. I assumed he was visiting somebody on the street.'

'Can you describe him?'

'Now you're testing me. Erm, tall, medium height, dark-haired.'

'What about his clothes?'

He screwed up his face. 'I didn't really get a good look at him. He was wearing some sort of dark sweatshirt and jeans combo, I think.'

'And you hadn't seen him before Tuesday?'

'No.'

'Any idea of age?'

He gave it a moment's consideration. 'Late twenties, maybe early thirties. Sorry I can't be more specific.'

'That's okay.'

He gave a light shrug. 'Well, if I think of anything else, I'll ring the station, right?'

'That would be helpful, Mr Hopkins.'

'Everyone calls me Ben. Apart from my pupils,' he added.

She warmed to his friendly smile. 'Thank you, Ben.'

She returned to her car. Ben was soaping his car again. He waved his sponge at her as she reversed. A bland description of a young man. It wasn't a lot to take back with her.

CHAPTER
TWENTY-ONE

It was half past two and Kate was getting antsy. If the perpetrator had changed vehicles, they no longer had anything to go on. Surveillance team or not, she knew the chances of anyone collecting Charlene's car from the garage again were almost zilch. There was a greater chance of them being spotted on a Sunday afternoon, rather than during the week, when people were at work.

Morgan plucked the wrapper from a sandwich. He stared half-heartedly at it. 'I suppose Samuel has nothing more to add to this.'

Jamie snorted. 'Let's face it, he's not really told us anything we couldn't have worked out ourselves. It's obvious the killer is arms-trained, but they needn't have been in the forces to learn those skills. You can learn shooting skills on civvy street. As for CCTV cameras, well, if the perpetrator is a local, they'll know where they're positioned, and if they're not a local, they could have checked out the locations while planning the attacks. Samuel's superfluous to our investigation.'

'He might come up trumps yet,' said Morgan.

Jamie was being deliberately unhelpful with his comments about the profiler. It was all part of some scheme to ensure she lost face when the investigation was passed over. Thanks to Samuel, Kate thought she understood what was motivating the killer. Their perpetrator was going through something akin to her own experience – a death, the loss of somebody close to them.

The aftermath of Chris's murder had left Kate unable to function properly, taking medication, burying herself in work. As she'd gradually accepted Chris's death, confusion had been replaced by a fierce rage to right a wrong, find out who had ordered his murder. She had been in that dark place, her focus only on the person or persons responsible for her husband's death. She suspected their killer wasn't so much guilty as full of vitriol and fury, lashing out uncontrollably. She shoved the chilling premise aside and concentrated on her task – searching for the catalyst that had sent this person over the edge.

Having exhausted case files regarding violent deaths, she turned her attention to local newspaper articles from the past year. Major incidents were often reported by the press. Chris's death had made the front pages. She clicked on to a copy of the *Gazette* from their archives and scrolled through headlines, searching for anything that would be construed as traumatic.

Emma's return interrupted her reading. 'The teacher spotted a young man vaguely matching the assailant's description.' She yanked off her jacket and explained what Ben had told her.

'He might have seen one of Charlene's sons,' Morgan said.

Jamie piped up with, 'Nah, mate. They were miles away on Tuesday. I've just this second finished speaking to them. Besides, what motive would they have?'

Morgan stared at his still-uneaten sandwich. 'Oh, I don't know. Charlene's husband died unexpectedly. Samuel said the killer had undergone a traumatic experience.'

'Lots of people die, often in tragic circumstances. Their relatives don't usually start shooting innocent people in the forehead with a captive bolt pistol. Our perpetrator must have experienced one heck of a traumatic experience to do what they're doing.'

Morgan crumpled the cellophane wrapper into a small ball and rolled it between his fingers before speaking again. 'Charlene's younger son was sent away for robbery with violence. A few months later his father dies. Now he's got out and his mum has undergone what sounds like major surgery. He could be a messed-up kid.'

Jamie sighed. 'Okay. I'll speak to their employers and make sure they were both at work like they claimed. I want to try Charlene's phone again. I got her number from her son, but it was engaged a minute ago when I tried it.'

'Morgan's right. It is best to double-check. We can't let anything slide,' said Emma.

The office phone rang, and Kate lifted her head in time to spot Morgan give Emma a small wink of thanks before answering it. Kate zoned out. Her team were only trying to make sense of what was rapidly turning into an illogical puzzle. She scanned the document half-heartedly until an electric spark shot through her entire body and she sat bolt upright.

'Kate!'

'Yes.' She forced herself back into the room. The answer was here. Morgan's hand covered the mouthpiece and most of the handset. 'It's Charlene Leith. She gave her keys to a neighbour.'

'Pass her over.'

She jumped to her feet, took the phone from Morgan and in a smooth tone said, 'Mrs Leith. Thank you for ringing.'

'One of my neighbours has just called me to say my car might be stolen.'

'I can assure you that isn't the case.'

The sigh of relief was audible.

'Can I ask who rang you?'

292

'Geoffrey Wilson. He lives opposite me. He said the police have been asking questions about my car and he saw them go into the garage. He wasn't sure how to contact me until he remembered I wrote my phone number on an old Christmas card I sent him, in case he ever needed to ring for help. Are you sure everything is okay?'

'Your car is in the garage and appears to be undamaged.'

'Thank goodness. The garage lock needs fixing. Ben said he'd take a look at it for me while I was away.'

'And I assume Ben has your house keys?' Kate caught Emma's eye. Ben had told her he didn't have them.

'That's right. Such a sweetie. He's been a great help recently. I've been unwell for a few months and Ben has done a few odd jobs for me; the ones my husband, Mick, used to do. I left my keys with him so he could water the houseplants and keep an eye on the place.'

'I understand you recently underwent surgery, which is why you're not at home.'

'I did. The surgeon says it'll be another four to six weeks before I'll be able to get behind the wheel again.'

'Do you plan on being away until then?'

'No. I told Ben I'd be back today or tomorrow, but it's more likely going to be later in the week. My sister wants to keep an eye on me for a while longer.'

'Mrs Leith, what do you know about Ben?'

'Why are you asking me about him?' A querulous note had crept into her voice.

'I wouldn't ask if it wasn't important. Could you help me out here and tell me about him?'

'I can't imagine what you think he's done. One thing's for certain, he wouldn't take my car without permission. He's dependable, helpful and pleasant.'

'Does Ben have anyone in his life?'

She heard a soft tutting. 'You don't know? It was all over the news at the time. I'm surprised you're even asking me.'

'Mrs Leith, I need you to tell me what you know.'

She huffed again. 'He was married. Before he moved into Scarratt Drive. He and his wife were expecting their first child when they got involved in a horrible accident on the M6. His entire family was wiped out. His sister, her children and, of course, his wife, were all killed. It happened about a year ago, I suppose. Of course, when he moved into the street, I recognised his face immediately. I'd followed the story on the news. I spoke to him a few days after he moved in. Told him how sorry I was. He was in a terrible state. He told me he'd had to move to get away from the press. He asked me not to give his identity away, and I didn't. The way the press hounded him was dreadful. The poor man didn't want it all dragged up again. He only wanted to start a new life. It's not much to ask, is it?'

Kate had not seen the coverage at the time, dealing, as she had been, with her own grief. Nevertheless, she'd just been reading about the four children and their mother, Rowena O'Bryan, from Canada, who'd been holidaying in Stoke with her brother. There'd been only one survivor. Douglas Benjamin Hopkins had emerged from the wreckage almost unscathed. The press had camped outside his house in the village of Draycott in the Moors, between Stoke and Uttoxeter. They'd pursued him for two weeks, until he disappeared from his house and his job at an engineering company. After that, there'd been little more about him, and gradually fresh news replaced the old.

The call over, Kate relayed the information to the team. She read out the newspaper article and showed them the photographs of the family prior to the accident, and one of Ben and his wife. Leaner and with longer hair.

Emma nodded. 'That's him. That's the man I spoke to.'

'I remember hearing about the accident, but I didn't recall any names. It was before I moved to this area,' said Jamie.

'It was all over the local news,' said Morgan. 'We should have twigged sooner. When the neighbour told us his name.'

'That's the thing. He was known to his neighbours as Ben Hopkins. The newspapers reported his given name, Douglas Hopkins. Benjamin is his middle name. Either he chose to use Ben after he moved house, or he's always been called Ben. I know other people who use their middle name rather than their first name. We were thrown off the scent,' said Kate.

'He wasn't teaching at the time either,' Emma said. 'Not that that excuses me not recognising him.'

'How could you?' said Morgan. 'It happened a year ago. You don't have a photographic memory. Don't blame yourself.'

'I read the newspaper reports. I saw the photos. I didn't get any inkling, no *wait a minute, this doesn't feel right* moments. My instinct let me down.'

'Emma, you've been under strain,' said Kate. 'Let this go. We are a team. We all missed it and for good reasons.' She gave a smile. Emma returned it weakly.

'Yeah. Okay. I still feel bad, though.'

'Don't.'

Jamie's eyebrows lifted. 'I've realised something else. Samuel was spot on when he told us the perp would have suffered a tragic loss. It doesn't get more fucking traumatic than this guy's story. Six of his family wiped out.'

Emma corrected him with a shake of her head. 'Seven. There was an unborn baby too.'

There was a tap at the door. 'I'm not interrupting, am I?'

'Come in, Samuel. We've had a breakthrough,' said Kate.

He came in eagerly, kicking Kate's case over as he tried to find a space against the wall.

She brought him up to speed. 'The accident took place just before quarter to six in the evening. According to witnesses at the scene of the accident, Ben stopped his people carrier in time to avoid hitting a lorry but was shunted from the rear and propelled into the vehicle, which was carrying lengths of metal poles. One of them crashed through the windscreen and speared his wife in the forehead, killing her instantly.'

The sleeves of Samuel's shirt rode up as he folded his hands to expose a green silicone wristband, the colour used for awareness in mental health. 'This is interesting. It would explain primarily why his victims were shot in the forehead and why all these acts happened at around the same time. When did the accident take place?'

Kate already knew. 'Last Monday would have been the first anniversary of their deaths.'

Samuel gave her a knowing look. 'Then I think we can establish the one-year anniversary was the trigger for the spate of attacks. What about his background?'

'We haven't had a chance to look into it yet. Papers say he worked for an engineering company. We know he's a teacher. We've yet to establish if he has any military or police experience,' said Jamie.

Samuel responded with a slight shake of his head. 'There might not be time for internet searches. Six people died in that accident, seven if you include the unborn baby. So far, he's killed five. There's every chance he'll strike again . . . today. He might be taking a life for a life. You should bring him in and charge him immediately.'

The last thing Kate wanted was another death because of her poor decision-making. They were close to catching him. Now was the time to exercise extra caution and ensure no mistakes were made. Dickson would want i's dotted and t's crossed. If they hauled

Ben in without concrete evidence, he could slip from their grasp. 'I don't want him to escape any charges because of our sloppiness.'

Emma's eyes flashed. 'Well, he lied about not having Charlene's house keys, for a start. Why would he do that if he wasn't trying to cover his tracks? He perverted the cause of justice. We could nail him on that.'

Kate nodded. 'You're right. We have enough evidence to bring him in for questioning. However, none of it proves he used her car or committed any crime. We can only place the vehicle at the crime scenes, around the time of the murders, not the driver. Even then, we don't have concrete proof. The CCTV images don't show the car's registration. The garage witness might have been mistaken. Nobody on Scarratt Drive saw Ben take or drive the Ford Focus. We have no witnesses to any of the murders and no weapon. We only have a profile which he matches, and a decent amount of speculation. Our sole hope is to obtain a search warrant and cross our fingers we can find something at either his house or in Charlene's car that gives him away. It's a tall order.'

'At least if we bring him in for interview, he won't be able to harm anybody this evening. It also buys us some more time. Kate?' Tension stretched Emma's lips into a thin line.

Mindful of the impact losing yet another innocent would have, Kate nodded. 'Agreed. Emma, Morgan, would you fetch him?'

Emma slid from the desk where she'd been sitting cross-legged. Kate noticed the sad look Samuel gave her as she brushed by him without so much as a backward glance.

CHAPTER
TWENTY-TWO

William was eager to get a warrant to search Ben's house. He was pacing the floor, his eyes shining. He seemed to have regained enthusiasm and youth.

'I'll organise it, and a forensic team to examine the Ford Focus. Will you let Mrs Leith know what is going on?' he said.

'Yes. What do we do if we can't find the weapon?'

'We'll cross that bridge when we come to it. Search his classroom at school, his locker, wherever else he might have hidden it, and do whatever you need to.'

'You don't think I'm being too hasty? If I've got this wrong as well, I may as well give up my badge.'

'Not this time. You've acted appropriately and reasonably. The theory is sound. We only need proof to support it, and we'll get you that. Now, get back to the investigation, DI Young.' His eyes crinkled as he spoke.

Jamie and Samuel were by the whiteboard, packing the space with their collective presence and blocking Kate's route to her desk. Samuel had added profile details to the board with red lines from each connecting it to Ben Hopkins's encircled name. He completed the word 'ex-military' and drew a final line.

'So, you were right about him being ex-forces,' said Kate.

Jamie answered. 'Ben joined the Army Reserve when he was at university, although it was still known as the Territorial Army back then. After he finished his degree, he signed up for the minimum four-year term. And get this, Lieutenant Benjamin Hopkins became a member of the Parachute Regiment.'

While the SAS was regarded as one of the world's most renowned special-forces regiments, the paras were seen as one of the toughest, most prestigious infantry regiments in the British Army and prided themselves on a rigorous selection process. Ben had the necessary training and background to have carried out the killings.

Samuel seemed more subdued than Jamie. His long neck was arched, head lowered, reminding Kate of the swans on the reservoir.

'Well done, Samuel. You were spot on,' she said.

He drew a question mark on the board. 'Something doesn't add up. He's clever. He'll have interpreted Emma's visit as a warning sign and planned an exit strategy. Yet when Jamie contacted the surveillance team watching over Charlene's garage, they said no cars had been in or out of the road since Emma left.' He faced Kate. 'I'm worried he's already packed up and gone.'

Kate got on the phone immediately. The connection was patchy, Morgan's voice urgent. 'His car's outside. Can't rouse him.'

Loud banging ensued, fists against wood, followed by Emma's shouts. 'Ben Hopkins, open up. It's the police.'

Morgan was back. 'Fucker's not answering. Have we got a warrant?'

Kate tightened her grip on the phone. The warrant wouldn't be ready yet. 'Break in regardless. We believe he has committed a serious crime, and that's sufficient reason.'

There was more shouting and a sharp crack as Morgan applied the enforcer. Emma's voice was loud in the background. 'Living room, clear.'

Kate could envisage the situation, listening to the dialogue and hearing the frustration in their voices as they confirmed each room was empty. Eventually, the shouting ceased. Morgan's angry voice returned.

'Kate, the fucker's done a runner. He was ready for us. He's fucking well disappeared.'

Kate looked at Samuel. 'What do you think his next move will be? Will he go into hiding?'

Samuel folded on to a seat, arms flopping on to his long thighs. 'No. He hasn't finished yet. He has to kill again, and probably today.'

◆ ◆ ◆

A forensic team had been dispatched to the house. William had organised extra officers to help Kate with the manhunt. For the first time in a year, she was back in front of a large unit, many of them from her old team. They'd moved into the briefing room. As large as it was, there were insufficient seats for all, leaving several officers standing. She felt a familiar contentment being back in front of faces she'd worked with before Chris's death. She'd missed this. She caught everybody's attention with a quiet 'ahem', before beginning.

'Right. You have in front of you a photograph of our suspect. Ben Hopkins is not to be underestimated. He's successfully evaded capture and, up until now, has been one step ahead of us. However, he has a weakness. A witness who spotted a man crying at Westport Lake has since confirmed that man to be Ben. Prior to breaking down in tears, Ben was overheard saying, "Don't make me do it." We can't be certain if this was said to somebody over a mobile device, to himself, or spoken to somebody he imagines he can hear – possibly one of the deceased members of his family. However, our profiler, Samuel Links, believes those words indicate Ben doesn't want to continue these acts of violence, yet he finds himself on a trajectory he can't control. To that end, there's a chance that, if cornered, he might weaken and give himself up. It is not a chance I am willing to take. It is my opinion that Ben is unstable.'

She pointed to a photograph on the board of a man and woman, both in their thirties, at a beach café. The woman was doe-eyed and dark-haired. The man had strong, angular features. 'This is a picture of Ben and his wife, Lisa, taken two months before the accident which saw Lisa and their unborn child killed. The same accident wiped out his sister and her four children. Ben was driving the family car at the time and sustained only minor injuries. Although we haven't yet been able to obtain a psychological evaluation or doctor's report following the accident, it won't require a great deal of imagination to work out how it affected Ben. Let me pass you over to Samuel, who has been working with us on this and created a profile that Ben fits.'

Samuel stood up, arms hanging loosely by his sides. 'Erm, yes. Thank you. To date, the perpetrator has murdered five people, each with a shot to the forehead with a captive bolt pistol. You may wonder why he has chosen this weapon over any other. I believe he chose *this* weapon because it is considered a humane way of killing an animal and he wants to execute his victims as humanely as possible. Ben fits the profile I put together. These are only my thoughts. However, I think the loss of his entire family has traumatised him to the point where he believes he has to take lives. It is my earnest belief he is taking one for each of those lost in that accident. Call it what you will, an act of God or fate, he perceived it to be arbitrary. Any one of those vehicles on the motorway that day could have been shunted into the lorry, nevertheless it was *his* car and *his* family who died, selected at random out of all the vehicles on the motorway. Consequently, he is also choosing victims at random. Remember, this is only my take on the situation.'

He paused to wet his lips, then continued.

'Although it's guesswork on my part, I think DI Young is in agreement with me when I say if the perpetrator is Ben Hopkins, he is choosing locations that he and his family visited prior to that fateful journey. Erm. That's everything, I think.'

Kate took over again. 'Jamie?'

Jamie spoke from his seat, arms resting on the table. 'It's not complete guesswork because we've spoken to one of Ben's work colleagues who is close to him. From the information she gave us, we have good reason to suspect Ben. He and his family visited all the locations where a victim was killed. That includes Blythe Bridge, where he first picked up his sister and family at the start of their stay in the UK. We also think we understand the relevance of the attack at the petrol station beside the M6. This is where they made a last-minute stop before the accident. Ben told his colleague, had he not chosen to fuel up there and instead done it later or even on the return journey, they wouldn't have been involved in the accident. He carried a huge amount of guilt about what had happened. All of which makes him a likely suspect in these murders.'

'Thank you, Jamie. Okay, we are working on the premise our perpetrator is Ben Hopkins. While his colleague has helped us identify some of the tourist spots he and his family visited, we can't be sure there aren't others we've missed.

'You should all have lists of the most popular attractions in and around Stoke-on-Trent. DS Meredith will assign them to each of you and you will stake those locations, emptying them of anyone who is there. The official line is you are clearing the area in order for a police exercise to take place. You will request that people do not pass on or share that information with any other members of the public as they exit the area. We can't afford for any members of the public to inadvertently alert Benjamin Hopkins.

'Should you spot him, keep him in your sights and alert the team. He is armed and dangerous, so do not approach.' She paused to drive home her point. Ben was clearly unstable and, now he knew they were on to him, he might shoot at any target, including a police officer.

'The killings began on a Monday, exactly one year from the date of the car accident. Ben *will* choose one of those locations and he *will* kill again unless we stop him. If Samuel is right and Ben is taking the same number of lives that were lost in the accident, we won't have many opportunities to capture him. Our belief is that once he has killed six or even seven others, he will stop and most likely disappear. To ensure he doesn't kill another person, you need to be vigilant. He is out there. We can find him. If there are no questions, take your instructions from DS Meredith, and . . . good luck.'

Leaving the briefing room, she took a deep breath. She hadn't been way off with her hunches after all. Ben had been largely targeting tourist locations, as she first suspected. Samuel followed her out. 'Kate.'

She spun on her heel. 'What is it?'

'I've been thinking further about the crying episode at Westport Lake.'

'And?'

'Ben's words. The fact he really didn't want to kill again. It doesn't fit with my profile of him as a calm, calculating executioner, especially in light of his military training. You see, his car was parked at the scene of the crime in full view of potential witnesses, which was a risk, and he isn't a risk-taker. It was in a disabled bay, opposite the playground. A playground where little Billy was playing alone.'

Her jaw tightened and she couldn't speak. Samuel's face was long; lines on his forehead spoke the words for him. 'Oh Lord, no. You mean he was going to kill the child and changed his mind?'

'I believe so. Maybe it was because he saw the child's mother at the last moment, or couldn't go through with it, but four children died in that car. I suspect he isn't only going to kill adults.'

'Tell Emma and Morgan. I've got to speak to William.'

CHAPTER TWENTY-THREE

Kate zipped up her protective vest. The others were preparing alongside her. The mood in the changing room was sombre but determined. Jamie cracked his knuckles and shook his shoulders like a boxer about to head into the ring. Kate had last-minute instructions for them.

'Samuel's bombshell has altered the way we handle this operation. It's not enough to place car parks under surveillance. Ben is determined. He knows we are on to him and, from what Samuel has deduced, is in a serious mental decline. He is likely to be hunting for children as well as adults. I've decided to double up teams where children or teenagers are likely to be found unsupervised. Primarily, the parks on the list, where there are children's play areas, skate parks, football pitches and so on. That means, Morgan, you and Emma will now both go to Burslem Park. Jamie and I will take Longton Park. I've requested extra officers to accompany those already heading to other locations. I'm not prepared to take the chance that Samuel is wrong about this. Okay, it's time to go. Can we check the comms are working?'

They went through the procedure and slipped outside. Kate piled into the lead vehicle with Jamie, who took the wheel. Neither of them said a word for the first few minutes of the journey. Traffic was heavy. Kate kept a visual on Morgan's car in her wing mirror, until the indicator flashed and it turned off the main road. A black Volvo, driven by one of her old team, moved into position behind them. It too would turn off in due course and head to one of the locations. Her mind raced as fast as her heartbeat. They had to get it right this time. Failure was not an option.

The silence was broken by Jamie.

'I was wrong about Samuel.'

'We all had our doubts about him.'

'Me most of all. I'll be the first to admit I was more than sceptical about his methods. I've not worked with a profiler before.'

'I've not worked with one like him.'

'If we catch this perp, I'm going to buy Samuel a drink.'

'Steady on. Don't go too wild.'

He didn't smile. 'I meant what I said about getting my act together, guv. I really like working in the team. It's been good for me. I was a bit . . . lost before I joined you.'

'Lost?'

'Well, not lost exactly. More, not settled.'

This was the opportunity she'd been waiting for. Now was the moment to press for information about Dickson. 'You worked with small units before?'

'Once. It wasn't the same.'

'Worked on anything major in the past?'

'Nothing like this. It was mostly undercover stuff.' He kept his eyes on the road ahead, which suited her. She didn't want him to suspect she was fishing.

'Ah, things you can't talk about.'

'Yeah, pretty much. I was glad to get out and join your team. It was messing with my head and my relationship.'

She didn't push him. Sometimes it was better to say nothing and see if the speaker would give any more details. Jamie did.

'Undercover's tough. You spend so much time living a legend, you start believing it yourself and forget your true identity. It puts a strain on your family life and, with Sophie falling pregnant again, it was a no-brainer to get out. Have you ever done any undercover work?'

'No. Always been crime squad.'

'I can see its appeal.' He flicked the indicator stalk and they turned off the roundabout on to a long street. 'Longton Park isn't far. Two minutes tops.'

'So, you wouldn't consider going back undercover?'

'You're joking. Boss was headstrong, to put it mildly.'

She was sure he was talking about Dickson. She see-sawed between letting the conversation drop and pushing it further. In the end, she couldn't help herself. 'The CIO who was killed last year, Heather Gault, worked covert ops. You ever work with her?'

He maintained a poker face. 'Yes.'

'You didn't mention it at the time of the investigation into the rape attacks.'

'We were on the same operation. She was removed and didn't see it through. I didn't think it had any bearing on the case, guv. Simple as that. She worked with you in the past too, didn't she?'

'True.'

He gave an eyebrow shrug.

'Point taken.' She allowed a pause before she casually asked, 'Why was she removed? I got the impression she was tenacious and thorough.'

'No idea. Didn't ask. I'm a soldier, guv. I do as I'm told and don't ask questions.'

This was one nut she wouldn't crack easily. They were level with the park and this conversation was at an end.

'You clear on what we're doing at the park?'

'As a bell.'

They'd already decided where they'd station their vehicle and how best to cover the area. It was now a matter of coordinating a two-pronged attack should Ben show his face.

◆ ◆ ◆

Emma and Morgan had also been discussing their strategies and then fallen silent on the car journey until Morgan blurted, 'Have you got a thing for Samuel?'

'Wow! Where did that come from?'

He gave a cheeky grin. 'Come on, all those sneaky glances between you, and don't think I didn't see him slip you a note the other day, like you were both schoolkids sneaking messages in class. It's obvious there's chemistry between you.'

'I didn't know you were so observant.'

'Sure you did. You've known me long enough. Well?'

'There might have been something if I hadn't knocked him back.'

'And the reason for that was—?'

'His behaviour's a little too out there for me. I can't cope with people who are up one minute and down the next. I need straight-forward men in my life.'

'Like me.'

'Of course, like you.' She gave him a light punch and he winced.

'Ow! That hurt. You work out too much. You have wa-ay too much strength behind those punches!'

'Shut up!' She laughed.

'He's an okay bloke, you know?'

'I know. In another life I might have gone for it. I'm not able to take on anyone who is so complex.'

'What about somebody who isn't complex?'

'You mean, a daft, easy-to-talk-to, not complex sort of person?'

'Pretty much.'

'I'd probably be better with that.'

He returned her a genuine smile. 'Fancy some company at the cemetery later, when we're done?'

'You remembered.'

'We've known each other since forever, Emma. I remember all the important things and I know what date it is; that it's been ten years since your mum passed away. And I can guess how difficult this case has been for you. A man taking revenge on the world, after the death of his family. A mother left childless, children without a mother and others without a grandmother. I'm not insensitive. I can tell from your face and your mannerisms this is eating into you. I didn't want to broach the subject sooner, in case I pushed you away with my clumsy questioning. I know how fierce you are, how protective you are of your image. Emma Donaldson. Iron Girl. You wouldn't have wanted me to see you were struggling.'

She stared hard at him. 'Even though we've known each other for so long, you still have the power to surprise me. Yes, the investigation has got under my skin. Big time. I can't understand how anybody thinks it's okay to kill an innocent person, no matter how screwed up they are. People die when they shouldn't. One minute they're with us, the next taken, often with no forewarning. Even though it can feel unfair, even though we rage against whatever deity or force that took them from us, we learn to accept. We live without them, even if, some days, it feels like the hardest thing in the world.' Her voice began to crack. Her eyes had become blurry through tears. She didn't want to break down in front of Morgan. Not him. She didn't want him to see how weak she could be.

He put an arm around her, pulled her towards him and dropped a kiss on her forehead. 'And some of you do a bloody good job of it too.'

She let him hold her for a while. They fitted together comfortably. It took a long minute for her to appreciate she was enjoying having his arm around her. No sooner had she recognised it than he released her and brushed a stray hair from her face. 'Well? Do you want me to come along to the cemetery?'

She gave a small nod. 'I'd like that.'

She stared out of the window. Every anniversary since her mother died had been horrible, accompanied by the horrendous memories. This year had been the worst. They had to catch this son-of-a-bitch today. There were no ifs and buts about it. She couldn't bear the idea of another mother- or fatherless child or, worse still, the death of a child. That wasn't going to happen. If she spotted him, she was going to use every ounce of speed and strength she possessed to nab him. Together with Morgan, there was no way this perp was going to evade capture.

Jamie got out of the car, arched his back and winced. 'Too much sitting around. I could do with a jog through the park. Not been here for ages. You?'

'Same as you. Used to run regularly around here.'

'That's the trouble with having kids and a full-time job like ours – you never have time for yourself. It'll be worse when the next rug rat arrives.'

'But you're looking forward to it?'

A look of pride wiped across his features. 'Yeah. Not more sleepless nights, though. Definitely not those.'

He nodded towards the grand residences opposite the park. 'Wouldn't mind a house like that for the kiddies. They'll be sharing a room for the foreseeable. To afford what we'd like, I'd need a detective sergeant's salary.'

'Why haven't you tried for promotion before now?'

'I did.'

He looked like he wanted to say more so she encouraged him. 'I'm surprised it didn't happen for you.'

'Yeah. Me too. In spite of all the hints dropped and promises of recommendation, nothing came of it. Bit of a bastard really.' He glanced at his watch. 'We should have time to check out the lay of the land and clear the park.'

She wondered if Dickson had been the person who'd promised the recommendation and then reneged on it. It would certainly explain the shift in Jamie's attitude.

Longton Park covered an area of forty-five acres, five of which were taken up by the two lakes. Kate and Jamie strode past the Victorian lodge along a path that curved beside wide-open green spaces where a dog chased after a frisbee and a small group of children were playing football. Over at the skateboard park came the sound of clattering wheels as two teenagers performed a series of manoeuvres and jumps. Nobody other than a fisherman, packing away his rod, was at the smaller of the two lakes.

'Not too many people about,' said Jamie.

'That worries me even more. Ben prefers to attack when there are no witnesses. This place is perfect for him. It's vast.'

'We'll start moving people out.'

'Yes, tell them what we agreed: a police exercise is about to take place, so we need to empty the park. Don't panic anyone. Make sure they are asked not to mention it to any other members of the public.'

Happy shouts reached their ears before they spotted the children, who were scampering from one piece of equipment to the next in the playground.

'I'll move the skateboarders, those kiddies and parents on,' said Jamie. 'Looks like the fisherman is already on the off.'

'Okay. I'll make my way around.'

The all-weather sports courts were abandoned, as was the bandstand. Kate could hardly remember the last time she'd heard a band playing on it. There was a flitting memory of a Christmas concert, her and Chris with hot dogs, and snow covering the bushes, lending its frosty magic to the event, but it quickly faded. She wasn't here to recall those events.

A squirrel scurried past, paused to study her then raced up the nearest tree trunk, where it clung to the bark, beady eyes still on her. Clusters of pale-yellow crocuses peeped out between tree trunks, their petals closing for the night. A cyclist rode past. She flagged him down, requested he head home. A spaniel, nose to ground and tail propelling in rapid, circular movements, hastened first left then right, following a wiggly, invisible trail. Its owner brought up the rear. Again, Kate showed her ID with a request they vacate the park.

Kate's senses were on full alert, every movement noted, every person in the vicinity eyeballed. The chances of Ben showing up here were as good as for any of the locations. If he did, they'd be ready for him.

◆ ◆ ◆

Similar in age to Longton Park but restored in 2012, Burslem Park consisted of a circular half-mile walk that allowed visitors to take in the gardens and lake, various sculptures and mosaics, including a pagoda and an extensive rockery constructed from Pulhamite through which ran an ornamental fountain. The focus of the park, the pavilion, was where Emma now stood. From here she had eyes on the iron bandstand and winding pathways. Morgan had headed to one of the more recent additions, the children's play area, to clear it.

She cast about the walkways in search of Ben. He was aware they were on to him. He could have changed his appearance, even be wearing a disguise. He was smart. He'd completely fooled her with his innocent act, which vexed her. The more she thought about it, the more she wanted him to appear so she could see the look on his face when she collared him.

A jogger came into view, running at a leisurely pace. Using the zoom lens, she snapped his picture with her mobile then blew it up to check the details. It wasn't Ben. She stopped the man, explained about the fictitious police exercise.

Two women, both pushing buggies, strolled by. She repeated her words and sent them on their way. The sight of babies didn't send her hormones racing or post reminders that her biological clock was ticking. One thing she was certain of, she didn't want kids. She'd already made her life choices and the force would always be her priority.

A couple of teenagers came flying along the path, one chasing after the other. When she stopped them, they told her they'd already spoken to another officer who had asked them to leave. Morgan was clearly on the case too. A second jogger headed towards her, explained she was already on her way home. If he'd chosen this spot, Ben would appear soon, when he believed numbers of visitors were dwindling and he had more opportunity to pick off a lone target. She flexed her fingers, continued her vigil. If he so much as put one toe in this park, she would nab him.

◆ ◆ ◆

Longton Park was also emptying. Only a few stragglers remained. A man on a bench came under Kate's scrutiny. His head was lowered over a mobile phone, both hands on it – a gamer. After she spoke to him, he got to his feet and trundled along the path, still focused on the game. Dogs were whistled to. Children hustled along the paths. She heard Jamie's voice in her earpiece.

'All clear at the playground.'

'Any sign of anyone else?'

'No. I sent everyone home.'

'Stay in position. Nothing to report here.'

She walked along the path, still signposted as a carriageway, the reminder of a bygone era. Repetitive quacking rose from the lake, the warning to fellow ducks that a predator was prowling nearby. Now was the time Ben would also be lying in wait. The paths divided again, and she followed one leading towards the centre of the park. There were no white-hatted competitors playing bowls on any of the three greens, and nobody sitting by the pavilions. There were no visitors at all in this part of the park, nobody, that was, until she approached the bandstand again, beyond the last strip of manicured lawn. A man was standing there, one hand angrily gesticulating as he shouted.

'It's one step too far. I don't care what you say. Not even for Gracie!'

Kate spoke quietly into her communications unit. 'I have a sighting. I repeat I have a sighting at Longton Park bandstand. Request urgent backup. No sirens.'

Jamie came over the airwaves. 'What's your location?'

'I'm by the bowling green pavilion with a view on to the bandstand. Suspect is in the middle of the bandstand.'

'Headed your way.'

'No. Stay in position.'

She crouched against the building in the hope Ben wouldn't spot her. She couldn't rush him on her own. She studied his movements carefully. Only his left hand moved when he spoke. His right arm appeared to rest across his body, under his jacket. There was every chance he had one hand on the weapon. He turned from her, paced to the end of the bandstand.

'Stop it!' he yelled. 'Just stop. Please.'

He was becoming increasingly agitated. A threat to anyone he came into contact with. Her only hope was that the other team members would arrive before he finished arguing with himself. It was not to be. All of a sudden, he strode down the steps in the direction of the children's play area.

'Suspect on the move. Calling all officers, suspect is on the move towards children's play area.'

She slid away, maintaining a safe distance behind Ben. If she spotted any stray joggers or visitors, she was prepared to shoot him rather than have another innocent person murdered. She accelerated her pace. Once he was closer to Jamie, they'd stop him together. He didn't falter, his steps firm as he strode towards the play area.

He dropped out of sight momentarily, causing Kate to sprint onwards to the turn in the path and to breathe again when she spotted him still alone.

'Suspect continuing on path towards play area.'

Ben continued at a pace then came to an abrupt halt. The arguing began once more.

'This is too much.' He appeared to listen to a tirade then said, 'But a child, Lisa? No. You're right. Our child didn't deserve to die. You're right. I should do this. It's the only way.'

She froze momentarily. Ben was talking to his dead wife. He was conversing with her like she spoke to Chris. Ben had tipped so far into mania he was now being governed by a voice in his head. One that forced him to kill. Furthermore, judging by what she'd heard, he was going to murder a child. There was no escaping the fact she and Ben were alike. The only difference was she hadn't killed anybody. A voice in her head whispered, 'Tom Champion.'

She hadn't pulled any trigger, but by allowing him to be tortured and forcing a confession, she had endangered his life. Moreover, she was sure he was dead. She wasn't so far removed from Ben after all.

Ben was off again. Jamie was in her ear.

'I'm in position by the play area.'

'No! Do *not* confront him. You are putting yourself in danger.'

'How else are we going to capture him?'

'Jamie, he's armed and dangerous.'

'We can't let him get away. He could kill a child. If not this time, then the next.'

'Get out of sight. He could shoot you.'

'Better that and you catch him than a kiddie dying.'

'Jamie!'

Contact was broken and she began to run. It wasn't time for heroics. Ben was a man on the edge. If he couldn't find a suitable target to kill, he'd murder whoever was there. She raced past the clock tower. Beyond it a scene was unfolding that almost caused her to scream. Jamie and Ben were grappling on the ground, hands scrabbling for the weapon that lay between them. She thundered towards them, couldn't decide from the tangle of limbs which body part belonged to whom. She couldn't shoot in case she injured Jamie, who, listening to the painful grunts, was getting a beating. Before she could launch herself into the melee, Ben grasped the pistol and hurled it with force into Jamie's face. Blood spewed from his lips.

'Officer down!' she yelled into the communications unit. Ben was speeding away.

'Jamie!'

He groaned. She had no choice but to leave him. She darted after her suspect, flying along the pathways, back towards the lodge and the entrance. There were numerous low walls surrounding the park that he could easily surmount, undergrowth he could hide in, and with him being trained in escape and evasion techniques, she feared her chances of catching him once she lost sight of him would be slim. However, she wasn't unfit and had staying power. She dug deep, arms pumping, as she ran the fastest she'd ever run.

'Suspect headed towards Queen's Park Avenue.'

She was gaining on him until he weaved to the left and dived off the path towards thick undergrowth and ploughed into it. She pursued him, mindful he might attack rather than make good his escape. The dilemma was whether she should take the chance and climb over the wall to hunt for him on Queen's Park Avenue or wait to see if he reappeared. She decided if she were him, she would have parked on the roadside. Now she'd be trying to get as close as possible to her vehicle under the cover of the bushes, rather than be flushed out on to a main road where she'd stand more chance of being taken down. If her hunch was right, Ben was still in the park, making his way to his car.

Decision made, she strained to hear any rustling that might give away his location. The rapid beating of her pulse in her ears made it almost impossible to detect any other sound. She'd called it wrong. Then there was the tiniest crack, a twig breaking, and Ben emerged from the undergrowth and raced away, back in the direction they'd just come from.

She was on the move in an instant. 'Suspect still in Longton Park.'

Morgan's voice was clear. 'Arrived and in position on Queen's Park Avenue.'

Officers were coming. More would follow. Ahead of her, Ben ran towards the clock tower. Her energy was flagging. Even with all her training, she couldn't keep up the sprinting. Ben was pulling away again, no doubt aiming for another exit point. More voices in her earpiece alerted her to the fact the others were now here. They could still catch him if they surrounded the park, but it was a huge ask. Her breathing became laboured and her limbs heavy. As she sucked in ragged gasps, she caught sight of motion. Jamie emerged from behind a tree and hurled himself at Ben, flooring him. Spurred on by the action, she made for them. Ben was fighting off a blood-stained Jamie, who clung to his leg and wouldn't release it. Ben raised the pistol and Kate shouted, 'No!'

Fuelled by a spurt of adrenalin, she sped towards the men. She reached for her weapon. There was no way he was going to kill Jamie. Eyes blurred by sweat, she found Jamie in a heap, face caked in blood and mouth open. She levelled her gun at Ben.

'I'm okay, guv.' His words were thick, but he managed to roll on to his side to get up.

Ben remained on the ground; his legs pulled towards his chest. His face crumpled. 'I never wanted any of this. Lisa said it was the only way.'

'Put the weapon down, Ben.'

He laid it down and she kicked it away from his reach.

'It was the only way for what?'

'For us all to be together again.'

'Benjamin Hopkins, I am arresting you on suspicion of the murder of Asif Baqui, Helen Doherty, Harriet Parkinson, Tobias Abrahams and Susanna Lopez. You do not have to say anything. But it may harm your defence if you do not mention when questioned something which you later rely on in court. Anything you do say may be given in evidence.'

◆ ◆ ◆

Jamie's right cheek had swollen and was already showing signs of bruising.

'Jeez, mate. I'd hate to see the other bloke,' said Morgan, standing by the ambulance tailgate.

Jamie gave a lopsided grin. His lip required stitching and he'd lost a tooth. The paramedics believed he'd broken a couple of ribs. Given they weren't sure of the extent of other injuries sustained, he was being admitted to hospital.

'Hey, make sure you get plenty of meds and a good night's sleep. Might be the last one you'll manage before the baby's born.' Morgan patted the door and moved away to join Emma.

Kate stayed inside the ambulance. 'How are you feeling, really?'

'Not too bad, guv.' His words were slurred.

'You did good. I'll be putting in a recommendation for you.'

'Really?'

'Yes. You showed fortitude today. We'd have lost him if you hadn't stepped in.'

He lay back on the gurney and shut his eyes. She decided the painkillers he'd been given were taking over and it was time for her to leave. She stood up. He didn't open his eyes, but he did speak, slowly.

'I do know why Heather was taken off the investigation. We were searching for underage sex-workers. She thought the person in charge was using the investigation for their own purposes, as a front, to find one girl in particular. She asked me what to do about some evidence she'd found pointing to him. I told her to drop it. She didn't, the silly cow, instead she challenged him over it. He denied it. Said it was for the best for everyone if she left the operation. We were told she'd asked to leave. I never questioned it even though I knew it wasn't true. I just do as I'm asked, you see?'

'And that was the end of it.'

'No. She kept digging. Unearthed the girl she believed was the real target and warned her off. The girl vanished after that. We couldn't locate her, or her pimp, and the operation got wound up.'

'Who was leading the operation, Jamie?'

'You already know who, guv, don't you?'

'Superintendent Dickson?'

'You're good, guv. I like working with you.' His eyelids fluttered as the painkillers took over.

'Thank you, Jamie.'

He didn't respond. She climbed down from the ambulance. Jamie had jumped ship. He was now working with her. She thanked the paramedics. Told them to take care of Jamie and made for her car. This wasn't over yet. Not by a long chalk.

CHAPTER
TWENTY-FOUR

Kate shifted on her chair. Ben, directly opposite her, spent most of the interview in tears, a broken man, willing to confess to his crimes but all the while adamant he wasn't wholly responsible. DCI William Chase had joined her on what would be their final case together.

Ben rocked backwards and forwards on his chair, a steady motion, fists bunched on his knees.

William tried for the third time to get Ben to answer intelligibly. 'You say your wife, Lisa, planted the idea into your head?'

Ben snivelled. 'She's been at me for months, non-stop. She convinced me this was the way to fix everything. She can't get any peace, you see? None of them can, not until I fix it.'

'When you say "none of them", who do you mean, Ben?'

'All of them: Lisa, Rowena, Kathleen, Dillon, Archie and Gr—'

The rocking intensified. His lawyer, a quiet, middle-aged man, cleared his throat. 'I think you'll agree my client isn't in a fit state to answer your questions.'

Kate levelled her gaze at the man before turning to the accused, her voice gentle. 'Mr Hopkins, Ben . . . would you like us to stop asking you questions?'

'I . . . No. It's okay. It's for the best.'

'I think your client has expressed a desire to continue,' Kate said, resting her arms on the table and leaning closer to Ben. 'You were telling us about the others. They were all involved in the car accident, weren't they? Your sister, your nephews and nieces, your wife?'

Ben stopped rocking and began nodding slowly.

'Can I ask you to speak, for the purposes of the recording, Ben? A yes or no will do.'

'Yes.'

'And Lisa got into your head.' She already knew the answer. Her own experiences with Chris made it easy to relate to Ben. She understood his pain, his frustration and how desperately he would have wanted to hear his family's voices.

'Yes.'

'When you told us she "can't get any peace", what exactly did you mean by that?'

'It was like she was anchored to me, forever. You can't imagine what it's like. She was there, but she wasn't. I know she's dead. I know she isn't a ghost, but I can hear her, all the time. Now and again, I can sense her, touch her. Her voice is in my head even when I don't want it there. Don't get me wrong. I want her to be alive so badly it rips me apart, even after a year, and part of me loves hearing her. It's so . . . real.'

Kate had to look away. It could have been her speaking. She felt exactly the same way about Chris and, even now, after this investigation, and seeing how it had destroyed Ben, she still wanted to hear him.

'It was Lisa's idea to make the attacks random. To choose a destination and a time, then wait for the first person to appear. She said it was fairer that way, that fate played a part. As it had with our family.'

William cleared his throat but didn't speak. Kate sensed him tensing beside her. There was no justification for Ben's actions. Moreover, he couldn't recognise his own accountability. At least she saw hers. She knew she was at fault, that she had crossed lines. Ben was lacking a moral compass. She still bore some trace of one.

'Lisa believed it would help me exorcise the guilt I'd been carrying over the accident, and free her.'

Lisa believed. Lisa. Ben. They were the same person. *Ben* had believed it would help him assuage the guilt. He was putting the onus on an imaginary voice, an invisible person. Kate dampened her dry lips. Was her quest to bring down Dickson really for Chris, or as revenge for her benefit? She rubbed her lips together again. Heat rose up her neck. She had to focus on the interview, not her own guilt.

'Is Lisa talking to you now?' she asked.

'No.'

'Do the others speak to you?'

'Only sometimes. Usually at night. The children come to my bedside and tell me they can't sleep and that I'm to blame. Mostly they talk to Lisa and she relays what they say.'

The man had clearly descended into chaos, allowing Lisa to be the malicious force in his life, whereas Chris had been the force of reason in hers. Ben had used his grief to destroy others. Kate had used hers to maintain a semblance of normality. It was only because Chris had stopped talking to her that she was sliding over the edge, doing things she would otherwise not do. Chris's voice had prevented her from becoming like Ben.

She watched him regain some calm, as William, the gentle father figure, coaxed him to respond. 'You're doing really well, Ben. We're beginning to understand what has been happening to you. Tell me, when you were at Westport Lake, you had an argument with Lisa, didn't you?'

'That's right.'

'Can you tell us what it was about?'

He lowered his gaze. 'I didn't do as she asked. She wanted to keep it true to the accident: two adults, four children. I should have chosen a child.'

'You refused?'

'Not exactly. I went to the playground to find a child alone. There was a little boy there. Billy. I couldn't do it. The last time I'd been there, Gracie and Dillon had played at the same playground, chasing each other and laughing. I walked away. I was going to leave altogether. Lisa and I had a bad argument. In the end, I stayed. Eventually a man came jogging past. I chose him.'

'What about Longton Park? Did you have any plans to kill a child there?'

He sniffed. 'Lisa insisted I went through with it. She said the babies, Gracie and Archie, couldn't pass over unless I did, and if I didn't, I'd hear them crying every single night for the rest of my life.'

Kate's palms were damp with sweat. She clamped them under her armpits. It could easily be her sitting in Ben's position. Ben had concocted a twisted, bizarre retribution for the deaths of his loved ones that made sense to him. What William, Emma and the lawyer would never fully comprehend was that Ben *was* in contact with his wife. She was real to him. He honestly believed shooting random victims would give him the mental release he desperately required. She understood him better than anyone in the interview room. She and Ben weren't poles apart. In fact, the more he spoke, the more she imagined she could hear Chris's voice returning. Whispers. Warnings to stay silent and not give away anything.

Ben's voice was quiet. 'There was a man at Blythe Bridge station on the phone. I shot him, and a woman at the Trentham Estate, the snowboard instructor and the woman at the petrol station. None of them suffered. Not like my family.'

'And how did you choose your victims, Ben?' William asked.

'By chance. Fate decided who would appear and die, not me.'

Kate sat rigid with fear. She'd almost crossed the same line. After all the dead ends and frustrations she'd faced during her investigations into Dickson, she'd even considered asking the same man who had tortured Tom Champion to kill Dickson. Chris's voice in her head wasn't as vindictive as the one Ben listened to. With sudden clarity she realised he hadn't asked her to pursue Dickson relentlessly. She had chosen that path. She and Ben could both hear the voices of those they loved, but while Lisa pushed Ben to violence and illogic, Chris had been pushing for Kate to be better than she would otherwise be.

Once they had his confession, she sped to the washroom, glad to be alone with her thoughts. She and Ben were almost two of a kind. Her haunted expression in the mirror spoke volumes. It was time to stop her vendetta against Dickson and move on, before she found herself on the wrong side of the interview table.

She reached for her buzzing phone. 'DI Young.'

Nothing but silence.

'Hello?'

A voice, timid, almost inaudible, spoke.

'My friend, Rosa, was murdered by a policeman. I know things, important things, and I have proof, but before I tell you, I need protection.'

CHAPTER
TWENTY-FIVE

There was only one person who Kate could turn to for help.

Bradley's voice was gruff with sleep. 'This had better be good.'

'I've got to collect an important package,' she said.

Bradley was quick on the uptake. 'What time are you picking it up?'

'Three hours. I'm already at the main depot.'

'Ten minutes.'

The line went dead. If Bradley agreed to look after Stanka for a few days, she could think of nowhere better than his house with its gated entrance and two German shepherd dogs that roamed freely in the grounds. Even though her eyelids felt weighted, her mind was wide awake, processing the information that had fallen into her lap. Time was of the essence and subterfuge necessary. Dickson couldn't find out. She had to act before he realised what she was up to or discovered Stanka's whereabouts. Following Rosa's death, the girl had taken flight from Leeds and Kate had arranged to collect her in three hours' time from the entrance to the North Pier in Blackpool. What happened afterwards depended on Bradley.

In spite of the urge to do so, she didn't vocalise her thoughts to Chris. The interview with Ben had frightened her and her only consolation was she hadn't descended into the same dark place as him.

'Haven't you, though? Here you are crossing a line again.'

Had she not been thinking about his voice during Ben's interrogation, she would have been surprised to hear Chris so clearly once more. She pressed her lips together so she couldn't reply and disagree with him. Her plan was the only way. She was fully aware of the correct procedure, yet following it was something she couldn't afford to do. She wasn't going to risk losing the last possible connection between Dickson and Chris.

There was movement on the surface of the reservoir water, silver ripples that spread out in an ever-widening circle until they melted away. Rain began to patter on the roof, its soft drumbeats in time with her heart. Apart from the paperwork and a debrief, her part in the investigation into the recent murders was over. There was every chance Ben would plead diminished responsibility and the outcome would most likely be unsatisfactory to the victims' families. Whichever way Kate looked at it, Ben was still responsible for the deaths of five people. She knew talking to Chris was unhealthy and, although she listened to his voice, she would never follow any advice that would result in murdering somebody. Ben should own his actions, like she had to own hers.

Car lights approached and the Range Rover turned into the car park. She slipped outside into the darkness to join Bradley. If he didn't agree, there could only be one course of action left to her – one she had decided upon, not Chris. And she would bear its consequences.

◆ ◆ ◆

Bradley had listened to her, then insisted on accompanying her to Blackpool, arguing his vehicle would attract less attention than her own. She'd dozed off at one point, coming to only as they were driving along the promenade.

'Sorry.'

'It's fine. I'm not much of a conversationalist,' he replied.

'You are sure Gwen won't mind?' Kate had found Gwen, his wife, to be somewhat standoffish at first.

'We've been through this. Gwen will be okay with it. We've got surveillance equipment and guard dogs. When I'm working, I'll make sure somebody is around to keep an eye on the girl.'

'It won't be for long.'

'Then you don't need to ask again.'

She eased back against the leather, as comfortable as Chris's office chair, and studied the skyline, a giant silhouette of buildings and, behind them, the iconic tower.

'You ever come to the illuminations?' she asked.

'Brought the grandkids a couple of years ago,' he grunted.

Kate had investigated the death of his son-in-law, Alex, and met his daughter, Fiona, and her two boys. She understood him to be protective of them all, the alpha male of the family, and knew better than to pry further.

Traffic was light. Two young women in thick jackets and leggings were being pulled along the road by two eager Staffordshire bull terriers. Blackpool had its darker side. Central Drive was infamous for its deprivation, where sex-workers had become prevalent around the junction with Palatine Road. She wondered if Stanka had been one of them. She would soon find out.

They got closer to the North Pier. She began scouring the pavement for a girl. Bradley pulled up before the main entrance. 'I don't want to scare her off. She's only expecting to see you. I'll wait for you both.'

She unclipped her seatbelt and exited on to the pavement, where brisk winds whipped at her face, making her hair dance.

She lowered her head and crossed the road towards the oldest and longest of the three piers, once a promenade, now full of attractions to entertain families. She stood in front of the Victorian-style entrance and looked left and right. There was no sign of Stanka. Then, out of the corner of her eye, she caught sight of a shadow detaching itself from the traditional sweet kiosk with its minaret roof, and walked towards it.

'Stanka?'

The girl was petite, not much taller than five foot, in grey joggers, face swaddled by the matching crop hoodie. Her voice had an accent Kate placed as Eastern European. 'We must go.'

'I've come with a friend. He and his family are going to protect you.'

'It's not enough.' The hoodie slipped to reveal a pretty face, narrow, heavy brows and dark shoulder-length hair. The girl's eyes grew large in the half-light. Her hand tightened around the handles of a small carryall.

'They'll keep you safe. Trust me.'

'You don't understand. I will be killed like Rosa.'

'No. I won't let that happen. *We* won't let that happen.'

'I have something for you. It is why he wants to kill me. Please take it now.'

She held out her free hand. Kate took the mobile phone.

'What's on this?'

'Video. Of the night at Maddox Club. Rosa filmed him.'

A van drove past. The man at the wheel turned to stare at them.

'Come on. We need to get you away from here.'

The girl didn't move. 'I must be safe. He's been looking for us since that night when they killed the boy who was with us.'

'Stanka, you can keep running or you can come with me. Which is it to be?'

The girl cast a look left and right, then stepped out from the darkness.

'See that Range Rover parked over there? That's my friend, Bradley. He used to be in the SAS, and he's trained in martial arts. He has friends too, who will also help to protect you. You are going to stay with him and his wife until I can arrange something else, more permanent.'

The girl nodded.

Kate waited until there was no sign of any traffic. 'Come on. Time to go.'

They walked quickly to the car. Kate put the phone in her pocket. It could contain the vital evidence she required rather than the circumstantial evidence she'd been accumulating. She knew exactly what she was going to do next.

◆　◆　◆

The night sky had passed its darkest moments and black gave way to indigo as dawn approached. The huge gates to Bradley's house opened with a tired groan and they drove into the grounds. The house was squirrelled away from public view down a rural lane and, as Kate emerged from the car to the distant honking of geese, she recalled her first visit here to interview Bradley's daughter, Fiona, about her deceased husband, and how she hadn't taken to the man. Now he was her sole ally in this turbulent quest.

The house wasn't as flamboyant or impressive as his daughter's, a grand farmhouse extended tastefully to match the original architecture. He went ahead to ensure the dogs didn't come rushing out, then waved them inside.

The large entrance hall was exactly as she remembered it, the rustic console table near the door containing a photograph of the Chapmans; Bradley in military dress, and glamorous Gwen in a russet silk dress that hugged her lithe frame and with blonde hair piled high on her head. There were other family photos: individual school photos of the grandchildren, a picture of the whole family when Alex had been alive, but the picture of Fiona and Alex's wedding, taken on a beach, had disappeared. The solid ticking of a grandfather clock filled the silence. Stanka was glued to the spot.

'It's so . . . big.'

Bradley made for the kitchen. 'In here.'

They followed him into the hub of the home, where warmth and the faint smell of herbs lingered in the air. Stanka still clung to her bag, eyes wide, hood up.

'The Aga's on if you need to warm up, Stanka,' he said, indicating the cream oven. She shuffled forwards, both hands on her bag. Under the lights she looked no more than a child. Kate felt heartsick that such a vulnerable young girl had been selling her body and had been so terrified for her life.

Bradley clearly felt the same way. He removed his waxed jacket to reveal a well-toned physique, biceps bulging from under a T-shirt. 'Welcome to your new home . . . for now. I'll introduce you to the dogs later. They'll be fine once they've met you. It's strangers they don't like.' He gave a conspiratorial smile in her direction. 'So, what do you want? Tea? Coffee?'

'Tea,' she replied.

'Kate?' It was the first time he'd ever called her by her first name. It felt intimate, a bond of solidarity between them.

'Same for me, please.'

'Do I tell you everything now or do I have to go to the police station? I don't want to go to the station. Farai said it would be dangerous for me to go there.'

'Does Farai know you rang me?'

'He gave me your number. He said you were the only person who could help me. He couldn't look after me any longer. It was too dangerous to be seen together.'

'Where is he?'

'I honestly don't know. We left Burnley . . . after Rosa was killed.'

'Did you ring the police to tell them her name?'

She nodded. 'Farai was angry. He said I was putting us both at risk. I didn't care. She was my friend. They needed to know her name.' She dropped her gaze and Kate extended her hand, put it on her arm.

'No station,' said Kate.

'Thank you.'

'I'd like to record what you have to say, if that's alright.' She pulled out her mobile, placed it on the oak-topped island. 'Come and sit down and tell us everything.'

The girl put down her bag and climbed on to a stool. Bradley said nothing as he rested against the worktop, arms folded, listening to every word. A muscle in his jaw flexed as she spoke. She told them about the night the young boy was murdered in the room next to theirs and how, afterwards, they'd been in danger. Kate already knew about this, but Bradley didn't, so she let the girl go at her own pace, recalling details that Kate would be able to use against Dickson.

'We moved from Stoke to Manchester where a police officer found us, but she was nice. She wanted to help us. I thought it was a trap. Rosa was sure it wasn't and went alone to meet her.'

'Where did she meet this woman?'

'At Stoke railway station.'

'Do you remember the name of the woman?'

'Rosa wrote it down for me, with the date and time of the meeting in case anything went wrong. I have it on a piece of paper in my bag. It was Heather.'

'What happened at the meeting?'

'Heather told Rosa the policeman who was looking for us was a high-ranking superintendent. She'd found a date-rape drug in his locker at work and was worried he was going to use it on us. Rosa told her about the Maddox Club, how she'd already slept with him. That he wasn't after her to rape her but to kill her.'

'And did she tell Rosa the name of the drug?'

'Special K.'

The same drug the girl had apparently overdosed on.

'Did Rosa ever take drugs?'

'Never. She didn't smoke or take drugs.'

'Can you explain why she died of an overdose?'

'No. I only know she was working. One of the other girls saw her get into a car with a client, and we didn't see her again. Then we heard she had been found dead.'

'Did the girl see what sort of car it was?'

'Farai asked her too. It was a white or silver estate car.'

'She didn't know what make it was?'

'Maybe Mercedes.'

Kate glanced at Bradley. Dickson drove a silver Mercedes E-Class Estate. It was, unfortunately, still circumstantial evidence. The say-so of a frightened girl, a sex-worker who'd lost her friend and who could, in a defence lawyer's opinion, be making it up. Kate wasn't sure she could put Stanka on a witness stand or even expose her to the sort of questioning that would be inevitable.

'Here,' said Bradley, placing two mugs on the island. 'Drink your tea.'

Stanka smiled gingerly and took the mug. It would soon be time for Kate to return to work. Between now and then, she had important decisions to make. Did she follow the right route, or did she choose the alternative? She watched Stanka sip the tea, dark hair falling around her elfin-like face, delicate hands around the bone-china mug. She'd already half made up her mind.

CHAPTER
TWENTY-SIX

Kate drove towards the blood-red waters. The sunrise was one of the most spectacular she had ever seen – the sky on fire with flames of orange, red and pink. She cast an eye over the reservoir in search of the swans but couldn't spot them. She turned her attention to the problem she faced – what to do with the information now in her possession.

She had her own career to consider, and yet she owed it to all those who had died at Dickson's behest to expose him for who he really was.

She was almost across the reservoir when she saw it – a heap of white feathers. It was one of the white swans she had grown so fond of. *No!* She came to a halt, threw herself out of the car and raced across to the bird. Its neck and head were twisted to one side, a red bib over its chest. A stone filled her throat and she crumpled against the wall next to it, unable to stop the sobs.

Fatigued, subdued and despondent, Kate climbed the stairs to her office. The loss of the swan had turned her upside down. She'd reported the dead cob to the authorities, who assured her the bird would be removed, yet she couldn't help but think about the female who would now be searching for her mate. It was heartbreaking to know she wouldn't see the pair together again. They weren't just wildfowl. She'd felt such affinity with them. Perceived them as an embodiment of her and Chris. Their togetherness had touched her. Now, like her, the remaining swan was completely alone.

'Morning, Kate. Why the sombre face? I thought you'd be celebrating,' said William.

'Not in the mood, William.'

'Come and have a chat.'

She trooped after him into his office and flopped on to the chair.

'You and your team did a great job. I'm so proud of you. You've done it, Kate. You've shown everyone. There'll be an official announcement later today but, from next week, you will be heading your old unit again. It goes without saying, you'll be highly recommended for promotion. Now is the time to seize it.'

She mirrored his smile even though she shared little of the enthusiasm he evidently felt.

'There's no stopping you now. You gave me the best leaving present possible. I can go out on a high. Thank you. So, do you fancy celebrating tonight, my shout – the whole team?'

The others would be up for it and deserved the treat. She thanked him.

'There's something else I feel I ought to come clean about. I should have spoken to you about it when you asked about your father, except the timing was wrong. You were heading the investigation. I didn't want you harbouring grudges. But . . . things have changed. I don't approve of the way you've been treated recently. I want to set things straight before I leave.'

Her body felt too heavy to move. She waited.

'The allegations levelled at your father were false, as you know. I should have guessed you'd get to the bottom of it. When you turned up with the photograph of us all, me, your dad, John Dickson and the others, I thought you had. You see, John Dickson was also a DI at the time and keen to climb the ladder. Your dad and he were both being considered for a DCI post until the allegations. By the time they got to the bottom of them, it was too late, and Mitch's reputation had suffered. John got the promotion.'

Kate's lips unglued. 'Superintendent Dickson made up the allegations?'

'Yes.'

'And you knew?'

'I did, and I'm ashamed to this day that I didn't say something about it back then. I thought Mitch would get promoted next time around and, of course, that didn't happen.'

'Why did you stay quiet?'

'It's difficult to explain. John had a reach; people in his pocket who could make things happen if you didn't play it his way. I didn't want the same thing, or worse, to happen to me. The job was all I had.'

'I don't believe what I'm hearing. You allowed it to happen. You should have reported him. Stood up to him! My father was your best friend.'

'And he forgave me. He understood the situation.'

'But you let Dickson get away with it. It was bullying. You helped him to become stronger. Did you believe he wouldn't use his *reach*, as you call it, over and over again to get what he wanted?'

'It was a long time ago.'

'You know what happens to bullies. They become bigger bullies.'

'That'll do. I know what I did was wrong. I've lived with the knowledge.'

'Tilly was right when she said you were only looking out for me to atone for your guilt.'

'No! I admit I became your self-appointed guardian. But it was only because I *wanted* to guide you. I've been proud of every one of your achievements. I look at you and I see Mitch. He might not have made DCI, but you will. I wasn't going to let history repeat itself, which is why I stuck my neck out for you in the superintendent's office. After you left, he took me to task over it. I stuck to my guns. Told him I wouldn't let him do the dirty a second time. He won't block you, Kate.'

They sat in silence, Kate realising her anger wasn't directed at William. Her dad had forgiven his weakness and she could be as magnanimous. Her rage was against the man who had targeted those people she loved most in the world.

'Okay. I think we're done here,' she said.

'Are we good?'

She nodded. 'We're good.'

'And you'll join me at the White Rose at six?'

'Yes.'

'Make sure the team knows.'

She left, fury directed at Dickson for his crimes bubbling like a boiling pan. He had to be stopped. William didn't have the guts to do it, but he was an old man. She wasn't scared. Not any more.

◆　◆　◆

Morgan and Emma were completing reports, a box of doughnuts the giveaway sign of relaxation and celebration.

'Help yourself,' said Morgan to Kate.

Emma rolled her eyes. 'He's already wolfed down all the chocolate ones.'

'I'm a growing boy,' he replied, patting his stomach.

'The only way you'll be growing is around that midriff of yours.'

'Yeah, but you'll still fancy me if I do.'

'In your dreams.'

Judging by the playful tone in her voice, Emma didn't mean it. Kate passed on the news about the celebration and decided to ring Samuel to invite him along too. He declined.

'I've got something on tonight.'

'Can't you reschedule? You're missing a treat, William's paying.'

'I can't. It's my Samaritan work.'

'Oh, I didn't know.'

'I don't talk about it much. I'm paying back to the community, so to speak. I know what some of these people are going through. I've been there myself. Still struggle some days.' The green wristband he wore took on a greater significance.

'Well, you're always welcome to drop by and have a coffee whenever you're passing.'

'That's kind of you. It's probably better if I don't.'

She looked at Emma, who was flicking small balls of paper at Morgan, who pretended he couldn't feel them. 'I understand,' she said.

Getting to her feet, she left them to it and headed for the changing rooms. She checked all the cubicles were empty before pulling out Rosa's phone to watch the video she'd seen several times already. It was shot in a bedroom. Rosa must have perched the mobile on a shelf nearby and set it off before she and Dickson had begun sexual relations. Why she'd chosen to do so was a mystery, unless she'd intended using it for blackmail purposes. Kate wasn't interested in the sex. Watching Dickson made her feel ill. What followed was even more stomach-churning.

Moans, then audible cries for help. Rosa's scared voice: 'What's happening?'

'Nothing. Ignore it.'

A high-pitched scream. Rosa pushing Dickson away.

'You must help.'

'No. It's normal. Ian likes it rough.'

Rosa kicking out at him. 'Go, or I'll scream too.'

'Listen, you little bitch, I paid for you. You do as I say.'

Grunting. Dickson pushing Rosa back down and continuing. Moans through the wall. All the while, Rosa's frightened face, staring at the camera.

Dickson making one final grunt and rolling off her. A kerfuffle. Shouts. Dickson leaping to his feet. Leaving the room. Rosa pulling the sheet up to her chin, staring at the camera. No more noise. A minute. Another. Then Dickson returning. Marching to the bed.

'Let's get one thing straight, you heard and saw nothing tonight, right? Anybody asks you, you say nothing.'

'What's happened?'

'Nothing.' Moving closer, tightening his hand around her jaw and squeezing. 'You say a word and the same thing will happen to you as to him next door, only it will be even more unpleasant. Do you understand me? I will send somebody to find you and have you killed.'

Dickson leaves again, presumably to help deal with the fallout next door, where a boy lies dead.

The video contradicted everything Dickson had told her during the investigation at the time. Moreover, it explained why he had shut Rosa up once and for all.

She pocketed the phone once more. William had spoken of Dickson's 'reach' back when he'd been promoted to DCI. She couldn't imagine how far it stretched by now. He'd recruited officers to find the girls, was responsible for the death of Bradley's friend, Cooper Monroe, was likely to be behind Rosa's death, and maybe Heather's too. There was no doubt in her mind he had also helped organise the concealment of the dead boy's body and the hitman who'd killed her husband. What she'd always suspected seemed more likely than ever. However, she couldn't fight Dickson in the courts. She would come out of it too badly. There was only one way, even though it might mean losing Chris's voice forever – to continue to play dirty.

◆ ◆ ◆

The takeaway van had shut early. The cheery tables had been cleared away. Kate sat on a nearby wooden bench. Next to her, Dan Corrance sunk further into his parka as if it were a magic cloak of invisibility.

'You are kidding me,' he said.

'Everything you need is on this phone and the USB stick.'

He couldn't disguise the glee in his voice. 'This will cause a major shitstorm.'

'Well, you have facts this time, a video with footage you can leak online, and a witness who is willing to talk to you. There can be no comeback. You have proof to substantiate your claims.'

'My editor will love this. But, Kate, why aren't you taking this to your lot? Get him charged.'

'No. I've gone as far as I can with this quest. There's no other way of stopping this man. Here's a phone number for Bradley Chapman. He'll work with you on this and give you whatever else you need. He'll ensure you speak to Stanka. What do you say? Are you sure you want to go ahead?'

'I say, fucking hell, this is gold dust, and, yes, I definitely do want to run with it. Thank you.'

She passed over the items she'd been keeping safe. 'Once this is exposed, he'll be less likely to harm you or any of us. Suspicions would rest immediately with him if anything were to happen to us.

Nevertheless, remain vigilant. Make backups of everything, protect it all and talk to Bradley. He'll have some tips on how to stay safe.'

'What about you?'

'I'm pretty much done. It's taken a year to get this far, and I'm worn out. I've lost the man I loved with all my heart. I can't get the closure I need. Dickson's beaten me. I'll never find out if he had anything to do with Chris's death, even if I continue searching for another year, or another ten years after that. It's time for me to give up.'

'I'm sorry you feel that way. Really. Maybe you should move on, though. You can't keep going over the same ground. You'll end up . . . well, you know.'

'I know. If your editor is willing to go ahead, text *yes* to my pay-as-you-go-number. If not, don't text at all. Goodbye, Dan.'

'Bye, Kate.'

She'd given away everything that had kept her connected to Chris. She supposed the evidence she'd collected was in good hands. Dickson would be revealed for the vile snake he was. If, afterwards, he somehow managed to get off any charges levelled at him, he'd still have the stigma of Rosa's video, combined with Stanka's recorded and written statement, which would prevent him from returning to his former position in the police force.

She walked away from the *Gazette* offices for the last time. Her quest was almost at an end. She'd lied when she'd told Dan she was beaten. Using the pay-as-you-go again, she dialled the number that would lead her to the finale. John Dickson answered the phone.

'Sir, it's imperative I meet you. This can't be discussed at the station. It's about Stanka. Would you meet me at Blithfield Reservoir?'

There was a long pause before he agreed. 'I can be there in an hour.'

'Thank you, sir.'

She reached her car, got inside, put her head in her hands. The image of the swan floated in front of her eyes. The sorrow it brought was unbearable. She was like its mate, forever pining until she died of a broken heart. 'Chris, it's now or never. I have to hear you again. I can't face a life without you. I simply can't.' When there was still no reply she sobbed again until she was wrung dry.

CHAPTER
TWENTY-SEVEN

Night was falling, bringing its dark world. She parked along a lit-
tle-used lane a couple of miles from the reservoir and removed the
lightweight bicycle from the car. It was imperative Dickson trusted
her and could see she wasn't a threat. This would be the only way.
She attached her cycling helmet, swung a leg over the crossbar and
began pedalling.

Moments later, Dickson's Mercedes whispered past her, heading in the direction of the car park on the near side of the reservoir.
She maintained her pace. It wasn't far. She was thankful that there
was no sign of the dead swan's mate.

After this meeting she wouldn't return here. Chris's voice had
joined others that local legend claimed lived below the water. If he
wouldn't talk to her here, he wouldn't talk to her anywhere. All the
same, she spoke to him.

'I promised I'd see it through to the end. I always keep my
promises.'

She crossed the causeway, wind stinging her face. Dickson
would be parked out of sight, more or less where she'd parked to
meet Bradley. She coasted over the final part of the causeway and
turned into the empty car park. Dickson watched her arrival and

opened the car door. She drew to a halt, then walked the bike to the water's edge, where she propped it carefully against the low wall.

He slammed the car door and clipped his way towards her.

'What's this all about, Kate? I knew you were taking your exercise regime seriously, but really, you rode here on that?'

'Yes, sir. I prefer it to driving. Riding gives me a chance to order my thoughts. It was Chris's bike,' she added.

Dickson gave a brief nod. 'Before we begin, I need to know you're not recording this. There are people who will go to extraordinary lengths to land me in it, so to speak.'

'I'm not one of them. I prefer to ask direct questions.'

'Be that as it may, hand me your helmet.'

She held it out for him. He took it, examined it for any recording devices then took it across to his car and tossed it in. He returned and indicated she should undress. 'Come on, show me you're not wired.'

He waited and with a sigh she undid the zip and opened up her exercise top to reveal a sports bra. Dickson's lips curled. 'You really should cut down on the exercise. You're nothing but skin and bones.' He took a stride towards her, placed cold hands under her bralette, felt around her breasts for devices before removing his fingers from her flesh.

'I'm commando if you want to check thoroughly,' she said, lowering her exercise bottoms and staring at him. He cast a disinterested eye over her.

'Turn around.'

She performed a slow full circle. 'I've not brought a phone either. Nothing. I wanted it to be just you and me.' She pulled up her bottoms and removed her cycling shoes for him to check.

'This is curious behaviour, DI Young. I'm starting to wonder if the investigation hasn't taken its toll on you and pushed you towards a relapse.' The fake concern didn't perturb her. It was only to be expected.

'Not a relapse, sir. I know when I'm beaten.'

He handed back her shoes and she slipped them on. 'Okay, enough of this charade. We've established you're not recording this, whatever it is. You invited me here because you had news about an underage sex-worker.'

'That's right. I know where she is.'

'Well?'

'First, I'd like to request a transfer. Get out of Stoke-on-Trent. Start afresh somewhere else altogether.'

He rested his arm on the wall, appeared to give it some thought. 'I've made no secret of the fact I've been concerned about your mental health for a while. A new start is a good move. I'll action it. You could have discussed all this in my office. You didn't need to play the spy or barter with me. I'm happy for you to put in for a transfer. Why drag me all the way out here?'

'I didn't want us to be overheard.'

'Everyone will know soon enough,' he said. 'When you clear out your desk and go.'

'My transfer comes with another caveat.'

His eyes narrowed. 'Don't play childish games with me, Kate. If you don't know where the girl is, don't waste my time any further.'

'She's back in Staffordshire and I can take you to her. I know how much you need to speak to her. After all, she knows what happened at the Maddox Club and has proof to support it.'

He folded his arms and stared hard at her. 'And?'

'I chose this location because it's in the open. There's no surveillance equipment in the vicinity or even along the road to reach the reservoir. There are never many people traversing the causeway at this time of night. Certainly none parked up, birdwatching. I run or cycle here most days. Sometimes, I even come here in the dead of the night, so you see, I know it's safe to meet and talk here. We're alone.'

'Get on with it,' he snapped. 'What is this about?'

She wasn't going to be rushed. 'I want to hear you confess to having had Chris killed. Then I'll get out of your life for good. I won't bother you or tell anyone about your part in the cover-up at the Maddox Club.'

'What are you talking about? Cover-up! Kate, I understand the investigation took its toll and you've struggled, what with everything else that's gone on in your life, but you really are starting to cause me deep concern again. I have no idea what nonsense you are talking about. I came along because your request sounded urgent, and now I find myself deeply concerned about your mental well-being.' There it was again, the fake sincerity. 'I admitted I was at the club the night of the murder. I told you everything I knew at the time of the investigation. I played no part in the boy's death. I wasn't even aware of it.'

'You can drop the act. Thanks to Stanka, I know *exactly* what happened there.'

'The testimony of some sex-worker who is probably also a drug addict, against a superintendent with an excellent work record. Shall we guess how that might pan out?'

'Not a testimony. There's hard evidence. A video Rosa filmed that night and gave to her friend for safekeeping.'

A vein pulsed in his head. 'What video?' he growled.

'One she filmed on her phone. It's conclusive. There's no mistaking what you were doing or what was occurring in the room next door. She left the camera and sound running the whole time.'

He turned away, back rigid with anger. She wondered if he was going to stalk off, leaving her high and dry. She had him on the ropes and had to keep hitting him, this time with lies.

'It wasn't Ian Wentworth's idea to hire the hitman who killed Chris. It was yours, wasn't it? You persuaded Ian to get rid of Chris because he was close to uncovering the murder at the Maddox Club. And Ian was so terrified of being caught, he agreed to your suggestion of hiring an assassin from the dark web. By the time he came to his senses, it was too late, and he could do nothing to stop it.'

He turned back. His lips twisted into a cruel smile. 'Now I know for certain you've got mental health issues.'

'Cooper Monroe told me that's what happened.'

'He can't have.'

'Why not? Because you had him killed by a prison guard? I'm afraid you had Tom Champion act too late.' The name caused a dark cloud to flit across his features. She'd married what little evidence she'd gathered with guesswork to wrongfoot him and, judging by his expression, it was working. She went for the jugular. 'Cooper revealed everything to me personally, in private, way before he was sentenced. So, you see, I've known about it for several months and kept the knowledge to myself.' The lie was thought through. Dickson had believed he'd covered all his bases. This revelation would undermine his confidence, weaken him. Weak opponents made mistakes.

Dickson's nostrils flared. 'It'd be your word against mine. Without Cooper you can't prove anything.'

She stared at him. 'A written statement from Cooper would change things.'

'You're bluffing.'

The lies kept coming. 'You're welcome to take a chance and test out your theory. You shouldn't have underestimated my tenacity, sir. You know I don't give up. I've been a busy bee since the murder inquiry at the Maddox Club. I've amassed quite a collection of confessions and statements that, when pieced together, make for interesting reading. It would certainly give a lawyer plenty of ammunition and see you squirm in court.'

'No. I don't believe you.'

She gave a light shrug. 'Fine. I'm not going to try and convince you otherwise. You see, I don't really care any more. I know what you did. You know what you did. I'm sick and tired of all this subterfuge. I want to move on with my life. I'm willing to trade – Stanka and the information I have gathered, in return for an honest answer. Then, as far as I'm concerned, this is over. Tell me, face to face, did you order the hit on Chris?'

'You know, you've become something of a thorn in my side ever since Chris's death. I guessed you'd be trouble when you refused to take time off like any normal, grieving widow. You tried to muscle in on the investigation into the train attack, pick out and pore over every detail that didn't sit right with you. Why couldn't you just accept what you were told?'

'I wanted the truth.'

'The truth!' He spat the words with contempt. 'Oh, please! You sound like your husband. He used the same argument. Said the public had a right to know "the truth".' He made quotation marks with his fingers in the air. 'Never mind how he went about getting it. Let me tell you about your husband. He was a weasel, a lying weasel who pried into business that didn't concern him. He was a parasite. He wasn't searching for *the truth*, only a scoop to make a bigger name for himself. Truth is a noble ideal. There was nothing noble in how he went about unearthing it. He was ruthless, devious, sneaky. He threatened me and my friends, and I don't take kindly to being threatened. We gave him a chance to back off. He was offered a substantial pay-off, which he stupidly refused. In the end, he left us with no other choice. He browbeat Ian and backed him into a corner, so Ian was prepared to do anything to get rid of your husband. The problem was, Ian lacked direction. I gave it to him—'

He hunched like a bull about to charge, eyes burning into her. 'There, now you know *the truth*. Give me whatever information you've amassed and tell me where the girl is, and I'll sanction your immediate transfer. Then, you and I are finished. If you ever try to come at me again, you know what will happen to you. You've been warned.'

'The same fate as Chris, Cooper and Rosa?'

'Come, come, DI Young. Don't play dumb with me. What are you up to now? Trying to make me confess to more deaths? That wasn't the deal.'

'You're right. It wasn't. Tell me, do you still keep vials of ket-amine in your locker?'

'Enough!'

'Did you play a part in Heather's death because she was on to you?'

'I said, that's enough. Where is the girl?'

'Did you have Heather killed?'

'The girl, Stanka. Where *is* she?'

Kate backed away, took a step towards her bike, felt under the handgrip and removed a minute recording device, the size of a paper clip. She held it aloft for him to see.

'I'm afraid I wasn't being truthful. See, I'm not the reliable Kate you think you know. The same Kate who plays by the rules. I don't roll over like my father did.'

'What the—?'

'Stanka is in a safe house. The wheels to bring you down are already in motion. The *Gazette* is running an exposé on you. They're in possession of the footage filmed at the Maddox Club as well as all the information I dug up on you. You're right, I don't give up. I've been digging since the beginning, building my case against you. Your lies and corruption will be plastered all over the papers. It won't be long before the nationals take up the story and, as the saying goes, mud sticks. You *will* face charges and you *will* be brought to justice. I'm not my father. I can't be bullied.'

He breathed heavily, shoulders rising and falling, then smiled.

'Kate. I warned everyone you were taking on too much.' He tutted. 'You were brave to come back so soon after Chris's death. Everyone could see the effect the pressure was having on you – the pills, the talking to yourself and then that mini breakdown in the train when you almost attacked a passenger. And since then, you've poured yourself back into work, relentlessly, day after day. There's been the intense pressure of not one but three heavy investigations, all to be handled by such a small team. Little wonder you were showing signs again of cracking. You've been burning yourself out. It's clear from your weight loss and your appearance.' He tutted again. 'It won't come as a shock to people when they discover you ended it all here.'

As he spoke the last word, he withdrew a gun from his pocket. Kate had little time to react. She threw her body to one side. The bullet whizzed past her to bury itself into the bank. She threw herself to her feet and hurled herself at him, knocking the gun to the ground with a clatter. It spun away and she reached for his arm to wrench it behind him, he kicked out, twisted away and reached for the gun. Kate couldn't see the weapon, only Dickson's snarling face as he pushed her into the ground. She bucked her hips, causing him to tumble, then kicked both of his feet with all the force she could muster. He fell on to his back then rotated quickly on to his side and rolled away. She spied the gun, now in his hand, and launched again at him, hands fumbling to grasp it. She sensed cold metal, grabbed for the handle. She felt rather than heard the shot. The impact punched her in the ribs, winding her, followed by the weight of the man as he slumped against her chest and slid down the length of her body.

She dropped down beside him. An artery had been punctured. Blood was pumping out. She needed to pack the wound. She pulled off her top, rolled it into a ball and pressed it hard into his chest. He groaned.

She didn't have her phone. Maybe Dickson had one. She patted his pockets gently. Nothing. It could be in his car. If she didn't keep up the pressure on the wound, he would die. If she didn't phone an ambulance, he would die.

His lips moved. 'I ordered the hit on Chris. Happy now? I'm not the only officer who doesn't play by the rules. There are others, worse than me. You're a lone soldier, Kate. You can never beat us all.'

'Shut up. I need to get you help.' She raced to his car, yanked open the door and began searching for a phone. There was one in the glove box. She tore back to him with it in her hand. Before she could dial for emergency services, she knew it was already too late.

She walked to the edge of the reservoir, looked across the water, where moonlight fell across it, and placed a spotlight on the female swan gliding alone.

'Fuck, Kate. What have you done?'

'Chris? I found out what happened. He admitted the hitman was his idea. We finally know we were right. I got you justice.'

Justice? This isn't justice. Not the justice I wanted. You've screwed up, Kate. You've totally screwed up. What are you going to do now?'

The anger in his voice chilled her. He'd never used that tone of voice with her before. This was a side to him she'd never come across before and she had no answer for him. Albeit out of self-defence, she had killed Dickson.

A gentle breeze blew against her cheeks.

The swan dipped its elegant neck and head underwater to feed.

Kate pocketed the gun, her mind spinning.

There was a way out of this.

But if she took it, she would never be the same person again.

ACKNOWLEDGMENTS

Huge thanks to Mr Grumpy for being my partner in crime and accompanying me on long walks around Blithfield Reservoir, at all hours, to get into Kate's head space. You can now return the kitchen knives to the drawer.

To Russel McLean – thank you for all your time, brilliant editorial input and entertaining chats.

To my fabulous agent, Amy Tannenbaum, who is not only responsible for bringing this series to the attention of Thomas & Mercer but who read through the script and offered sound advice on language and structure.

To Victoria Haslam, editor extraordinaire, and her ace team at Thomas & Mercer – thank you for all the passion and expertise you have injected into this book. To the eagle-eyed Sadie Mayne and Sarah Day, whose skills I admire hugely.

To every member of my street team for supporting me on this venture and the numerous book bloggers who help get my work out there. I shall never tire of saying what a phenomenal job you do and how grateful I am to you. There are too many to mention (apologies to those not named): Emma Welton, Zoe-Lee O'Farrell, Donna Morfett, Jacob Collins, Nigel Adams, Kate Everleigh, Kirsty Whitlock, Charlotte Baddeley, Nikki Jablonski, Linda Hill, Jacqui Turnbull, Stephanie Lawrence, Alison

Stockley, Melanie Robertson-King, Javier Fernandez Perez, Ann Jones, Debbie Smith, Misty Manoogian, Annette Angelx, Vicki Wilkinson and wonderful Nicola Southall.

To you, my readers, who motivate me every day with your kind emails, messages and comments. You make writing incredibly worthwhile.

ABOUT THE AUTHOR

Carol Wyer is a *USA Today* bestselling author and winner of the People's Book Prize Award. Her crime novels have sold over one million copies and been translated into nine languages.

A move from humour to the 'dark side' in 2017, with the introduction of popular DI Robyn Carter in *Little Girl Lost*, proved that Carol had found her true niche.

February 2021 saw the release of the first in the much-anticipated new series featuring DI Kate Young. *An Eye for an Eye* was chosen as a Kindle First Reads and became the #1 bestselling book on Amazon UK and Amazon Australia.

Carol has had articles published in national magazines such as *Woman's Weekly*, featured in *Take a Break, Choice, Yours* and

Woman's Own and in *HuffPost*. She's also been interviewed on numerous radio shows, and on Sky and *BBC Breakfast* television.

She currently lives on a windy hill in rural Staffordshire with her husband, Mr Grumpy . . . who is very, very grumpy.

To learn more, go to www.carolwyer.co.uk, subscribe to her YouTube channel, or follow her on Twitter: @carolewyer.